Forw

CW01456610

Dear Reader.

To help you understand the story behind this story — and by that I mean how, perhaps, just perhaps, how this novel may have come about, I suggest we travel back together to 2028, where a maniac with a time machine is on a mission.

Coked out of his mind from abusing an 8-ball he acquired from Route 36 in La Paz, Bolivia the day before — in 2024. We watch as our maniac sets the dials to travel back to San Francisco in 1965. There, we witness him grab Hunter S. Thompson by the scruff of the neck and drag him out of a house party where he is about to cop a beating from the Hell's Angels.

After some persuasion involving an impossibly complex philosophical, socio-political diagram that he has drawn out with lines of coke on a table in a coffee shop, our maniac convinces Hunter to travel with him, far back to the Villa Seurat in Paris in 1936. Together, they snatch a particularly morose Henry Miller out of the public bar of a hotel around the corner from his apartment, where he has spent the afternoon drowning his sorrows to a barely interested, particularly buxom barmaid — meandering across and rummaging through the machinations of the end of his second marriage.

The maniac, Thomson, Miller, and the barmaid — who joins them for the hell of it — I mean, why not? When you have a time machine you can do whatever the fuck you want, all crash together back in 2028 at the maniac's apartment in Barri de Gracia with a balcony and a fantastic view of la Sagrada Família.

Sitting together in the kitchen around an art deco Laminex table, they devour a feast from McDonalds that our maniac has ordered in. We watch as Miller, seemingly spellbound; slowly turns a half-eaten Big Mac around in front of his eyes. While glancing occasionally at the now almost finished servings of chicken nuggets, dipping sauces and French fries on the table in front of him, we hear Miller mumbling that the meal is "a cuisine, a feast of a truly extraordinary nature".

We are transfixed as our maniac, without warning, launches into a passionate and outrageously comprehensive explanation of his life; his world, his travels, and the slings and arrows that fate has hurled at him — as well as every fine detail he can remember about J.D. Salinger's *The Catcher in the Rye*.

Exhausted, and three shared bottles of 2018 Ornellaia DOC later, we see our maniac dragging himself out of his chair, and to the astonishment of his guests, with one great swipe of his arm wiping the table completely of the burger wrappers, wine bottles, fine hand-cut crystal classes, and discarded empty double-chocolate-sunday-plastic cups, scattering it all about the floor. We see him exit the room and return a moment later wearing a red hunting cap, striding back into the melee — his expression one of haunted anguish. He has in his hands a 16" MacBook Pro, and under one arm; two simple, straight, small glasses over the necks of two unopened bottles of Pernod Absinthe, and under the other, a loaded double-barrel shotgun.

Placing the laptop on the table and a bottle in front of each of the two men, we watch as he opens the computer to the blinking cursor of an empty Microsoft Word document. We jump back in fright as our maniac suddenly leaps up onto his chair and, sobbing now in utter exasperation and waving the shotgun wildly about, demands that Hunter S. Thompson and Henry Miller "Write it down! Write it all fucking down!" — that they must tell the story, his story; of what has become of him, of his world, of Western Civilisation.

Together, they must write this book.

But. As I said. Just, perhaps.

A.C.

Except, of course, for actual locations and the obvious description and references in general terms that relate to the ego-maniacal sociopathic miscreants that are destroying Western Civilisation, this book is a work of fiction. All names, characters, and incidents are the product of the author's imagination and are used fictitiously, and any resemblance to actual persons, living or dead, business establishments, organisations, events or locations are purely coincidental.

The Beating Room

Copyright © by Alexis Caulfield

2024-E5

All rights reserved.

The reproduction or utilisation of this book, all or in part, in any form by any electronic, mechanical or other existing or hereafter invented medium, including xerography, photocopying and recording on any information storage or retrieval system, is forbidden without the prior written permission of the author.

For Jim

You stand in full view before my eyes. I am on the point of parting from you. I see you choking down your tears and resisting without success, the emotions that well up at the very moment when you try to check them. I seem to have lost you but a moment ago. For what is not a moment ago when one begins to use the memory? It was but a moment ago that I sat as a lad in the school of the philosopher Sotion, but a moment ago that I began to plead in the courts, but a moment ago that I lost the desire to plead, but a moment ago that I lost the ability. Infinitely swift is the flight of time, as those see more clearly who are looking backwards. For when we are intent on the present, we do not notice it, so gentle is the passage of time's headlong flight.

Letter XLIX, De Brevitate Vitae (On the Shortness of Life) — Seneca

Introduction

It was a time when The Truth had grown accustomed to The Darkness. Perhaps they were even lovers as they lay there, filthy, slumped back against the wall of the grotto they had crawled into. Now, completely corrupted in compromise and deceit, when The Truth raised its downcast eyes and glanced furtively out towards the light, it shivered. With nothing more to give since Hope had drained away, The Truth just floated about, wallowing in the warm, putrid tide of low self-esteem that had poured in to replace everything that mattered.

The West had become a place where men were weak, and when Right and Wrong — reborn as identical twins — shared drunken, joyous evenings, arms around each other's shoulders laughing and singing, twisted up in mutual admiration and disgust. It was a time when Relativism, having banished Logic, Diligence, and Discipline into purgatory, was now firmly in charge, its laughter could be heard echoing amongst the sharp slaps and cracks as it whipped and flogged a beaten and weary Civility into submission.

The world had changed, as it always does, now into a place where Mediocrity and Resentment found themselves — inexplicably — at the table where all the decisions get made.

"How did we get here?" they asked each other, bewildered.

At first, they were confused then excited, and then, of course, as it dawned on them where they were, their eyes narrowed with vicious intent as they gazed hungrily at the feast of revenge that The Meritocracy had been forced to serve up to them. Revenge for their version of The Truth — a version that they had beaten and bloodied so badly, it was unrecognisable. Of course, they were not very bright, never having gotten past the most basic of urges — when to shit, when to fuck and when to eat. And like so often is the case when the universe is tilted and influence ends up where it was never meant to be, Mediocrity and Resentment set about in a rage, destroying everything that worked and replacing it with "stuff" that sounded good.

And so it all began.

Contents

1

The Third Quarter

September 20, 2025

My eyes opened slowly to a blurred haze. I closed them and opened them again, but it made no difference. A white shape moved across in front of them — a person — no words. A damp, warm cloth gently wiping my face. Blinking, the shape moved away again as my eyes began to focus. Curtains, heavy-bright-sunlight-framed, forming a silhouette hiding their colour. A faint beeping, bustling — muffled voices, the cold odour of disinfectant and sounds of quietly managed professionalism.

A hospital.

I tried to roll over, but nothing happened. My mind slowly recalibrating itself to the scene. The crisp, sharp white fabric of the nurse's uniform moved across in front of the curtain again — inches from my face. Staring, I realized everything all at once, and a wave of horror washed over me. I started to sob, but all I could hear were strange whining and grunting sounds.

How? Fuck! How?

A warm hand on my arm. A cold, wet sensation rubbing on the inside of my elbow, a sharp prick, a needle. Fading back now, a floating, building pleasure accelerating in intensity towards something impossible.

Gone now. Drifting…

... sitting perfectly still in an old wicker chair against a wall... strange, it was the chair my grandfather had died in. Equally odd, in a chair against the wall to the right of me was a very old Indian man. He was just staring at me, his face an expression of kind, sad judgement. His skin was tanned and deeply crinkled and his hair was tightly bound in a bright orange pagri with one escaped silver-grey lock falling down the side of his face — his old tired eyes sparkling.

In front of the chair I was in was a naked woman sitting up in a bed, washed into shadows formed by fractured angles of bright sunshine that cut across the room from cracks in the curtained window on the side wall. The light was exaggerating the shadows, contrasting as it fell, illuminating one section of large fluffy white pillows that she was resting against, as well as across her chest, stomach, pelvis, and part of her right thigh — her face, completely in the shadows.

My eyes grew accustomed to the scene, recalibrating, smoothing the extremes into some generic exposure. I could see her head was lowered forward, and she was looking down. Her gaze seemed to be falling between her legs, at her bald pubic mound glistening and swollen red.

"Nothing like a bit of self-abuse", she said absentmindedly. Her voice was young — perhaps in her mid-twenties. She slowly lifted her head, bringing the top part of her face into a single sharp shard of light, the lower part remaining in the shadows. She had sparkling-clear-sapphire-blue eyes, juxtaposing against porcelain pale skin. Virginia? I thought.

She looked like she could be one of those girls you pass in the street, just so beautiful that you instantly fall in love, never to see them again.

One tear from a woman could drown him
Zorba The Greek — Nikos Kazantzakis

I reached over slowly and snapped the switch on the tall lamp next to me, the pale-yellow light filling the shadows and washing out the shards of sunlight.

The first thing I noticed was a heavy, leather cuff attached to her right wrist, its patina of dark, worn age mixed with sweat contrasting against the shiny stainless-steel rivets, latch, and small padlock that connected it to a silver steel chain. The chain ran across the bed sheets, looping down to a heavy metal plate attachment that was bolted to the concrete wall behind her. I looked up from following it just as she reached over to the bedside table, fumbling around for something — her hair falling across her face. A pouch of tobacco and cigarette lighter, the chain running rattling across the steel frame of the bed. Pushing herself up now into a more seated position and flicking her hair back, the light struck her face properly for the first time.

I just stared.

She started the process of rolling a cigarette, a Tally-Ho paper hanging by its corner from her cherry-red-plump-lower lip as she reached into the pouch, drawing out a wad of tobacco. Plucking the paper from her lip, she teased the tobacco out evenly along its length and, in one movement, rolled it into a perfect cylinder and swiped the paper's edge across her wet tongue, like she had done it a thousand times before.

Reaching down onto the bed, she picked up a green BIC cigarette lighter and, flicking it into a burst of golden sparks and flame, lit the tip of the cigarette and turned her gaze directly at me for the first time. Staring straight into my eyes, she exhaled a long jet of translucent blue smoke and smiled.

Terrifying.

Her teeth had all been ground into razor-sharp points. Grinning full-faced at me now, enjoying the shock she saw in my expression — sharp, glistening white teeth. I knew, but I couldn't remember how, that she had managed to bite the cocks off three men in one night before the resulting blows to her head had left her in a permanent state of psychosis.

She just sat there smiling at me, smoking. Her polished, pointy, sharp teeth glistening between two slashes of lipstick that had been applied in such a way as to perfectly describe her mental state... her eyes sky blue, her breasts gently rising and falling with each breath she took.

Drifting. Burleigh Heads. Gemini Court. Pandanus palms. Janelle, lean, tanned, lying on her back topless on my towel in the hot summer sun, my Tubeline twin-fin lying next to her. A phone box. "Bro, if she cheated with you, she'll cheat on you…"

September 21, 2025

Slowly, my eyes opened as someone was lifting my arm. Nighttime? Daytime? I was shaking and felt as if I was sweating all over. I could hear myself moaning as if I was somehow separate from my body. I could see the curtains now; they were a dull green colour under the fluorescent lights. Nighttime, I decided.

Lost. Sleep.

My eyes opened again. The curtains were pulled back, a generic rectangular red brick building beyond the glass. I tried to move again, but once more, nothing. No choice but to stare at the wall.

Time ticking. Toying with me, my mind. How?

That fucking wall, it was everything I could see. How long had I been here?

Staring at the bricks I decided that the wall was a perfect testimony to disgrace, the disgrace endured by whoever life had forced into designing it, and to the sad resignation of the person who had found themselves with no fucking choice but to build it. Brick by brick. Completely void of even the slightest expression of artistic licence or soul, its perfectly proportioned mix of function and economic rationalism told the story of the desolation, the destruction of the dreams of two men. It was a story that neither of them, in the eternity of their youth, would have ever thought even for one moment would be theirs — that their lives would come to this — this monstrosity designed and built into existence. More than anything else, it was a monument to the dreams of men being savagely beaten down by choices and fate.

Staring, thinking — my choices, my life, my fate. Sam's life, Sam's fate.

I felt completely numb. Moving my eyes down, I noticed two clear plastic hoses snaking out from under the covers and disappearing over the impossibly white sheets and down out of sight beside the bed — one dull red, the other pale yellow.

As I stared at the tubes, my reality once again dragged itself out into the spotlight of my mind and stood there grinning grotesquely at me. Unable to move — I could feel a tear slipping down my cheek.

How? Was all I could think.

I forced my eyes away from the tubes and back out onto that wall. It had started to rain outside, darkening the colour of the bricks beyond the reach of the soffits from about halfway down.

She is crying again, I thought.

I remembered back to the last 15 years of my adult life before my mother had died and how she and my father had treated me so terribly. She was always somehow implying that I was not a good person and that I needed to "fix" something while at the same time apologising for how poorly she had managed my childhood years. It was quite the paradox: an apology for years of parental failings delivered through a framework of ambiguous accusations. No matter how hard I had tried to understand why for the last season of their lives both my parents had thought so little of me — what it was that I had to fix — the answer eluded me until the very last days of her life. Absurdly, it was at a time when her mind no longer had the order nor the intent required for us to finally understand the truth together, or for her to grasp the enormity of her and my father's failings — or of the extent of my hurt.

The irony that it took the combination of imminent death, stalking guerrilla dementia, and a morphine-induced haze for my mother to choose to say enough words, however upside-down, back-to-front, and sideways, to finally explain to me why, was not lost on me. For her to choose a time when she had become so undone, had fallen apart to such an extent, that there was no more time left for a rational setting-of-the-record-straight, for me, was just heartbreaking.

It was all over one of those things that happen in friendships and in families, those seemingly innocuous incidents that come along and float about between people and then, usually, drift off into the past — forgotten.

Usually, but not always.

Sometimes, for any of a thousand possible reasons, a best friend, or a brother, or a sister, or an uncle attaches themselves to it and sets about twisting and pulling it out of shape until, perhaps over many years, it becomes so large and distorted that it is unrecognizable compared to what it once was — a monster that takes up so much space in the gaps amongst and between relationships, that the people involved can no longer even see the truth past it, the good in each other beyond it.

When my mother explained it to me, I had been surprised and saddened that something so benign had been deliberately nurtured into such a malignancy. That something that should have been almost an irrelevance within the lifetime framework of a loving family had managed to seep and spread through the machinations of our interlocking lives, affecting everybody, hurting everybody.

Watching the rain, I remembered the last time that I saw her alive and awake, just before she slipped into that dark, sad coma that heralds the end of a cancer patient's life. I had said to her that when she died and went to heaven, God would give her complete clarity about us, about her and me — about the truth. That he would hold her gently in his arms and comfort her, and she would finally understand — without even the slightest doubt — just how poorly she had treated me and just how utterly sad it had made me, her son — always my mother's little boy. And looking into her old, tired, confused eyes, I had continued saying that for me, for the rest of my life, whenever it rained, it would always be her tears falling from heaven as she looked down upon me, knowing in her heart that they, of course, had my complete and unconditional forgiveness.

They were my family.

September 22, 2025

"Hello? Sir, can you hear me?" My eyes opened. My mind blurred. Drugs? Sleep? Both? The nurse's uniform came into focus. She bent forward and gently pulled and pushed me into a slight roll away from her. I could see her face for the first time. She was about 30 years old and dressed like she was from a First World War movie set, some British colony from the 1930s — her hat a perfect white triangle with a colourful embroidered patch in the centre, her hair a remarkable construction of bobby pins and tightly-combed-hair-sprayed order.

She smiled a kind smile at me. She looked Thai or Vietnamese — the generic simplicity and honesty of Southeast Asia clear in her face. It was not that unsettled, somehow contorted confidence that set the background to many Western women's faces — like a working man in a rented suit trying his best to be absorbed unnoticed into the ceremony of his child's graduation.

"Are you in much pain?" she asked. I couldn't feel anything at all. I tried to talk, but nothing happened. I don't even think my lips moved. "Do you know where you are?" I stared. "You are in Bumrungrad Private Hospital," she said.

Thinking. Bumrungrad? "To nurture the people". Bangkok. Of course, I was in Thailand — I could be nowhere else.

"The police said it was some accident that happened to you, Sir. Do you remember? Sir, can you remember anything? They said you were drunk from the whisky, and you tried to get your wallet and fell off the balcony. They said it was a huge miracle that you landed on the canvas back of the lorry".

She was staring at me as if waiting for me to reply. I just looked at her. I couldn't believe what she was saying, what I was hearing — my whole body began to shake. She motioned to someone beyond me and leaned in again. I could feel another person helping her roll me from my side further onto my back. The ceiling.

White cork tiles. Rectangles. Perforated bubbles. I could feel her reaching for my arm again.

Spiraling down now. Gone.

> I can't say what made me fall in love with Vietnam. That a woman's voice can drug you. That everything is so intense. The colours, the taste – even the rain. Nothing like the filthy rain in London. They say whatever you are looking for you will find here. They say you come to Vietnam, you understand a lot in a few minutes, but the rest has got to be lived. The smell, that's the first thing that hits you – promising everything in exchange for your soul. And the heat – your shirt is straight away a rag, and you can hardly remember your name, or what you came to escape from.
>
> The Quiet American — Graham Greene

… a memory so clear I slid gently into it, nestling comfortably into its arms. Sitting by a fire on the sand dunes, just up from the ocean at Wooli on the New South Wales mid-coast.

September 16, 2024

Staring into the flames of an open fire had always brought me closer to death.

My mind invariably wandered across the intense landscape of my life, stopping occasionally to stare quietly, savoring a moment of pleasure or kindness before moving on. And horror. There was always the horror.

For most of my life, I had known how I would die. A blessing in some ways.

Now I had one year to go. 365 days.

My thoughts on how I would choose to use those days completely crowded out everything else from my mind. Only the important things now: my children, my wife, my brother and sister. Or not? Perhaps you realise it is only you in the end — it has always only ever been you. Alone. What is life anyway if it is not just staring into a dark pool of memories — time spent, people, places, feelings, pleasure and pain — memories that can only ever really be yours alone. Most are lost, sinking to the depths over time with only a few of the more intense, bright, shiny, polished, and repolished fragmented bits and pieces floating amongst the most recent ones on the surface and just below it.

Sitting by the fire, I mused at the absolute clarity my situation afforded me. Was my wife strong, or was she just numb? I couldn't tell anymore. She had been raised by soulless parents without any faith in anything, without any tools to even access emotional depth or romance. She had made her choices as best she could, and those choices over time, those decisions throughout her life, had led to the stripping away from her of anything soft, everything vulnerable and organic that love, or pain, or regret could attach to.

I knew my choices now would have almost no effect on her emotionally. And I knew my brother and my sister would be okay

— they had had a lot of practice when it came to loss and pain.

My children were all that really mattered.

365 days. Was it even possible? Probably, but there was a danger. The empty spaces between the words, the paragraphs and the chapters — those moments terrified me. I knew that in the minutes, hours, and days when I was not focused on my writing, the emptiness would grab me by the back of the neck and drag me in front of a mirror, forcing me to look at myself, and it would be there, in the reflection, that despair would be waiting.

A year to write a book.

It was not a long time, but enough. "The task at hand expands to fill the time available," someone had once said. The trick was to have enough distractions to fill in all the gaps — to avoid that mirror. Perhaps relentless wild, savage sex with a young woman paid was an option. Definitely, but maybe just one part of a larger plan. Add alcohol, food, drugs, and violence — all to excess — and now you're fucking talking. In any case, it was the most reasonable solution to avoiding the horror of dealing with the gaps I could come up with.

I was 61 years old and would be dead at 62. One more birthday.

In 61 years, I had led a life that many would judge as better than most. A life of "drinking life to the lees", of "piling life on life", as Tennyson would have encouraged it. It had been a long time since I had had to answer to anyone. A life of freedom. And the girls, the beautiful girls. Since I was just 13 years old and spent a whole hour in the dark of night kissing the beautiful Nikki Hocker with her flawless complexion, her blond hair, and her ripe full 14-year-old body — well beyond her years. That had been the start, igniting a fire that had raged in me ever since. I smiled, thinking back at my bushy blond hair and lean, tanned teenage body as I remembered their perfect breasts, their sweet slippery warm perfumed centers, their smiles, the way they fucked, the way they cried, and the way they laughed. And, of course, the way they lied.

They always lied — it was just part of them.

These beautiful girls. So many, so much, so often, for so long — all now reduced by time to a life lived in an instant of yesterdays. A young man trapped in an old man's body with only the memories left.

The young woman — paid, drifted back into my thoughts. Purely transactional — both parties happy. Perhaps more than one, I thought. Perhaps three — one more than any man could ever possibly justify. Staring into the fire, I absentmindedly reached up and touched the dressing on my neck, immediately regretting it, flinching with the pain. You can have one thousand problems in life until you have a health problem, and then you only have one.

Staring back into the flames, I drifted back to my thoughts. A gentle and complete dive into the waters of ubiquitous hedonism; of gorging wine, drugs, rage, food, and flesh — like a one-year oeuvre of the now. Of immediate need and gratification — without any gaps, without even one moment of time available for the intrusion of even a single piercing shard of regret or thought about the important things, about God, about what I had lost, about what should have been, about the end. About my beautiful wife, and about my three beautiful sons and the tears and the pain and the loss they would inherit from me, as I, too, had inherited from my younger brother Sam.

Son, it's Sam. There's been a tragedy.

Is he dead?

Yes...

I looked up from the flames of the fire and gazed at a passenger jet passing high overhead through the late afternoon sky.

You can actually feel a broken heart. It is a dark grey cloud, a soft, heavy weight that settles down upon you and doesn't leave. With distraction, it becomes lighter, airier — but in the quiet moments, it comes back heavy again, weighs down upon you, engulfs you, suffocates you with feelings of loss. Taking a deep, slow breath, I stared at the jet, marveling as I always did at the way its fat, heavy carcass floated across the sky, defying any sense of reasonableness, winking at me with mesmerising regularity.

So many flights I had endured to deliver the excitement and peaceful isolation of foreign lands. The best seat rows with the extra legroom. I took a long drink from my beer, Tooheys Old — a dark ale I had poured from its small bottle into a glass to savor its smell.

Watching the plane.

The number of times I had jetted out wrestling with equal parts: stoic reserve to fight through the physical strain of it all, and the excitement and anticipation of landing somewhere different. Above all, memories of Southeast Asia.

I smiled at my theory that there was nothing more beautiful than a pretty woman stowing her overhead luggage.

I watched the jet get smaller and smaller — full to the brim with promise, fading slowly away. The take-offs, the landings. The freedom you feel like no other that comes with being alone, a stranger completely responsible for only that one day, that moment, in a place removed from everything repetitive, monotonous. I thought about Heathrow, Menara, KKIA, Changi, Tan Son Nhat, Suvarnabhumi, Don Mueang, and Madrid–Barajas. One by one, I walked through the terminals in my mind, savoring familiar memories: the rude, aggressive men on the customs desks in Morocco — the women all asking for bribes, the gorgeously beautiful uniformed young men and women at Madrid-Barajas, and the outrageous politeness and civility of the staff at Heathrow.

Eventually, and of course, inevitably, my thoughts took me to Thailand, to the tired halls of Don Mueang, and finally to Suvarnabhumi with its golden serpent-wrestling Gods.

The seemingly endless taxiing upon arrival — "Surely we could have flown the last 10 kilometers" would always come to my mind. Standing in the aircraft, the painful wait on the tarmac for the passengers in front of me to start moving — uncomfortably pressed up against them, hand protecting my phone and wallet from the thieving wretches, anticipation screaming in the motionless silence. Once out, maneuvering around the dawdlers and the "open-mouthed Renault drivers" standing in the middle of the travelators — like they were on a fucking ride — staring vacantly off into the distance. What kind of life is so mundane that there is no urgency to break out into Bangkok? Their genuinely surprised expressions — the only real sign they are actually alive — as they are jolted out of their grey reverie when I asked them politely to move to one side so that I could pass.

I knew from experience that the days of short border queues at customs in Bangkok International were long gone. Relativism had seen to that. Now, according to the commercials on television, "everyone could travel" — but fuck me, I wish they wouldn't. I knew that every person I passed on my way through the terminals was one I didn't have to stand behind in a queue.

When I reached Customs, I was always careful to note which line was twice as fast as it fed into two and not one, utterly disinterested, stamping, ridiculously tight-canvass-cotton-uniformed Customs officials. Then, through to the baggage area, the endless carousels fading off into the distance in each direction. And then watching — always in disbelief — those few mind-numbingly stupid people standing right up to the baggage carousel blocking everyone else's view. And then moving on past the uniformed touts, stuck in their decades-old purgatory of offering their over-priced limousine taxies, and then through the farcical security/quarantine gates — always green — and finally upstairs, and upstairs again to the top floor at the end, and then out! I would burst through the doors at the entrance to the departure lounge on the top level and outside as if I could not bear the anticipation for even one second longer.

Like I'd been holding my breath since I left Australia.

Instantly, the warm, moist, scented Bangkok air would engulf me, and I would just stop. Right there, in the middle of everything. Thailand. I had never arrived until this moment; it had always been the same. No other place on earth I had ever been to felt or smelt like Thailand.

Standing there, still, I could feel her, hear her, smell her, the country and all her promises, gently reintroducing herself to me. Like an old lover with a kind, knowing smile. She understood. She was there for me. Instantly, everything would slow down: my heart, my thoughts, my every movement, as if her heavy, fragrant pizza-oven heat was a tonic, an antidote to my life of disappointment, dutiful urgency, meaningless days, responsibility, and pain. We had grown together over the last 25 years, learning much from each other, and although we both had been ravaged — at times savagely — by all that life had done to us, we were still, at our core, old, familiar friends. A lot of both of us that was once out and open and free was hidden now, for one reason or another, but everything was still there. Somehow, even though the years had worn our sharp edges away, had disinfected and plastered over the cracks in our character, our souls remained unchanged.

Ravaged. That was the word. Life, commerce, "progress", had done that to us. Patpong was a good example — once a poorly-lit, organic, heady mix of clubs, colour, and trinkets — the same faces whose stories you watched evolve year after year. The short, heavily muscled, somehow strange-looking young man growing older, the ladyboy with the thick white plastered face makeup. The smells, the raw chaotic vibrance of colours and movement, the thumping music — an essence unique to that place — now quickly being covered over by the malignant cancer of consumerism with its glittering shop fronts and bright lights opening up onto clean sidewalks replacing the bars and the clubs with their shining poles and the dark alluring depths they faded back into.

The smiling girls with their freshly washed hair rushing through the crowd to get to their bar, stopping only briefly at a statue temple for a quiet, solemn prayer to Buddha on the way to their club to dance almost naked in front of older men. A whole generation who could sense death's presence, and who had enough life experience of helplessly watching their options fall away to justify the desperation in their eyes and the fists of Baht they clutched. All that was being replaced by homogenized tourists who didn't know any better, who thought "this" was it, this was all it ever was.

The New Zealanders, the Australians, and the British backpackers were long gone, replaced by different faces, faces that now shone with the ignorance of base, pedestrian hunger, and greed: Chinese and Russian faces, Arab and Pakistani faces, Indian faces. They were there not to immerse themselves in the beauty, the fun, and the tranquility of the place and its people, to connect and engage as we had done — as I had done. To dance with the girls on a Patpong bar swinging my suit coat above my head — the girls and security going along with it, hysterical with laughter. But to ravage and feast, to destroy and to devour whatever had been left behind by time and the change that it always brought with it.

To me, in those times, Thailand had been a place of depth and colour, of peacefulness and flavor, of innocence, simplicity and kindness. A place that these Russians, with their round, squashed heads and lined brows searching for meat, wearing their fake gold-embossed white Versace T-shirts stretched tight across their fat abdomens, and their sparking skin-tight clothing — just never quite pretty —girlfriends could never understand.

Not to mention the Chinese. I had Chinese friends — people who had looked after me for many years on my visits to China.

A handful of kind, clever people intent on shaking off the dirt and the grime of their provincial, pre-industrialised collective childhoods, and embracing all of the opportunity that Deng Xiaoping's version of capitalism had brought with it. But they were the exceptions, not the rule. I remembered back to just one of the many taxi rides I had endured in China, travelling from Shanghai to Ningbo. The driver's phone had rung, and as he spoke, the taxi had filled completely to the brim with the stench of his breath — heavy and thick with the smell of stale tobacco filtered through the meat that I swear to God must have been rotting between his teeth for months.

And now they were travelling, these Chinese!

Let loose on the civilians, the delicate nuances of other countries, other cultures! Staggering around Bangkok, desperate to shed a lifetime of thought control and to understand this thing, this "freedom". Scrounging and conniving, spitting and snorting, stuffing as much as they can take into their mouths and into their pockets while they wipe decency and civility off their filthy chin with a dirty 100 USD note.

And then there were the Arabs: fat-black-bearded men, wearing their faith on their bruised foreheads — their ghoulish cloaked wives dutifully floating along behind them like big-black-un-dead ducks. Thin hawk-like Israelis sitting quietly in the corners silently watching them. I like old Arabs, but I don't like young Arabs — there is no fucking peace in young Arabs. And the Pakistanis and the Indians. My God! These "Tony Montana" peasants of the world contriving every next move with awkward, embarrassing, loud enthusiasm as they lurch into modernity.

None of them could even comprehend what Thailand once was, even if you could transport them back into it. They were the uninvited visitors who failed to realise the party was over and that Thailand had moved on. Who flopped down into their chairs and could only see flesh, and money, and brands, and excess as they tore what was left to shreds and picked through the scraps and bones of a place so different that it was derelict now from what it once was, now wrapped in the cloaks of post-modern, relativist fucking misery.

I had been fortunate to first start visiting this place so long ago — back in a time that could be marked by elephants roaming Sukhumvit and when it was cheaper to station policemen with white gloves on raised concrete cylinder blocks in the middle of Bangkok intersections directing traffic than it was to install traffic lights. A place so simple and kind — a place that those who were not there at that time would never believe or understand. And then, as I kept coming back, clinging to her in desperation as she faded away — savoring the occasional glimpse of her past that she offered up, that had survived.

The joy of days full of genuine happy smiles from strangers — now all but gone. That peacefulness that, as a man in the West, you only encounter occasionally when you pass someone in the street — older like you, and you both just smile at each other — gone the ego and competitiveness of youth. Back then, Thailand was a place where it seemed this was everywhere, with the old and the young, with men and women, as if the Thai people were born with this simple kindness and peace within them. Now almost gone. Washed away by the disease of Western "Progressivism" and the consumerism, greed, and selfishness that it brings with it.

But it was not all bad.

The paradox was that although the cost of "progress" had been her soul, her simplicity — it had been a price well worth paying.

These changes appeared to have brought with them some peace and opportunity for the next generation of Thailand's boys and girls, smashing some of the chains of poverty and circumstance that had bound them to the sex industry. This was a silver lining — a beautiful thing — for this country that I held so dear to my heart. It had always saddened me that generation after generation of Thailand's young people had been sacrificed on the altar of greed, corruption and financial expediency. The sex industry was still there, but now it seemed very different. Thailand's young people were out and about in suits — selling high-end property and setting up exclusive bars and restaurants and businesses with a distinct air of confidence and drive.

There just seemed to be far fewer people involved in the sex industry because they had no choice.

Standing outside the massage shops and the clubs there were clearly far fewer teenagers with sad resigned expressions drawn from having no option but to have sex with strangers so they could help feed their family. When you walked past these places now, the girls outside appeared to be older and more brash, laughing and joking amongst themselves and with the constant stream of passing tourists. Some of them had even taken up knitting for God's sake like our grandmothers used to do in the west!

The Western liberal elites, of course, never visited Thailand.

Thankfully, most of these ignorant assholes still deemed it to be just one of those dirty, squalid little Asian countries. Any improvements to the living conditions and opportunities available to Thailand's people were only ever going to be an accidental bi-product of the influence of the new globalist world order. Making life better for the weak and disadvantaged was never, ever, their goal — although that was the flag they committed all of their atrocities under. For all of their farcical compassion shouted from the rooftops, by virtue of every selfish self-centred action they took, they clearly never showed any genuine interest at all in helping the truly disadvantaged of any country, ever.

Ye shall know them by their fruits. Do men gather grapes of thorns, or figs of thistles?

Matthew 7:16 King James Bible

Over the years, as I had watched these people destroy my Australia, I had grown to loathe them. I had categorized them into three separate homogeneous groups — describing the generals, the sergeants, and the foot soldiers, defining each into their own tier by the role they had played in destroying the best country in the world.

The generals, the people responsible for creating this fucking catastrophe, I called the Zealotribe. These were usually academics, politicians, or senior public servants, along with the very wealthy, who developed and leveraged — always for their own benefit — as much selfish stupidity and fear as they could. They were ideologues, the zealots who, with almost religious fervor, latched onto ideas or narratives such as "climate change", or "the patriarchy", or "covid mandates", or "pronouns", or "multiculturalism", or "substantive equality", and popularised them, loading them with perceived virtue that they then used for their own ends. They were the people who normalised being transgender at twelve years old, and who sanctioned double mastectomies and the chemical castration of children with hormone blockers purely to gain social credit amongst their equally deranged peers at meetings and at dinner parties.

In general terms, they took an idea that they simplified to such an extent it could be digested easily by the masses — invariably replacing something that worked, with something that sounded good.

They always ignored the subjective complexities or the scientific and social nuances of the subject of their argument and, charging it with emotion, fear, and blame, delivered it in terms of the idea being an absolute, incontrovertible and indisputable truth.

More often than not, their carefully selected narratives had very little in common with actual facts or science, an anomaly they managed cleverly by using terms like "the science" instead of "science".

No longer with their roots in the principles of morality, nationalism or civility, the vast power and influence of the media and the political machinery of Western countries had become available for purchase to the highest bidder, which included foreign governments with nefarious intentions. It was much simpler and significantly cheaper to have the West destroy itself from the inside than to wage war on it.

Acting with selfish, malicious intent, motivated through simple stupidity or greed, or both, the Zealotribe built their strategic distractions around a complex framework of "false dilemma", "strawman", and "appeal to authority" fallacies. This allowed them to create narratives for their own ends; the perverse manipulation of almost any concept into something that was loaded on the one hand with terror, judgement, and blame, and on the other, with retribution, rage and the emotional allure of enhanced social status — a combination that was like honey to a bee for the mindless masses.

And the results of their grandiose narcissism? Farmers forced to blockade highways all over Europe to resist Government policy designed to destroy the very food chains the people of these nations survive on. Illegal migrants assisted across borders in their millions by Leftist governments and the United Nations through its clandestine subsidiary: the International Organisation for Migration. And police standing by, watching fascists who call themselves anti-fascists, beating up people in the street who resist the blue pills that their globalist overlords are determined to shove down their throats.

Parasitoids.

They enforced their dogma with an absolute and ruthless aggression that saw anyone who even questioned their logic, their ideology, treated with contempt — first laughed at, and then very quickly attacked by the savage mob until they lost their voice, their friends, their career — and increasingly even their freedom. They were almost always identifiable by deliberately choosing to ensconce themselves in jobs beyond any real objective accountability. They preached from ivory towers where they rarely, if ever, paid any price for being wrong.

The Zealotribe would never travel to places like Thailand, for fear that they would be labelled as being uncultured, or worse — too poor to be able to afford to travel to the more enviable latest-must-visit Eastern-bloc European destination. They much preferred the people in these Southeast Asian countries to be seen as remaining "exploited" and "poor", another stereotypical victimhood group they could use to shore up their diabolical narrative. Their motive, as was always the case for all such allocations, was to add one more high-horse to their teeming stables of moralistic judgement against Western civilisation — one more high horse that they could ride trampling through the dazed multitudes — skulls crushed under pounding hooves.

The closest these assholes ever got to "Asia" was overpriced organised walking tours in Japan.

The tier below them I called the Followerati — that group of middle-level public service managers and supervisors and private sector small business owners and professionals whose careers and social lives depended almost entirely upon them being seen as devout disciples of the Zealotribe. Their role was to implement and spread, on a practical level and as loudly and enthusiastically as they could, as much of the ideology developed by the Zealotribe as possible. It was their job to transfer whatever insane strategic narrative that was being espoused by the Zealotribe into populist, suburban thinking — to turn these ideas into actionable, street-level strategies and procedures.

To achieve this, any aspiring members of the Followerati quickly developed the not insignificant skill of being able to completely ignore any information, logic, or facts that they might stumble across that could be construed as being even slightly in opposition to the Zealotribe's agenda.

During "Covid", they implemented their support for "lockdowns" fiercely. Behaving in a manner that was exactly the same as informants in Nazi Germany, this Gestapo of the New World Order reported their neighbors to the authorities and aggressively chastised and bullied people who disobeyed or even just questioned any of these intemperate mandates.

They ignored the almost complete lack of difference in death rates compared to previous influenzas or the lack of effectiveness of their measures as evidenced by comparative death rates reported in countries that implemented none of these archaic, barbarous strategies. At the same time, they refused to even acknowledge the insidious side-effects that were resulting from their belligerent demands; like family members deprived from spending precious time with elderly parents dying in nursing homes, the significant number of businesses that people had put their whole lives into that were being destroyed, as well as people losing their homes, the breakdown of marriages, kids being isolated from all of the social and other benefits of going to school, and the spike in suicides. They happily enforced people's basic human right to decide what they put in their body being taken away from them — pugnaciously coercing family and friends into getting the Covid vaccine. They demanded that people lose their jobs, and cancer patients needing hospital treatment be locked out, refused treatment, until they complied with vaccine mandates.

Like the members of the Zealotribe, for them, there is absolutely no value, no social or career currency to be earned, from visiting places like Thailand.

The Followerati's loud and enthusiastic support, the overbearing conversations they had with their neighbors, all their bumper stickers, and all the fucking signs they put on their fences and in their front yards signaling how virtuous they were, brought the simpletons, the masses—the group I called the "Echochamberists" into the fold.

Unlike the Zealotribe and the Followerati, the Echochamberists flocked to Thailand in droves in their endless desire for tick-the-box travel. In fact, they were so thick on the ground you had to kick them out of the goddam way half the time. This group could be homogeneously identified as the safe, comfortable, unthinking multitudes whose perspective on the world was drawn almost entirely from conversations with the people they interacted with within their work and their social echo chambers, as well as from the six o'clock news that they watched religiously on their huge televisions that proudly hung on a wall where once previous generations had had bookcases.

In their quest to position themselves perfectly in the safe centre of the bell curves of social acceptance and financial security, they embraced and consumed, without even a second thought, whatever narrative the people on the television spoon-fed them. Grasping and holding dear to themselves any opportunity at all for the victimhood that always unpinned the Zealotribe's ideology, their natural state was "wilful ignorance", with their only real passion being the desire to remain completely uninvolved in anything that could be remotely construed as being real, controversial or outside of pulp, populist thinking.

They were utterly dedicated to an absolute commitment to their roles as malleable, compliant drones. The Echochamberists fell into a broad spectrum of socio-economic classes, from simple people just wandering from day-to-day, to reasonably wealthy retirees and workers in safe positions in large organisations or government departments who had no interest in ever questioning the dominant paradigm and absolutely every reason, financially and socially, to accept the dominant narrative as unarguable fact.

They were a diverse group, motivated by everything from intuitive disinterest, all the way through to being overwhelmed by utter terror at the thought of being seen as not part of the herd, of being socially ostracised, or of having their completely egocentric daily-weekly-annual plans and routines upset in the slightest way.

Without even one original thought, they could often be seen wandering around the most heavily documented and promoted tourist attractions in Thailand, like "the floating markets" or "the elephant sanctuaries". Most were very happy with their careers, having carefully positioned themselves beneath the raging currents of original thinking or responsibilities that were tied to anything remotely subjective, where the slightest wrong move could upset their career and knock them out of the grey, safe miserable cocoon they had worked so hard to ensconce themselves in.

Immersed in this cloud of wilful ignorance, the Echochamberists focused only on the prize: that weekend's social gathering, the next holiday, or the next investment property, all underpinned by an absolute commitment to never having to think about anything real or important.

Unfortunately, you encountered these seemingly immortal fucking assholes everywhere in Thailand striding out in their expensive zip-off-quick-dry-hiking trousers and Teva sandals, boasting endlessly about how lightly they packed, eating their couscous and their salads, sipping their soy fucking lattes and their herbal teas.

The one thing all three tiers had in common was that they all held closest to their hearts a complete and absolute contempt for my Australia — for the mums and the dads and the families, for traditional values, for the truth and science and facts and merit.

Relativism had given birth to them as new money, and instinctively, they hated old money.

Sitting by the ocean staring into the fire, my thoughts wandered back to Patpong. The acrid stench of rotting waste interplaying with the spicy scents of street-vendor-cooking-cart kitchens and the exhaust fumes from the endlessly knotted traffic. Sitting, sipping an espresso, watching a jealous Thai girl in a tartan mini skirt and long-white-knee-high-laced silk socks with little bows on them screaming and snarling at her boyfriend on his back foot. The statue of Satan, the lord overseer of that place that was always near the entrance to the Lucifer Bar, smirking across the whole debaucherous landscape. No pants — what's the point? — this is Patpong. Awkward, almost embarrassed stance — he simply could not help himself. They are so beautiful that his lust overrides everything. It is beyond his control. He has abrogated all responsibility to his DNA. Self-consciously, he hides his hard-on, eyes blood-shot with the impious insanity that is eating his brain and the alcohol-soaked sleepless nights.

That statue now, nowhere to be seen.

And the smell — now just a hint of what it was. Everything real almost all gone as the new commerce with its trappings of expensive knock-off clothing, shoes and handbags displayed behind clean glass and faux respectability grabbed simple opportunistic crime by the scruff of the neck and re-organised it.

I used to always get a haircut there, in Patpong, if I could possibly justify it, at the hairdresser next to the 7-Eleven. Pat would smile as he charged me twice what he charged the locals, and we would both burst out laughing — still a fraction of what I would pay in Australia. I wondered if it was still there. Probably not — Covid's henchmen of deceit, vested interests, and scripted fear and confusion would have well and truly laid waste to both Patpong and Pat along with his hairdressing shop. I would sit back while Pat cut my hair and watch the constant stream of beautiful young women — all always with a ready, friendly smile for me as they came in, getting their hair washed and blow-dried in preparation for their night's work on the poles. I remembered on one occasion, mid-way through my haircut, a particularly beautiful Kathoey had started singing "I Will Always Love You" by Whitney Houston — only to be sobbing with emotion by the end of it amid cries of loving, caring support and hugs from the rest of the girls.

Only in Bangkok. Only the Thai people.

The fire was very low now, just the glowing embers and occasional small flame flashing against the white ash. I sipped my beer.

I always arrived in Bangkok at nighttime. I remembered what it felt like there, just outside the entrance to the departure lounge at Suvarnabhumi airport. Standing there, still, feeling her warmth engulf me, always somehow managed to make my pain fade back, not away, never away, but back.

Sam.

After a while, she would slowly return me to the present, with her blaring horns, the strange terrazzo floor patterns, and the yelling and excited waving and flapping from the taxi drivers at the drop-off rank on the top floor — desperate for my attention. All this amplified by the shrill whistles of the traffic control police reminding the drivers that the window of opportunity between dropping their fare off and illegally sneaking in that elusive return passenger back to Sukhumvit, was closing quickly.

At this point, there was often a moment when I would stop and deliberately notice the travelers walking towards me, past me into the departure lounge. They were all the same. To my mind, they all carried a burden much heavier than their luggage in the way they walked and the expressions on their faces. They were leaving paradise. It was over. The current of life and responsibility was drawing them back. No matter where they were going, it was worse than here. To be arriving, to be at the start, was so much better than to be leaving, to be at the end.

Gathering myself back to the present, I would cross the road in a gait brimming with contrived confidence and determination — I wouldn't even look at the oncoming traffic. I knew what a fucking zebra crossing was for! For anyone watching me, it would be absolutely clear that as far as I was concerned, there was not even the slightest damned opportunity for any driver to pretend that that zebra crossing didn't exist. The cloak of colonial superiority, inherited from arrogance, gunpowder, and history, was still recognised — rightly or wrongly — this air of superior civility was still respected, almost feared, in places like this.

From there, I would negotiate myself and my luggage through that devil of a one-way, silver-turntable gate and then onto the drop-off taxi rank. I had always done this. It had nothing to do with the 100 Baht I saved by avoiding the designated taxi rank on the lower floor — for me, it was all about the quiet feeling of experience, of knowing a better way that was outside the bland, grey bureaucratic systems that the miserable compliant masses cling to with such fear and determination. It was about beating the system. I had always railed against any form of control — State or otherwise, no matter how trivial.

"On the meter?", repeated enough, quickly removed the scammers from my options, and after a nod and a smile, a quick look over the taxi to make sure it was relatively new and clean, and then "Sukhumvit Soi 15, Highway, I pay the toll". And I was off — hurtling through Bangkok's veins, the huge sparkling LED billboards and the glittering showrooms with their lime-green-Lamborghinis and mat-black-Ferraris, and eventually into her capillaries and deep into her heart.

The dirty darkness, pulsing with colour, life, and promise.

I missed Thailand, sitting there by that fire. I missed my tailors, the girls dancing on the poles to the thumping music, the spicy food, the Singha beer, and the ladyboys that hung around Sukhumvit at Soi 7. The way they looked at you was like no one anywhere on earth — they just stared, unwavering, straight into your eyes. They used that smouldering gaze to leverage your imagination, to describe in the most explicit detail, without even a single word, the erotic promises they offered. The way we always laughed together when they reached out to touch me and I walked on by.

I missed the temples and the bottles of red Fanta and the Jasmine necklaces hanging from the rear-view mirrors on the taxis and the bustling street stalls with their strange smells and smiling, welcoming faces. And JPs off Soi 31 with his wonderful hearty welcome and his delicious Beef Wellington, and the Next 2 restaurant at the Shangri La, with its endless plates of perfectly cooked Foie Gras, drizzled with a balsamic Jus — the Chao Phraya river almost lapping at your feet.

And the rain. I missed the Bangkok rain.

Gridlock.

Sitting in a taxi.

The night-time neon transforming into bright brush-strokes of watercolour against the dark shadows and black asphalt, slipping and sparkling across the windshield.

Great big, fat droplets of water plopping down to black mirror puddles, splashing into kaleidoscopes of colourful fragments of reflective neon in suicidal delight.

Thunder rumbling.

Traffic slowly, patiently, peacefully finding its way.

No rush, no pressure, no obligations.

Heaven.

To miss something that has gone forever has so much more of a heavier weight of sadness to it than to miss something that you know one day you can come back to. More than that. I missed the person I was when I first started going to Thailand so long ago. That person, in that place, at that time. I knew deep down that that person was gone forever and that, for me, Thailand would never be that way again.

The plane was now nothing more than a tiny, faded flashing light. I wonder where it is going, I thought. Completely irrational feelings of loss and hopelessness washed over me. Gone now. Searching feverishly, almost desperate, but I could see no sign of it. As if it had never been there. Those passengers, oblivious to my world, now contemplation for someone else further around the earth's curve.

I shifted in my chair. 365 days. This timeline had been brought into sharp focus by that feeling. You know that feeling you get when the news is so personal, so upsetting that you can actually feel your blood become cold instantly in your veins? Like when you ask her: "Did you fuck him?" and she answers simply, quietly, "Yes", and your whole body chills, and part of you just dies, forever, under the weight of the loss and the sadness.

I am tired of it, that feeling. The core of it all, of course, was my younger brother Sam. He had taken his own life at 26. He was my friend. He was my best friend, and now, almost 30 years later, my heart was still broken completely in two. That cold feeling in my veins still clinging to me.

I missed him so much. It was strange; just as much as I missed the times we had together, I missed all those years of his life that we never got to share.

Some fucking maniac telling me, "Alex, you mustn't let Sam's death define your life."

Fuck off. Just fuck off!

After a lifetime of the gods appearing out of nowhere and beating me savagely, I was well aware of the contempt and rage they are capable of. Beyond my children, all I had left was fear and sadness. Like a mistreated dog, I had been waiting quietly for what these Gods have planned for me next. But no more. No more. I prodded the fire gently with a stick, causing a log to shift down into the flames sending a stream of smoke and bright golden sparkles floating up into the night sky.

I had zero interest in sitting back comfortably and allowing chance to dictate what happened next. I was fucking done with that.

I could hear the sound of my wife and the others talking and laughing, drifting outside as if carried on the smell of the roast lamb and rosemary simmering in the oven — sounds and scents mixed, floating back across the breeze to where I was sitting.

Tomorrow was a red-letter day, I thought. One of those sharp fractures that defined a life — a thin, jagged line drawn across the cosmos, a crack between birth and death that separates the before from the after, that changes everything forever. I stood up, placed a few pieces of old dried hardwood on the fire to keep it going, and wandered inside — into the maelstrom.

2

Two Dogs Caged

September 24, 2025

My eyes opened slowly. How long had I been here? Without words, everything I knew seemed to be standing still. I could feel something new though — a tube in one side of my nose. Is that how they're feeding me?

No visitors. At least that horror had not been imposed upon me, thank God. That would be the only thing that could make this worse — to see their faces. Simon had given me a full twelve months, but that time had passed. Surely they knew where I was now and it was only a matter of time before they came to Bangkok? The police would have found my name in the wallet and in my passport. Surely they would have contacted my family by now? I wondered for a moment if Simon was still alive.

Staring at that fucking wall, I had no choice but to close my eyes and back away from it, the fluorescent lights, that room, back into my mind, my thoughts.

September 16, 2024

… Sitting quietly eating dinner, smiling when I'm expected to. I could still smell the fire outside and hear the ocean crashing onto the beach beyond that.

Small words, swallowing. A sip of red wine.

Eight chairs, seven people. Sharing a meal with an eclectic assortment of monsters: my wife, three younger women, a middle-aged man, and an older woman.

The three young women — Amy, Lakshmi, and Donna, all worked with my wife at the Department of Social Services, and the man, David, was Amy's boyfriend. He worked at a different Government department altogether.

The older woman, Robyn, was my wife's manager at work and inexplicably to me, was someone she held an almost unhealthy admiration for.

When Amy wasn't out driving around aggressively in her government car screaming and snarling at people in traffic — urged on by the empowering-women-motivational-career podcasts she listed to — she was most easily identified by the blood splashes and spatters that she got on her kitten-heel-stilettos from clambering over work colleagues and clients, gouging, and stabbing, and kicking for the next promotion into a deeper more rewarding section of the Government pig trough.

David had been married before and was quite a bit older than Amy, although strangely, he didn't seem to own anything. He rented an expensive two-bedroom apartment where he sub-let the spare room to an endless stream of foreign boarders, all of which always had two things in common — they were all females, and they were all half his age. In what was clearly an excuse for his abject financial failures, he was forever telling anyone who would listen that money wasn't important to him while, in the next breath, talking about a long list of moronic business ideas that, of course, he needed funding for. Like, instead of tuna and mayo sandwiches, he wanted to breed tuna and feed them mayonnaise.

Perhaps the thing I liked least about David was that from what I could tell, he was never to be found when it came to all of the boring, arduous responsibilities that being a good parent required — like dropping off and picking up his kids from their friends' houses. In fact, from everything I had heard, he only ever seemed to spend time with his young teenage daughters from a previous marriage when it involved doing things that allowed him the opportunity to hit on the mothers of his daughters' friends. He was one of those people, one of those "friends", those men you are forced to endure in life that you know, given the slightest opportunity, would go behind your back and try to fuck your wife.

He was the epitome of the weakness that had developed in Western men — that indulgent irresponsible escapism, that they had allowed themselves to be overwhelmed by. He always struck me as being about as cunning and convincing as a rat with a gold tooth, and I despised the man.

The older woman, Robyn, was the great matriarch of not only my wife, but of her three psychopathic friends. Before her role in the government, she had been a lecturer in the sociology department of a university where she had enjoyed a long career in "Feminism and Gender Studies". During this time, she had displayed an utterly myopic dedication to a lifetime of indoctrinating young women to mistreat, belittle and destroy any and all of the young men who were unfortunate enough to find themselves in their company. She proudly wore a small pair of taxidermied human testicles hanging down from a gold chain around her neck although, curiously, I was the only one who could see them.

Lakshmi had recently been the subject of a particularly nasty workplace incident when, as she describes it, she had been summoned to a meeting with, not one, but two senior Human

Resource Officers where she had been asked about the two-hour lunch breaks she had been taking with her new girlfriend.

Apparently, they had asked her a direct question about why she was taking two hours for her break instead of the prescribed one-hour lunch break.

In her formal complaint on the matter to the Manager of Human Resources, Lakshmi had outlined that she had felt bullied and victimised by being asked such a direct request for an explanation, and that, as far as she was concerned, the question was clearly racially motivated.

The Manager, along with the Department Head, had, after some deliberation and a not insignificant amount of confusion and anguish over the intersectionality implications of defending the rights of a young gay ethnic woman versus those of not one but two older women who were career Human Resource professionals, referred the matter to the Ethics Committee. Strategically, this allowed them to wipe their hands of any involvement and, as such, safely avoid the career minefield that the volatile conundrum presented.

If only the young woman of colour had been just a white CIS-gendered male, the course of action would have been simple — crystal clear, they had mused at the time.

The Ethics Committee consisted of an assortment of volunteers who were completely homogeneous in their makeup in three distinct ways.

Firstly, and perhaps as a direct reflection of the Department's almost rabid push for equity and equality, none of the members possessed any qualifications at all that related to the role — all members were almost perfectly equal in the lack of qualifications they possessed for the work that the Committee undertook.

It was comprised of a broad cross-section of staff from various areas within the organisation, including Accounting, Public

Relations, Corporate Services and Payroll. Donna, who was seated at the dinner table between Amy and Lakshmi, was a member of the Ethics Committee. Although she was only 24 years old, she was very mature for her age, having backpacked around New Zealand for two months and having read "everything Naomi Wolfe had ever written".

She was a very progressive young woman in her third-year apprenticeship as a motor mechanic in the organisation's Carpool Workshop. As an expression of her independence and free thinking, she only ever wore cherry-red, eight-hole Doc Martens boots. Although she was physically capable of only being able to do about 50% of the work that the job demanded, she was quite pretty, and photos of her were often included in organisational publications where she was lauded as being a "Jewel in the Crown" of the Department's push for Substantive Equality in mission statements, programs, policies, procedures, and guidelines.

The second and perhaps the most obvious characteristic that the members of the Ethics Committee all had in common was how much they all enjoyed the regular opportunities that sitting on the Committee offered them to avoid having to do the work and deal with all the responsibilities involved in the jobs that they had actually been hired to perform.

And the third? They all, every last one of them, savoured, in fact relished, the status and the power that being on the committee gave them. They all enjoyed seeing the fear in the eyes of their colleagues and the contrived-completely-unwarranted-ridiculously-friendly conversations that being on the Committee elicited from their work colleagues in casual interactions around the biscuit jar in the tea-room.

The position, indeed, was one of great power. After all, "Ethics" was just moral philosophy, a malleable, murky discipline where both expected behaviours, as well as the punishment for failing to comply with those expectations, were subjective and always in a state of flux. It was not like there was such a thing as right and wrong anymore — that was all so "old school".

And that flux? Those ever-changing sets of expectations, rules, sanctions, and punishments that swirled around the organisation intertwined with all of the opportunity that came with the endless organisational restructures? All of that discretion fell squarely under the control of the hallowed members of the Ethics Committee.

They had come to a time when no one dared speak his mind, when fierce, growling dogs roamed everywhere, and when you had to watch your comrades torn to pieces after confessing to shocking crimes.

Animal Farm – George Orwell

After much deliberation across a number of meetings and discussions, the Committee decided youth and skin colour trumped two old white women and that Lakshmi had indeed been bullied.

Upon her return from two weeks mandated stress leave with full pay, Lakshmi had been allocated half a day a week — every Friday afternoon for "as long as she felt she needed it"- as a "safe space" for her to attend a 45-minute counselling session with a psychiatrist that the department had contracted on their payroll, specifically for situations: just, like, this.

The two senior HR representatives responsible for what everybody around the water coolers was describing as "that outrageously aggressive racist attack", were both recipients of formal written warnings, and they too were sent off once a week, in perpetuity, to a firm of consulting psychologists — also on the Department's payroll.

It was put to them in no uncertain terms that "they needed to get the bottom of where their aggression and racism was coming from, and hopefully, the sessions with the psychologists would equip them with the learning tools they required to better understand the needs of all stakeholders involved in the work undertaken by the department, with the goal that eventually they would become better team players".

As senior Human Resource Managers, they were also given the responsibility to redraft the Key Performance Indicators in the Position Descriptions for the jobs they held, with it being expressly noted that those redrafts include a set of Mission Critical Behavioural Standards around their interaction with the Department's internal and external stakeholders. It was explained to them by the Ethics Committee that those KPIs were to include the addition of detailed, quantifiable expectations and requirements with regards to body language, verbal cues, and eye contact; "behavior and limitations". As part of this process, they were also encouraged to explore possible guidelines around "wardrobe colour choices" on any days that involved disciplinary responsibilities in the performance of their roles, with a clear emphasis on the suggestion that the colour red should be avoided at all times.

Two months later, the more senior of the older women committed suicide over the incident — falling forward in front of a train at a suburban train station. Leaving a note, she expressed her profound regret that she had failed not only women in general but also the lesbian community and people of colour — that she had fallen into the trap of not "checking her privilege" — and went on to outline how she could see clearly now that she had become part of the problem and not the solution. Her untimely demise left her position in the Human Resources department vacant — an opportunity for a small promotion pounced on by the remaining older woman who professed that, with the guidance and support she had received from the team of Organizational and Behavioral Psychologists, she had "risen to a higher plane of consciousness" and was thrilled to be promoted into the still warm, albeit somewhat haunted role that her colleague had vacated.

In the meantime, Lakshmi, who had broken up with her girlfriend over "the sheer stress of it all", had been placed on a schedule of large doses of anti-anxiety medication by the Consulting Psychiatrist. As a result, she had been reduced to an almost comatose state — a strange mix of jumping and screaming at the slightest movement or comment from a colleague, and barely being able to function, barely able to even move at all.

Intriguingly, she still took two hours away from work for lunch.

She also now never left her apartment without wearing a surgical mask which she only ever took off to eat. Apparently, the two-hour lunches "helped her relax", and the mask made her feel safe, somehow protected — a barrier between her and the world and all of its "aggressive, racist savagery".

A short time later, the newly promoted older woman, who everyone now agreed was "operating on a higher plane of consciousness", perhaps in an effort to foster reparations of sorts for her past transgressions towards the young woman, successfully lobbied to have Lakshmi promoted into a more senior role in the organisation, on a significantly higher pay grade. In her words; in the more senior role, Lakshmi would have more capacity to influence organisational culture, while at the same time enjoying having less work to do — essentially putting her under less of the "stress of it all". Everybody agreed that this was a great idea, with the general consensus being that, of course, the higher up you got in the organisation, the less actual work you had to do.

Someone even suggested that Lakshmi be appointed to the Ethics Committee — something still under deliberation and discussion amongst various Managers, Directors, the Department Head, and, of course, the Ethics Committee itself.

Unfortunately, all six of these people were regulars around my dinner table and sitting there, I fucking hated them all.

"How was your conference?" Amy asked. I had just returned that day from an overnight "online business" conference on the Gold Coast. I smiled at her.

"Not surprisingly full of self-obsessed wankers" I replied, remembering all the gratuitous hand-shaking and embarrassing egotistical displays of materialism and self-promotion that I had endured.

"If they were all self-obsessed wankers, were you the keynote speaker?" she said, a smile on her face. I felt my wife's silence just before I heard the scorn from Robyn as she started to chuckle uncontrollably. Interestingly, she stopped, but then, unable to let the opportunity to release a little more of her hatred, the old woman chuckled some more.

My wife sat still, silent.

I looked at Amy. "That's a nasty thing to say, Amy. Is that what we are doing? Are we saying nasty things to each other?"

She shifted in her chair, still smiling, poking the roast lamb that I had spent the afternoon preparing with her fork.

"I mean, it seems a strange fucking choice for us to be doing that", I continued on, "you being my guest and all, and me having gone to the trouble of cooking such a lovely meal".

Silence now, the old woman's chuckling had faded away, and she was just sitting looking at me — her eyes sparkling with delight in anticipation of witnessing more hurt and pain — more of a man being humiliated at his own dinner table. A second course of misery before dessert, perhaps, she was thinking.

"Can I ask Amy, as we're doing this, is your half-wit public servant of a boyfriend aware of exactly just how much a filthy slut you are?" I had always held simple contempt for public servants — people who worked for the State, for the government. Who the fuck chooses their one shot at life to be spent working for the fucking government?

"That while you were waiting for your plans to destroy his marriage — and, by extension, his family, you were scouring online dating sites, fucking an endless stream of men, and rating them back to my wife based on cock size?"

David, Amy's boyfriend, looked up from his drink, his face suddenly pale with anger. I looked into his eyes, waiting, watching.

I could almost see pride and alcohol pushing his fury forward like jeering school children, while feelings of confusion and uncertainty wrestled him back. He was glaring at me as if perhaps he was not quite sure what I had just said.

David was a talker. You meet them as you wander through life, and they are invariably all the same. Middle-aged, his general expression was that of an alcoholic — that mixture of equal parts conjured arrogance and earthy fear that compete to hide low self-esteem. Bold statements of athletic prowess woven into a fabric of drawn-out, repetitive stories of such a pedestrian nature that it makes your eyes water to endure them. The venal dolts, as I liked to call them. The wasters of lifetimes that fill in all the gaps in the world as they weave slightly unsteadily to get their next drink, their protruding stomachs leading the way.

The jeering schoolchildren won, and he stood up violently, his chair crashing back against the sliding doors and onto the floor.

"You OK up there, Dave?, I said from the other end of the table.

"Fuck off, he snarled, a handful of Amy's hair now in his fist, twisting her about like a rag doll while she said his name over and over. It was actually a pleasant surprise to see the real David emerge for the first time since he had been forced upon us. A completely different, honest David tearing through the dusty veneer of the self-effacing, sugary-sweet David that we were all accustomed to enduring with his contrived dopey smile, downcast eyes, and worst of all, his almost melodic baby talk — which was most unsettling to hear coming from a man well into his 40's.

My wife sat motionless, silent — a silence that only a husband can know — her choices made. She sat looking straight into my face, her eyes burning with rage.

Amy's whimpering and crying mixing with David's confused, angry, snarling questions, his face inches from hers, dragging her from side to side by her hair. The old lady's face was white. I caught her eye: "Loathsome fucking bitch", I whispered clearly at her — a slight smile on my face — snatching an opportunity from the camouflage that the chaos offered me.

"I..." she started saying.

"Just on that", I interjected quietly. "Robyn, have you ever, in your entire life, considered starting even just one fucking sentence with absolutely anything other than the word "I"? Just a thought", I said, smiling.

Suddenly, David stopped reefing Amy about by the hair and, letting her go, picked up his chair, and they both sat down. He glared at me; the pale face of adrenaline-fueled, unconsidered rage that sits right at the edge of explosive violence had gone, submitting instead to the far less dangerous red face of simple anger.

Silence. Everyone sat blank-faced, staring at each other. Lakshmi sat, elbow resting on the table, her fork hovering midway between the plate and her still gaping mouth, half full of food.

Suddenly, as if on cue, there was a knock at the door.

"Oh, good, he's here", I announced, rising from my chair and starting towards the door. David stood up, forced composure taking hold.

"We're leaving", he said. I spun around and, without a word, hurled my half-full beer bottle as hard as I could, delighted as it smashed into his face, dropping him to the floor. Amy screamed and lunged out of her chair to him.

Opening the front door, I ushered Peter in. Peter was approximately 6'4" tall and weighed about 150 kg. He was missing most of his teeth and had that look about him of someone who perhaps had been born with fetal alcohol syndrome — his face and expression clearly offering up a low intellect, chiseled into features distorted ever so slightly, a face imperceptibly at odds with the eye's expectations.

In his hand, he carried an old blue plastic bucket stained with use and, in places, drawn white with stress. We smiled at each other as he walked straight past me, without a word, into the kitchen and proceeded to fill the bucket to the brim with water from the faucet. Everyone was staring at him. I had met Peter after placing an ad on a few ".onion" sites on the dark web outlining my plan. To be honest, I was fucking horrified at the number of people who had responded to the ad.

"Alex, we need to call an ambulance!" The sound of my wife yelling at me repeatedly drifted into my world. "David is really hurt", she said kneeling over him, and then glancing at Peter, "Who is that?" she demanded, almost as an afterthought.

Happy that his bucket was full of water, Peter came out of the kitchen and over to the dining table, water slopping everywhere. Walking to where Robyn was sitting, he carefully pushed her plate of half-finished dinner to one side and placed the bucket on the table directly in front of her.

"I don't want tha…", she started to say with her usual forceful, overbearing confidence that always struck me as being in complete contrast to her tiny-brittle-boned-vulnerable-old-woman stature.

Without a word, Peter's powerful right hand grabbed the old woman by the neck and plunged her face into the bucket.

Lakshmi screamed. Finally, I thought with a smile, something from Lakshmi that, for once, was not an overreaction. Kate had jumped to her feet and had both hands uselessly around Peter's powerful forearm, desperately trying to help Robyn. Peter, holding the bucket with one hand and the old woman's neck with the other, was now smiling at me full-faced as we both watched, grinning at each other above the chaos as the old woman thrashed about. My wife, now flailing hopeless fists at Peter's face while Amy knelt over David, yelling incoherently, and Donna and Lakshmi sat, screaming.

I slowly dragged my mind back to the present and looked up from my meal across the silent dinner table — my reverie of Peter and his bucket fading back away from me along with the unkind humiliation. Over time, their preoccupation with belittling me had impacted me less and less. I had realised long ago the best revenge was when you honestly didn't care anymore, but it was never easy.

The old woman had stopped chuckling now and was looking at me with her small, watery eyes, a slight smile lingering at her mouth. Amy and David had moved on to some other, as usual, mind-numbingly-fucking-mundane conversation about something someone irrelevant said to someone even less relevant about something completely uninteresting, while Lakshmi sat, soaked in her quagmire of psychiatric drugs, fork hovering, dripping, chewed loudly, staring off into some private middle space.

My wife still, sitting, quiet.

> It was a good hanging. I think it spoils it when they tie their feet together. I like to see them kicking, and above all at the end, the tongue sticking right out, and blue, a quite bright blue. That's the detail that speaks to me.
>
> 1984 — George Orwell

There was never an exception in this for her — she always stood by her family and her friends — never me, her husband. I wasn't certain if it was yet another consequence of the putrid quagmire within which she had been raised — taught to value her independence more than her marriage — or it was simply a conscious choice she had made. Sitting there, I wondered if she knew the saying wasn't "blood is thicker than water", but the complete saying meant the exact opposite; "the blood of the covenant is thicker than the water of the womb". That a choice, a bond made, is stronger than one simply inherited.

A choice of a husband, a family, a life.

Probably not, and even if she did, it wouldn't have held any reference for her.

They were starting to clear the table. I stood up slowly, tired now. As I walked past her to the kitchen to make a scotch and dry, Robyn looked over at me with that expression that she had of smug satisfaction, satisfaction for whatever measure of credit that she felt she could claim for her part in facilitating any misery that I was enduring in my life.

As always, I ignored her. Walking from the kitchen into the bathroom, I punched two Panadeine Forte out of the pack for the pain in my throat and threw them back with a glass of water from the faucet. I then wandered outside with my drink into the cool night air and slumped back into my seat, happy the fire was still crackling away.

I just sat, quietly enjoying the sharp sounds that the large broken chunks of ice were making in my drink, clinking against the hundred-year-old hand-cut Waterford crystal. I bought all my crystal from second-hand shops because that was the only place you could buy truly beautiful hand-cut crystal. The new stuff — even Waterford and Stuart — was cut by a machine and didn't have the character, the sharp edges and corners, and the small mistakes of uneven spacing that good hand-cut antique crystal had.

The gentle ocean breeze and the sounds of the waves finishing up and slipping silently back into the sea drifted up to me — drowning out the background murmur of contempt and disregard as the table was cleared and the dishes were washed inside.

It was only 8 pm, but it was pitch black beyond the reach of the fire's glow, the flames extinguishing the stars in the night sky.

I could feel the salty ocean breeze against my face, cool and finely strained through the casuarina trees as it wrestled playfully with the heat from the fire at my feet. Staring into the flames, I slipped quickly back into a state of quiet contemplation that soon, as it always did, tempered into a haze of self-indulgent loss and regret.

The trick, I thought, and I believe I had done it, was to pick the perfect timeframe. Enough time to have the confidence that I could live in reasonably good health, regardless of how much physical abuse I subjected myself to, with a fair degree of certainty. The mistake, I had decided, was to assume that anything more than that was a bonus. I mean, what if in twelve months, regardless of my absolute dedication to hedonism, to the perfect mix of personal enjoyment and self-destruction, irrespective of the women and the drugs and the cigars and the alcohol and the violence, what if I was still in reasonably good health? What then?

Fuck that.

I had reasoned that if I managed it well, surely I would be out of money, broke, destitute — and I had decided long ago that there was almost nothing worse than being desperately poor and old. The worst by far, of course, in this scenario would have been having no choice but to return to them and the quiet resentment, the palpable disrespect from those I loved, for abandoning them. There would be little consideration in their minds about why I had made the decisions I had. No balancing up and accounting for the horror that I had faced or of the disinterest verging on contempt they had all shown me in the third decade of my marriage, of our family in their teenage years.

There are times when a man has to fight so hard for life that he has no time to live it.

Flower Horse – Charles Bukowski

No measuring up against my extraordinary love for them on the other side of the ledger — the absolute commitment of a life spent encouraging them, ensuring that they were not raised like I was, or God forbid, the way my wife had been raised. Every day, I smiled when my children said "I love you" to my wife with genuine, honest intent. Everything that I had done to ensure they had the confidence, education, and grounding they needed to truly launch like rockets into wonderful lives of joy, satisfaction, and happiness.

Back when they had preferred to be with me, before they were happier when I wasn't around.

The thought of suffering at the hands of the world, of being absorbed out of obligation back into the lives of the people I loved, could not even be a consideration. My timing had to be perfect. I needed to manage the next twelve months so well that they took me perfectly to the end. So perfectly planned that my body literally failed on day 365, and without even one dollar in my pocket or even one cold beer left in the fridge, I sat down, thought of Sam, and took my last breath.

My drink was empty. I climbed slowly out of the chair and, pushing some sand with the inside of my foot across the glowing embers of the fire, walked back towards the now silent, black house. I had an early start, and it was getting late.

I mused at the idea of people leaving and others retiring to their beds without giving me even the slightest thought of a "thank you for dinner" or a "goodnight". It occurred to me that I was never lonely when I was by myself, only when I was with others. The only thing worse than being despised, I thought, was being irrelevant — alone surrounded by people, especially if they had once loved you.

September 25, 2025

Perhaps it was these thoughts that triggered a change in the tone of the endless beeping that ushered the nurse back to my side — again, no words, just an adjustment of my pillow, a cold alcohol wipe, and the needle prick, slipping away…

… Sam, sitting. Morning sunshine. His hands shaking slightly as he rolled a cigarette. His smile. His damaged finger. The expression on Mum's face in the back of the police car with Dad. Sam's funeral.

Mum, tears. Dad, broken, forever.

Drifting now.

… the little old lady in Guangzhou so many years ago. Sitting, staring at my phone on a bus, enduring the 3-hour ride to the Canton Trade Fair from my hotel in Foshan. We were stationary, caught up in the twisted, snarling traffic that always defined that journey, when I looked up and out the window into a scene that no one in their right mind could ever conjure up.

It was a vacant block of land, framed by those dirty, tiled multi-level apartment buildings that China is full of, with their silver-iron-bar-reinforced windows designed to deliver equal certainty that no one could ever break in, and that absolutely every living creature inside would burn to death if the place ever caught fire.

In the foreground, straddling the sidewalk and almost encroaching onto the road, was a pile of pig snouts approximately four meters high and six meters in diameter. The lack of smell on what was a hot day made me think that they must have been dumped there sometime during the evening by a factory worker looking to save time and money disposing of them through a more legitimate method. The rest of the site was strewn about with various piles of dusty rubbish and dirt, and in the middle of all this chaos was the little old lady.

She was standing on the very top of one of three of the larger mounds of dirt that were distinct from everything else in the scene. The tops of all three mounds had been meticulously cleared bare of weeds and rubbish. Each one had been planted with three neat rows of what looked like baby lettuces, all bright green — almost as if they had tiny electric lights inside them in contrast to the slurry of the greys and browns that made up the balance of the scene.

She was standing there all bent over in a blue cheesecloth dress, her old frame distorted and twisted up with the forces of life under the weight of her years. Standing there, still, looking down intensely at her work, she was the definition of determination, of hope, hope almost for the whole nation. Hope that the civility of honest toil and patience would win against the mad greedy scramble into China's version of an industrial revolution — the scramble for the next higher series black BMW.

She was going to draw something good out of this godforsaken outrageous scene of human failing. No matter what — she was going to win.

Sleep.

3

No More Beef Fingers

September 17, 2024

I rose early — my bag, hidden in plain view, had been packed for a week. It was an old, tattered suitcase with the brand Aladdin crudely printed across the front of it. A dull peach colour, with scuff marks and well-worn corners, it defined its owner as hopelessly poor and uninteresting — struggling from one day to the next. I had bought it two weeks ago from a thrift shop on James Street in Sydney for $12, choosing not to take the Tumi that I had purchased at ION in Singapore twelve months earlier — its sleek black lines, shiny ballistic nylon, and my initials embossed in silver discreetly in the corner painting a somewhat different picture of its owner.

Everyone was still asleep as I wheeled the battered suitcase quietly down the hallway towards the front door. I had heard the Uber arrive 5 minutes ago, its tyres crunching on the gravel emphasising the silence of its electric motor. Opening the door, I waved to the driver holding up my index finger, indicated that I would be one minute, and leaving my bag there like a holding deposit for him, walked quietly back to my eldest son's room.

Opening the door, I stopped, looking at him sleeping. He was a huge lug of a man now — at least 6'2", lean and broad-shouldered from his determination in the gym. What had happened to my little boy who used to follow me around wearing nothing but a diaper and an inquisitive smile? How had he become this, this behemoth? Breathing quietly, his unshaven chin, his outrageously hairy long legs, and his bare muscular back, all curled up in a ball, sound asleep. My beautiful son. My Thomas. So handsome, with a sharp mind and a fantastic sense of humor.

He was a most unusual young man — like a light switch, he was either "on" or "off". When he was interested in something, I had never seen such determination, such "focused agitation" in anyone I had ever met. He literally twitched and flickered and bounced with the energy of concentration. It was like no matter how simple or how vast the concept or task that had grabbed his attention was, he was completely engaged with exploiting every avenue of thought and analysis about it, from every angle — a white-hot focus until it had run its natural course and then all of a sudden, it was gone — burned out.

Whispers of blue smoke drifting off into the past.

And when he relaxed, he had this incredible ability to withdraw into his own mind, his own world — far, far further back than what most people ever could. Into a place that must have offered a level of peace, of solitude that I could not even imagine, a place I wished I could go to in my mind, a place that I envied. When he was like this he was completely lost to the world and anyone around him. I had watched people who didn't really understand him, try to lure him out from that place, into the day-to-day trivialities of their world — watched them become frustrated and confused by the lack of connection he was able to make available to them.

There was rarely anything in him between these two extremes.

Although over the years that process of him growing into a young man had, as an inevitable natural consequence seen us drift apart, standing there looking at him, I truly believed that no kinder soul had ever lived on this earth and that no dad had ever loved his son more than I loved this boy. I was so proud of him. Walking over to his computer, I took a hand-written note out of my pocket, placed it under the keyboard, and then turned and walked quietly back out. I could feel the tears coming. I closed the door, watching him sleep through the gap until the last moment, and moved on to the bedrooms of my second and third sons.

To my surprise, my second eldest son Liam was awake, propped up in bed, looking at the screen on his iPad — two or three books written by great minds probably centuries ago were scattered about his pillows.

"Hi, Dad", he said. I was shocked to find him awake but was careful not to show it. I smiled at him. "Hey, buddy, how did you sleep?"

"Great, thanks", and then that smile. Clear eye contact that quietly stated the confidence he had had since he was a small child, an intellect that had a manner that was almost a challenge, almost a threat. He had a mind akin to a hi-tech machine of razor-sharp analysis and determination powered by a mental engine that spun and whirred — a frictionless masterpiece that he fed with books and carefully chosen conversation. An outrageously accomplished, well-rounded young man who only ever put down his blood-spattered keyboard and took a break from the knowledge battlefield to offer the most patient, attentive assistance to anyone who asked it of him.

Already at 19 he was his own man — so much so that I felt that there was almost nothing left that he needed from me, that as his father I could teach him. Over the years I felt like he had gone from listening with wide-eyed attentiveness, eager to learn from every word of advice or instruction I gave him, to now just politely referencing my words against his established mindset on any given topic.

He was both humble and brave, and he outright refused the automatic presumption of value in the bright, colourful accolades bestowed on the so-called experts, by the so-called experts —

those achievements that so many wore proudly around their necks. Even at such a young age, he knew these honors and the esteem that came with them were often bestowed by fools upon fools within the hallowed echo chambers of prosaic mutual stupidity — it was ubiquitous.

We had both laughed, drawing the same conclusion as we had walked out of the Tate Modern into the London sunshine — a busker playing an almost perfect Johnny Cash version of "Hurt", one of my absolute favorite songs. We agreed that the place was just another monument to the now completely accepted ridiculous notion that all people are equal — this evil relativist deconstruction of the meritocracy with its celebration of mediocrity that the postmodern high priests were forcing upon us.

To propose that people who are not born artists can simply attend a university or some sort of "art class" or just practice "kindergarten art" year after year and "become" artists; writers and painters, was just ridiculous. To ignore natural talent, natural gifts.

Liam understood that an artist is born. They spend their whole life knowing what they are, and they either bus fucking tables in a coffee shop and live it, regardless of all of the sacrifice and the hardship, or they deny it and spend their entire fucking lives gnawing on their soul for breakfast every day — as accountants and carpenters and doctors.

I walked in and kissed him gently on the forehead. He smiled that beautiful smile at me. "I'm going out for a while, buddy", I said, struggling hard to appear calm and relaxed. "Catch up later. Love you, son".

"Sure, Dad, love you too", he replied smiling — his eyes already back to the screen; the concept or the opinion, the prey, that he was about to either devour and make part of him — or discard in polite contempt, depending on the measure of value this mind of his attributed to it.

My youngest child Ethan was the last door on the left — I opened it quietly. The room carried the faint perfumed odour of lemongrass and jasmine and was crammed full of beautiful things — each carefully placed so as to project a general aura of peace and tranquility. He was in a deep sleep, his cherry red lips slightly parted, his curly blonde hair tussled around his face, and his blue eyes softly closed.

This beautiful boy, this younger version of me. I looked at his hands, his fingernails perfectly manicured, his skin pale, translucent, and his light pink pajamas with colourful pineapples printed all over them. He would be okay this artist, this passionate, determined soul. I remembered that I had once asked him, "What would you do if you were in the Hunger Games?" He had thought about the question for a moment and then looked at me and smiled;

"I would eat the poison berries, lie down on the grass, and look at the the sky."

Even at 17 he was so mature. For him that day had already come, that day when a boy becomes a man. That day that all boys face when they realise that no one knows the answers, not even their father, when it dawns on them that their parents know as little as they do, and they suddenly become men. I knew that everything that happened in his life, even what I was about to do, would be transformed into art by him, a story for his adoring muses.

He was such an interesting mix of sensitivity and belligerence, of art and contempt and passion — I had never met anyone like him. "I love you, Ethan", I whispered, staring at him. He didn't stir as I closed the door quietly — tears in my eyes — and headed out of the house to the waiting Uber.

Walking across the gravel, I noticed the lingering smell of the fire from the night before still hanging in the air. The cool ocean breeze made me feel alive and determined as the driver placed my bag in the trunk, opened the door for me, and we drove away from my world and into another.

September 26, 2025

What was that terrifying sound? Someone was screaming. Why doesn't someone shut them up? Move them into another fucking ward — don't they have a special ward for everyone who's fucking screaming? A screaming ward? Muffled cries like someone was being torn apart while smothered under a pillow. Gasping, whimpering screams. I opened my eyes. My throat, my God! And what was that pain in my leg — like it was on fire?

I realized the screaming was me — my damaged body trying to thrash about on the hospital bed, a voice trapped inside a corpse, animal-like cries of pain and fear escaping my mouth. Hands grabbing me now — strong hands, a man's hands, at least two men pinning me to the bed and holding out my extended arm. A sharp sting, a warm flood of pleasure as the pethidine surged into me, through me, overwhelming the pain and fear, floating down now, through the bed.

... my Dad's face. Sam, always Sam. Soft tears. Floating again now.

... "I would like to declare to the house a proposed Bill born of this world of so-called "equality" through which we stagger — forging ahead through the melee, suffering the blows of restitution from all directions. I propose that all female bathrooms, both public and in businesses, be equipped with specially placed cameras that capture, in all their glory, the vaginas of their patrons while seated, and further, that the images of those vaginas are fed live directly up to digital screens placed on the outside of every cubicle door!"

The house roared with laughter and shrieks of protest.

"In this day of enlightenment where Relativism relegates everything to be the same as everything else — this great big melting pot of equality — I propose that the women in our society should get to enjoy the same appreciation of their genitalia as the men do! Hanging their dicks out all in a line along those glistening white rows of urinals."

Another roar from the audience.

"For all to see!" I yelled triumphantly.

Mayhem. Papers, pens, whatever lay at hand, hurled into the air now raining down from the galleries.

"Let them, too, judge each other as men do. Let them stare curiously at the simple, neat bald smooth slits of some and at the Hannibal-Lector-feasting-aftermaths of others — with their flaps and folds bursting forth 'willy-nilly' in all directions!"

"Willy nilly, I say!"

Pandemonium.

Looking around the chamber, I noticed there was a single spotlight falling on one seat. Focusing, I realised it was the old Indian man wearing a bright orange pagri that I knew I had seen somewhere before. He was just sitting there perfectly still under the spotlight — his expression I could only really describe as a powerful sadness steeped in deep thought. Standing there, my eyes locked on his as if we were somehow separate from all the chaos I had created, I racked my mind. I just couldn't remember how I recognised him, where I had seen him before. So strange.

Hesitating for a moment, I gathered my thoughts and went on.

"Now, don't get me wrong, y'all," I grinned, faking a Southern American drawl just for the hell of it. "I love me a vagina as much as the next man. In fact, like most men, I hasten to add, they mean more to me than life itself in all their warm, slippery, scented loveliness. I am far from casting aspersions! No! My brothers and sisters! Not aspersions — Substantive Equality! That's what it's all about! That's the key! That's where we are all heading!" I was almost screaming now — my suit coat bunching up on my shoulders as my fist pumped the air above me.

There was a small trickle of members filing out of the House now, but most were standing and hooting in appreciation, with the few sitting, scowling in their well-rehearsed roles of subservience to their ever-watching PC masters.

"In fact, my friends", I continued, my mouth so close to the microphone to be heard that you could hear my lips and the whiskers on my chin scraping its silver-metal-honeycomb surface, "I further propose we develop a kind of mandatory automatic insertion tool — triggered by the woman sitting down! With a set..." I hesitated for a moment. Fuck it, I decided. "A set of kind of tubular expansion caliper plates positioned just below the camera that measures the very diameter of the woman's hole! Under a certain reasonable Newton pressure, of course!"

The crowd was hysterical. Looking around the gallery I noticed that the old Indian man was gone now but in his place was a large colourful bouquet of flowers that were melting under the spotlight, as if they were made of wax.

Looking back at the chaos, I continued.

"And displays THAT measurement underneath each glorious picture on the respective cubicle door screens!"

My voice could now be barely heard above the uproar.

"A 'slut-o-meter' we shall call it — a kind of a humble brag to the body count — not unlike the well-hung man leaning back at the middle urinal and proudly offering a clear view of his heavy cock to the miserable wretches lined up on either side of him! Girls with larger openings boasting just how free, just how fucking emotionally removed they are from the burdens of all of these old-fashioned ideas of "pair bonding" and "love" that society now holds in such contempt! And rightly so! Exploit the moral fatigue! Fuck oxytocin, I say! Fuck love! Fuck monogamy, and civility, and honesty, and decency, and commitment — and all that old-fashioned guff that has held the female of the species back! Fuck it all!"

"Liberation! Liberation is what it's all about!" I screamed into the microphone.

Amongst all of the chaos, I hadn't noticed the house Speaker had left his chair and, coming up to my side, was asking me something, his hand on my shoulder.

"Excuse me, Sir? Sir?"

I opened my eyes.

"Would you like the steamed chicken and vegetables or the braised pork with rice?" the air hostess was asking me with a smile.

"The pork, thanks", I answered as I cleared my eyes, reality settling down on me. Sitting up, I brought the back of my chair upright and lowered my tray table.

"What would you like to drink with that, Sir? We have cola, apple or orange juice, wine, beer, or water?"

"I'll have a beer, thanks", I smiled back — the brand didn't matter; I was just chasing the alcohol.

I watched as she carefully placed the tray onto the impossibly small fold-down table — each component of the meal separated into its own allocated space. Then came the can of Asahi, popped open with the ease of someone who had done it a million times, and the clear plastic cup followed by two blocks of ice.

My father putting ice in his beer on a hot Australian summer's day

when I was a kid.

"Thank you", I smiled at her. Smiling back, she was already moving on to the person sitting behind me.

"Would you like the steamed chicken and vegetables or the braised pork with rice, madam?"

Elbows tucked into the tiny space allocated in Economy, with only my hands moving, I managed to get the little bottle of hand wash out of my pocket and open the lid, deliberately listening for the pressure change. I always had a few spare empty bottles at home that I bought from 7-Elevens in Thailand to use for hand wash. Thailand was the only place in the world where I had ever seen them. They were originally full of Johnson & Johnson baby oil, but after squeezing out the oil, giving them a good rinse, and removing the label, they were perfect for use as a hand wash bottle. They were very slimline in your pocket, and the lid was small and very secure.

After washing my hands and maneuvering the bottle back into my jeans pocket, I tore open the plastic around the bread roll. Carefully separating the bread roll into two halves, I unfolded the slippery-silver-golden-origami foil that encased the butter block and, in screaming defiance of the lectures I had had to endure from my Doctor about my cholesterol levels, spread all of it as evenly as I could across the two halves. I then peeled up the silver aluminium edges of the cardboard lid on my meal, took the plastic fork out of the paper envelope, and started to eat slowly.

What was it about aircraft meals that I enjoyed so much? Reaching for the can of beer and pouring it across the ice, I retreated back into my thoughts.

I had decided on Thailand for many reasons. Thailand was one of the few countries in Southeast Asia that was not a Third World country as defined by nations that had obtained their independence after the Second World War. She was, however, like most third-world countries, identifiable in large part by corruption and a weak Rule of Law that tends to nurture the essence of places like that.

I recalled the police stand between Soi 13 and Soi 15 on Sukhumvit, where uniformed officers handed out 500 Baht littering fines daily to people just walking past as an entrenched, apparently sanctioned form of corruption.

You didn't have to litter. You just had to walk past on the sidewalk.

They even had their own brick booth built, apparently to keep them shaded and comfortable in the implementation of this ruse. I needed a place that was like this — a place where corruption was available to everyone, a place where expediency and tardiness flourished amidst a landscape of hazy laws and lazy, opportunistic officials.

Thailand was not perfect. Life had taught me that there was no such thing as permanent perfection and that everything was always in a state of change. Natural laws always make enduring perfection in anything an unattainable illusion, something that, if you never took the time to understand, made for a very miserable life. Perfection always required the coming together of opposites on a continuum — and although in transition they occasionally crossed over into the same space for just a brief moment, any sense of perfection having a permanent state was just simply not possible. The bad in one thing was often the good in another, and to take one away usually takes the other away — each referenced the other at two ends of the same continuum, constantly moving along it.

For example, the obstinate belligerence that made my wife almost impossible to communicate with was also the ground in which her unwavering discipline for exercise and fitness had its roots.

Freedom and civility were perhaps another good example. My definition of the perfect country was one where you had the freedom to buy fireworks over the counter whenever you wanted, but a place also where people stood to one side of the escalator to allow others to pass. I have never found this country, and I have decided that it doesn't exist, at least in any permanent state. Like a linear see-saw, there is only ever a brief moment in time when the balance of perfection is achieved, where people both understand what a wonderful thing freedom is and, at the same time, choose to take responsibility for themselves in relation to everyone else — to be "civil".

History has shown that golden periods in time — like Rome in the 200 years at the time of Christ, or Lee Kuan Yew's Singapore at the turn of the latest millennium, end as suddenly as they appear. Inevitably, freedom, inclusion — being granted a seat at the table — becomes a tool used by the ignorant, the spiteful, and the opportunistic — a chance to exploit and take advantage of civility, to push others under — to get the upper hand.

Human nature.

Eventually, like what was happening under the new world order of the Zealotribe, freedom was used by ugly women in comfortable shoes and short beta-balding men with large briefcases as tools to exact revenge for a fictional version of their lives they spend a lifetime of bitterness and misery concocting.

Nestled inside an echo chamber crowded with fellow miscreants from all walks of life, they took control of my Australia. They set about abrogating all responsibility for their failures, concocting complex systems of accusations and blame underpinned by almost childlike superficial arguments.

They conjured up great grievances by manipulating history and twisting logic. They traveled back and forth through time, superimposing cherry-picked sets of standards and "values" from the present onto a period in time that was generations ago, leveraging some perceived injustice from the past to improve their social status and boost their bank accounts and their careers in the present. Social and financial reparations demanded for things done centuries ago, to people, and by people, all long dead. People labeled as guilty, and forced to pay a price for things they never did, to people who never suffered, by people who never even took responsibility for their own behavior, or the behavior of their own children.

The most effective way to destroy people is to deny and obliterate their own understanding of their history...He who controls the past controls the future. He who controls the present controls the past.

George Orwell

"Another drink, Sir?" the hostess was asking, jolting me back from my thoughts. "Gin and tonic, thank you", I replied. Regardless of how physically arduous it was, I loved flying. It was like getting a haircut — you were forced to just sit and relax. There were no other options.

I retreated back into my mind.

These pairs of opposing forces, I had come to conclude, encompassed everything. Everything was assessable and defined against its own unique continuum that extended from one extreme to the opposite extreme. Good/evil, day/night, alive/dead, lazy/dedicated, happy/sad, moral/amoral, honest/dishonest, fat/fibre: endless examples of how all of life can be defined by where it sits somewhere on a bell curve — on a continuum between a pair of opposite extremes.

The eternal natural seesaw of Yin and Yang — Quantum Photon Entanglement.

Nothing sits outside this world of opposites. The masses in the bell curve, clinging to habit and monotony forming the great knotted ball of mediocrity in the middle — climbing all over each other, using their fear and their comforts as footholds in their quest to stay away from the edges. And the rest of us? To varying degrees, we allow ourselves to slide, to drip, and to seep into the tapers on either side — expectations pricked.

For me, this phenomenon of bell curves and balance had become very real, very personal, very suddenly.

The memories and the regrets had joined together and formed ranks facing off against the opposing forces of opportunity, the future, choices — the merchants of the options of what to do with what was left. For the first time in my life, the forces stood equal. Balanced. At 61 years old, the protagonists of this natural balance that judges and decides all things had quietly encircled me without me even realising it — some were glowering; some looked like they cared, smiling quietly; others just stood there staring at me, giving nothing away.

There is a sadness in realizing that the person you have become is not the person you once wanted to be. It is the sadness of looking back on your life and seeing all the ways you have compromised, all the dreams you have let go, all the parts of yourself you have lost along the way. And in that sadness, there is a sense of mourning, not just for the life you could have had, but for the person you could have been.

T.S. Eliot - The Love Song of J. Alfred Prufrock

It is a point in a lifetime that begins at the end of life's blissful years, a clock that starts at that exact moment the penny drops, when you realise that the reliable endless line of years ahead of you has finished — it has come to an end. A profound awareness brought about by old age or some horrible news that weighs up your past against your future and announces that they are equal — or worse. You realise for the first time that every step, every day you live from now, takes you down a gradually increasingly slippery twisting slope where both sides are lined by death's foot soldiers in all of their grotesque uniforms, patiently waiting for you to slip, for their opportunity to be the one to win your soul.

Like you wake up one morning and you realise that your future is behind you.

It feels like the beginning of the end is probably the best way of explaining it — a point in your life when it hits you that the past is going to be bigger than the future from here on. I mean, you wake up, and suddenly you're in a different place, and everyone is younger than you. Everything you thought and said and did yesterday is gone. You're invisible. You feel like tomorrow has forgotten you, and if you dare to wander into it, everyone you encounter will be slightly uncomfortable with you being there. All of a sudden, you lose everything.

Gone overnight.

I mean don't get me wrong, it's not like a ship on the horizon getting slowly further away. Bang, it's gone — it's a fucking car crash. One day, when you talk, people smile and listen, and the next, nothing — worse — uncomfortable disinterest. Wandering along that continuum from birth towards death, life, fate, time, they all make you realise that getting old is a fucking nightmare.

I found myself looking down at my meal tray and the carefully balanced utensils and packaging left over. Delicious, as always, I thought. I actually think there is a linear relationship between how hungry you are, how much you are at the mercy of the airline — trapped in a chair, miles above the earth in a silver tube — and how enjoyable the food is. Under any other circumstances, it would probably be very average.

I turned my head and gazed across the empty seat next to me, past the young woman curled up in the window seat and out into the clouds, plump and silvery-soft against the endless afternoon sun as it chased us around the globe. Refocusing from outside, I studied the woman's face as she slept. She looked Thai, but her pale skin made me think that perhaps she was half Thai and half European. I reached over and, quietly lowering her tray table, placed the meal tray that the stewardess had left on the seat between us onto it, and went back to my thoughts.

I had decided that, in many ways, Thailand and Australia sat on opposite ends of one of these continuums — although the march of the apocalyptic horsemen of post-modernism was making sure that Thailand was quickly moving in towards Australia and the grey misery of the socio-political centre-left.

The obvious difference between Thailand and the modern Western world is that in countries like Australia, corruption is hidden in plain view, integrated like a cancer into the framework of the rule of law that sustains it. In Australia, the State and the large private sector monoliths are granted exclusive access to the financial pig-trough, and all the opportunities and excesses that it offers up. In these modern Western countries, through their structure, and their resources, and their lawyers, and their lobbyists, these privileged few thrive and wallow in their greed, wastefulness, and incivility, taking full advantage of complying with the requirement of the law while giving its intent, not even a moment's thought.

Take whatever you can, exploit the system at every opportunity — that is the battle cry.

The "State Pathocracy" — the pathological bureaucracy — gorges itself on the hard-earned income of the masses, feeding its voracious appetite for more staff and more control. Shifting its focus incrementally away from serving the people and turning it internally upon itself, eventually the taxpayers becoming almost incidental in the process — just a funding bloc.

150 years ago you didn't have to ask permission from the government to go fishing, own a property, build on your property, renovate your home, use a transportation vehicle, start a business, get married, own a weapon, hunt, cut hair, sell products, protest, grow your own food, sell that food that you grew on your own property, or even just set up a lemonade stand. Now, you virtually can't do anything without asking for the government's permission first...If you still think you're free, you're deluding yourself...You're a free-range human in a tax farm.

Truth-to-the-rescue @ Instagram

Concerns and complaints from individuals and businesses trying to navigate the endless green tape, red tape, and piles of obfuscating paperwork falling on deaf ears. Or worse, administrative failures being responded to with ever-increasing numbers of formal Government enquiries and reviews that cost a fortune in taxpayer funds but never ever result in anything reasonable or just.

Tails wagging dogs.

To me, to work for the government, for the State, was just one step away from being on welfare — the rations of slavery. It was just backdoor socialism. Bourgeoning State employment numbers, more and more people becoming directly dependent on Government handouts — instead of a welfare cheque, a fortnightly salary cheque.

> *Socialists don't like people to do things for themselves. Socialists like to get people dependent on the State. You'll never build a great society that way.*
>
> Margaret Thatcher

Actually, in my opinion, to work for the government was worse. I mean, someone on welfare, apart from using up public funds, at least does not have the opportunity to do direct damage to a country and its people — doesn't have important responsibilities that they can fuck up. The lack of accountability in the public sector actually caused pain and misery to everyone else. These lazy fuckers that work the system doing the very minimum, clocking in, clocking out, exploiting things like "flexi-time" and "penalty pay rates", and State funded outrageously leveraged superannuation algorithms. Their jobs, their income, safe and protected from recessions and government-inspired ruses like pandemics and blunt-instrument interest rate rises, while everyone else lives under stress and the daily threat of losing their employment, their businesses, and their homes.

And the inevitable talent-fade these organisations suffer as a result of distorted hiring policies like Substantive Equality, or just capable people joining them and allowing themselves to drift lazily — to be absorbed into the culture of generically low expectations that is fostered by the sheer critical mass or the monopolistic nature of these organisations. That haze of "secure mediocrity" big companies and government departments seem to nurture as these people quickly give up on thinking and striving for better, and instead, acquiesce to the ethos of doing the minimum and just counting down their days to retirement.

Any reasonable person understands and would absolutely support "equality of opportunity" because it's logical and decent, and good for a society. It offers the chance for the very best — the smartest and the most talented, the most dedicated — to achieve success, regardless of where they are from, what colour their skin is, or what religion or what sex they are.

But equality of outcomes? Substantive Equality? The ideology that was the power base for the rise to authority and influence for many of these people? Just fucking ridiculous.

For Australia, it had been a disaster.

By definition, if you override the principles of merit, the most talented, capable people lose out on positions of influence to people with less talent who are less capable. Quotas are filled though a process that places a distorted selection bias on constructs that have no bearing at all on the job's requirements; things like the colour of someone's skin, their sexuality, their religion or their gender. The results of this stupidity not only harm the people who should have been given these opportunities based on merit, but are damaging for the whole of society. They affect everyone who has to endure the consequences, the sub-optimal outcomes that these people produce that are in some way less than what they could be, what they should be.

At their most dangerous — at State level — ideologies like Substantive Equality create government bureaucracies that produce significantly less than the best possible financial, social, and foreign policy — while never paying any price for their failings and their mistakes.

The US government can't go bankrupt because we can print our own money...the---ahh... so the...I mean...again...the

government definitely prints money and it definitely lends
that money by selling bonds...ahhh is that what they do?...
they, they, umm... they yeah, they ummm, they sell bonds,
yeah they sell bonds...the language and the concepts can
be confusing but there is no question that the government
prints money and then it uses that money to umm ahhh so
umm yeah I guess I'm just I can't talk I mean I don't get it, I
don't know what they are talking about like cause its like the
government clearly prints money, it does it all the time...

Jared Bernstein 2023 — Chair of the United States Council of Economic Advisors
Qualifications: Bachelor's Degree in Music

No wonder in Australia and in other Western countries there had been a huge increase in people becoming homeless and living in tents. They were everywhere — the parks and the riverbanks were covered with them — mums and dads and kids forced to live in fucking tents because of incompetent people developing and implementing poorly thought-out wasteful government policy. Imagine being a parent, trying your hardest to get ahead, and having to tell your children that you were now all going to have to live in a tent. A fucking tent! In a park, with no toilet or running water! In Australia!

Just ridiculous.

And these callous, selfish fucking dolts — they never connect the dots as they drive past the parks full of tents and the homeless people lying on the sidewalk with their cardboard signs. They never accept any responsibility — just take, and take and take. More investment properties, more shares in their portfolios, more cookie-cutter-mindless-social-media-posting holidays. They choose, they make the deliberate choice to not see past themselves, their self-interest, and their ideologies.

These State agencies were full of the technocrats that caused people's children to be terrified and to wear fucking surgical masks to school for no reason at all, with their draconian just-plain-fucking-stupid mandates during "Covid".

Assholes...

I know what I'd do if I was in charge. I would force every person hired as a Parking Inspector — you know, those assholes who drive around in air-conditioned fucking cars all day fining people hundreds and hundreds of dollars for parking in the wrong place? And force every person employed in that bursting bulge of mid-level-management in public administration that is responsible for most of government wastage and expedience. I would force every single one of these fuckers to sign an employment contract that had a special clause in it. In order to get the job, the Position Description would include a requirement that as part of the role, they accept that once a week; let's say every Friday, one of them would be chosen entirely at random, and that person would be publicly flogged in the town square on Saturday morning — for the pleasure of the people.

The fucking crowds would be huge, people looking for some recompense, some fucking retribution against these assholes who applied for jobs like this and the system that they represented.

I'd go. I'd go to every single one of them — sit in the front fucking row. Assholes!

In Australia we spend $8B every year on policies and programs supposedly to help the lives of indigenous Australians. And year after year nothing ever gets any better for them. Greedy, lazy, white bureaucrats and so-called "Indigenous Leaders" skim it all away, hijacking it into pork-barreled programs that "sound good" — nothing more than outsourced get-rich-quick schemes that absorb the lion's share of the funding.

Yeah sure, they'll argue on and on and fucking on with micro examples about how much good they are doing, but the endless misery of women and children being beaten and raped within a haze of violence and substance abuse in squalid, concrete-slabbed-corrugated-iron hovels in filthy Aboriginal settlements continues on. It's honestly as if this fucking nightmare remains deliberately unaddressed because its continuation provides the justification for the endless gravy train of taxpayer funds that these profoundly selfish parasites feed off.

And it's not just the governments in Western countries. Big business is just as bad. Huge mining companies buying up massive tracts of farmland under the guise of investment in cattle stations and farms — they even show their prize bulls at the State Fair for fuck's sake. Meanwhile, they quietly babysit the vast coal reserves just below the surface, beyond the scrutiny of the members of the press who they bought years ago, their "Primary Producer" status offering them substantial tax advantages while hindering any native title claims.

At the same time, they fly their environmental colours and "acknowledge the traditional owners of the land" at every opportunity — on every fucking document and from every virtue-signaling flagpole available to them.

I mean, they're fucking mining companies! What the fuck are they doing buying farms and showing prize bulls at annual fairs? Why does no one in the press ask these questions?

For decades these companies have decimated small countries in Africa as the oligarchs that own them sit by their fireplaces in their mansions in the mountains on Lake Thun, instructing their lawyers to drag out lawsuits for decades and to do everything they can to make sure that any actual payouts, any actual compensation imposed on them as penance for their belligerent treachery, is only pennies to the estates of people who they have blinded and killed by their gas leaks in their greedy fucking quest for more.

But in Thailand, the rule of law is different. It is weak and malleable, and as a result, its base-level generic corruption offers up a strangely organic, altruistic equality. Everyone in Thailand, at least to some extent, has access to manipulating the system to their own ends. Everyone is equal in the grey haze of flexible laws and the purchase of discretion, with many, especially the police, having an air of sloppy opportunism about them as they allow themselves to be distracted away from poorly rewarded diligence towards other, more lucrative opportunities.

All things considered, Thailand was a good choice in terms of a place that would offer up not only extensive, affordable options to fill in the gaps so that I could avoid that fucking mirror — without the overarching threat of a diligent legal system — but also a place where any police investigation would be lazy, cursory at best, and would draw the simplest conclusions. Although she was hurtling quickly into the abyss of Western modernity, Thailand still had a comforting mix of opportunistic freedom and civility about her.

Enough for what I had in mind, anyway.

The girl curled up against the window next to me woke up with a start as if from a dream where she was falling — dribble glistening on her chin. Looking a little embarrassed, she wiped her chin on her sleeve away from me and, after taking a moment to gather her thoughts, noticed the tray table with the meal in front of her and looked over at me. "Thanks", she said with a smile, wriggling about adjusting her skirt under the table.

"My pleasure", I said, sounding a little more friendly than I had intended. She laughed, but her smile was simple and kind. A Thai smile. I guessed she was about 23 years old, but, like most Asian women, it was very difficult to tell. They seemed to reach 18 or 19 years old, and then they tended to look as if they were in their mid-twenties until they were well into their 40s before they started to noticeably age, and you would guess they were maybe 35. It was only when they got into their late 50's or even early 60's that they suddenly started to look their years.

Carefully removing the foil lid from her meal, she started eating, gazing out the window at the clouds.

Watching her, she ate slowly, the way people used to eat — the way Europeans eat — without the voracious, embarrassing urgency with which fat people consume food. It was as if she was just nourishing her body, almost out of obligation, because she had to.

'Tell me what you do with the food you eat, and I'll tell you who you are. Some turn their food into fat and manure, some into work and good humour, and others, I'm told, into God. So there must be three sorts of men. I'm not one of the worst, boss, nor yet one of the best. I'm somewhere in between the two. What I eat I turn into work and good humour. That's not too bad, after all! '

He looked at me wickedly and started laughing.

'As for you, boss,' he said, 'I think you do your level best to turn what you eat into God. But you can't quite manage it, and that torments you. The same thing's happening to you as happened to the crow.'

'What happened to the crow, Zorba?'

'Well, you see, he used to walk respectably, properly — well, like a crow. But one day he got it into his head to try and strut about like a pigeon. And from that time on the poor fellow couldn't for the life of him recall his own way of walking. He was all mixed up, don't you see? He just hobbled about.'

Zorba The Greek — Nikos Kazantzakis

Well, enough putting it off, I thought to myself. Fuck it. I'd been putting it up and putting it off for almost 40 years now. I unbuckled my seat belt, stood up, took my laptop out of my bag from the overhead lockers, and sat back down again. I dropped the tray table, flipped the lid, pressed the button, smiled a moment later at the picture of my family on the desktop — taken in much happier times — clicked on the MS Word icon, clicked on "New", and there it was. The cursor. Blinking. Not like it used to — not like a challenge, or a threat, or an embarrassment for what hadn't been done — not like a barrier to anything moving forward. Now, it was blinking like a lighthouse, full of hope and positivity, welcoming me home.

Three hundred and sixty-five days, and I didn't have a moment more to lose. The starter's gun went off, and I started to write.

MEREDITH DEW AND
THE WITCHES OF CRACKLEWOOD FOREST

CHAPTER I

None of the moon shone in the sky above the small country town as Eugene Lumpthistle made his way along its dark, deserted streets. The town was Applecreek Grove, and the year was 1789. Nestled into the edge of a forest, the town survived for the most part on the proceeds of apple growing or, more correctly, the proceeds of its apple cider factory. The apple cider factory had been the birth of the town and the backbone of its economy since 1629.

It had all begun in the early 1620s when a middle-aged gentleman by the name of Edward P. Fizzlebub pioneered his way into a then little-known part of the country, and upon finding a creek and declaring the surrounding land to be "good apple country", set about producing what the world has come to know as;

FIZZLEBUB'S
APPLE CIDER
"The world's first and only TRUE cider"
Edward P. Fizzlebub
There's a little Fizzlebub in all of us!

For that is what appears on the label of every bottle. But enough for now of Mr. Fizzlebub and his cider and back to Eugene Lumpthistle, whom, for all you know, l introduced, forgot, and is now wandering aimlessly about Applecreek Grove in the dark for no apparent reason.

Living as he did on the outskirts of a small town with a tiny population, Eugene was not just another lad of lanky build and lumbering gait, but he was THE lad of lanky build and lumbering gait.

He had said goodbye to Charlie Smigley in front of "The Last Picture Show Theatre" at a quarter past ten and was heading for home as briskly as his lanky legs would propel him. As he walked along, there was one question uppermost in his mind: should he save himself the extra two miles' walk and take the short-cut through Cracklewood Forest?

Cracklewood Forest surrounded the town of Applecreek Grove and, in part, extended into it. In the early days, parts of the forest closest to town had been cleared, leaving a stand of trees about 800 yards wide to protrude in amongst the houses as one side of the town grew around it. How large the forest was no one really knew, and that was probably because everyone did know that it was a dangerous place to go wandering into. Once one had walked the length of this protruding stand of trees and started into the forest, it got darker and darker very quickly, which meant it became easier and easier to get lost. The forest was said to become so dark, in fact, that lanterns were needed to light the way even during the day if one was to journey deep enough. As a consequence, few ventured into the forest, for over the years, the majority of those who had, including those with lanterns, were never seen again. Legend had it that Edward P. Fizzlebub was one of the few exceptions, for he would often disappear for days at a time into Cracklewood Forest, and although over the years there had been much speculation, thoughtful chin-scratching, and wisely espoused theories, no one really knew why.

Eugene pressed on into the night, his hands burrowing more deeply into his coat pockets as gusts of cold wind stirred the trees along the footpath and lifted leaves from the sidewalk to send them cart-wheeling across the road in front of him. Thunder rumbled in the distance.

A large drop of water plopped onto his cheek, and his stride took on a note of urgency. Two hundred yards ahead of him was the alleyway that marked the fork in his journey. The ally lay between Kosinkie's shoe factory and old Miss Peterson's place, leading away from the road and into Cracklewood Forest. He arrived at the entrance, still undecided on the path he would take home.

It was not only the forest at night that concerned him, but there was also the graveyard to consider. It was old, having not been used for years, and contained no more than about twenty or thirty graves, with one of these being the final resting place of Edward P. Fizzlebub. Although the memory of Edward Fizzlebub was held with great affection and reverence by the towns' people, there was no need for them to tend his grave, as a larger-than-life statue of him stood in the middle of town in a grandiose expression of their eternal gratitude to the man and his achievements.

That the graveyard was small and discontinued did not, to Eugene, detract from the fact that it was none the less a graveyard and one that he would have to pass through at night in the middle of the forest. The main problem was that there was no way around this particular part of town, for to cut through the end of Cracklewood Forest and avoid passing through the graveyard would mean having to leave the path, which to him, did not seem like such a bright idea. Even though it was the easiest section of the forest to negotiate, the possibility of getting lost was not inconceivable, especially at night.

He stood there cloaked in darkness, listening to the wind in the trees and watching the leaves shift restlessly about on the grassy lane as his mind debated the pros and cons of the two ways home. Thunder cracked and rumbled louder than before; the storm was closing in. All of a sudden, he made up his mind.

"After all", he thought to himself, "What am I afraid of?" He strode briskly down the grassy lane and entered into Cracklewood Forest as thunder broke loudly overhead.

The path was about one yard wide, covered with fallen leaves, with occasional tufts of grass popping up wherever they could. With his hands still wedged firmly into his coat pockets, he moved along with a steady, stilted kind of upright jog. The wind picked up and began to whip through the trees, the rustle of the leaves rising to a crescendo. Leaves and twigs showered down from every direction as the drops of rain came in gusts that came and went, suddenly dropping off again.

Eugene ploughed on, knowing that at the pace he was moving, it would not be long before he reached the graveyard. Although the rain seemed now as if it had begun to ease, this gave him little comfort, for he had the distinct feeling it would be much easier on his nerves if he were to glide through the forest under the camouflage of pouring rain.

Eugene stopped abruptly just as the storm seemed to die down almost completely, leaving what was left of the wind in the trees to shake the droplets free of the leaves, mimicking the sound of rain. The forest canopy had suddenly opened up, and he found himself standing on the edge of the graveyard. Breathing heavily, he could feel his heart pounding as fear and exhaustion settled down on him at once. In front of him was a patch of ground about forty yards across and about the same in width. Through the darkness, he could only just make out the great oak tree that stood in the centre, and around the tree, scattered about at varying distances, the grey, motionless headstones.

What was that? He thought. Did he just see something move? Surely it was just his imagination, he decided, peering into the graveyard as intensely as he could.

The sky was deeply overcast. The headstones distinguished almost solely by their slightly lighter colour than the darkness about them. Eugene stood stationary, watching. His mind suddenly calling back the tales of Witches he had heard while growing up. Witches that supposedly dwelled in the forest waiting to gobble up little children.

Stories of Meredith Dew.

He knew the rational explanation for these stories was to keep young children out of the forest and thus prevent them from getting lost. But standing as he was on the edge of the graveyard in the middle of the night, in the middle of the forest, his attempts at rational thought were, at best, furtive and unconvincing.

Standing there, one story from his childhood, in particular, came back to him about Edward P. Fizzlebub and a band of Witches. Rumor had it that Fizzlebub had managed to purloin the recipe for a magic potion from a band of Witches and had used this concoction as the secret ingredient in the creation of his Apple Cider. The oldest rumor in the town was that this sorcery was still used to this day in the brewing of the cider. The formula for this potion was said to have been passed down from Fizzlebub to Fizzlebub. It was said that the secret remained closely guarded by those Fizzlebubs who had inherited direct responsibility for the brewing of the cider and that this was the case right up to the present day with Wilbur P. Fizzlebub the 3rd, the last remaining Fizzlebub, who currently ran the factory.

The truth was that drinking one of Fizzlebub's ciders did bring about a state of mild euphoria and an almost imperceptible loss of the ability to concentrate. This, of course, made his cider very appealing in a confusing sort of way because the memory between drinking his cider and a couple of hours later, never really rang quite true. Over the years, many people had tried to understand the effect that the cider had on them, but no matter how hard they tried, any real attempt seemed to be stifled by what could be best described as a sort of blurred apathy of the mind.

A large droplet of water slid from a leaf above and landed on Eugene's nose, dragging him back from his thoughts to his current predicament. He looked about, listening intently, "No Witches?" He thought to himself, "Good". Suddenly, he was off! Bounding through the graveyard with all the speed he could muster – his arms pumping now, his jacket billowing around him. But he had hardly travelled a third of the way across when suddenly his left foot came down into nothingness. He found himself falling forward, plunging face first into a void as black as pitch, then THWACK! He came to rest on his face in black, oily mud.

Forcing himself to roll over so he could breathe and clearing his mouth and his eyes of mud with his hands, he lay perfectly still for a moment, shocked, trying to comprehend what had happened. The ground had just disappeared beneath him. Turning his head and looking up at the overcast sky framed inside a perfect rectangle, he realised with terror what had happened. Lying there watching grey clouds glide past in front of the stars, he realised he was at the bottom of a freshly dug muddy grave. "Why the devil was there an open grave in this place? It hadn't been used for years", he thought to himself.

Then he heard it — the sound of cackling, shrill as hyenas and as harsh as crows. It seemed to be coming from all directions. Dark shapes appeared silhouetted around the edge of the grave above him, voices over voices intermingling with laughter. Eyes glowing the colour of pale green and red, looking down at him. Eugene tried to scream, but no sound came out. The shapes above must have seen his expression, and the cackling rose again to a chaotic chorus.

Without warning, the laughter stopped. The two shapes that stood at the end of the grave above his feet parted and up moved a slightly more stooped shape than the rest, its eyes glowing a deep, bright red... It stood apparently leaning on some sort of staff, peering forward down into the grave.

And then it spoke. Its voice was all at once strangled and seething with anger, a frightening old throaty rasp, "One hundred and sixty years!" and then it began to chant;

"CURSE THE TOWN,
CURSE THE FOLK,
CURSE THE FRUIT,
WITH WORMS TO CHOKE.

SNARE THE PREY,
THE NEEDED SPICE,
IN HOLLOW GRAVE,
WITH MOON AND VICE.
WITHIN THE WRETCHED PIT,
IN FUZZLEBUB'S HOLE,
TO RETURN THE POWER,
THAT HE HATH STOLE."

As soon as she had finished, the others all hissed in unison and then just as quickly fell silent again. Light rain started to fall.

"Let's take him now", chortled one with green eyes.

"Quiet hag!" hissed the one who had rhymed the verse, "Lest you wish to become a hog." A frightening hiss issued forth from the one who had been reprimanded.

It was now more than apparent to Eugene, who had been lying motionless at the bottom of the grave, para- lyzed with fear, that the one with the brightest eyes was the leader, the leader of a band of Witches. She spoke again.

"I am Gagglebroth! Queen of the Morgriouse Clan, con- troller of mortals. Who be our little mud worm?"

Eugene lay still, too frightened to answer. His whole body aching from the fall, his eyes stinging from the mud, and his heart pounding with fear.

"Who be you!" repeated Gagglebroth, this time a com- mand more than a question. All of a sudden, he found the strength and presence of mind to stammer an an- swer.

"Eug-Eu—Eugene La—La—Lumpthistle."

"And what be your errand in the forest on a night such as this?" The dark shape hissed back menacingly.

"Errand?"

"Errand worm. What be your purpose?" replied Gaggle- broth, beginning to glower.

"Just taking a shortcut home", said Eugene shakily. For a moment, everything was silent as the slight rain fell softly.

"Out worm!" Commanded Gagglebroth. Eugene felt himself being lifted, floating by magic from the grave. No sooner was he out when Gagglebroth suddenly thrust forward with her staff, and he was propelled backwards into a tomb stone, the air in his lungs expelled from his mouth with a loud Oomph as he bounced off the tombstone and fell forward onto the ground with a thud, and lay there gasping for breath.

"What do you want?" Eugene forced himself to ask, scared but feeling he had to at least pretend not to be quite so frightened as he was.

"Hold your tongue, or I'll have it removed, you miserable bag of blood and bones! Beetlecrunch! Garblebilk!" directed Gagglebroth.

Two of the Witches, the other one with red eyes and the one with green eyes approached him. "An ear, we'll want, something in case that meddling Dew turns up. Bring him!" And with that, Gagglebroth looked warily about and, turning quickly, disappeared into the darkness with surprising speed, the remaining three of the brood slipping into the forest after her.

"Please let me go", pleaded Eugene, getting a closer look at his two captors. Their faces taught with haggard, leathery, wrinkled, scared skin, sickly grey in colour. Their noses, one bulbous, the other hooked, both covered in warts and glistening weeping sores. Their mouths were nothing more than a slash within thin, pale, sickly lips. He leapt up to try and run away, but the one closest, the one with the green eyes, grabbed him by the shoulder with a talon-like grip and, with surprising strength, forced him back down against the tomb stone.

"Be still, you little dog." Said Beetlecrunch, her breath wheezing in and out, a cloud of foul odor settling down on him.

"Just an ear", taunted Garblebilk, extending the

pointer finger on her right hand. A long, slender, hooked nail protruding from it. She drew her arm back, then flashed forward. Eugene felt a numbness on the left side of his head, then, feeling the sensation of blood running down the side of his neck, screamed. Ignoring him, Garblebilk picked the severed ear up from the ground and placed it in a leather pouch under her cloak.

By this time, Eugene had begun to whimper. "Be quiet, you little runt", hissed Garblebilk, her pale red eyes scanning the perimeter of the graveyard, seemingly peering through into the forest as they started forward, all but dragging Eugene between them.

"Tears tart the stew", cackled Beetlecrunch.

"You too!" snapped Garblebilk.

"You're not Gagglebroth. You're not the boss of me, cow!" spat Beetlecrunch, her voice horse with rage.

"Meredith, Oh, Meredith?" mocked Beetlecrunch in a soft whisper. Garblebilk stopped abruptly, her eyes ablaze with anger as she glared at Beetlecrunch, who swallowed dryly, realising she had taken things too far. Just as suddenly as they had stopped, they started moving forward at Garblebilk's lead, Eugene reluctantly between them, pondering the significance of what he had just witnessed. Then, out of the blue, he had an overpowering urge.

"Meredith Dew!" He yelled as loud as he could. "Meredith Dew!"

At that moment, almost as soon as the name had escaped his lips, a light came from behind them. Eugene turned to see a door had opened at the base of the large oak tree, and a light from inside spilt out across the graveyard sending elongated shadows out from the tombstones in front of it.

"Run, cow!" rasped Garblebilk, rushing forward into

the forest. "Dew has awakened. Gagglebroth will turn your hide to bacon for this."

All of a sudden, the witches were gone, and Eugene, standing alone in the middle of the graveyard, noticed the funniest-looking fellow he had ever seen suddenly step out of the light from inside the tree. He was four feet tall, or there abouts, and looked like a pear on legs. His shock of hair shone like gold in the light. His body was plump and round, getting plumper and rounder as you followed it down till it got to his waist, where it was plumpest and roundest of all.

Under this remarkable torso were two thick, short, stumpy legs that disappeared just below the knee into two enormous bright purple leather boots that must have accommodated two equally enormous feet. Eugene could not see his face with the light behind. Suddenly, the man called out.

"Someone holler, someone yell", and then came the sound of snorting and snuffling followed by, "Witches in the night, I freshly smell!"

He started walking towards Eugene.

"You know mine, I know not yours. State your name and why with all cause".

"Eugene Lumpthistle", Eugene answered nervously. The strange little man from the tree stopped a few feet in front of him and snuffled once or twice as he studied him. Eugene stood staring at the strangest face he had ever seen.

The fellow had eyes that were oval in shape and decidedly sleepy-looking. Under these eyes sat the most ridiculous of noses. It was almost perfectly round and was almost the size of a peach. Eugene could not take his eyes off it. It vibrated when the funny little man spoke and jiggled about when he walked. Standing there looking at the strange little fellow,

Eugene concluded that if this fellow ever sneezed, it would truly be something to behold.

They stood staring at one another in the star light, the rain falling softly around them. Then, all of a sudden, Eugene felt a cold chill run down his spine as a horrible, gut-wrenching scream of pain drifted out of the forest across the night air, turning instinctively in the direction it had come from.

"Beetlecrunch or Curdleslop, no doubt. Punishment for allowing you to wake me. I assume it was you who dragged me from some much-needed sleep? We haven't been formally introduced. Meredith Dew", said the funny little man, tipping the small leather hat that sat in the middle of the untidy shock of golden hair.

"Eugene Lumpthistle", said Eugene, starting to feel slightly more comfortable when yet another scream more horrible than the last rang out, followed by a flash of crimson light from deep within the forest.

"My! Gagglebroth is upset. You must be quite important. Good heavens, man, why are you covered in mud from top to toe?"

"They cut off my ear and took it!" protested Eugene, sounding somewhat dazed and confused.

"Let me see." Said Meredith. "Indeed they have. Well, no time to lose, young fellow, follow me."

And with that, Meredith Dew turned and lumbered back toward the doorway in the oak tree. Certainly not wanting to go back into the forest and not knowing what else to do, Eugene scurried after him, holding his handkerchief over what used to be his ear.

4

Karl Marx in a Flower Garden Wearing a Purple and Yellow Sundress Being Raped over a Huge Bible by a Pudgy Technocrat

Looking up, I glanced at my watch — I guessed I had been writing for a little over three hours, and my mind was numb. Saving my work and shutting the computer down, I motioned to the hostess walking towards me.

"Could I have a gin and tonic on ice, please?"

She smiled. "Yes, I'll just be a moment sir," replying as she walked past me without missing a beat.

Sitting there sipping my drink, I started thinking about my life again. I knew full well that it was only my past that sustained me — memories of places, of my family, us laughing, living close together in those balmy days. The excitement of tomorrow's opportunities — that anticipation — now replaced by memories. My wife, before the endless years of grey repetition had taken their toll — when she at least tried to feel love, tried to love me. My children, when they were younger and looked up to me, before they began to argue with me and started noticing all the failings I endured as a result of life taking so many pieces away from me.

When they had needed me — before that long feeling of loneliness in their company, which, regardless of my clumsy attempts to keep things alive, to reconnect with them, eventually grew into a perpetual awkward silence.

It was strange the way, over time, my kindness towards them seemed to feed their disdain for me. Like most husbands, I had endured the suffering of "the doing of things" to keep the machinery of marriage alive, of managing my wife's wrath.

I had always believed — better that; to suffer the abuse than to live that other life, that life of strategised, contrived manipulation; splashes of disinterest, and metered-out psychological abuse, which I knew was probably the most effective way to stave off the natural contempt that showing kindness and decency seemed to bring out in women.

"Treat her mean, keep her keen," I think is the term used to describe it.

In most instances, I don't think a man can make a woman happy. I think it's a trap, an impossible quest that men take on, this belief that they have the power to make a woman happy. No matter what he does, no matter how hard he tries, I think only she can make herself happy. As men, I think the best we can do is to give up, and simply be kind and supportive.

The greatest question that has never been answered, and which I have not yet been able to answer despite my thirty years of research into the feminine soul, is: What does a woman want?

Sigmund Freud

In a less complicated, simpler approach, and without any spoken agreement, my wife and I seemed to have settled on "selective resignation". A life where we each resigned in just enough circumstances to keep the relationship alive while choosing carefully when to hold our ground, just enough to stay sane. Picking your battles, my father would have called it.

However, occasionally, the bile would rise up in her, and even if I decided I would agree with everything she said in a discussion, to completely disregard any opinions or ideas that I may have had just to diffuse the situation, she would still find some obtuse angle of argument that she would leverage into an almost incendiary, seemingly uncontrollable rage. She would then invariably refuse any more discussion, preferring the matter to remain unresolved, simmering in a pot of resentment until she felt like dishing it up again.

While I waited, her weapon of choice during the truce was always the same — she would use my kindness against me, refusing to let me hug her or do anything for her to try to fix things — even if she was in the wrong — even, if she later apologised and admitted she was in the wrong. I mean fuck, can you imagine that? That someone that said yes to marrying you, would use your kindness and desperation to fix things — to just make things better — as a tool to hurt you?

Logic twisted 180° forcing you to constantly have to apologise for defending yourself against the endless cycles of completely unreasonable contemptuous fucking rage. Without children, there is no way on earth you would tolerate it — you would just walk away. I mean, you wouldn't even look back, not even once — you'd just fucking walk away.

Women can be scary fucking creatures.

The saddest times were when she walked away from me in her mind, when she retreated into the romance in the words of a song from her past or the hollow timber strumming of an acoustic guitar — jealously guarding those thoughts, those memories from any sharing, a deliberate barrier built between them and me — me and her.

It was strange; whenever I heard her singing to music I had put on while I was cooking, I would feel a great connection and actually fall deeply in love with her all over again. And whenever I saw her put in her noise-cancelling earbuds to block out my music, my heart would sink so fucking low. Completely irrationally, I would feel like everything was lost.

She did not marry me for love. I knew that because of the way I had so often seen her look at a man playing the guitar in the street — any man: old-young-fat-handsome-ugly. After all, real love is not superficial. She looked at them in a way she had never looked at me, as if their tune was a magical key that opened a secret door to her heart, a world for her that was as far away as possible from the strains and the stresses of the things she had chosen, the plans she had put in place, her choices; the mechanics and the logistics of a marriage, of becoming a wife, of being a mother, of managing money and time and responsibilities and obligations, of having to fuck the same man year after year after year after year.

She couldn't possibly have married me out of love — I don't play the guitar.

Sitting there, I thought back to better times with my family. My sons, when they would jump up onto my chest and hug me with their little arms and legs, fitting around me perfectly, like a warm, soft, beautiful puzzle piece I hadn't realised was missing. Before they challenged almost everything I said and, finally, no longer sought my opinion on anything. Before time and inevitability took everything away.

That.

That's what people mean when they advise you when you have young children to "pay attention because they grow up so fast". That banal, pedestrian, endlessly repeated fucking cliché is nowhere near clear enough to express something so important as what they are trying to say.

What they should say is: Notice! Every moment of every day with them! Notice and carefully, deliberately collect and save the memories. I mean, I know that children must grow up and become themselves, but what you don't expect is not only how quickly it happens, but that it finishes, it ends — this growing up business, and when it does? You lose them! They are only entirely yours for about twelve to fourteen years, and then they turn around and they walk away. They turn their backs, and they fucking walk away! All those beautiful hugs and giggles and tickles and kisses and smiles — gone! Finished! From then on, from that moment forward, they only occasionally turn around from their world to give you an awkward hug or a smile, and in that smile, if you are really, really lucky, you may, from time to time, glimpse love.

I read once that by the time your child finishes school, you have spent 98% of the time you will ever spend with them. I'm telling you, it's a fucking nightmare. You feel so empty, so lost and alone. You have all this love; just thinking about them brings tears to your eyes, but they're gone. It's over. All that's left is the occasional fitting of you into their life.

That outrageous paradoxical realisation that we all must face; that we will always love our children so much more than we love our parents — but so will they.

This is just one of the ways that time hacks away your options, savages you, while you are busy living your life, day after day, and not noticing it. When you are taking everything for granted, and you suddenly wake up alone — regardless of how many people are around you, under the same roof — and you realise that all you have left are the most mundane of choices; when to eat, when to sleep, what to wear. Time, the most ruthless of adversaries, has taken it all away from you and given it to your children, leaving only memories and the most painful of regrets. You end up in what is called zugzwang in the chess world. No matter what option you choose, things can only get worse.

People spend their whole lives chasing money, thinking wealth is the path to happiness. But the irony is that you can have more than enough money and still be profoundly unhappy and lonely.

Wealth can be a path to fun, but fun and happiness are two entirely different things.

I was grateful in a way because absurdly, without the disdain that came from my children as they became older and from my wife reaching a point where she had nothing left to plaster over and hide just how miserable and bored she was, a point where it felt like she actually hated me, I couldn't be here on this plane.

Silver linings.

If, instead, they had stayed close to me. If my wife had had the strength not to give up, to not give in to accepting days of vanilla repetition. If she had chosen to be absolutely determined, as she once had been, to work with me to seek out new and exciting ways to make the endless days interesting and wild. If my kids had stayed connected. If they had been able to find that balance, to share their love and focus between the boyfriends and the girlfriends and the goals and the dreams with me, as deeply as they once had, I would not have been able to make the choices I had made. I could not have been here now.

The changes in people are so subtle, so incremental, that no one ever really notices it happening until it has happened, and it's over, finished, and everything you loved, everything that was special to you, all of that wonderful opportunity is lost, left behind forever in the past, in your memories.

I took a sip of my drink. And it wasn't like the world we were in was any help to a husband and a wife trying to raise children in a traditional family. My world, the place that my parents raised me in before the Zealotribe got control of everything, had been a simple place, binary: good/bad, right/wrong. Deception and deceit, when you did encounter them, were obvious, striking exceptions to the normality of things.

Ideologues were rare and were generally viewed as lunatics.

Not like today, this cesspool I had been forced to raise my children

KARL MARX IN A FLOWER GARDEN

in, where you go to a dinner party, and some fucking maniac wants to spend the whole evening trying to convince you to vote one way or another. Or when a man with a beard wears a see-through evening gown to a television premiere, and instead of people having concern for his mental health, he is praised for his bravery.

My world was gone; Herbert Marcuse and his merry band of miscreants from the Frankfurt School had certainly seen to that. While the captains of industry were busy building Western Civilisation, Marcuse, Adorno, Horkheimer, and their disciples set about taking control of the young minds of the next two or three generations of wide-eyed, ingenuous university students. In the end, the unguarded backdoors in traditional conservatism — those provisions of flexibility, kindness, and welfare that are built into the system of conservative civility, were smashed open in a zombie apocalypse of emotionally charged Cultural Marxists.

Without faith in anything, spiritual or otherwise, they saw no reason at all why they themselves should not be the centre of the universe.

Your soul is now your gender, and you get to decide what it is. You're the God now, encourage the High Priests of the Technocracy, the Pathocracy, as they stand around warming their hands at the fire of indulgent self-righteous rage they have stoked under the bubbling cauldron of social media.

Sixty years later, their work was done — the Meritocracy is destroyed, and Relativism had given birth to the monsters of Progressivism, the Pathocracy, Substantive Equality, Identity Politics, and Political Correctness.

And the West is all but destroyed.

Seemingly endless waves of indoctrinated Ideologues launching themselves into the world.

Skinny-bearded-beta men put their hair up in buns and, together with fat-pasty-pale-skinned white girls, got themselves jailhouse tattoos, and while enjoying syrupy-sweet-lattes and smashed avocado on toast, set about planning the tearing down of as many social and economic fences as they could. Their arrogance and their collective sense of entitlement ensured they didn't even for a moment consider why these fences existed, why they had been built in the first place, what greater purpose they may have had.

Where once these people served our coffees or fixed our computers, or sold our wives dresses in department stores, or processed our new driver's licenses, or returned our library books back to the appropriate slot on the shelf — or just simply stayed trapped in their homes by their anxiety, their eating disorders and their low self-esteem playing Dungeons and Dragons, they now emerged as the leaders of the technocratic revolution.

And they hated us.

Where once the wisdom rested naturally with people who had lived and learned over a lifetime, it now sat with fifteen-year-olds with blue hair. Their gender deliberately ambiguous, their focus on cultivating an expression of aloof, disdainful disinterest. They set about reinventing and rearranging the tools of discourse and technology while disregarding any value at all in the virtues of effectiveness, or outcomes, or of taking responsibility.

At every turn, their goal has been to undermine decency and civility. The men scrawny, pudgy, dressed in bikie-hacker-pantomime Jack boots and black hoodies, the women boasting about how many men they had spread their legs for.

Terms like "body count" and "slut shaming" were coined.

Most of them, of course, held daytime jobs working for the State — public service jobs that offered such low levels of expectations in terms of outcomes and accountability and such high levels of flexibility and forgiveness that they had ample free time to invest in indulging their conjured rage and implementing their misguided agendas.

Their schemes generally boiled down to executing the tried and proven politics of incremental Progressivism while the rest of us were actually at work — keeping the lights on; creating and building and maintaining. Like malicious hackers, they became experts at exploiting the "Complacency Ladder", searching for what they saw as weaknesses in the "code", scampering up the ladder and holding their new position for just long enough for us to no longer have the time or the energy to fight back against it — long enough for it to be established as a new baseline of social or economic "normality".

Overnight, they became the victims, the oppressed. Suddenly, they could blame the "patriarchy" or the "extreme far-right," or "racism", or "greedy capitalism", or any science that wasn't "their" science for all of the misery their personal shortcomings in life had dealt them.

There was no longer anything wrong with eating the whole block of chocolate instead of just one or two pieces. The problem wasn't that they were morbidly obese, that their Body Mass Index was 35. The problem lay in the discrimination they had to endure because people's perspectives had been distorted and manipulated by that other science and those horrible people, those doctors, who said they were unhealthy and were "fat-shaming" them.

Instead of exercising self-control and hitting the gym, and working hard, they embraced this New World Order of Relativism, where there was no need to take responsibility for anything. Virtually overnight, to be held accountable for almost anything was to be victimised, discriminated against, bullied.

Suddenly, everyone was anxious; everyone needed a safe space.

There was no right or wrong in the New World Order — only opinions and ideas. Words were seen as being exactly the same as actions. Everybody got to choose to be a victim, got to choose their claim to victimhood. Suddenly, everybody could be oppressed — the ultimate in egalitarian equality. Except, of course, for the oppressors. The oppressors, not surprisingly, happened to be the same people who created, built, and maintained their homes, their sewerage systems, their cars, their computers, their transport systems, and their health systems — the people who secured their fucking safety.

So suddenly you were fearful; everyone was watching you, everyone could see if you were a bad person. The ethos was that you had better cross over and join the bullies; you better join the side that was judging, attacking, or you'll be attacked — you'll lose your job, lose your friends, be ghosted, be laughed at, dragged before the courts. If you don't join them, or if you even question this brave-new-world order, how do you expect to protect yourself, protect your "social currency" that has become all that really matters to you?

The truth won't protect you. You will be an outsider, outside the echo chamber. Someone to be dealt with. Someone to be punished. Logic or science, or even common sense won't protect you. These things have no value anymore.

But I thought racism was over? I mean, wasn't it? Hadn't it been declining into oblivion for decades before the media started their prolific campaign telling us we were all raging racists?

But women and girls have been getting into university at higher, and ever-increasing rates than men and boys in the West since the 1970s?

So what? That's not the fucking point! Haven't you been listening? Women are the victims, and men are the oppressors — these are the rules now, so just shut the fuck up with your facts and your logic and your questions! No one can hear you anyway — surely you know that by now.

Become a victim — I have a higher moral status than you because I'm a victim. I am entitled, I get to tell you what to do, what is right, and what is wrong because I'm more of a victim than you are.

What a fucking mess.

> The greater part of the population is not very intelligent, dreads responsibility, and desires nothing better than to be told what to do. Provided the rulers do not interfere with its material comforts and its cherished beliefs, it is perfectly happy to let itself be ruled.
>
> Aldous Huxley

The elites started to lose control with Brexit and Trump, so they tapped into wokeism and cancel culture as predicates for censorship, and then the gloves were off. The most effective way to destroy a society is to gaslight them in terms of their understanding of the truth — especially their history, and the most effective way to do that is through taking away their freedom of expression.

Enter organisations like "News Guard" and the "Global Disinformation Index" with completely arbitrary, almost inconceivable social and economic power and influence, funded by George Soros' "Open Society" and by the unsuspecting taxpayer.

Censorship doesn't protect the vulnerable; censorship allows the oppressors to rewrite history to the benefit of their narrative, their objectives, and, of course, to the detriment of the people.

And that's EXACTLY what they've done.

Joseph Goebbels said: "We do not want to be a movement of a few straw brains, but rather a movement that can conquer the broad masses. Propaganda should be popular, not intellectually pleasing. It is not the task of propaganda to discover intellectual truths... You can't change the masses. They will always be the same: dumb, gluttonous, and forgetful... Make the lie big, make it simple, keep saying it, and eventually they will believe it."

Hitler in Mein Kampf said: "The State must declare the child to be the most precious treasure of the people. As long as the government is perceived as working for the benefit of the children, the people will happily endure almost any curtailment of liberty & almost any deprivation."

Threaten the children by threatening the future. Threaten the climate, the planet. Tell them they are all going to die — cooked to death from the sun or killed by a virus.

Pit them against each other. All that is needed is fear and hatred.

All the State, the Pathocracy, and the Zealotribe have to do is convince the masses that they are the victims of a looming catastrophe that needs to be stopped. It doesn't even matter how glaringly false or contrived the narrative is. The people crave freedom from responsibility; they crave to be controlled, the freedom of letting it all go, and will quickly embrace the framework of rules and instructions and the perception of safety and certainty offered up by the Mother State. They will happily, wilfully, and deliberately ignore all the facts right there in front of them, embracing the State's carefully articulated narrative.

The party told you to reject the evidence of your eyes and ears. It was their final, most essential command.
1984 — George Orwell

They won't read the government-mandated label on every box of surgical masks that says, *"Not for medical use,"* or *"Does not offer any protection against viruses or bacteria"*.

Surgical masks only assist in preventing you from spreading disease if you're sick and coughing over other people — assist in preventing surgeons from breathing fine droplets of water into open wounds. If you're not sick, they do almost nothing that is preventative, and certainly nothing to stop airborne viruses and bacteria from making you ill — these things just pass straight through them — "Like a fly passing through a hole the size of a football field" a doctor had once explained to me.

In hospitals, the most basic level of protection for airborne viruses and bacteria is P2-rated masks, and even then, P3-rated is recommended — with a positive-pressure P3 full body suit as the only truly effective way to actually guarantee virus transmission prevention — the gold standard.

And yet they will sit in their cars, alone, wearing a surgical mask.

Feeling safe, protected, virtuous.

They were both right, Goebbels and Hitler; that's why they were able to roll up their sleeves and get so much work done, so much horror done. When you boil it all down, people are gullible and, above all else, crave the safety of the herd.

"Climate change": where once you were accountable to God, now you are accountable to nature.

Racism, Capitalism, Sexism. The power gets shifted from the people you vote for to the people that you don't vote for, to the "experts", to the technocrats, the post-modernist High Priests in Brussels and the UN, because only they can "set you right" by the new moral order, offer you the path to the redemption that you crave for all of the harm you have done to nature, to people of colour, to women, to the trans community.

You thought you were just going about your days, didn't you? Getting on with life. Live and let live and all that. Well, you weren't, you racist, misogynistic climate rapist. I know this is who you are because you're white, you're male, and you're straight, and that's what white straight males are! That's your identity; that's your politics! We are here to explain very clearly, to teach you in no uncertain terms, just what a horrible person you have been while you thought you were just getting on with your life.

You just need to know your race, know your place in the globalist moral hierarchy. Wake up! It's not about equal justice under the law anymore — that's all gone now. That's so fucking yesterday.

We need to be ruled by the victims, by a victims' hierarchy — whoever was victimized the most should have the most power. And if you males are killing yourselves four times more often than females are; those women and girls that you have trampled underfoot for generations, then that's just karma. Our fucking Karma running over your fucking Dogma! Collateral damage for progress, our progress, our science, our truth!

Mass manipulation "Mass Formation" through Marx's false consciousness. The masses embraced the whole "Carbon Footprint" smoke and mirror show. In fact, they became almost pathological in their determination for self-flagellation, self-effacement — to take on the moral responsibility for the pollution of the world's environment — diligently, loudly "reducing their carbon footprint", "doing their bit", "counting their carbon credits", "being environmentally responsible". And they did this how? By demanding paper straws and separating their beer cans and their cardboard into recycling bins with a satisfied, proud, neighbourly smile across the fence.

British Petroleum, the second-largest non-state-owned oil company in the world, with 18,700 gas and service stations worldwide, hired the public relations professionals Ogilvy & Mather to promote the slant that climate change is not the fault of an oil giant, but that of individuals. It's here that British Petroleum, or BP, first promoted and soon successfully popularized the term "carbon footprint" in the early aughts. The company unveiled its "carbon footprint calculator" in 2004 so one could assess how their normal daily life – going to work, buying food, and traveling – is largely responsible for heating the globe.

Rebecca Solnit — The Guardian 2021

BP spent $200 million on a campaign that was so successful and duplicitous that it even won the prestigious international "Gold Effie" award for advertising.

*2007 Gold Effie Award Ogilvy "Beyond Petroleum" campaign for British Petroleum

Dear reader, I must pause here to ask you: Did you read that, or are you just drifting across the words? I mean, did you really read that! Those last 2 paragraphs? If you are going to take the time to immerse yourself in my pain, to wade though this outrageous, self-indulgent diatribe, then I beg you — please read it again.

They made it up! They made it all up.

With the winds of rage carefully and cleverly manipulated away from the sails of the average person's indignation, governments and big businesses were freed up to continue unabated in their destruction of our jungles and the filling of our oceans with plastic.

Have you ever looked into the eyes of an orangutan? Have you seen what the Governments of Borneo have done to them, to these beautiful creatures? To their jungle? Have you ever snorkeled around the islands off Kota Kinabalu and watched the clown fish deftly maneuvering between and around the empty plastic bottles, the dead coral, and the discarded diapers on the ocean floor?

The Zealotribe and the Followerati, building and rebuilding the deception, conducting the orchestra of Echochamberists as they diligently obfuscate any cracks that appear in the deception, any facts that slip through the propaganda network.

Diversions. Gaslighting. Loud statements, refusing even to acknowledge that elephants exist, elephants that are standing right there in the middle of the fucking room.

Pointing the finger of blame at the poorest countries around the world that are struggling to bring about their turn for their industrial revolution, to get toilets into people's homes, struggling to get gas so they can do two things at once and not have to tend a fire to cook dinner, or to provide heat to the freezing cold rooms their children are trying to sleep in.

Marx explained it perfectly in *Das Kapital*. I mean, for fuck's sake, it's all there. It's not hidden. Everyone's heard of it, but of course, no one's fucking read it; they're too busy watching reality television. No one wants all the trouble that comes with having their slumber disturbed, of having their eyes opened.

Marx said: the Bourgeoisie's strategy is to make the Proletariat, the people, feel responsible for their own misery. Make them feel like it's all their fault, that they can make a difference, that they must make a difference, that it's all up to them. Fleshed out and subsequently termed "False Consciousness" by Marcuse and Lefebvre, it was a blueprint to manipulate people into unknowingly participating in a system designed to cause them to misunderstand their genuine interests and to fail to recognise oppression.

And the people bought it all. Every single word of it.

They wanted to buy it. They wanted to be given a simple suburban solution, given a way that they could "just do their bit" and then forget about it. Forget about their oceans being filled with plastic, forget about the orangutans being slaughtered for palm oil plantations and concrete condominiums.

The cherry on top was that built into the solution, was an outrageously conspicuous, big, bright, yellow refuse bin the masses could wheel outside once a week, like a golden glowing light of social virtue, for all their neighbours to see.

Nietzsche said that you could tell much about a man's character by how much truth he could tolerate: which is very interesting. You know, there's another idea. In the, in the, Great Western tradition that the truth is the way and the path of life and that no one comes to the Father except through the truth. I believe that to be the case because I don't think that you can manifest who you are without the truth. And so I think it's literally and metaphorically true that the pathway to who you could be if you were completely who you were is through the truth. And I would say, and so the truth does set you free, but the problem is, is that it destroys everything that isn't worthy

in you as it sets you free, and that's a process of burning.
Jordan Peterson

Humanity. Weak, wilfully ignorant, self-centered, gullible, selfish fucking dolts.

And on they march, orchestrating, feeding off the destruction of the planet, the oceans, the jungles. The governments and the monolithic global business and media oligopolies — the master puppeteers — constantly changing the language, increasing and refreshing the fear, ramping up the severity of the narrative. Global Warming becomes Climate Change becomes Climate Catastrophe — personal, individual responsibility at the forefront, with ever bigger, broader, closer threats.

Milestones of predicted environmental catastrophe pass by — empty, unfulfilled, unquestioned — smothered by the sheer volume of the noise of it all.

And marching behind them? The people. Like Hollywood zombies, they shuffle forward, heads down, gazing at their screens — the coalesced glow of the choreographed news feeds lighting the way.

The Echochamberists, especially, having "done their bit", reveling in not having to think, not having to notice.

They ignore logic — the rampant waterfront development in low-lying coastal areas of Florida and its sky-rocketing prices — all paid for and held as collateral assets against 30-year mortgages by the savvy banking sector that reports record profits year after year after year.

They ignore the news reports that break through the big-tech-media veneer to tell them about the astonishing failures of the recycling industry, about the thirty shipping containers sent every month from the US to the Philippines to meet US Environmental statistical obligations — before first being burnt into the atmosphere and then dumped into the ocean there. Or the overflowing warehouses of so-called recycling material that no one knows what to do with.

The environmental cost before and after the life of electric cars, that's another one of their fucking outrageous deceptions — these assholes sitting at traffic lights in their electric cars, looking down their noses at everyone else, on their way home to plug them into coal-fired power stations. The environmental and human catastrophe associated with the battery systems from the lithium strip mining in Chile and the "conflict minerals" — the horror of twelve year olds getting injured and killed in accidents while mining the cobalt in the Congo — the minerals that are then shipped all over the world on diesel tankers.

They completely disregard the fact that the world's mineral supplies are just a tiny fraction of what's required to be able to ever produce anywhere near the green battery utopia they boastfully predict is coming. Or the fact that just to charge 30 heavy-duty electric trucks has a five-megawatt application that requires more draw on the power supply than an entire average US city!

Not to mention the endless circular arguments around trying to figure out an environmentally safe way to dispose of the battery systems — the environmental costs after the life of these vehicles — once the cars and trucks are scrapped.

But to these assholes, this type of detail is irrelevant as it is contrary to the idea, and the idea is everything to them. They have no grasp of — or even interest in — reality. It sits beyond the idea, behind it.

The list of incontrovertible evidence of the stupidity of all of this is endless.

We don't know where the carbon dioxide is from. We can't measure the warming of the oceans. We have terrible temperature records going back 100 years...This isn't data, this is guess and there's something weird underneath it, there's something weird that isn't oriented well towards human beings underneath it. It has this guise of compassion, or we're gonna save the poor in the future. Its like that's what the bloody communists said. And they killed a lot of people doing it. And we're walking down that same road now with this insistence that you know, we're so compassionate, that we care about the poor 100 years from now, and if we have to wipe out several hundred million of them now well that's a small price to pay for the future utopia. We've heard that sort of thing before... And that's exactly what's happening now with organisations like the WEF.

Jordan Peterson

In the same way that vegetarians are always incapable of refraining from telling you that they are vegetarian in the first thirty seconds of a conversation, the Echochamberists, emotionally charged by the group-think, shout out how wonderfully environmentally conscious they are with their endless judgement and badgering of people when they bump into them at dinner parties and on suburban street corners.

I motioned to a passing hostess to ask her for another Gin. The girl beside me interjected, "Make it two", and smiled at me. I smiled back. I introduced myself, and we talked for a while. I was actually really surprised to find her sitting next to me. Typically, in this situation, it seemed all that fate ever cared about was making absolutely fucking certain that whoever I sat next to on a plane was not a pretty young woman. More than that, fate seemed to go out of its way to sit me next to someone that by the time I landed, for any one of a million reasons, all I could think about was strangling them to death with my bare hands.

Anyway, it was nice; she was nice, and we talked for a while before I reclined my seat, closed my eyes, and wandered back into my thoughts.

All this was basically Relativism's clever capacity to substitute knowledge and facts with ideas. These "ideas" are now the absolute orthodoxy of the Zealotribe and their minions. Their ideologies are supreme; nothing can challenge them.

Their "ideas" are all about goodness, virtue, and the best outcome for all — they embody the betterment of humanity. To argue against any of these ideas, to argue against any of these assholes, means you are not only wrong but that you are fucking evil because you are standing in the way of "progress", of a better world — of the very future of civilisation. To even question these ideologies means you want bad things for people, and you must be stopped; no, not just stopped, you must be silenced so that no one can get to hear what you have to say.

How dare you present facts, significant research, that show children raised in a home with both a mother and a father are clearly statistically better off — measured against a whole range of metrics — than children raised by single mothers? Or say anything that contradicts the promoted paradigm that multiculturalism is wonderful.

For these psychopathic fascists, the idea, the ideology, is absolute, unchallengeable by any criticism or dissent. It is inimical to reason itself. It is the antithesis of reason.

The idea is all that's important.

With an ideology, evidence is irrelevant, and therefore, rationality and reason are irrelevant because you cannot have reason without evidence and without the cornerstone belief that truth and lies are different from each other — something that has been completely destroyed by Relativism.

I mean, fuck, if you are exasperated, suspicious, inquisitive, confused, or just stupid enough even to suggest that you have evidence that challenges one of these ideologies — that you have data, for example, that illustrates that the earth was warmer many millennia ago — you are shouted down as a liar or worse, someone who clearly wants to hurt the planet, people, the future, hurt the children. There is something wrong with you — you are a monster!

The critical mass of these suburban ideologues believe they stand for reason, the truth. At the same time, they behave as if there is no fucking difference at all between truth and lies and behave as if evidence is irrelevant. Men can be women and women can be men — and anyone who questions that is a sexist, hateful homophobe.

People: false consciousness, the eagerly manipulated masses, the Pathocracy, and Mass Formation. I felt like I was abandoning my world, my dad's world, the West, Australia, but fuck it, I figured you had to know when to walk away. I mean, this shit was like a fucking tidal wave — there was nothing except the inevitability of Rome burning to the fucking ground that was going to stop it, put an end to it.

And that's what would happen; that's what always happened.

Historically, it has always been the same: the Hellenistic Era, the Roman Empire, Weimar Germany. In every single case, in the eleventh hour of these great civilisations, men were dressing like women, and women were dressing like men, and everyone thought they were so fucking sophisticated and cosmopolitan and tolerant and open-minded. And without exception, the government of the time was supporting it all by ploughing the economy forward at breakneck speed, spending and debasing the currency like drunken fucking sailors. In every case, it was almost as if no one wanted to give anyone any opportunity to stop and think, to question all the madness.

And every single time this has happened, what did the outcasts, the disciples of the power of heroic masculinity do? They gathered around the edges, outside the culture, biding their time massing in preparation — the Visigoths, the Vandals, the Huns — the list went on and on and on.

And that's what it felt like now.

I hate democracies. They are absurd lowest-common-denominator fucking death sentences to any civilization.

"Oh! I know! Let's let the fucking imbeciles have a say in all the decisions". A ridiculous concept. Imagine if you took that approach with a company or an army? I mean less than a century ago, only landowners could vote in America, and in the Republics of ancient Greece, where democracy was born, this absurdity that the literal masses could have a say in a democracy would have been considered outrageous — with only "citizens" being allowed to vote.

> I don't believe in liberty or democracy.
> I believe in actual, sacred, inspired authority:
> The divine rights of natural kings;
> I believe in the divine right of natural aristocracy,
> The right, the sacred duty, to wield undisputed authority.
>
> DH Lawrence

I looked down, and my hands were shaking. Fuck, I was a wreck. I was so glad I had walked away from it all and was sitting on this plane.

I was done. Exhausted.

I don't think I could have lasted even one more day. Fuck it all. Historically, the last 200 or so civilizations had endured an average of 336 years, so I figured we were almost done anyway.

The West, in my mind, was finished. Over. All that was left was the nebulous echo of Western values drifting in a universe amongst the damaged scraps of fading and unjustifiable optimism. A group of elites that were wealthy and powerful enough to remain hidden in the shadows had wrested control from the people, deciding that the "Consent of the Governed" was too dangerous to tolerate. They had successfully established their legions of drones, their tyrannical gangs of mindless Ideologues; the Zealotribe, the Followerati, and the Echochamberists, and in the process, decoupled the traditional pluralist system — that judicious measured process of honest, informed discussion and equitable influence — from the increasingly homogenised global system they were building.

I had watched the governmental structures and institutions across the globe being captured, hollowed out, and turned into paradoxical inversions of what they were designed, what they were intended to be. This wasn't an accident. This was the deliberate, carefully orchestrated, systematic destruction of the traditional power base of the people across almost all the world's separate sovereign States, with only a few world powers like Trump in the US and Putin in Russia brave enough and strong enough to resist it.

The WEF (sic World Economic Forum) actually posits that it is the new World Government together with the United Nations ... these are both "supra-State" ... that new corporatism socialism fusion. Because the UN is intrinsically socialist; headed up by the former head of the Socialist International, and the World Economic Forum which is intrinsically Corporatist; its basically a trade union of 1,000 of the largest transnational companies in the world...have formed an alliance and they're the ones propagating a lot of these globalised structures using the organisational model of the European Union. So the EU is the political predicate for the new global organisational structure that's being proposed. Both the United Nations and the WEF self-proclaim that they represent the new world government – so they're not hiding it.

Dr Robert Malone – Peak Prosperity Podcast. December 24, 2024

The truth was that most people in the population had no useful role. They hadn't noticed or didn't understand any of it, really. Through no fault of their own, they had not been given the motivation, the perspective or the insight, to seek out or see this stuff, to be interested in analysing anything beyond the immediately apparent. Sitting there, I wondered if these elites were actually being influenced by the thought that this could all change, that they were actually terrified by the prospect of some looming global "French Revolution" moment.

Regardless, none of it mattered now. Let the 'Cluster B' personality psychos burn the whole lot to the fucking ground.

Fuck them all.

5

Blue

Sitting on the edge of my bed in my hotel room on Soi 15 —blue lights and stainless-steel fittings setting the theme, the lighting somehow pushing everything out of focus. The room could be spotless, or it may not have been cleaned for weeks — you would never know. Having removed the cans and bottles of drink from the bar fridge, they now sat stacked neatly in a row on the shelf that ran almost the full length of the room under the television set. I had asked the taxi to stop at a 7-Eleven and a Subway on the way to the hotel from the airport. The fridge was now full with half a dozen Singha beers, a half-eaten steak and cheese melt sub loaded with jalapenos, and two unopened packets of double-milk chocolate Tim Tams I had brought with me from Australia.

Just the essentials.

The air conditioning was well and truly kicking in, and, as always at this place, there was a faint smell of moisture or mildew in the air. The Dream Hotel was somewhere I knew well, having stayed there many times before — back before my world had disintegrated. Those were happy, carefree days. Days that had that baseline structure of normality, a general sense of a never-ending future, the subconscious expectation of a familiar, uncomplicated framework about them — boxed up neatly by the daily repetitive fulfillment of a thousand mundane expectations. That sparkling spinning cube, those life-sized blue-striped tigers, and those wonderful breakfasts served graciously by smiling staff.

For all those times I had come to Thailand — at least twenty five — I had never once been unfaithful to my wife. Everything I had seen there made me feel that perhaps I was one of only very few men in the whole history of Thailand to have achieved this.

I had withstood such temptation beyond description — a temptation that only a man who had lived it, who had been there during those times, could understand. I looked down at the young woman kneeling on the carpet in front of me. Somehow, she sensed I was watching her, and she slowly drew her mouth back from giving me head and looked up at me, smiling. Her silken complexion and small, perfect breasts just so cute. I smiled back and, reaching across the bed, passed her a pillow. Her lips were red and wet. Smiling at me, she took the pillow and putting it on her thighs in front of her, went back to work. I took a sip from my beer and, reaching down, tapped her on the shoulder. She drew her head back once again, exposing my hard wet cock, and looked up at me with that smile.

All patience; there was no rush here.

"Perhaps you should put the pillow under your knees? It would be more comfortable for you".

She started laughing in a slightly embarrassed way for not having understood at first, placed the pillow on the carpet, kneeled back down onto it, and, giving me one last friendly smile, cupped my balls with one hand, and reached for my cock with the other — the shaft disappearing impossibly down her throat. She was good, working deliberately, rhythmically towards her goal — the speed increasing very slowly as she skillfully moved her mouth and her hand along my saliva-slippery cock. Taking her time — total focus, like a tradesman or an artist who took great pride in their work.

I told her I was coming — purely out of courtesy, but she didn't miss a beat. Withdrawing almost completely in her rhythm to swallow my cum with each deep motion, finishing me off gently, carefully avoiding the now sensitive tip except for the gentlest of tongue work to clean me up. Wow. Perfect, I thought, as she gracefully got up to her feet, smiled again, and walked naked except for the briefest of white panties away from me to the bathroom — her perfect little ass, just mesmerising.

I loved that she didn't close the bathroom door behind her. There was an honesty, a giving, in her leaving it open. A deliberate message that we shared a type of kind, unthreatening familiarity that can only come between two people who had done something like what we had just done — and from someone who had genuinely been happy to do it. She had told me she was 28 and I loved that the age difference between us seemed almost irrelevant to her — I was over twice her age. In most cases, Thai people were like that — they didn't tend to be so absolute, to place the same emphasis on age in general as you find in Western countries. Her name was Waan, which she had said apparently means "sweet".

On the flight, once I had dragged myself out of the dark reverie I had allowed myself to slip into to pass the time, we had talked for hours. I had been surprised but delighted when she had told me, after checking her phone while we were standing in the queue for Customs, that she had mixed up her bookings and couldn't get into her hotel until 2 pm the following day and had asked me with a big friendly grin if she could store her bags at my hotel. I had especially liked the grin. A smile is easy to fake, but the smiling eyes that come with a grin have an honesty, a giving that comes from the heart.

I slowly stood up and, walking over to the fridge, placed my empty beer in the small waste bin under the shelf, took another, opened it with the back of the spoon from the tea and coffee set, and walking back to the bed, sat down again, now with my back against the headboard.

Thailand. The perfect place for personal worlds to be dismissed — deliberately, and completely ignored. Histories, promises, expectations, and consequences smothered over by the blanket of distance, the sense of pure opportunity, the heat — just the smell of the place. I took a long drink from my beer. Visions of sweat beading on silken, smooth, firm, caramel skin, like waves, washing over the stale acceptance of yesterday and tomorrow, drowning out the fake smiles and stilted mechanical laughs of worn-out obligation and the endless contrived conversations of everyday life and work.

Relaxed, smiling, slippery pleasure — metered out in thousand-baht blocks.

Dutiful Western men relinquishing their honor and their conscience, if but for only a brief time, letting themselves cascade into that void, into this world of simple, peaceful pleasure.

After an eternity of God knows what she was doing; water running, cupboards and draws opening and closing, toilet paper tearing, finally, the toilet flushed, and she came out and started to dress. I watched her quietly as I leaned back, drinking my beer. She had a beautiful tattoo that covered most of her shoulders and her nicely muscled back, and reached around to her flat stomach.

Noticing me watching her, she started laughing as she wriggled into a tiny pair of what looked like sleeping shorts she had taken from her suitcase, still topless, her long, straight, silky hair swaying across her perfect breasts. She allowed herself to turn around during the little jumps and pulls and squirms as she pulled the shorts up — her stomach muscles twitching and flexing against her ribs — finally presenting her perfect ass to me in those cute brief white panties disappearing underneath her shorts with the last wriggling hop.

It was just too much. 25 years, 365 days.

I put the beer down on the sideboard, stood up, and walked over to her. Her smile had changed now, like she knew exactly what she had done and was happy with herself. Drawing her towards me from behind, I cupped her small, firm breasts and hard little brown nipples, massaging them. She sighed. I reached down to her waist and undid the bow in the tie-string on her shorts. Bending down, I tugged them aggressively on each side until they were down under her hips and then slid them down to her ankles.

25 years.

I walked her around and pushed her forward onto the bed on all fours facing away from me and, reaching under, grabbed and massaged her breasts some more. Lowering myself to my knees on the floor, I ran my hands down her torso across her sharply corrugated rig cage onto her hips and buried my face into her panties.

That smell. It's like no other. Driving an urge so animalistic, so primal, that a man, for just a few moments of savage sexual blindness, will risk losing everything: a wife he loves, his beautiful children — even his very life — responding to it.

365 days.

I reached up, grabbed each side of her panties, and ripped them down to her bent knees, burying my mouth and my nose into her pussy from behind while she moaned and squealed. I licked and sucked and flicked my tongue around the surface of her pussy and then pushed it deep inside her and then as far forward and up as I could, searching for her clit, as I reached up with my right hand to her breasts. She was moaning heavily now and moving back into me with each push of my tongue. Standing up, I reached forward with my right hand, pulling her right shoulder towards me so she couldn't move away, and with my left hand grabbed her opposite ass cheek so she couldn't twist sideways. In one smooth movement, I pushed my rock-hard cock deep inside her — all the way up to my balls into her wet pussy. It was unexpected, and she let out a loud moan.

I was fucking her now — I was fucking them all now.

All those beautiful girls, all those sweet, alluring glances, I had resisted. Topless on poles, smiling, well dressed as we passed in a crowded shopping mall in Sydney or sat opposite each other on the sky train. Memories, laughing together in a dense crowd during Songkran, the rain softly falling as she — perhaps only 18 years old — smiling that beautiful smile, staring right into my eyes, inches from my face, as if it was just her and me in the whole world, the crowd pressing us so hard against each other my feet were lifting off the ground, wiped that white paste on my cheek. 25 years, 365 days.

Whimpering and moaning loudly now, she reached back and, grabbing my hip, started pulling me harder into her. Bringing her hand up back behind her, she put her fingers in my mouth and then, reaching back again, this time between her legs, began working her clit. She was rocking with me now, moaning softly with each push. I reached my hand up underneath her and, encircling almost all of her tiny throat, squeezed just enough for her to feel the strength, to taste the fear. Instantly, she responded by pushing harder and faster back into me — her rasping breath and moaning becoming louder and more intense. Eventually, I came, grinding hard into her, spurting my cum as deep into her centre as I could.

Everything slowed down to nothing as I gently lowered her down onto the bed, holding her close to me, onto our sides. We just lay there, breathing.

25 years of temptation, finished. 365 days, started.

What had I done to be here? Why me and not Sam? My world. Was it a blessing to see things as they truly are, or a curse? Was this, what I had just done, a reward, or was it a punishment? "You can't miss what you never had" came to my mind. Now that I had had it, would I miss not having it for the last 25 years?

After a few moments, she rolled over — my cock now soft, slipping slowly out of her. I reached over and gently drew a perfect sliver of jet-black hair that had fallen across her face away, and placed it behind her ear. Her lips moved, and she opened her eyes and smiled at me in a way that was so genuine, so real — a smile with nothing behind it except kindness and simplicity. I smiled back.

Thailand.

It had only been three and a half hours since we had landed on flight SQ714, and although the digital clock on the shelf said it was only 10:15 pm, with the combination of the flight, the beer, the sex, and the three-hour time difference, I was exhausted. I fell asleep.

What? That's it? You want more? Sitting there in your shitty house in the suburbs with your fat husband and your average children making up the fucking numbers trying to decide when you'll start your next diet, or secretly wondering if Sally was right and Roger at the dog park really is interested in you. Porn? Is that what you want? There's no fucking porn here, it's just a story. It's just the story, the truth. Fuck! How do you even live with yourself? It's your miserable fucking life that makes this porn. Your fear. Your fucking choices. Your weaknesses.

And anyway, that's the end of it. So you can just fuck off.

September 18, 2024

As was not uncommon for me, a familiar, dull, background nagging feeling of rage was dragging me back into the world that was awake.

I opened my eyes. The sound of Bangkok traffic drifted up from the chaos below. Rolling over, I looked at Waan lying next to me, naked, her young body and pale skin flawless in the morning light. Thinking back to last night, her skin was so smooth, so silken, it was almost like it was electric when I touched it. What I had done to her! My God. Yet here she was, sleeping gently, her beautiful young face against the white cotton, her perfect chest rising softly with each breath. She had been so giving. Not even a single word of resistance or complaint as I pushed hard, deep inside her body.

Slowly climbing out of bed, I wandered naked into the bathroom. I sat down and let the shit go.

Blue lights.

> I don't have fun. Actually, I had fun once, in 1962. I drank a whole bottle of Robitussin cough medicine and went in the back of a 1961 powder-blue Lincoln Continental to a James Brown concert with some Mexican friends of mine. I haven't had fun since. It's just not a word I like. It's like Volkswagens or bellbottoms, or patchouli oil or bean sprouts. It rubs me up the wrong way. I might go out and have an educational and entertaining evening, but I don't have fun.
>
> Tom Waits

When I came out, Waan was still asleep, so I quietly took out my laptop, sat down at the small desk, and started to write.

Chapter II

The door to the Oak tree closed surprisingly quietly behind Eugene as he hunched down and entered. Squinting, he held up one hand to shield his eyes from the bright light inside.

"Sit, sit", said Meredith, motioning for Eugene towards a shiny red chair.

Removing the hand that had been shading his eyes but still squinting, Eugene looked about the room. In front of him was a shiny circular silver table, and around the table, three more chairs, each a different colour. The light in the room was coming from what looked like a glass sphere the size of a large melon that was located about a foot from the ceiling and, as far as Eugene could tell, did not seem to be suspended by anything and was just floating midair. His gaze switched to the curved walls of the room encircling him. It had a rough yellowy-green surface that glistened in the bright light. "Sap" Thought Eugene. They were inside a living tree, so of course, the walls were alive. He looked over to where he had entered but could see no sign of the doorway.

His attention switched to Meredith Dew, who stood hunched over the table in front of him, going through a sack, muttering to himself, the light floating above his head forming a shining bright halo out of his shock of golden hair sticking out from around the small leather hat that sat on his head. Eugene studied the funny little man properly for the first time now that he could see him clearly in the light. Above his tired-looking, oval-shaped, deep brown, almost black eyes sat two large, bushy silver eyebrows, his big round nose hovering above two thick, pink lips. He wore a vest that looked as if it had been woven from finely spun gold, and over the vest, a rather worn-looking brown leather jacket that matched the hat on his head. He was wearing baggy trousers that seemed to alternate from a deep purple to deep green to deep blue in colour as he turned in the light, the trouser legs disappearing into two large leather boots which matched his hat and coat. The boots did not have laces and could be best described as a pair of moccasins but boots, folding back just below his knees.

"Ear", he repeated to himself over and over as he arranged an assortment of crystal jars and glass vials containing what appeared to be different coloured powders and liquids on the table.

"Ah!" He exclaimed. "This should do the trick, at least until we get to the stump", said Meredith, turning from the table towards Eugene, his nose taking far longer than it should have to vibrate to a halt.

"Any idea why?" asked Meredith.

"Why what?", said Eugene.

"Why you had your ear stolen by Gagglebroth and Co.?"

"All I know is I was on my way home when I fell face first into an empty grave", Eugine replied.

"Grave?" Meredith said urgently, lifting his head up towards Eugine suddenly from his jars, his nose wobbling about.

"Yeah, then the next thing I know, there's all these red and green eyes peering down at me."

"Do you know whose grave you fell into?"

"Fizzlebub's, I think, judging from the rhyme the main one chanted", said Eugene, the funny little man's intense line of questioning starting to make him feel a little uneasy.

"Do you remember anything about the rhyme, any of the lines, anything at all?" Meredith asked urgently.

"Well", said Eugene, falling silent for a moment while he stared up at the light, thinking. "First, what's her name? Gargl…"

"Gagglebroth."

"That's it. First, she said something about 160 years. Then she started the rhyme. Something about putting worms in the fruit, then, something, something, 'the needed spice' then it ended with "in Fizzlebub's hole, to return the power that he hath stole. Or something like that anyway."

Meredith sighed. "I suspected something like this might happen. As we used to say back in the old days, 'Yesterday's deeds with stealth and slight oft expand under tomorrow's light.'"

"What do you mean you suspected something like this might happen?" interjected Eugene, shocked, taking his handkerchief away from his ear to look at the blood. "I was just trying to get home from the bloody movies! What's all this got to do with me?"

"Fizzlebub! The old fool." Meredith yawned, revealing to Eugene as he did so that his tongue was bright blue in colour. Eugene had thought he had noticed this earlier but had put it down to a trick of the light.

"What about Fizzlebub, and why is your tongue bright blue? And you said something about a stump before, what stump?"

"Ahhh. One blunder at a time. Questions, questions, questions. But I suppose with a missing ear, it's not surprising", said Meredith rather absentmindedly, yawning again as he turned away. "All in good time. Won't be a moment", he said, removing a funny-shaped black key from his pocket, muttering to himself as he did so. Eugene didn't catch what he said because his words were made incoherent by yet another loud yawn. Crouching down, Meredith pushed the key into what looked like the ground, turned it twice, and an oval-shaped door opened silently upwards towards them.

Eugene sat speechless as he watched the funny little man disappear through the trap door in the floor, followed almost immediately by the ball of light which drifted down from the ceiling and through the trapdoor silently as if it had a mind of its own, leaving him sitting by himself in almost complete darkness. Sitting there pondering it all, he noticed the jars and vials on the table emitting a soft glow in their respective colours. Thirty seconds later, the light floated back up through the trapdoor in the floor followed closely by Meredith Dew carrying a small silver bowl.

"Sorry about that", said Meredith. "Just woke up. Still not thinking straight. Didn't alarm you too much, I hope? Now, where were we…"

"Fizzlebub, or more particularly, his grave."

"Ahh, yes… Fizzlebub, that wretched fellow."

Eugene detected a distinct note of distaste in Meredith's voice.

"Late one night a few years ago", began Meredith, as he started mixing an assortment of powders with dribbles and splashes of liquids into the little silver bowl, "I was out looking for mushrooms. Not just any sort of mushrooms, you understand, but a particular type. They appear to only spawn once every 160 years or so." The mention of 160 years pricked Eugine's already keen interest in what Meredith was saying.

"Anyway", continued Meredith, "A while back, I discovered that these lovely mushrooms go marvelously well in my Boobleberry pies, so I thought this time round I'll pick myself as many as I could so I'd have some to store so I can use them later on when there are none to be found."

"What do you mean this time round?", asked Eugene, inquisitive but sounding suspicious. How could anyone experience something that only happened every 160 years more than once?

"This may seem a bit bizarre,
as if your mind may have gone too far.
It may take a little while to comprehend,
but all in good time, my newfound friend,
all speed with little haste,
for I fear we have little time to waste.
They have your ear, though it could be worse;
we must stay on our toes to prevent the curse.
I speak in rhyme some of the time,
sharpens the thought, and nimbles the mind."

As Meredith finished his little outburst, he pulled a golden flask out from beneath his coat and, removing the silver cork, poured a dash of the contents into the bowl. It spilt from the flask like water in slow motion — like water turned almost to jelly. It was clear and sparkled as the light caught it. Eugene sat quietly, his eyes mesmerized by the slow-flowing liquid.

"Mushrooms!" burst out Meredith all of a sudden, as if the thought had been eluding him for some time. "As I remember, the night was a splendid one for picking mushrooms; the moon was full, and I had just finished a particularly delightful Boobleberry pie. I was strolling through the forest very quietly, mind you, and had just about picked half a sack full when I spotted some movement ahead of me. Creeping forward carefully, I spotted old Fizzlebub, and curious as to what he was up to, I decided to follow him at a safe distance."

"After a while, I realised that he himself seemed to be following something or someone, for he was creeping very slowly — stopping and listening and moving forward again very carefully. After a short while, I saw the glow of a fire up ahead and heard muffled voices. I couldn't hear what they were saying, but from their cackling tone, it was clear that they were witches, and as I moved in closer, I recognised one of the voices was Gagglebroth. I moved to one side to get a bit around Fizzlebub for a better view of what they were up to. What I saw, I did not like the look of at all."

"Gagglebroth and Enchantlure, that's the name of another one in her brood, were huddled round a cauldron hanging above a small intense fire. Up to no good, I thought to myself, couldn't be any other way with those two. You see, Gagglebroth is the eldest of the brood and by far the most powerful, but Enchantlure is almost as bad and, in some ways, worse. She is the second eldest, and as her name suggests, she has the gift of enchantment. Which means to say, Eugene, my lad, that if you ever happen to find yourself in Cracklewood Forest and you meet the most beautiful of young ladies dressed in a nightgown that doesn't quite seem able to cover everything all at once, chances are you have found Enchantlure, though more likely she has found you. Catch her gaze, and you can consider yourself dinner."

Meredith paused for a moment and spooned some of the contents from the bowl he had been mixing into a small, flat rimmed container he produced from somewhere inside his coat. Holding one hand over the container, he closed his eyes, and his nose began to vibrate as he started to speak:

"Element of sound, element of skin,
Element of ear, to hear within,
Libdiddle thib wibble, mexious billbybubble,
make the ear, to relieve the trouble."

With that, he lifted the container and, reaching over, pushed it onto the side of Eugene's head. It made a suction sound, and when he took his hand away, the container stayed attached to the side of Eugene's head.

"What will that do?" asked Eugene pensively.

"It will stop the bleeding and, with any luck, give you a brand new ear", said Meredith, replacing the crystal jars and vials back into the sack."

"What do you mean *with any luck*?"

"Well, you see, Alchemy's my game. Turn anything into anything with the right substances. But this spell business, I'll have to admit, I've never been terribly good at, more Gagglebroth's line, if you know what I mean."

Eugene sat silently for a moment with the shiny steel container suctioned to the side of his head.

"What about Gagglebroth and Enchantlure and the cauldron?" said Eugene.

"I'll tell you as we go", said Meredith, picking up the sack from the table and opening the door in the floor as before.

"Go where?" asked Eugene.

"To the stump! Hurry now; no time to lose! Gagglebroth has already got a good head start."

"What stump?"

"Time enough for questions later; follow me!" With that, Meredith Dew picked up the small sack that contained the jars and began to disappear down through the hole in the ground, the light following after him.

Eugene, with little choice, followed the light.

6

Breakfast – but not at Tiffany's

September 27, 2025

Eyes opening. I was staring at that brick wall again, but it was different now. Incredibly, it seemed to be moving, transforming before me, changing while I watched. Astonished, I could see intricate patterns now in that prosaic brickwork: of people's faces, of an olive grove across the hills of Cordoba, of the worn, shiny pillars and striped arches of the Mesquita. Seneca, as a little boy in robes, running down a cobblestone street, laughing. Did I once tread the same worn polished-stone streets as Seneca? Did he, like me, have eyes filled with tears at Cordoba's incredible beauty? How had they done this, this architect and this bricklayer? Had I got it wrong? Were they, in fact, great artists? How could they do this with just bricks? Was I awake or was I dreaming?

I could feel my leg was worse; the pain intensified as if it was joining forces with the burning in my throat — a storm of pain brewing that felt like it was everywhere.

A faint squeaking noise brought my mind into focus, offering a distraction from the misery, as a white shape glided across the room from the left. A bed, wheeled in front of my gaze, between me and the window and that canvas of a brick wall, that extraordinary art that I was now convinced was there. There was a long lump in the middle. Someone was in the bed, but all I could see was a human outline swaddled in knitted cotton blankets over blue-trimmed white sheets. The person pushing the bed who was now plugging things in and moving around it was someone I had never seen before — an older man in a blue uniform with a kind face. Whoever was in the bed seemed very slight — perhaps a child? No. Surely there would be a separate ward for children?

Time so far had failed in its promise to temper my despair. Although the needles still came, they seemed now to disorient me as much as they faded the pain back, like it was actually confusion that now eased the pain, inducing a lazy, nagging determination in me to try to separate dreams from reality, to bring into focus the blurred lines between them. I could feel a new level of pain engulfing me. Days? Weeks? I had no idea how long I had been here.

The old man glanced at me and smiled as he walked away — exit stage left — and again, I was alone in my mind.

September 18, 2024

Closing my laptop, I went to take a shower. When I came out, Waan was already dressed, fresh, and clean — sparkling like only youth can manage. There was that smile again, one that is normally reserved only for the young and the carefree — with all of their life still ahead of them. She walked over and kissed me on the cheek.

"Breakfast?" I asked.

"Hello, Mr. Alex. Back again!" said Noi as we arrived at the breakfast reception area on the first floor, smiling at Waan as if she also was an old friend.

"Hi, Noi", I smiled back. "How have you been?".

"Wonderful, Mr. Alex, thank you. Can I have your room number?"

"614", I replied, and she proceeded to take us to our table.

"I will ask Prem for your usual coffee, Mr. Alex", and smiling at Waan, "Can I offer you some coffee or tea?"

"Green tea, thank you", answered Waan, excusing herself as she walked off to the bathroom.

It was only about ten minutes before I noticed Prem emerging from the kitchen to deliver my coffee to me personally, his great, gleaming-white-teeth-smile splitting his face as he welcomed me and proudly placed the small cup and saucer on the table in front of me. Matte olive-green with a glossy orange nebula pattern on the fine porcelain cup. Years ago, when my father died, I had requested the twelve-piece set from my mother: six cups and six saucers. "Susie Cooper - Member of the WEDGWOOD Group England" was printed on the base. I had given Prem two cups and two saucers to keep in a safe place for me for my coffee when I visited the Dream Hotel. I know, I'm a bit strange like that — I have always been outrageously particular about things like coffee cups, crystal glasses — even the cutlery I used. I mean, life is way too fucking short to drink even one glass of wine out of something that isn't absolutely exquisite, to have to stir even one cup of coffee with a teaspoon that hasn't been nurtured, curved, and scalloped into a thing of beauty, a work of art.

Prem had responded to my patient instructions with polite attention, and it was only because of the pride he had in himself and in his work that he had come to get the mixture and the process exactly right — like he saw it as a personal challenge. As a thank you, I always gave him a 2,000 Baht tip after every breakfast. Over the years, Prem and I had become friends, occasionally sharing a beer together when his shift finished, in the balmy evening heat at the FLAVA bar on the 11th floor of the Hotel, overlooking the shimmering swimming pool.

After a short conversation, he left, and I sat quietly, sipping my coffee. It was perfect. Two squares of Lindt milk chocolate and a generous dollop of sweetened condensed milk, drowned in three steaming shots of espresso, each one infused through a fresh, thin slice of bird's-eye chili.

I called it "Saigon Sludge".

Sipping my coffee, solitude and circumstance once again nudged me towards thinking back over my life, tentatively checking its pulse. I remembered back to my father grinding the coffee beans in the old yellow Bakelite grinder in the family kitchen in the home I had grown up in on the outskirts of Sydney. How he would spoon the ground coffee into a saucepan of water on the stove and watch it carefully so it didn't flow over the edge as it started to boil. Then he would tap the saucepan on the edge of the stove — always twice — and pour it into a cup through a strainer.

He used to call it "Cowboy Coffee".

My father had never travelled out of Australia. I thought about what an insular life that would be, what an insular person that would cause — my father had indeed been that. I had known many people in my life who lived like this, allowing themselves to slide into this particularly empty world. This loading up of the bricks of reasons, real or imagined, mortared together by excuses and obtuse-angled-logic into great walls built to hide the horizons, walls with a door fiercely guarded by the two stormtroopers of fear and familiar comfort, to prevent any boundaries from being even visible, and especially from that door ever being opened.

I sipped the coffee. The bite from the chili was only faintly noticeable as it was rounded up and pushed back into submission by the sweet, strong brew.

One of these coffees was never enough, but that was all I ever had. Only one. I knew that discipline was the only way to keep that delicate balance from pleasure tipping over into disappointment. I knew that with every moment of pleasure, happiness — real satisfaction and peace — gets pushed slightly further out of reach, as was the irony of all the seven deadly sins. Deadly because passions for anything, if not brought to heel by discipline, when indulged, only served to push satisfaction further away, leaving in their wake just a bigger "normal" — emptiness — and an ever-growing feeling of loss.

People often confuse pleasure with happiness, but I had learned that they were opposites. Pleasure, fun, could always be found alone: food, the body of a stranger, alcohol, cocaine, 'retail therapy', any number of indulgences, all of which faded quickly, meaninglessly into the past, leaving behind nothing but the desire for more. But happiness required all of the hard work, all of the patience and discipline involved in creating and nurturing real achievements and genuine relationships with other people, and the satisfaction and the joy that comes from those achievements and those relationships.

In the end, the gluttonous collapse into a desperate sobbing heap of fat, disappointment, and sweat, with contentment crouching just out of reach in a dark corner, smiling back at them.

To reinforce my philosophy, I had a regime where I only drank instant coffee from day to day at home. This way, the disappointment that so many other coffees offered up when circumstances backed me into a less than ideal corner did not have too much of a painful sting attached to them.

But I knew this place, this man, this Prem, and this coffee.

I had a similar relationship with some maniac who kept a block of Philadelphia cream cheese in the refrigerator especially for me to enjoy with my steak at that little restaurant — that ridiculous little restaurant on that busy dusty intersection past the Big C Supermarket in Kota Kinabalu in Borneo. There, by some outrageous twist of fate, a local man had managed to source high-quality, thick-cut New Zealand ribeye and, more importantly, had somehow figured out how to cook it correctly.

Steak. Turn it twice and leave it the fuck alone!

If you become an expat, if you are brave enough to uproot yourself and take the time to settle quietly into some other country — the more different, the more "foreign", the better — to become part of daily life in that place, you find these things hidden in the detail. It's amazing, they just happen. They rise to the surface in a casual conversation at a train station or as you wander past them to buy your groceries. Surprising, bright, sharp flashes of knowledge and enthusiasm grown there — perhaps transplanted from a faraway place — that somehow break through the cracks in the concrete of tradition, misunderstood language, rubbished sidewalks, and blaring horns — warmly nurtured into flower by some local who is resolute to be a little different from everything their life had been determined to make them. In absolute defiance of everything expected of them — they notice, they listen, they think and astonishingly, bravely, they do.

Waan returned from the bathroom just as I was using one of those lovely long-handled teaspoons they have there to scrape out the delicious chocolate-chili sludge that my indulgent formula always left behind in the bottom of the cup once the coffee was finished. Smiling, she picked up her plate and headed off to the buffet in search of sustenance.

She had told me she was a student studying Exercise Physiotherapy at QUT in Brisbane and was returning home for the end-of-semester break to visit her parents, who lived in one of the outer suburbs of Bangkok — somewhere out near the Chatuchak markets, she had said. I knew the JJ markets well, and when she had mentioned them, my mind had wandered back to an old dusty, dirty sign that read 'No Cock Fighting' with an image of an angry rooster that I had seen there hanging on two pieces of brown twine, about a million years ago. I had remembered it was covered in cobwebs, just above head height in one of a thousand narrow walkways. Back to the smells and colour and clamor of the stalls that made up the biggest markets in the world; packed with fake Nike T-shirts, incense and soaps, celadon ceramics, tasty but game-of-roulette-poisonous food and drinks, jewelry, and hundreds of clothing designers desperately trying to become anything other than just a needle in a haystack. Back to the woman near the south entrance selling the most beautiful ivory jewelry displayed on a burgundy velvet board, furtive, watchful in her fear of being caught.

As Waan walked away, the sound of the young couple at the table next to me drew my focus — they were arguing.

"Of course, there is a wage gap, Jay. Don't be ridiculous," the woman was saying.

"Bullshit, and you should have more common sense than to believe that crap. Everyone's a fucking victim, aren't they?" The man responded, "It's just a victim mentality, and your friend has bought into it, the whole box and dice".

"The world is not against men, Jay, and she is not playing the victim," the woman retorted. There were some brochures on their table that looked like they were from a trade fair. I guessed they were work colleagues. He was Caucasian, about 28; she was about 25 and looked middle Asian, but both had strong south London accents.

"Again, bullshit. The world is totally against men. You just don't see it — and the deck is especially stacked against men who are white." He continued. "Joanna's a female and in a wheelchair for fucks sake. She gets to tick every fucking box — everybody wants to hire her, and for her to bitch that the 'patriarchy' is holding her back is just fucking ridiculous. Sorry, but it is."

As interesting as the conversation was, I was hungry, and pushing my chair out, I wandered over to the buffet — time for something to eat. My process was always the same — simple, tried, and proven. First, I went over to the chefs and ordered two fried eggs, flipped — getting past any potential language issues by motioning with my outstretched hand turning over. Then, I walked over to the toaster and placed two slices of wholemeal bread onto the slow-moving conveyor. Walking away to pour myself one of those amazing fresh orange juices you can get in Thailand, I kept a close eye on my toast. I knew from experience that if the Chinese magpies were lurking, my toast would disappear the moment it fell into the tray. Our Chinese cousins still had a generation or two to go before they truly understood what was going on around them, what was right and what was wrong — until they had the confidence and the patience to embrace a system of polite civility without automatically feeling the need to just take from it.

Carrying my juice over to the two trays of bacon, using the tongs, I placed four pieces of the crispy bacon onto a plate and took the juice and the bacon back to my table — ever watchful of my toast. The couple next to me were still arguing. I looked at them, but they ignored me. Placing the plate of bacon and the juice on our table, I smiled at Waan and, walking back, collected my toast just as it fell into the tray, along with two foils of butter, and went back to my table to butter my toast. Then I headed back to the chefs, who invariably were just placing my eggs onto a small plate and passing them to me with a friendly smile.

Back at our table, Waan was busy working slowly through a huge plate of food — she was so slight it defied logic that she would ever be able to eat it all. It was an eclectic assortment of steamed rice, a blueberry Danish, Chinese BBQ pork, a small box of cornflakes — but no milk or bowl, an unopened container of strawberry yoghurt, some salad, a hashbrown, and a huge pile of corn kernels. Looking at it, no matter how hard I tried, for the life of me, I could not find any common logic in the mixture beyond the simple concept of "fuel". It was not bacon and eggs, a sausage and a hash brown, nor was it fruit, and yoghurt, and muesli — the Yin and the Yang of breakfasts. It was the type of assortment that one might expect a homeless person may have chosen, given the opportunity for a meal in a place such as this.

But Waan was no starving wretch. She was wearing a tight red cotton singlet top — no bra, her tiny nipples sharp through the fabric, a crisp white linen overshirt — unbuttoned; CK designer jeans that looked new; a fine tan coloured leather belt with a small, shiny, gold plated buckle that looked Italian; a simple 24K shiny yellow gold necklace with a single large pearl on it; and neat slip-on fine tan leather shoes — almost like what a ballerina might wear but shiny leather.

"Now you're just being silly," the girl at the table next to us was saying. "Of course, the world is geared towards preferential treatment for white males; you can't deny the 'Patriarchy' exists, or the 'Wage Gap' for that matter; it's just ridiculous. Just look at who owns all the real estate and who gets all the highest paying jobs."

"You need to think this shit through Sarah," the man answered.

"There is no 'Wage Gap'. Women just make different choices. They choose different careers than men; they work different hours — generally, men are more driven. Men are more interested in things, "stuff", and women, generally, are more interested in people. They take time off to have kids, shit like that. Maybe a small group of highly driven males fall into the category you are talking about, but most men are at the very fucking bottom of the food chain", he answered with a mouth half full of salad. "How many women do you think choose to work at sewerage treatment plants or lonely twelve day fortnights on mine sites? What about high-paying, dangerous jobs on oil rigs or high-rise construction? How many men choose to work as nurses or social workers, or secretaries? How many women choose to work 70, 80, 100 hours per week in a high-stress office environment? It's just fucking choices."

He went on.

"Think about it — they get paid the same hourly rate for the same job. If companies could get away with paying women less for the same job — which is fucking completely illegal in most civilised countries anyway I might add, they would just hire women because they would be cheaper, and the company would make more money."

Astonishingly, not only was Waan's plate now almost empty, but she was pushing her chair back and setting off for still more breakfast. Perhaps a bowl and milk for the tiny box of cornflakes that was sitting there next to her teacup unopened, I thought, or at least a teaspoon for the yoghurt — also still sitting there untouched?

"Most men lead a life of quiet desperation." I can't remember who said that, but it's true — just look at the statistics", the guy was saying. "Almost 70% of people who are homeless in England are male. More than 75% of homicide victims are males, and more than 99% of people who die in the workplace are men. Males make up only 42% of higher education students, and yet, STILL, all the focus is on improving women's access to university! In classrooms, boys are treated like they're dysfunctional girls — they're put on fucking drugs if they move around in their seat too much, if they fucking fidget. It's just crazy... Four out of five suicides are men and boys, for fucks sake. Why do you think that is? Don't the fucking assholes responsible for this bullshit have brothers? Sons? Fathers? Husbands, for Christ's sake?"

He suddenly seemed to realise how animated he had become, and, glancing over, I saw him consciously relax his shoulders and reach for his coffee cup. She, on the other hand, had a look on her face as if she was just annoyed at what he was saying — as if she was not really listening to the points he was making, more just waiting for the opportunity to argue her thoughts on the subject.

"I mean, all you have to do is look at marriage," he continued in a more subdued tone. "Why the fuck would any man ever want to get married in today's world? All she has to decide at some point is, 'Damn, I've had enough of this whole working together, compromise thing. I'd prefer just to do exactly whatever I want whenever I feel like it. He gave me the kids, has been a good loyal father, and has provided well, but, hey, I don't really need him around anymore, so fuck it, I'll just get a divorce. If she leaves, she gets everything, well, almost everything, and if he leaves, he gets almost nothing, so he's always trying to make it work while she's always got one foot out the door. This shit defines how people interact in relationships. So. She leaves, and he gets his whole world ripped out from under him — everything he has spent his one fucking chance at a happy life building up and maintaining — gone. The future he's been dreaming of, of just him and her, when the kids have grown up, and the house is paid off, travelling around enjoying life, finally with enough time and money to do some of the things he thought they BOTH wanted to do together — vaporised, overnight. She takes most of everything; hell, she goes for the kids as well because then she gets even more. He knows he's completely fucked if he tries for custody of the kids because he knows that judges award custody to the mother in like 95% of cases."

Boet, my man, never sign a contract with someone who is rewarded for breaking it.

A South African mercenary I found myself sharing a large plastic jug of Long Island Iced Tea with, in a bar in Mogadishu one sweltering summer's afternoon.

"So there he is, alone, poor, his dreams over, the last shittiest season of old age with all its health nightmares is all he has left, along with half a home at best — and now there's an impossible mortgage on the other half, and he's having to ask permission to see his own fucking kids every other week."

I caught the girl's eye; she looked angry and a little confused, suddenly out of her depth. His statistics and the obvious thought he had put into the subject had thrown her. The guy saw her looking at me, and he turned to follow her gaze.

"Well? Am I wrong?" he said to me.

I looked at her, then back at him.

"I think you're right, but from what she's been saying, with all due respect" I said glancing at the woman and then back to him "I think you're wasting your breath trying to explain it to her."

"And why is that?" she said, immediately arcing up.

"Because it's pointless trying to convince someone of something if they're determined to misunderstand you. I mean what he has been saying are just simple truths. Facts. But because it doesn't fit into your world, because it's different from what everyone in your social life and everyone at work talks about and believes, the impression I get is that even if you accept what he is saying as factual, you're just going to refuse to engage with it, refuse to accept that it's a problem. I mean I feel like I've heard enough of your conversation to be able to say that people who talk like you, in my opinion, are all the same. Anything different from your current viewpoint, anything that contradicts the group-think, that could in any way unbalance your world or jeopardise all of the benefits you are enjoying from it, is something you just aren't interested in. Sorry. So. As I said. I think he's wasting his time." I finished with a cold smile.

"Bullshit!" she replied. "Clearly the world is dominated by white men, you can see it everywhere. It's people like you are the ones not interested in facts." She was clearly pissed with me, which I guess wasn't surprising, but I ignored that and went on.

"OK. For the benefit of doubt, for the sake of argument." I replied. "Let's assume people who believe what you believe don't see the stuff he's talking about because of the whole frog in a pot thing".

They both looked puzzled. "Well, you know, if you put a frog in a pot of boiling water on a stove, it jumps straight out. But if you put a frog in a pot of cold water and turn on the heat, it just stays there and slowly cooks and dies."

He was nodding like he understood — she was just sitting there, arms folded, glaring at me.

"Everything he's saying, his statistics, I think are dead right, but these changes have happened slowly over time and people just don't notice them. I mean, I think most people just get on with life — they just ignore all this stuff he's talking about. I actually think in the West, suicide is the biggest killer of men aged between 21 and 45, but people just don't seem to care. People never even talk about it. Government funding for women's health — in terms of research, education, and on-the-ground delivery — is consistently orders of magnitude higher than it is for men's health. I think people like you just float along, drawn into whatever narrative seems to be the most popular and suits who they are in their lives. Most people don't really care about anyone outside their immediate world. I mean, I guess it's just selfishness and convenience — and fear. I think there is a shitload of fear in there as well."

"I think most people, don't want to see this stuff because if they do, then it draws them away from the world that they all feed off — like I said before; their friends, their work colleagues. To have different opinions makes you an outsider. You're scared of being laughed at for having a different opinion on stuff like this or worse, being ostracised — so you just ignore it. Being accepted and being liked means more to you, is a bigger driver for you, than the truth — than bothering to be aware of what's true and what isn't. Or maybe more accurately, the fear of being rejected or disliked, the fear of being judged by your friends as being outside the dominant consensus of opinion is what frightens you the most."

"Bullshit again" she shot back. "I'm an engineer — I deal in facts all day long. Facts matter to me."

"Perhaps, but maybe it's easy for you to just ignore these particular facts?" I replied.

I went on.

"He's right about it being a very small group of highly driven males that fall into the category you're talking about and that most men are at the very bottom of the ladder in Western society. I mean they are literally treated as disposable, literally treated with contempt. I mean, the whole four out of five suicides are men and boys thing, unless this stuff impacts them directly in a really obvious way, unless they're out there with a dazed expression on their faces getting semi-colon tattoos on their fucking wrists, most people just don't care. You're an engineer, you do the math. Why do you think four out of five suicides in places like England and Australia are boys and men?"

She was just staring at me now. The guy interrupted.

"Just on that, even the men", he said. "Which is really fucking crazy when you think about it. In today's world, most men have to deal with so much animosity, so much fucking resentment and abuse from society in general. They're just desperately trying to pay the mortgage and escape with their dick still attached to their body. They know intuitively that the world is against them. They can tell by everything they read, every ad on TV that portrays men as stupid or untrustworthy or inconsiderate or useless, every time they get ignored or sneered at by some twenty-something girl from behind a counter. But they don't have the time or the skills to figure out what the fuck is happening to them."

Waan returned and, placing a fresh orange juice in front of me and a bowl of pistachio ice cream on the table in front of her, proceeded to eat delicate, small spoonfuls, slowly, as if to savor every last drop of it.

The man and the woman had both stopped eating and were staring at me now — him with a kind of self-justified confidence having found an advocate for what he was saying, and her, staring at me with just simple, raw animosity.

Suddenly, I was annoyed. I mean, for fuck's sake, I was so sick and tired of seeing that look on women's faces. That expression that said that they really would prefer not to have to look at you, and especially they would very much prefer not to have to talk to you.

"That, there", I said, pointing at her.

"That's a nasty look. A look like that takes practice — you must have sisters."

I laughed. I mean, I didn't give a shit — she was a stranger to me. I decided to take off my rose-coloured glasses and put on my bile-tinted monocle.

"You're looking at me like you don't like me, actually, like you hate me, like I'm somehow your enemy. You don't even know me. It's cognitive dissonance. It's like, no matter how much logic or how many facts are thrown at you, they all just slide down the Teflon wall of your mind. It's almost like you're programmed, hard-wired to support this psychopathic narrative — this destruction, this fucking casting out and destroying of men. Like, why the fuck is that? Do you think your friend and I are just making this shit up?

"I mean your so-called Patriarchy; let's start there, hey? All of your freedom, all of your safety, and all of your authority are given to you by men."

"Oh, that's just fucking bullshit...", she interjected, standing up as if she was about to march off.

"Sarah, we're just talking." the guy said in a calming tone.

"No, let me finish, just think about it." I said, as she sat back down reluctantly, albeit on the edge of her seat.

"The bad guys exist; they just fucking do. It's not the fault of the good guys that some guys are just assholes that would rape and enslave women given the slightest opportunity. I mean its just not reasonable to hold the majority of men responsible for the behavior of what is clearly that minority of men in the world who choose to be assholes."

"I think if you're really honest with yourself, you'd agree that most guys are the good guys. Most guys, by far the majority of men, even if they didn't know you, would intervene — would be prepared to risk their life to protect you if you were being threatened in the street."

I stopped and just looked at her. "I mean, you know that, right?"

She was staring at me blankly, refusing to concede anything.

I went on. "Think about it. Without the significant majority of men — the good guys — protecting you from the bad guys, women would live a brutal and terrifying fucking existence. If men didn't protect women, who would? Women? I don't think so. It's just simple biology. Most men, say four out of five, are much stronger physically than women, much more capable of inflicting physical harm — it's just the way it is, it's just nature."

I went on. "By protecting you, men give you all the freedoms that you have; it's the good guys who have always made the laws and who have always enforced the laws that keep you safe. They do that. Women can't do that."

Violence is the gold standard, the reserve that guarantees order. In actuality, it is better than a gold standard, because violence has universal value. Violence transcends the quirks of philosophy, religion, technology, and culture... Without *action, words are just words. Without violence, laws are just words...Violence isn't the only answer, but it is the final answer.*

Jack Donovan

"There's a natural physical power imbalance between men and women that is, just the way it is. To deny that and say men and women are equal is just fucking silly. Even men and men aren't equal, even women and women aren't equal. Intrinsically, naturally, you have no authority, no freedom, and no safety except the authority, the freedom, and the safety that men give you — that the good guys give you."

Although she had shifted back from the edge into her seat, she was still clearly furious at me. In response to the raw savagery of what I was saying, to how volatile the discussion had become, his body language and the expression on his face had changed as well. He looked like he wanted to at least nod in agreement with what I was saying, but seemed reluctant to even move.

I went on. "I mean, up until very recently, men's and women's roles were, to a great extent, an arrangement of mutual consensus. The world was a very different place for most of history to what it is now — much more difficult, far more dangerous and threatening — and as a result, the physical inequality between men and women was much more emphasised. I mean look who traditionally has gone off to war — dying in their millions, sacrificing their lives to protect the women and children at home?"

"This role that men played was never imposed by authority, it was imposed by consent. Actually, men took a very paternalistic view on how women and families should be treated — you know the whole 'women and children first' thing and all that. Historically, generally, men have treated women with an incredible amount of deference. And women wanted men to play that role, they wanted to be protected, they wanted to be provided for, they wanted to make sure their children were safe — and men did everything they could to provide that security. It was only very recently that all this changed — when the world became a much safer place — which by the way, was the direct result of the intentions and the efforts of this so-called 'Patriarchy'. Men just want women to be happy. They want them to love them, they want their approval. That's the whole raison d'être of being a man, just to be needed by someone else."

"Where you've been misled," I continued, "where third-wave feminism has fucked it all up for women, is telling you that that authority that men have naturally through their size and their strength — through their fucking testosterone — carries implications with regards to dominance and control. Most men don't see this relationship like that. For most men, protecting women, protecting their freedoms and their safety, and making sure they have authority, making sure they have a say in the world, is a natural function. They see it as a good thing, good for everybody. Even more, they see it as a fucking responsibility and are happy to do what they can to make sure these rights are supported."

"What's that quote, 'Feminism has liberated women from the natural dignity of their sex and turned them into inferior men' or something like that. The bottom line is, if you removed that authority that men naturally have from our society, then your life would be a nightmare. That's this fucking "Patriarchy" you're complaining about."

Calming down, I smiled at her and took a sip of the orange juice Waan had put in front of me. My throat was starting to hurt now from all the talking I was doing. I took just a moment, a fraction of time just to myself, pure focus, enjoying the sweet flavour, the feeling of the cold juice running down my throat.

But it was just too seductive to stop. I was wasting my time but had to keep going — boots and all. I knew from experience that no amount of discussion would make any difference to the view this woman had of the world.

"So yeah," I continued, looking at her. "I think all of his statistics are correct and the blame for all of this shit really lies with the masses, the benighted fucking herd. I'm sorry, but it lies with people exactly like you who make a conscious decision to ignore facts, who float through life at a kind of superficial level, who choose to remain ignorant because then they can play the victim card and benefit at the expense of other people who suffer because of it." I continued calmly, looking at her.

Under the spreading chestnut tree, I sold you and you sold me.
There lie they, And here lie we, under the spreading
chestnut tree.

1984 — George Orwell

I turned my back on you, and you turned your back
on me under
the "goose stepping, twelve stepping, tea-totalitarianist"*
pathocracy.

*God is in the House — Nick Cave and the Bad Seeds

I would probably have preferred if fate hadn't put them at the table next to mine, however, I had to admit I was enjoying the distraction, enjoying myself belittling the masses, belittling her, and it didn't seem to be bothering Waan. These lazy, opportunistic people who were too stupid to realise the costs that society suffered as a whole, that their boys and men suffered, and subsequently that they suffered, because of their short-sighted selfishness.

Their cruelty.

I had a great contempt for the Echochamberists that I had spent my life developing, nurturing. I fucking hated them. They were responsible for 90% of the world's misery. 90% of Sam's misery.

The hottest place in hell is reserved for those who in times of
trouble retain their neutrality.

Dante

157

"And you just don't want to challenge it — people like you don't want to challenge it. I mean, think about it. That way, they will never get called out or embarrassed. Instead, they are going to get included and invited and welcomed — floating along, reveling in their feelings of pretentiously fabricated moral superiority. They choose to remain deliberately disinterested in why so many men compared to women are homeless, deliberately disinterested in what's causing men and boys to kill themselves at the rates that they are."

"But it's as I said", smiling, "frogs in pots."

"I think a lot of it is actually deliberate" the guy said. "I think a lot of this stuff is about rage and revenge from a twisted perception of what the world used to be like. Like you said before, about how dangerous the world was for most of history. How, because of those circumstances, roles were naturally different, and for the most part, men and women not only accepted them, but actively supported playing those roles. I think modern day feminists forget all that and view the world through a kind of distorted, deliberately fallacious, self-serving lens — this whole oppression thing. To be honest, I believe that in today's world many women are fully fucking aware of what's happening to boys and men, and that in fact they're actually quietly enjoying it."

"Fuck Jay, how could you even say that?" the woman responded — clearly furious and feeling outnumbered in the discussion.

"Because it's everywhere — I mean its so fucking obvious how badly your average male is treated — how could women not see it?" he replied.

I interrupted. "Maybe the best way to look at it is a series of simple questions", I said, smiling coldly at the woman who was just sitting stoney faced now, staring at me.

"For example, if a girl wants to go out with a guy who is older, it's just a preference, right? But if a guy wants to go out with a girl who's younger — he's a creep. Agree?"

158

Caught off guard they both nodded — a little embarrassed looking at Waan.

Waan started laughing without looking away from her now half-finished bowl of ice cream. Clearly she had been following the whole conversation.

I went on, "Or if a girl doesn't want to date anyone under 6' tall, it's a preference, but if a guy doesn't want to date a girl who's fat, he's shallow. Agree?"

The guy threw up his hands. "Exactly, this is exactly what I was trying to say," he said. "But it's more than that. These days, if he doesn't want to date a trans woman — and I'm talking here about a dude with a fucking dick — he gets called an asshole and a transphobe".

"That's right", I said, lowering my voice a little in response to the disapproving look I had noticed our table was getting from a woman a couple of tables away.

I went on. "Or if a girl wants a guy who is confident and strong and takes charge, it's a preference, but if a guy wants a girl who will submit to his lead, he's a misogynist." I mean, that's the way it is, isn't it?" He was nodding, but she was sitting there staring at me, steely-eyed. "Or if a girl sets boundaries, she's strong and empowered, but if a guy sets boundaries, he's controlling. You see what I mean?"

"Fucking A man", said the guy. "I mean, just that boundaries thing. I would just walk the fuck away from a girl if she wanted to spend time with a guy from her past — even if it was just fucking 'coffee', no matter how much I cared for her. I mean, not one man, not even one man on this planet who still has his fucking balls, would be happy with someone that means a lot to him, spending time with another man who has fucked her, who has had his dick in her mouth. No man with any self-respect at all wants that — that's ball-breaking bullshit right there."

The girl looked very uncomfortable now — but fuck her, as far as I was concerned, she was part of the problem. And he was right, of course. I would fight for my wife, beside my wife, give everything I had, but there was no fucking way I would ever fight over her. If some other guy got her attention, he could have her.

I continued his argument.

"And any woman worth having would absolutely, 100% be completely aware of that, and she's just fucking gaslighting him if she tells him, 'he shouldn't be bothered by it', that they're just 'friends', that he 'really should work on his own self-esteem'." The guy was becoming quite animated in his agreement, now nodding and moving around in his seat.

I went on.

"And just on that, the majority of men that a woman has in her personal life — that are outside, separate from her relationship with her partner — are there because they think there is a chance they might get their dick sucked. The moment they realise that that's not going to happen, they disappear from her life very quickly. How long that process takes is completely up to her."

I looked at her. "I mean, you know that right? All women know that. I mean they fucking deny it and say 'Oh no he's just a friend' but they fucking know that's how it works, they just don't want to admit it."

I had once seen a pretty woman in a bar get approached by a really handsome, tall, well-dressed guy. Like there was just nothing guileful about him. He was wearing a $5,000 suit, obviously spent a lot of time in the gym, and had one of those kind, handsome smiles — everything about him was what women found attractive, what men wished they could be. After no more than ten seconds, the woman had held up her ring finger to show the guy she was engaged, or married, or whatever. I mean fuck, there was just no way her partner could have measured up to how special this guy was. He was fucking perfect. I mean, she was friendly and all about it, but not at all flirty. To me, it showed such strength, such dedication and love for her partner that even though she was alone, she didn't want to engage on any level at all with someone who was clearly interested in her sexually. Even just a conversation was a betrayal to the man she loved. It was honestly one of the most beautiful things I had ever seen.

I continued. "I guess what I am saying is that the world is constantly encouraging girls and women to make these choices, to be empowered, strong, and independent, while at the same time telling boys and men who want to make the exact same choices that they are manipulative, misogynistic assholes suffering from "toxic masculinity" and they need to fix themselves. That's the fucking essence of it all — men are constantly being told they need to fix themselves, that they're somehow broken."

He was sitting up now looking at her, on his face a smile of almost embarrassed vindication. Her expression was one of equal parts anger and defensiveness that seemed not only to be aimed at me but at him as well now — her breakfast untouched on the plate in front of her.

All of a sudden, he looked at his watch. "Anyway, sorry guys I have to go. Sarah, I've got a zoom meeting with Patrick at nine and I'm already late." Draining his coffee cup he stood up. "Nice to meet you man," he said to me holding out his hand for me to shake. "Sorry you had to put up with our ranting and raving" he said to Waan. Waan looked up from her bowl. "No problem" she said, as if she couldn't care less, and went back to her ice-cream.

"Well, I hope that's sorted that out then! See you tomorrow morning when we can resolve the whole Arab-Israel thing." I said to him with a smile.

He laughed and looking over to the woman said. "Does it suit you if I knock on your door at 10:30 Sarah and we can leave then?" he asked.

"Okay" she answered reaching for her knife and fork and starting to eat without even looking at him.

After he had walked away, she looked up from her plate at me. "You know, you might have a point with some of this stuff, but at the end of the day, in my opinion, men still have it better than women in many ways" she said, her demeanour a little calmer now, perhaps because he had left and it was just us.

I smiled coldly at her. "It's as I said before, no matter what arguments you hear people make, no matter what facts they put in front of you, you're never going to change your mind. In your world it's just not in your best interests, I get that. People like you justify your opinions by latching on to first level thinking and refusing to look deeper. It's simplistic and superficial, and its created a fucking nightmare for men and boys. You rage against any suggestion of increased funding that is focused on helping boys and men — deliberately choosing to interpret these efforts as an attack on women — as an attempt to try to take something away from supporting issues affecting women and girls! Its 'Zero-Sum Empathy', this idea that empathy is a limited resource, and that helping one group of people means hurting another. Its fucking insane."

I could have sworn that her smile back at me was an expression that confirmed absolutely what I had just said.

A little annoyed, I went on.

"Actually, the only thing that I can think of, is that up until now guys had that one superpower of choosing who they married. Women got to choose who they fucked, but men got to choose who they married. But as your friend pointed out before," I continued, "even that's been taken away from them now. In today's world, in the West, what guy in his right mind would want to get married? I mean, who wants a woman who reaches a point in her life where she decides that it's about time she found a partner to settle down with, to give her a couple of kids and some security? A woman who's incapable of forming any sort of strong emotional connection with him because she's been through 15, 20, or 30 other guys before she got to him? A woman who has no problem at all, the moment their marriage has some money behind it and the kids are sorted, with walking away without even a second thought — taking away everything he's spent most of his life working towards?"

"That's some fucking price to pay for something that all those other guys before him got for free."

"How can you say that? There's no difference in bonds between a man and a woman, between who leaves who in a marriage," the woman said, just as Noi arrived at our table.

"How is your breakfast, Mr. Alex?" she was tall for a Thai, with a friendly, open smile.

"Fantastic as always, thanks, Noi," I replied. She glanced at the woman we were talking with and, turning her smile towards Waan, placed her palms together at her chest, nodded her head down in a slight bow, and walked away.

"There is a difference actually" I replied after Noi had left. "It's like your friend was saying before, the dynamics are completely different. If the woman leaves, she gets almost everything, and if he leaves, he gets almost nothing. As he was saying; like where is the equality in that? The guy's always trying to make it work while she's got one foot out the door."

The woman continued, her attitude more matter-of-fact than aggressive now. "Maybe there is some truth to that, but you have to admit that there's no difference between men and women and how many people they have slept with when it comes to who decides to leave who in a marriage."

"No, I think there is a difference, maybe you just haven't thought about it" I replied. "I mean, firstly, just look at the numbers, like how many average guys get to sleep with even ten women in their lives? Even five? An average-looking woman can sleep with as many men as she wants. So, by definition, women who choose to sleep with lots of men get laid a lot more than your average guy does — so just the numbers are different."

"I agree," said the woman, looking up from her plate. "But if both a guy and a girl have each slept with, say, ten people, then there's no difference, is really what I'm saying."

"Well, I don't think that's strictly correct either; there is a difference. Whether or not that difference has any impact or not on who leaves who in a marriage might be debatable, but there is a difference" I replied. "Those guys that you were talking about before, that have all the money and own all the property, let's call them the Alpha males — the guys with the six packs, the Porsches, and the perfect teeth. Let's say they make up maybe ten percent of men. Is that reasonable?"

"I guess," she replied.

"These assholes get to fuck whoever they want, don't they? They're more than happy to pick up an average-looking woman in a bar and spend the night with her. I mean, they might prefer an alpha female, but they are perfectly happy fucking an average-looking woman."

"So an average looking woman, who obviously can easily get laid whenever she chooses, by the time she's slept with ten men, has to have slept with at least two or three of these alpha males. Would you agree?"

"I suppose so", she said.

"Okay, so let's look at an average-looking guy. We've already established that he's lucky if he gets to sleep with five, not to mention ten women in his entire life, but for argument's sake, let's say he does get to sleep with ten women. How many really hot alpha women do you think would be on his list? I mean, he has no fucking six-pack, no serious money, no dazzling smile. Maybe one in his life before he gets married, if he's lucky? Probably none?"

"So you see, it's not strictly even; it's not exactly the same. The point I'm making is any woman who has slept around a lot will have had experiences, have memories of big, strong, handsome alpha males that they have had sex with, that are always going to be there, wedged between her and the average poor-miserable-soft-bellied-bastard who ends up marrying her. But the guys? Not so much."

"Maybe. But I don't think this stuff has much of an impact on the thinking, you know, makes that much of a difference to your average woman," she replied a little coldly.

"Perhaps," I said. "But maybe your opinion might change after you've clocked up ten or twenty years of married life, of trying to connect with the same 'average' man".

Waan took advantage of the break in the conversation to declare with a big grin that she was full as she picked up the small unopened box of cornflakes and the still-sealed tub of yoghurt and put them in the tote bag she had brought with her from the room.

Standing up I smiled at the woman. "Well, at least you can't say breakfast was boring" I said, struggling to sound like I cared at all about how she was feeling.

She stayed seated and continued eating her breakfast, and without a word, dismissed us with a cold smile, as we walked away.

Thanking the waitresses as we walked out, I tipped Noi, and leaving Prem's tip at the concierge desk for her to give him, we went back to my room.

Sitting down at the desk and opening my laptop, I was immediately distracted by Waan. Gazing over the top of the screen, I watched her as she stripped naked, and after putting on a red bikini under some tiny denim shorts and a singlet top, walked over, gave me a kiss on the cheek, and said she would be at the pool. I smiled and, looking down, started to type.

CHAPTER III

Four miles away from Meredith and Eugine, deep inside Cracklewood Forest, was a cave with an entrance that was so well camouflaged that unless you were a witch, you would be completely unaware of it. Inside this cave was the stinking lair that had been Gagglebroth and her brood's home for hundreds of years. A spell woven by Gagglebroth made the entrance to the cave appear as solid rock, no different from the rock about it.

The area was covered with giant Oak and towering Boobleberry trees that did their best to shut out the light, leaving a kind of murky grey twilight that blended together rather than distinguished the shapes of the forest. The forest floor was a thick carpet of fallen leaves through which, like great pillars, the tree trunks rose up. So dense were the trees and so poor was the light that it was impossible to see more than twenty or thirty feet in any direction.

Through the entrance to the cave was a short stone corridor that opened up into a large chamber. In the middle of this chamber was a long timber table, a sharp golden crystal, two feet in height, balancing at its centre. Around the table were six chairs. All had been carved from solid pieces of timber. At the back wall of the cave were two more doorways. One chair much larger than the rest stood at the end of the table, and on it sat Gagglebroth. Hunched forward, she looked like a giant spider deep in thought.

To the right of Gagglebroth, on a similar but slightly smaller chair, sat Enchantlure, second eldest of the brood, second in power, second in command. The chain of command was largely dictated by their ages. The eldest being the most experienced therefore the wisest and most learned and consequently the most powerful. First came Gagglebroth, the eldest at 1,747 years old, then Enchantlure at 1,592, Garblebilk at

1,473, Elixius at 936, Beetlecrunch at 647, and Curdleslop at 621.

Over on the left side wall of the cave, a large fire blazed in a hearth carved directly into the rock face. Garblebilk stood by the fire. In hushed tones, she directed Curdleslop and Elixius between insults as they erected a spit above the fire; Enchantlure watched them closely. Chained to the wall near the entrance was a rather unhealthy-looking pig. The hog was squealing softly, occasionally sounding as though it were speaking, its squeals sounding like the word "please", for it was actually Beetlecrunch begging for mercy. In her fury at the news of Beetlecrunch's stupidity in mentioning Dew's name, Gagglebroth had turned Beetlecrunch into a pig and was now preparing to roast her.

The fire prepared and the spit erected, the Witches retired to their respective seats on either side of the table. They sat in silence, not daring to speak should they arouse Gagglebroth from her thoughts and, in so doing, become another focus of her wrath. The crackle and pop of the fire echoed softly inside the cave as the smoke spiraled up towards a hole in the roof, shifting and moving like a wraith departing on a mission of terror.

Enchantlure leaned slowly over to the bowed head of Gagglebroth and whispered softly. A moment later, Gagglebroth raised her head. She sat upright, her eyes glowing mendaciously against the flickering shadows. Her gaze fell on Beetlecrunch, the hog cowering back against the wall, slobbering, its eyes expressing a plea for mercy through a mask of dread and terror.

Slowly, Gagglebroth's eyes dulled to their former brightness, and she extended her right arm towards Beetlecrunch, her fingers outstretched.

"Out from Hog and back to form,
You miserable sniveling wretch,
But one more blunder, small or big
And you WILL find yourself forever
Living life as a wretched pig!"

An orange light flashed about Beetlecrunch, followed by a swirl of smoke. The smoke dispersed to reveal Beetlecrunch down on all fours in her natural but not much prettier form, her eyes still wide with fear, her mouth still slobbering. Gagglebroth waved her hand, and at this gesture, Beetlecrunch scuttled to the table, sitting on the seat furthest from her, the very seat that had once been Curdleslop's, who now sat sniggering quietly to herself at Beetlecrunch's misfortune.

Gagglebroth began to speak in a sharp, commanding voice.

"Dew has our prey and with that, the ingredient we have been waiting for for over 160 years. Our power against the mortals must be returned in full!" her voice rising to a scream as she crashed her fist down onto the table with surprising force.

Pausing, she inclined her head slightly towards Enchantlure, who hissed the name she sought. "LUMPTHISTLE", said Gagglebroth, sounding irritable in her distaste for the name. "Who is now, need I remind you?", her eyes moving to Beetlecrunch, who sat in the far corner with her head bowed. Curdleslop sniggered again. Gagglebroth's stare snapped to Curdleslop. "One more noise from you, my dear", her eyes beginning to darken once again as her anger began to rise, "and it won't be Beetlecrunch squealing above the coals."

"The smile disappeared from Curdleslop's face, and a ghastly grin stretched across Beetlecrunch's, out of Gagglebroth's sight. Gagglebroth paused a moment before continuing. "Who is now in the company of that meddlesome Dew, who now either knows, has guessed, or who at least suspects what is afoot."

"Therefore, our task has become a little more urgent."

"Lumpthistle's heart is by far our best option as I don't need to remind you, the likelihood of retrieving the Black Book or the crystal from Dew is not good, to say the least. But with this second chance to retrieve our blackest power, we can finally defeat Dew once and for all and avenge our sister's death."

All were silent for a moment as they thought of Malichara, one of the broods who they all assumed was killed by Meredith Dew when the book and the crystal were stolen.

"For two hundred years, we have had to rely on powders and potions due to that meddlesome thief, but the hour has finally arrived for all to be returned! I do not wish to speak with Lumpthistle again. If any of you miserable hags get the chance to take his heart, just take it! At all costs. We need our spells back!" she said, smashing her fist down on the table again.

"There's a promotion in it for whoever brings me his heart!" Gagglebroth's eyes were raging red now, as the ears of the rest of the brood pricked in unison at hearing the word 'promotion'.

With this, Gagglebroth stood and raised both her arms, her staff in her right hand high in the air. The rest, including Enchantlure, bowed their heads in acknowledgment as Gagglebroth departed the main chamber disappearing through the doorway to the left of her chair on the back wall.

Enchantlure lifted her head and, slowly looking around the table at the rest of the brood, took over proceedings. Her voice was not as deep as Gagglebroth's, but its tone was just as venomous.

"Garblebilk, you and Curdleslop go find a Boughglimmb. Spread the word that Lumpthistle belongs to us, or at the very least, his heart. Inform them that if they should find him and are unable to control their hunger, every last one of them will be hunted down, their throats slit for their blood, and their bodies diced and stewed. Even if every tree in the forest has to be burned to the ground to do so. By order of Gagglebroth! And the same goes for any Snizzlegrubs", she added as an afterthought.

Curdleslop nodded and, pushing up on the table to drag her old frame out of her chair, shuffled over to the doorway on the right at the rear of the cave. The doorway led down some stairs and through to a storage room with walls lined floor to ceiling with wooden shelving that was crammed full of ingredients: powders, liquids, and jars full of the strangest looking things, all used in the concoction of various magic potions and spells. Among the ingredients were also stored in various cooking pots and the witches' food supply. To the casual observer, the food and the ingredients were indistinguishable from each other and, in fact, in many cases, were one and the same.

Through the doorway, Curdleslop passed down the winding stone staircase and into the room. Inside, the room was lit by a torch burning brightly in the left-hand corner high up near the ceiling. The light from the torch danced and reflected off the smooth crystal and stone jars that were stacked row upon row on the shelves. Taking a sack out from beneath her cloak, she walked over to the shelves and started to methodically remove lids and pour a variety of contents into empty stone jars she drew from the leather sack: a handful of dried toad eyeballs into one, two carefully plucked mushrooms glowing purple into another, and a dollop of a thick flowing green liquid that made a hissing noise when the stopper was removed from a crystal canister that she drew right from the very back of a shelf against the stone wall.

Apparently happy her work was done there, she crouched down directly below the second shelf from the floor, which contained a row of small leather pouches. One by one, she opened each pouch, peering carefully inside. One emitted a bright blue light that flashed up through the shelves and the bottles and jars, casting sharp flickering shadows about the room. Another, when opened, emitted a shrill, terrifying scream, causing Curdleslop to immediately pull the drawstrings tightly closed, silencing it. After a little while, her green eyes narrowed in concentration at the contents of the latest pouch she had chosen and, satisfied, stood up and added it to her sack.

On the floor against the back wall was a pile of leather flasks that contained Witch water, a mixture of swamp water and rat blood. Curdleslop grabbed the closest one, slung it over her shoulder by the leather strap, and, picking up a small cauldron from the stack near the doorway, left the room.

When she returned from the storeroom to the main chamber, Elixius was gone. Enchantlure sat on her chair, giving Beetlecrunch instructions to go and watch the stump but to stay out of sight. Beetlecrunch left quickly with a piercing glance at Curdleslop. Curdleslop shuffled quietly to the front entrance under the impatient stare of Garblebilk, who followed her outside.

Enchantlure remained in the cave. She lifted a large cauldron half full of liquid and suspended it above the fire on the spit. Although the Witches appeared old and frail, they were capable of great physical strength. She had been instructed by Gagglebroth to brew two potions — a "potion of illusion" and a "potion of confusion", and this stinking broth was the base she would add to create both. When strained and dried, it became a powder that, when sprinkled on something or someone, made them appear as whatever the sprinkler desired, but only to the eyes of mortals.

Gagglebroth was sitting quietly in her chambers, a private lair of sorts that had been used by all the great witch queens before her. It was a sacred place where no other members of the brood, not even Enchantlure, were permitted to enter. None had even seen inside, for a spell known only to Gagglebroth prevented all but her from even seeing the doorway. It was a circular room with a cone-shaped roof lit by a sphere of light that floated about three feet from the ceiling. The glowing ball had been acquired by Dealthmorgrious from a Glock by the name of Methadiouse Flinckle, who had had the misfortune of being cornered by Dealthmorgrious herself during the Great Fire Wars.

On the left-hand side of the room, about halfway up the wall, was a large, round, black hollow, and below that, carved into the rock, was a stone basin. Fed by a hidden spring, the basin was full to the brim with a still pool of silver shimmering water that crept silently over the lip of the basin and flowed noiselessly down the wall, trickling softly around the edge of the floor, eventually forming into a perfect circle around a bonsai Boobleberry tree that was over four thousand years old. From there, it flowed on as a tiny stream in a channel that wound across the room, finally disappearing into a hole on the opposite side of the chamber.

On the other side of the room, to one side, stood a perch for a bird, a golden pulpit beside it, empty for two hundred years awaiting the return of the "Black Book." On the wall, about halfway between the perch and the spring, hung a large oval crystal mirror. In front of the mirror in the center of the room was Gagglebroth, sitting on a sparkling crystal throne that was refracting a myriad of colours around the room from the ball of light above. Directly above the throne in the cone-shaped roof was a hole through which the leaves and branches of the trees above could be seen in the murky grey light that was morning in Cracklewood Forest.

The hole in the roof was controlled by the same spell as the inner door to the room itself; nothing could see into it or pass through it save Gagglebroth. She was sitting there, staring at herself in the mirror. Thinking. After some time, she reached over and slowly lifting the lid off a metal box that sat on a table next to her, plucked out a small black feather. Opening her mouth, she placed the feather on the tip of her long, black tongue and then closed her mouth and her eyes for a short time before opening them again, removing the feather and muttering quietly:

"Black as night
In feather of birds
Take to flight
To gather the words"

At this, Gagglebroth's form on the throne quivered and flickered like a candle against gusts of wind from all directions, and then shimmering like jelly, her form began to shrivel and change shape until she had completely transformed into a large black raven, it's eyes glowing a deep red.

The bird looked into the mirror, Gagglebroth's true form stared back; the reflection had not changed, these magical crystal mirrors showing any illusions created by the Witches in their true form.

Jumping off the throne and with two or three large flaps of her shiny black wings, Gagglebroth was gone, rising swiftly up and twisting out through the hole in the roof and into the grey morning light.

7

In the Beginning.

June 18, 2024

I met Simon at a soup kitchen I worked at in Sydney. I went there every second Friday morning for six months with my eldest son Thomas. Tom wanted to join ASIO when he finished his university degree, and we had agreed that it might help his application if he was seen to be a more rounded person. We decided it would be a good idea for him to get more experience dealing with not only people from all walks of life, but also specifically to be exposed to all of the drama that is generated when 200 homeless people with completely diverse backgrounds, burdened by all sorts of social, substance and psychiatric luggage, get together under the one roof. I wasn't wrong. It was incredible just how much you learnt about yourself and humanity when you made toast for 200 people over a three-hour period: eight toast slots, one tub of butter, one tub of margarine, five different spreads, and four different types of bread.

Simon was about my age, my size and my weight.

He had once been a lecturer at Macquarie University in Sydney until his life spiraled out of control after he was accused of raping a female student in his office when she came to request assistance on an assignment — sex that he says was consensual, but something the courts in their assessment of the evidence decided was rape. After spending a little time with him, I came to the conclusion the courts were probably right. Seven years in the Long Bay Correctional Facility — one of Sydney's largest prisons, saw Simon become addicted to methamphetamines and, two weeks before his release date, be diagnosed as HIV positive. He was always coming up with different stories about why he needed me to give him money.

One day, I suggested that we go outside to the smoking area to have a chat. It was early, with only a few people around and none outside at the back where the smoking area was. I suggested that perhaps I could help him out with some cash if he was happy to do something for me. His immediate response was to take a step closer to me and smile, thinking I wanted sex. "No, no, you have it wrong", I said, laughing and putting my hands on his shoulders, guiding him back away from me. "I am happy to give you $1,500, but I need you to give me certain documents."

During a 10-minute conversation, I explained to him exactly what I needed. It was simple — he had to give me everything he had for me to become him.

I explained I needed any addresses he could remember that he had lived at; the approximate dates he had lived there; any references he had from previous landlords or jobs; any old driver's licenses or passports if he had them; his Medicare card; and an extract from his Birth Certificate — the original would be better — worth an extra $100 to him I had said. I explained that I also needed any letters from the Australian Tax Office or Social Security or both — one definitely had to show his Tax File number — any old bills or even letters that he had addressed to him for electricity, phone or gas, any old or current bank account details or cards, and lastly, and most importantly, a piece of A4 paper with 20 original versions of his signature on it.

He was eager for the money, and it took no persuasion at all from me for us to reach an agreement. With the thought of a $1,500 taste, he became very excited and started tripping over himself to organise how long it would take to get everything together, and when and where we could meet up to finalise the deal.

"I have to go to my sister's place to get most of it — she looks after all that stuff for me", he said.

"Sure, I understand Simon, but what are you going to tell her you need it for? Won't she think it's suspicious that you want all this stuff?" I asked.

"No, man, she won't even know. I know where she keeps it. I haven't got a key, but the laundry door has been broken for years. You just lift and pull, and it opens. I'll just go over tomorrow when she's at work. She won't even know I've been there. I'll call the house first just to make absolutely sure she's not there."

"Remember, there's an extra $100 for you if you can find the original of your birth certificate. An extract will be good, but the original is much, much better", I responded.

"Okay. I know she has another lot of papers in a drawer in her bedroom, which is all the important family stuff. I'll check there as well" he replied.

The trick was that I needed him to stay quiet about our agreement — and alive — for a minimum of 15 months; I needed three months for applications and preparation and twelve months after that. I had to figure out a way to minimise the risk of an overdose as well. We agreed on a simple solution — in return for him giving me everything I needed to use his identity, I would give him an initial $300 cash (plus an extra $100 if he got hold of his original birth certificate), and then every three months after that, he would email me to prove he was still alive and everything was okay. I would then transfer another $300 into his account, and this would happen four times.

For my purposes, he only needed to stay alive for 15 months. Beyond that, whether he lived or died became, to me, the same as I was sure it was to most people on the planet: irrelevant.

I had started with the smaller building blocks — things like renting an apartment in Simon's name. I found a place that was cheap because it was above a massage shop on a main road in a suburb called Paramatta in Sydney and had been vacant for months. It was easy because the owner was a typical slumlord who just wanted the money every week. The only challenge was that he wanted a cash-in-hand deal for tax purposes, so he didn't have to declare the money from the rent as income. I had to convince him for it all to be done properly so I could get the paperwork that I needed for the next step up the system's ladder. In the end, getting him to agree to a standard NSW Residential Tenancy Agreement only cost me an extra $20 a week.

Equipped with the lease documents, I slowly began to emerge from myself and become Simon. I connected the power and gas to the apartment in Simon's name, followed by signing him up for a mobile phone plan using the utility contracts and an expired driver's license he had given me. The Medicare card was the next big step, but with the motivation of an extra $100, Simon had pulled a rabbit out of a hat and delivered his original birth certificate which had made the process much easier than I had expected. Then a bank account, followed by a new driver's license with my face on it, and finally, the big one; a passport in Simon's name with my photograph.

Identity: complete.

I needed absolute freedom from everyone for what I had planned, and this was the best way I could think of achieving that. Being Simon, I could go anywhere and do anything. Not only would I be completely removed from any contact with anyone unless I initiated it, but none of what I did would have any connection at all with my family or my life before now. No one would be able to find me and mess it all up. I wanted to be relaxed, completely cut off from everyone and everything, and God forbid I ended up in more trouble than I could manage, as Simon, none of it would be tied back to my wife or my kids.

It's strange; when you have nothing, you really do have nothing to lose. What you once would have believed was beyond you —

something that you thought you would never have been able to do — becomes the next natural step.

Over the three months I spent building Simon in the basement, I tried to spend as much time with my sons as possible — hugging them and holding them, discussing philosophy with Liam, talking to Ethan about his life and his friends, and playing computer games with Tom.

In essence, this boiled down to me clumsily inserting myself into any gaps I could identify that I felt circumstance allowed in their timetables.

With their lives constantly pulling them away from me, it wasn't easy, but I persevered. I hoped that one day, these times spent together would become precious memories for them. I contrived as many opportunities as possible for us to connect closely — on anything I could think of — regardless of the cost. I was happy to spend whatever it took to create moments where they at least seemed happy to spend time with me.

Ethan was the most difficult because he always seemed to have something very specific he had decided to do and I often felt like was intruding, like spending time with me was something he was just not particularly interested in. I was aware that it was just the age he was at, but it broke my heart nonetheless. I knew it was a poison that one day he would have to swallow, that by the time he grew out of it and looked around for me, I would be gone and it would be too late.

The more time passed, the more I allowed myself to notice everything about my children — savouring every moment with them. Although often feeling very disconnected, I would sit with them and just focus, deliberately trying to block out everything around us while we were together, enjoying them, consciously immersing myself in my love for them, laughing together.

I could always make my children laugh, and being able to do that — to laugh together — staring into each other's eyes, was really something special, something to stop and notice and appreciate. The throbbing pain in my neck, a constant reminder of what was coming.

One of the most satisfying aspects of becoming Simon was quietly taking the time to come up with creative ways to shed all but a few of the "friends" that I had almost inadvertently accumulated on social media.

As the years pass, you connect with these people out of nothing more than that tired, weak acquiescence that settles down upon you when you are overwhelmed by life's challenges. Too busy gasping for air to notice the complete absence of anything real or authentic in these relationships when you respond "Yes" to their friend requests.

I started out by posting repetitively the sort of crap that I had had imposed on me over the years; about how I would know who my real friends were by those who reposted some senseless article about something obscure, and also demanding that only real friends would reply "yes" to my post to prove that they actually read it. Interestingly, this lost me almost none of my "friends" count. However, I felt confident some had probably switched off or silenced my posts — preferring to appear to still be connected as friends. I hadn't offended them enough to make them feel that they had to make a statement by being seen to deliberately turn their back on me and walk away.

Not fucking good enough — so I upped the ante.

I raised the subject of the overwhelming illegal refugee boat crisis Australia was facing, explaining that we had application systems in place for people to follow if they wanted to migrate to Australia. I pointed out that the vast majority of these people arriving in boats, based on their nationality, were passing through as many as five or even ten other countries before they reached our shores, meaning they weren't really refugees, or that at best, they were "economic refugees". I argued that by crossing the borders of so many other countries where they could apply for residency but chose not to, they were just migrants looking to bypass Australia's migrant application system — queue jumpers.

I went on to say that under the traditional definition — before the Zealotribe manipulated the terminology to "Asylum Seekers" — a refugee was someone fleeing their country, someone seeking refuge from some persecution or horror — someone whose life was in imminent danger. Further, I stated that anyone in such circumstances would happily accept the safety offered by the first country that they could get to.

I continued on, saying that I thought the only sensible solution to the problem was for the Royal Australian Navy to blow two or three of the smaller vessels out of the water with rockets, killing everybody on board, and post video footage of it on the Australian Department of Defense YouTube channel. I argued that the calculated killing of fewer than 100 people would act as a strong deterrent for those considering this option, along with the people smugglers they were paying. I went on to say that in fact, in the long run, this solution would save the lives of the more than 1,000 people on average that drowned every year trying to make it to our shores.

As expected, this saw a satisfyingly significant drop off in my friends' count by those wanting to send me their strong message of objection — albeit by proxy. I assumed the obvious lack of direct engagement on the subject was not just because they didn't want to get involved in an argument, but also because they were in a state of confusion, wrestling with the pragmatic logic of the line of reasoning I had proposed. I could almost see the meme with them stressing about which red button to push; save 1,000 lives every year — year after year — or not murder 100 people.

Kant and his "categorical imperative" would have had a ball with that one.

Even after this, though, there were still a few 'hangers-on' — 'friends' who I really felt I had nothing at all in common with. These were people I had accumulated like mud on my boots, people who I knew disagreed with me — based on the most superficial of idiotic arguments — on almost everything I believed to be important, so I brought out the big guns.

Interestingly, I was very pleased to see my final post put an end to almost all of them, leaving behind only those few that I would genuinely have chosen as people I would actually enjoy sharing a meal with.

I stated that in my opinion, democracies were fundamentally flawed because they gave stupid and wilfully ignorant people a say in things.

I went on to say that although "Benevolent Dictatorships" like Singapore under Lee Kuan Yew were the gold standard in terms of providing the optimal system of political governance, democracies could work under certain conditions. I suggested that for a democracy to be effective — to produce high quality outcomes for its people — a regime should be implemented whereby everyone wanting the right to vote, should be subjected to passing an IQ test. I explained that I thought that a pass should be defined as being both; any result equal to or above the average of 100, and, scoring in the top 10 percent of the population for the Abstract Reasoning component.

I argued that this would prevent not only the obviously stupid people from voting, but it would also stop all those smart people that you have to interact with in life who have no common sense at all.

Strategically, I was confident that this would include all of those people who read the post that I knew would be immediately "offended" by it — unable to even consider its merits. In my mind this group could be perfectly defined as those people who consistently misinterpreted any luck they enjoyed in their lives, be it by the circumstances they were born into, or getting carried along by a general current of positive economic osmosis like a stock market or housing boom, as some sort of personal achievement they attributed to their own cleverness.

They were the people you had to interact with in life who had never created anything and argued belligerently about something based on only those elements of the subject that were immediately apparent — who could see only the most obvious aspects that they had been spoon fed by the television or their friends. Those people who had no capacity at all to grasp the subtleties and contradictions, the subjective ramifications, motivations, and implications that underpinned relationships and problems. The masses that were incapable of second or third level thinking, that never made the connection between the Zealotribe's agenda of destruction and control, and the ever-increasing examples of societal misery that we all had to endure because of it.

In the post I went on to describe them as those people who we all knew would become paralysed with confusion if you swapped their house key for their car key on their key ring — stop those bastards from having a say in how the country was run.

As the pièce de resistance, I added that part of the testing process should include the Myers Briggs personality assessment test, and that anyone who the test classified as ENFP should be summarily executed as soon as possible, to protect the rest of society from their impractical, unproductive, ridiculously enthusiastic stupidity.

Over those three months, I also spent as much time with my dear friend Angus as I could. Angus was my closest friend, one of only a few I had. Once a highly paid engineer working for Lockheed Martin as a missile defence analyst, he had decided he wanted to be a doctor, so he left his job, studied, passed the exams, graduated, and became a doctor.

He was very well-travelled and one of the few doctors I had come across who hadn't gone into medicine for the money.

A few years earlier, he had been working as a junior doctor in a hospital when he had asked my advice on something. He had to make a choice between a promotion into anaesthetics as a specialisation along with moving forward with a woman he was thinking about asking to marry him, or, the prospect of just walking away as a GP to some African pot of misery and despair, or some jungle in Southeast Asia where he could "make a difference".

It was indeed a conundrum.

The meals we shared together were always very special to me — our philosophical arguments, his determination to always do everything perfectly, and his complete lack of respect for the 80/20 rule I lived my life by. Although we were very different people, we had in common a passion and rage for the endless, alluring choices and opportunity costs that were constantly offered up over the ridiculously short lifespan the gods had granted us. I knew I would miss him dearly and that what I had planned would hurt him. Although he had other friends, I felt that we had a very special relationship — both of us very unique — a friendship based on a great mutual respect and a shared pragmatic perspective of the world.

At dinner one evening, over a bottle of St Henri Shiraz (it always made me smile that he confused his bottles of St Hugo with my bottles of St Henri), I had finally decided my answer to the choice he had to make and vigorously espoused the joys and virtues a marriage and children and a career path in a hospital.

Two days later, my mind just refused to let go of it — like a dog with a bone — and I wrote him the following email:

Subject: I've changed my mind

Run, run as fast as you can!

Become everything you can be, everything you should be, everything men were meant to be.

Help children, help mums, help brothers, help sisters and wives and husbands, that without you, would be finished. Dead to their devastated, dust-mouthed few.

Stuff yourself with the greedy satisfaction of making a difference until it dribbles down your chin and you are bloated with happiness.

Gorge yourself on the bravery that will overwhelm you from only ever having to worry about yourself and your patients — your work.

Fuck women, fuck nurses and waitresses and doctors, and daughters and mothers.

Stagger from one self-indulgent 15-hour surgery to another, falling into a deep sleep in a mosquito-netted cot after a day of 300 small-arm inoculations and 1,000 of exactly the same questions from loving mothers and fathers, changing the lives forever of people who will never pay a bill or even know your name.

Live your life so perfectly that everything just falls into place without even one moment of thought or effort: a roof over your head, a hot meal, strength, your body, time, bills, friends, laughter, companionship, rest, joy.

Get drunk with warm beer, get drunk with the smile of a little girl, alive because of YOU.

Never read the Financial Review again, or worry about a negotiation, or waste your time trying to convince anybody of anything ever again.

Like magic, rooms and beds will always be provided for you, and food and drink, and the faces of interesting people – no more myopic fat white zombie, uninspired, poorly thought out, belligerently stupid conversations ever!

No more civilised tolerance like cancer eating you up from the inside as you watch their mouths move, silently screaming in disbelief at their stupidity.

Walk away from them all to the people who are meek, who are honest and real, who make you the simplest food and deliver it with a caring smile, who look at you with such genuine kindness and appreciation, that you can feel peace for the first time in fucking years.

Let humility well up inside of you pushing out any pride or fears or regrets and leaving no room but for true understanding, peace and happiness.

Be healthy for the first time in years.

Time. Sitting. Watching. A dewdrop, a flower. Rest after the storm, a hot cup of instant black coffee in a steel mug on a cool morning. Notice a blood splash on your boot.

The cleanest air.

Not a computer or a smartphone or a dumb phone, or a phoney anywhere for miles and miles and miles.

Let the months and the years drift by always in the knowledge that that other life, the one where you always feel empty but comfortable, alone but stifled, overweight but hungry, is always just an elephant a camel a boat or a plane ride away.

Alex

Strangely, I believe both pieces of advice were equally sound. Yin and Yang.

While I was becoming Simon, I badgered Angus out to dinner three times, dragging him away from his new family and the constant challenges of searching-for-veins-in-small-children-and-fat-people and the always-under-pressure-arithmetic complexity of dosages and body weights and pharmaceutical and chemical equations that the job involved.

Over this time, he had become a father, and watching him prepare dinner with his beautiful French princess and looking into the eyes of his gorgeous baby son, I was glad he had ignored my email.

Over these three months, it was also becoming more and more challenging to connect with my wife — she had become almost robotic in the day-to-day machinations of living a life so full to the brim with grey, repetitive monotony that there was simply no room in it at all for any colour. When you get older, it eventually dawns on you that some things just aren't worth a lot of words. On those rare occasions that I heard her laugh, the sound was strangely empty, hollow — her smile no longer ever reaching her eyes.

I spent a lot of the time organising my affairs for what the future held. This involved sending carefully crafted emails that, to their recipients, were probably seen as a little strange, raising eyebrows in terms of their excessive detail and apparent superfluousness. But these emails were, in fact, seeds that I knew would one day blossom into new meaning. Pennies would drop. Necessity would dictate they be searched out and re-read, providing information — patterns of logic and blueprints of understanding. They would serve as instructions that would assist in the process of cauterising those elements of my world that were finished while managing the maintenance of those that still held some value for the future.

8

Sam

September 28, 2025

Awake or asleep? I couldn't tell anymore... My reality had become blurred and disconnected — my dreams and visions seemed so real. I tried to roll over, but nothing. Pain. My eyes opened slowly, and my life — everything — came rushing back at me, carried on the harsh fluorescent light of the room.

The first thing I saw was a face I immediately recognised — the face of a very old Indian man staring straight at me. Where had I seen him before? In my dreams? Was my mind playing tricks on me?

He was real. He was sitting in the room with me, sitting on the edge of the bed that had been rolled in next to mine — the sheets hanging off the side, his legs dangling, his bare feet at least two feet away from reaching the floor. He was so small, so fine and frail. His deeply tanned, leathery skin hung loose and wrinkled off the sharply angled bones of his arms and legs that protruded out from the blue hospital gown. A smudged, faded red dot was nestled amongst the wrinkles on his forehead. One slip of silver-grey hair had escaped from underneath the tightly bound orange pagri on his head and had fallen across his temple and down the side of his face. That bright orange pagri — I was certain I knew him — or at least I had seen him before, but could not get enough order to my thoughts to remember when, or where.

He was just staring at me with eyes — an expression — that was unlike anything I had ever seen before, rocking slightly forward and back, his lips moving with the sound of some strange muttering — some sort of chanting. Was he moving? It was so slight, it was almost impossible to tell, but I was convinced he was. The only reason why it wasn't as fucking terrifying as it should have been, this old man sitting only a few feet away staring at me, was that his expression was of complete peace and kindness. It was difficult to explain, but he had an aura about him, like he was the place where everything good came from. It was like he was looking not at me, but at who I was.

I stared into his kind face deliberately, intensely, to try to focus my thoughts away from the pain. Two uniforms appeared between me and the old man — a nurse and another uniform I had not seen before. My leg — my God, the pain. Muttering in Thai — the urgency in the hushed tones indicating something serious was happening.

It dawned on me that perhaps a new, fresh, rancid blanket of horror was about to settle down onto my world.

Someone grabbing my arm roughly this time — now two more hands pinning me to the bed. Cold, hard rubbing on the inside of my elbow, staring past them into the old man's eyes — clinging to him in my mind. A sharp prick, that warm flood of pleasure streaming through my veins up my arm and coursing through my body.

Peace.

I've only had a couple of times in my life when I was carefree, like a period of a couple of years when I thought 'You know what, I haven't really any responsibilities, I'm making enough money, I'm hanging out with my friends, I'm seeing these chicks here and those over there'. You know, whatever it was, for a couple of years I felt okay, which is very rare for me.

And then he died.

And I have never trusted happiness since. I have to really force myself to think that things are going to be okay – in terms of worrying about my family or myself or my friends or whatever. Yeah, I've never been the same since my brother died. There's a melancholy in me that never goes away.

Billy Bob Thornton

September 17, 1994.

The day my brother Sam died, my life changed forever. At the time, death and I were distant strangers — no one really close to me had died.

To say Sam's death had a profound effect on me is an understatement. It affected me so much that from that point on in my life, there was a sad undercurrent in every moment, of every day. Even when my mind was preoccupied with other things, it was there, like a baseline where all of happiness drifted out of focus and became less intense, a background feeling of loneliness to my life, regardless of who was around me or what I was doing.

In a way, being immersed in such sadness for so long gradually made me fear my own death less and less. It was as if the original size and shape of the fear of my death, the mass, the sharp edges, and angles, were being worn away by the relentless feelings around the loss of him, feelings that returned every morning when I opened my eyes, and with every sunset, and every time I looked up at the Southern Cross, or opened a beer. Like we were still somehow connected, and with time, as I aged, the void between us was closing, and once the two sides met, everything would be okay again. It was strange how everyone else who lost someone close to them seemed to cope so much better than me. Were they stronger, were they just better at it? It was as if they were very upset and sad, but with each day, each passing year, it seemed to hurt them less and less. Not that they cared less, I'm sure they didn't, but the sadness in them seemed to fade away in linear proportion to the time that passed.

Many people had told me that I needed to "talk to someone", that "you mustn't let Sam's death define your life", implying that there was something wrong with me that needed to be fixed. I could never understand this. Well-meaning fucking assholes. I mean, what is some psychiatrist going to say to me? What words, and in what fucking order would they say them, that would help?

People were always dunking words in a bucket of clown makeup and pouring them all over me. Words that fell about like litter, swirling around on the ground at my feet. I guess deep down, I felt like if I wanted to heal, I would, but in my mind, perhaps going down that path would take me further away from him, and this was the last thing I wanted.

He was five years younger than me when he died. The perfect example of a little brother.

My little brother.

I cannot imagine a more tragic set of circumstances in terms of things being left undone between two people who were close. With the horror and torment of hindsight, I was disgraced and appalled at how much and how often I had let him down. Of how I may have been able to prevent it, of what I could have done, what I should have done, how I should have helped, and just how weak and fucking selfish and immature I had been. Perhaps that was the problem, regret. What do you mean, perhaps? For fucks sake, of course that was the problem. It was almost all about regret. And although my father had tried to console me many, many times by telling me I did more for Sam than anyone else had done, my heart remained broken more than thirty years later at the thought of just how much I had failed him.

The paradox, of course, was my remaining brother and sister, my wife, and especially, my three sons.

Suicide is a contagion; it's a contagious fucking disease.

People think: why? Why didn't she just talk to me? Didn't he love me?

They don't realise it is possible to love your family so much that it brings tears of joy to your eyes just to think about them, and at the same time, have the thought of committing suicide dawn on you in such a way that you see it as a precious, beautiful, freeing, glowing, happy thing. Something to be rushed towards

— so enticing in all the joy, all the relief that it promises. They don't understand that the last thing someone wants to do once they have decided to kill themselves is tell anyone. At that point, the idea of suicide has become so seductive, so beautiful, so inviting; the very last thing they want to do is risk someone stopping them.

People who have not reached this point don't understand that it is possible to have money, to have love, and respect but still be so profoundly sad that suicide is like a golden door in a dark, grey room — beckoning for you to just walk through it. This deep sadness can come from anything — feelings of being disconnected, of the loss of someone, of not living the life you dreamed you would, of being constantly disregarded by just one person special to you, of having to fight endlessly to be heard, of your life just generally becoming less and less.

And, terrifyingly, this deep sadness can come from nothing at all; it can just settle down on you.

Just the impact I had endured from the almost 20 years on antidepressants, trying to just stay alive on a day-by-day basis, had been devastating — lost wandering in a sea of emotionless mediocrity. All the while not realising that the drugs also had the insidious side effect of robbing me of the memories of my children growing up.

But.

No longer taking them and looking back, I was absolutely certain that it had been only the drugs that had kept me alive. I knew it was only the drugs that had prevented me from taking off my seatbelt and driving into a thousand different power poles that my pain and loss had tempted me with during that time. No matter how tragic the cost, I had my children, and my children had had me, their dad, growing up. And this was everything.

Right from the start, I had made the conscious decision to build my world around my kids — doing everything I could to strengthen them as individuals, as well as in their bonds with each other — in preparation for the day that that inevitable horror, that loss, found the opportunity to reach out and touch them. I had made it my focus to do everything I could to make them feel loved and to teach them to love and support each other in preparation for when I knew their world also, would fall out from underneath them — when their words would become strangled in their throats by those feelings of shock, fear, and disbelief.

Over time, as life's inevitable bittersweet cruelty had taken my children away from me, taken away their reliance on me — day by day, piece by piece — I had done everything I could to fight to stay with them, to stay as close to them as I could for as long as possible. That strange paradox of pain and loss wrestling with feelings of joy and wonderment, as they became adults. I had done everything I could to continue to have a positive impact on them, continue to guide their thinking — to give them some chance of making it through the tragedies and losses that I knew time would inevitably bring with it. Some chance of getting to the other side, to the light, and in doing so, permanently severing the rope tied to the anvil of despair that had pulled me, alone and completely unprepared, down into the hopeless, dark depths of depression when Sam had died.

March 12, 2025

I took a sip of my coffee and dragged my gaze back from the blue sky — down through the palm trees, down past the ocean, across the sand, and sidewalk, and the crawling traffic on the road — away from the everchanging landscape of Patong beach and finally down to the blinking cursor. Reaching out, I moved the laptop closer and began to type.

Chapter IV

Passing through the door in the floor of the oak tree, Eugene climbed down a wooden ladder and found himself in what appeared to be a small storage room with a tunnel leading off to one side. The ball hovered above Meredith Dew, its bright light illuminating the room about them. Most of the room was taken up by six large wooden rectangular tables covered in all sorts of things, most of which Eugene didn't recognise. On the table closest to him was a large brown frog with piercing yellow eyes. Sitting perfectly still, its wet skin shining and its bulbus throat ballooning out, becoming almost completely transparent with each breath it took.

In the centre of the room was the only round table, and it seemed to be made from what looked like steel or perhaps even silver. Meredith strode straight over to the metal table and started grabbing bits and bobs – even another smaller version of the frog that Eugene had noticed, although this one was light blue in colour with shiny black eyes – was snatched up and stuffed along with everything else he selected into what seemed to be an endless supply of pockets inside his coat.

"Right!" He exclaimed suddenly, lifting his head — his nose jiggling and bobbing about almost in slow motion for far longer than Eugene expected it to.

"That should do it. This way!" He said, striding off so quickly into the tunnel that Eugine almost fell over trying to make sure he wasn't left behind, the light hovering above them lighting the way.

The walls of the tunnel were the colour of dirt, though they were smooth and shiny, like they had been coated with something clear and hard. The floor of the tunnel was covered in pink pebbles that looked like quartz and reflected softly in the glow of the light. Eugene noted that the pebbles crunched under his feet but not under Meredith's.

Walking without a word spoken for fifteen minutes, Eugene listening to the rhythmic crunch of his boots, when suddenly his mind returned to the story Meredith had been telling about Edward P. Fizzlebub.

"So what about old Fizzlebub and the Witches?" asked Eugene, trying to sound casual as he tried to keep up with Meredith.

"Fizzlebub? Ah yes, Fizzlebub! Well, as I was saying, Where was I? That's right. I followed the old fool through the forest where it turned out that he himself had been following Gagglebroth and Enchantlure, who at that stage were huddled around a fire, up to no good as usual. For a start, they were popping the very same type of mushrooms that I had been out picking into a cauldron that they had hung over the fire. You see, I was close enough to notice their distinct smell amongst the putrid reek that was drifting out from the pot. They have a very distinct smell, you know, especially when they are being cooked. It's a little like roasted raspberries when they've been garnished with frog liver."

Eugine thought that that sounded disgusting but chose to remain quiet, as much as to ensure the story continued so as not to offend Meredith.

"Anyway", said Meredith. "From the angle that I had secured, I could see Fizzlebub crouching down behind a tree on the edge of the firelight off to one side, his beady little eyes and ears taking everything in. Then Gagglebroth spoke to Enchantlure, 'You've done well, my dear.' she said in that wicked voice of hers, 'Just think of it. Our very own little band of slaves.' Then they had both started laughing."

"Where does that go?" Interrupted Eugene as they passed another wooden ladder that came down on the left-hand side of the tunnel. "And when can I take this confounded thing off my head? It's starting to hurt", he said, tapping the cup that Meredith had attached to his head over his missing ear.

"That goes to another outpost", said Meredith. "I have them all through the forest. Never know when they'll come in handy. Oh, that", he said, pointing to the side of Eugene's head. "Soon enough, my young friend. Remember, just like all good things, replacement ears take time", as if losing and replacing an ear was a common occurrence.

Suddenly, Meredith stopped. Eugene had to stop abruptly to avoid walking into him. Meredith began to sniffle and snort, his head tilting back as he moved it from side to side, his magnificent nose following a split second after it.

"What is it?" Whispered Eugene uneasily, peering into the darkness ahead.

"Nothing?" said Meredith after a moment in an off-hand sort of way. "Thought I could smell a snizzlegrub. Must have been mistaken." And with that, he turned and started moving on again, walking a little faster than they had been up until now.

"What's." Eugene found he was whispering. He cleared his throat, trying to keep up with Meredith.

"What the hell's a snizzlegrub?" He asked in his best attempt at a calm voice he could muster. Suddenly, a high-pitched screeching growl sounded from the tunnel behind them. Eugene spun around, terrified, looking back into the dark tunnel, trying desperately to see what was making the noise, which now being accompanied by the terrifying sound of something that was obviously of quite reasonable size scuttling along the tunnel towards them.

"Quick, behind me!" Yelled Meredith, bouncing along in front of Eugene. Out of the darkness and into the light came the most hideous-looking creature Eugene had ever seen. It looked like an enormous worm with an open mouth gleaming with long, sharp teeth. It was about four feet long, pale grey and green in colour, and ran on two short, muscular back legs, its front legs held up like arms in front of it like bunches of shiny vicious claws. Behind its powerful legs dragged a wrinkled worm-like body that tapered off into an eel-like tail.

It was racing towards them with its elongated teeth and claws thrust forward in front of it as Meredith's hands fumbled desperately in the pockets of his leather jacket. Eugene began to scream. The thing was only ten feet away from them when Meredith finally pulled what looked like a shiny black ball out of his pocket.

"Close your eyes!" He yelled as he threw the ball at the creature. Eugene saw a bright purple flash through his closed eyelids, which was quickly followed by a screaming wailing sound. Opening his eyes, Eugene watched as Meredith stepped forward towards the creature, waving his hands about to disperse the purple smoke that rose up and clung to the ceiling, forming a cloud of eerie mist. Stepping forward behind him, Eugene peered gingerly over Meredith's shoulder.

"Snizzlegrub", said Meredith yawning. "Usually would have picked it up earlier. Happens a bit when I've just woken up. Takes a few days to get the senses straight, you know. Well, nothing for it but to get it out of here before the ghastly thing stinks the whole place up."

Walking around behind it and bending forward, Meredith picked the end of the creature's tail and began to drag it in the direction that they had been going, its arms and head bobbing about limply as it slid along the gravel on the floor of the tunnel.

"Where do they live?" asked Eugene, following a few yards back, unnerved by the creature's open, dead eyes that seemed to be staring back directly at him.

"On the forest floor, in pits under the leaves. Protects them from the boughglimmbs."

"How'd it get in here, and what's in heaven's name is a boughglimmb?" Eugene asked, feeling quite uneasy at the thought of a creature worse than the one that Meredith was dragging behind him.

"Most likely tunneled under the tree into that outpost back at the ladder we passed", said Meredith, sounding slightly preoccupied.

"Couldn't it have just dug into this tunnel?" Eugene glanced back at the darkness behind them.

"Not through these walls", said Meredith proudly as he tapped the wall with his free hand. "Developed this coating myself. There isn't anything that can get through this stuff!"

"What's a boughglimmb?" Inquired Eugene again, though he was not sure he wanted to know.

"Nasty creatures. Live way up in the boughs of the Boobleberries and the Great Greys."

"Great Grey's?"

"Great Grey Pine trees. Enormous, some of them."

"Boughglimmbs?" Said Eugene, becoming confused.

"No, the pine trees", replied Meredith.

They arrived at the entrance of another tunnel that went off to the right of the one they were on. "Come, and I'll show you."

"The pine trees?" Asked Eugene anxiously.

"No, the boughglimmbs", answered Meredith, his face an expression of comical seriousness, his large bulbus nose wobbling about.

Nevertheless, this answer terrified Eugene.

Entering the new tunnel, they walked for about five minutes, with Meredith dragging the corpse behind him before the tunnel opened up into another storeroom similar to the first. Again, a wooden ladder came down from the ceiling. The light followed Meredith up the ladder as Eugene watched from below, surprised at Meredith's strength as he pulled the body of the Snizzlegrub up behind him. Reaching the top, Meredith took a key from his top left breast pocket and, in almost one movement, opened the latch above him and continued up, disappearing quickly through the hole.

Not wanting to be left behind in the darkness, Eugene reached for the ladder and scampered up as quickly as he could and out through the hatch at the top, only to find himself inside another tree. Meredith had dragged the limp body of the creature to one side and, with the key still in his hand, pushed it into the wall of the tree and turned it once. Then, removing a small black cloth from his trouser pocket, draped it over the ball of light, which blacked it out completely. Once done, he pushed, and the door in the side of the tree swung silently outward. It was very dark outside, though not quite as dark as it was inside the tree. Eugene peered out into the night; he could see no shrubs or bushes but only dark grey and black tree trunks thicker than he had ever seen, crowded closely together. He realised that they had indeed travelled deep into Cracklewood Forest.

Meredith moved past him through the doorway, dragging the dead Snizzlegrub behind him.

"Watch", he whispered to Eugene. He moved out about ten feet from the tree and dumped the creature on the leaves. Returning, they stood together, peering from the doorway at the ghostly corpse on the ground.

"You going to kill a boughglimmb?" whispered Eugene.

"Can't. Gagglebroth."

Eugene found the wait unsettling. Then, out of no-where, at great speed, dropped what looked like a huge spider, startling Eugene into a yell. He threw an arm up as he jumped back, knocking the black cloth from the ball. The light burst forth, flooding from the door and lighting the creature for an instant as it pounced on the dead snizzlegrub.

Attached to its dark body that shone almost irides-cent pink in the light were four sinewy limbs, each with a single long, shiny black talon on the end. A thick, green web-like rope that originated from the base of the back of its terrifying head brought the creature to a slow, almost elastic halt as it sat motionless, stunned by the light for a split second. Eugene stood looking on in horror as the creature quickly came to its senses and, gouging and hook-ing its four talons into the corpse of the Snizzle-grub, turned its head to glare directly at Eugene and hissed, "Lumpthistle!" before, clutching the corpse, springing back up into the darkness above.

Meredith silently shut the door. "That, young fellow, was a boughglimmb. They have obviously been informed about you. The Witches are moving fast, and so must we! Quick to the stump!"

They made their way back down into the tunnels, and rejoining their original path, Meredith continued with his story about Gagglebroth, Enchantlure, and Fizzlebub — Eugene struggling to keep pace with the funny little man.

"Anyway, there I was watching the witches, when suddenly there was a scream followed by a type of horrible wailing coming from somewhere far off in the distance. Both Gagglebroth and Enchantlure started cursing and left to investigate, Gagglebroth saying it would be best to leave the brew simmer a while anyway. When they were gone, I watched Fizzlebub move stealthily into the clearing. After looking around to make sure he was alone, he grabbed the cauldron off the fire and started running back towards town as quickly as he could. I only discovered years later that what he stole was an elixir of enchantment. Feed one drop to somebody, and they are your slave for as long as you want them to be. But he was seen, not only by me but most likely a boughglimmb."

"So that's what he uses in his cider. It wasn't just a story after all", said Eugene, thinking out loud.

"I'm afraid not", said Meredith, coming to a fork in the tunnel and looking decidedly unsure as to which way to proceed. He chose the left. "By stealing the potion, Fizzlebub unwittingly took the power of potions that the Witches use over mortals such as yourself and when part of a Witches power is taken from them, they lose the ability to use it. Though I fear that is not the worst of it."

"Two hundred years ago, there were seven in the brood, and one of them was called Malichara, a particularly nasty piece of work. Anyway, one day, Gagglebroth found her dead on the edge of the forest, and unfortunately, for some reason, the Witches thought it was me; however, I am convinced it was the work of that idiot Fizzlebub. The witches and I have fought a running battle ever since, and it is only pure luck that has kept me alive. You see, there is a book, the "Black Book." This book contains spells and potions that are at the very heart of the coven's power, and because Malichara had the book when she was killed, they think I have it. Needless to say, they would do just about anything to get it back." They arrived at another fork in the tunnel. Again, Meredith looked unsure which way to go before choosing to proceed to the right."

"But that, unfortunately, is not the case. I don't have it. The book, I mean." He paused for a moment. "You see, the way I see it is that Fizzlebub disposed of Malichara and stole the book, and it is hidden either somewhere in that confounded apple cider factory of his or somewhere in the forest. The silver lining is that along with stealing the potion, the idiot unwittingly stripped the witches of most of their power. All this obviously has not augured well for the poor folk of Applecreek Grove, with the Witches more than happy to cast their wrath at every opportunity towards the town and its folk such as yourself."

"Can we please stop for just a moment?" Said Eugene, almost completely out of breath with the exhaustion of the pace they were moving at.

"It's not far now; we're almost there", replied Meredith, his pace unchanged.

He went on. "If a Witch's magic is stolen, until they get the magic back, or a curse made at the time the magic was stolen is fulfilled, they are without that power. You see, if they curse in rhyme in a moment of anger, the curse sticks until it comes to pass. The rhyme you heard at the grave was the very same curse I heard Gagglebroth chant when she discovered the

Elixir had been stolen one hundred and sixty years ago. Such a curse that takes so long to come of age may give them back their entire power, and this, my young friend, would give Gagglebroth the power to reproduce the book. So you are the key to them getting back their entire power! Which we cannot let happen, for it will be the end of Applecreek Grove – indeed, the end of us all!"

They hurried on, Meredith's torso wobbling about generously above his eerily, silent foot-falls. Eugene was puffing and wheezing now as he wondered what Charlie would have to say when he told him about all this – that is, if the witches, snizzlegrubs, or boughglimmbs didn't get him first. Without warning, Meredith burst into rhyme.

"Oh me, oh my!
Oh my, oh me!
To be asleep in
a hollow tree.
Out of wind,
out of rain,
with belly full
and witches slain.
With that bubble pop
and fizzle gurgle
that from nature's heart
I like to burgle."

Half an hour had passed since they had seen the boughglimmb when, after many turns and winding tunnels, they came to a crossroad. A ladder came down in the middle. Four tunnels met at the ladder from four different directions.

"Finally, we're here", announced Meredith triumphantly. "The stump!"

Climbing the ladder, he removed a different key — a shiny gold one this time, from a pocket inside his coat. Inserting it into what once again seemed to Eugene, who had followed him up the ladder to be a nonexistent keyhole, he turned it three times. A door swung silently open. Eugene followed Meredith, though, finding himself in a large, circular, brightly lit chamber. The bobbing light did not follow them through the doorway, though, as this room was already lit by another glowing ball already suspended in the center of the room that was similar to the one they had left behind, though twice as large. The room was full of long rectangular tables, all crammed with an assortment of wooden bowls of various sizes and crystal jars full of liquids and powders of every conceivable colour.

Pots boiled and bubbled on stands above flames that issued forth from tubes that came out of the floor. Tubes, some clear, others like copper, wound their way from bowls to funnels, carrying liquids from pots to beakers and back to pots; others led to vats that stood against the circular wall down which ran at least fifty shiny silver pipes of varying sizes around the room.

A complicated-looking machine sat in the middle of the myriad of sounds and colours that confronted Eugene. Cogs turned belts, and belts turned wheels. Steam burst out occasionally from hissing valves as a hydraulic ram rose and fell at its center. A long steel tube extended from the side of the machine, and from that, dripped a clear liquid into a glass bottle with a funnel-shaped neck.

The room was at least fifteen yards across. Eugene tore his eyes from the kaleidoscope of chemical activity that surrounded him and looked at the wall that encircled the room. It was silvery grey in colour, the colour of very old, dry wood.

"We're inside another tree." He muttered aloud, still finding it hard to believe.

"Well, a stump, to be exact", said Meredith, startling Eugene from his thoughts. "It was the mother of all trees. That's how the forest started."

"Oh", said Eugene. "How did it die?"

"The Witches", said Meredith in a forlorn sort of way. "Still", he announced, chirping up, "First things first. As I remember, you've got a slight problem with your left ear."

"It was bloody well cut off and stolen", said Eugene, feeling the matter of his ear was not being treated seriously enough.

"Let's take a look, shall we?" A morbid eagerness had possessed Meredith's dopey, oval eyes as he ushered Eugene to a bright green table. Eugene sat gingerly on a matching stool and awaited his fate.

Meredith pushed gently on the center of the disc, resulting in a short hissing sound as air rushed in to fill the vacuum. He removed the disc, revealing a small, fury, pointed ear not unlike that of a fox.

"Mmmm. Interesting. Can you hear anything through it?" He asked Eugene, with a tone that was a perfect mix of curiosity and doubt.

"Yes", said Eugene. "Marvelously well, actually!" He added, at this stage, quite pleased with the outcome. He reached up with his left hand to touch it, and Meredith took one pace back. His hand falling upon the fury mutation, he quickly jerked it back, screaming, and leapt to his feet.

"What have you done? What have you done to me, you bizarre little man?" Yelled Eugene.

"Nothing that can't be undone", said Meredith calmly, ignoring the insult and moving forward cautiously to examine the ear more closely, his brow furrowed.

"Well, I'd like it undone now. Do you have a mirror?"

Meredith lumbered over to a large wooden chest that sat beside a rather plush-looking bed. He opened the lid and shuffled through the contents, muttering to himself as he did so.

"Ah!" He said as he pulled a small hand mirror from the chest. It was set in a silver frame with a long, slender handle. He handed it to Eugene. "Crystal, you know." Eugene took the mirror and raised it. He studied the small fury ear on the side of his head.

"Well, how do we fix it?" Enquired Eugene, calming down as he placed the mirror on the table.

"Quite easily when the time comes."

"What do you mean when the time comes?" asked Eugene, beginning to become hysterical again at the thought of having to spend the rest of his life going round with a fox's ear attached to the side of his head.

"It's almost morning, and we must make the most of the day. Unfortunately, we have bigger fish to fry, my young friend", said Meredith, looking about the room, his mind seemingly immersed in other thoughts.

"But what about my ear?" Protested Eugene.

"That is exactly my point!" Exclaimed Meredith. "There is no way of knowing how much power will return to them now that you've lost it and they have it. Though I would guess they need more than just your ear. We must move quickly to defeat them. Unless you'd prefer to spend the rest of your life in the tunnels or go it alone in the forest", said Meredith, becoming annoyed at the delay.

Eugene was quiet for a moment as he realised his plight. It was either Meredith Dew or the witches and the boughglimmbs.

"Where are we going?" He asked quietly.

"Out into the forest, where your ear may actually come in very handy."

Eugene cast Meredith a skeptical glance.

"Ever heard of someone sneaking up on a fox?" asked Meredith, busily packing a sack with assorted bits and pieces.

"What about the boughglimmbs? Asked Eugene, alarmed at venturing out beyond the safety of the tunnel walls.

"Nothing to fear. They sleep during the day, and for some reason, I've rarely ever seen them in this part of the forest anyway", replied Meredith, removing the silver flask from the cuff of his boot and filling it from the glass bottle that stood by the machine. Again, Eugene was mesmerised as he watched the strange shiny liquid float slowly from one container to the other.

"What is that stuff?" Asked Eugene, referring to the liquid.

"Stagglebubble", said Meredith, finishing filling the flask up and lifting it up in front of him, staring at it in admiration.

"The base key for every element combination nature has to offer. Just think of it as very special glue", said Meredith, placing the glass bottle back next to the machine.

Eugene could contain himself no longer, "Who or what are you?" He said, trying to sound polite.

"I'm a Glock", Meredith responded proudly.

"The Glocks of the Great Northern Forest as we were known", his voice becoming distant.

"Were known? What happened? And which Great Northern Forest?" Asked Eugene, curious to know more about this funny little fellow who held his future in his hands.

"All gone now. Destroyed by the Great Fire War, which was followed closely by the Great Explosion, which, incidentally, wiped out all of my relatives."

Eugene looked nervously about the room at the gurgling, bubbling display of endless concocting that was going on before him.

"What sort of explosion?" he asked nervously.

"Stagglebubble machine – just like this one actually." Answered Meredith rather wistfully. "Old Great Grandfather Antle Mexiouse Dew. Tried to refine the machine. Always was one for taking things that one step too far. You see, pressure's the key to the whole thing. He managed to increase the pressure, but what he hadn't counted on was the machine taking a direct hit from one of Deathmorgriouse's fireballs. With the added pressure and heat from the fireball, the machine just went boom." Meredith paused in his packing, his sad expression filling in the silence. He continued, "And let me tell you; when a Stagglebubble machine goes boom, it really goes boom!"

"Who was Dealthmorgrious?" Asked Eugene, wondering how he could know so little of the forest's history.

"She was the leader of a great band of Witches. They arrived out of nowhere in their thousands and tried to move in and take over the forest. We fought them long and hard. 33 years it went on, but it all ended with the explosion – I mean, for both sides, it wiped out most of the forest. I'm all that remains of the Glocks, Gagglebroth and her mangey crew are all that are left of the Witches, and Cracklewood is all the remains of what was the Great Northern Forest."

Meredith yawned, then began speaking again, though this time more urgently. "Still!" He said, "Enough talk for now, for it seems we are once again at war, and you, my friend, are the key to it all. Dawn will be upon us soon, and we must hurry, for we'll need all the help we can muster."

"What are we going into the forest for?" Asked Eugene, becoming excited at the prospect of adventure in spite of his fear and the ridiculous ear on his head.

"Ziffleweave lives in the forest, and he can be a big help, presuming we can find him." Meredith had become intense, his nose quivering as he paused.

"Still, time will tell. It usually does." This last comment confused Eugene, for it seemed to be unrelated to everything else that had been said. Eugene was about to ask another question when Meredith spoke again.

"Hungry?" He asked.

With everything that had happened since he had fallen into the grave, Eugene had quite forgotten about his stomach.

"Starving!" Replied Eugene, as if he had just been reminded of something that he had been meaning to ask for some time.

"Good", said Meredith, "Let's eat, then we'll be off!"

9

Where's the Fucking List?

So time passed, sweetly poisoned by memories.
Zorba The Greek — Nikos Kazantzakis

Closing the lid of my computer, I looked up and out again across the beachfront counter of the café in front of the Baan Laimai Hotel in Phuket. The sun was low in the sky, the Andaman Sea was sparkling, and there was a gentle ocean breeze in my face. The yachts of the rich and famous defined and separated the blue sky from the darker blue ocean, where they blended on the horizon.

It was 5 p.m., and I had just ordered a Singha beer. The beer was cold and soothing to my throat in the balmy afternoon sunset heat — the sting from the western sun on my face. It was strange. Singha beer has always tasted best in Thailand. Whenever I drank a Singha beer in Australia, unless I recalibrated my mind to "Thailand," to the heat, the smells, the smiles, it tasted pretty average. But if I focused my mind, dragged the memories of that place forward into my consciousness, and then raised the bottle to my lips, it always tasted so much better.

The slow flow of traffic along the esplanade road in front of me was always interesting to watch, and I could still hear the loudspeaker shouting from the little red open-backed truck that had passed by almost ten minutes ago: "Bangla Boxing Stadium, tonight…".

At least some things never changed.

Halfway now. 182 days.

I had parted company with Waan in Bangkok exactly six months ago. We had spent three days and four nights together, and looking back, I had to admit that it was one of the best times I had ever had. We were always laughing together, and the sex was fantastic — she had given up her lean, taut young body enthusiastically and completely. She had been amazing.

Up to you

I had left Australia with a budget of about $120,000 AUD to last me for the next 365 days. This worked out to a minimum of about 7,000 Baht per day, and I knew that in Thailand, if I managed it carefully, this would be enough to ensure that my time spent would be in completely stress-free comfort, often luxury. I was on a mission. Simon had me hidden from everyone, and the last thing I wanted to be worried about was money.

All my adult life until this point, there had been this undercurrent of financial strain pulling my focus away from the important stuff and forcing me into endless days of doing things I didn't want to do to keep myself and my family just out of reach from the sharp claws of the system.

People who said money wasn't important really were assholes. They were inevitably relatively wealthy people who had either been insulated from poverty their entire lives — born into the right family — or they had started life without wealth and had been too ignorant or arrogant to take any notice of the lessons that life had offered up to them along the way, or had at least forgotten those lessons.

Instead, they chose to push back that terrible feeling of not knowing what fate poverty had in store for them tomorrow, for their children, or what it feels like to be tied to endless days of stressful work completely at the mercy of people and a system that couldn't care less about them. They liked to forget all of that, liked to stuff all of these distasteful thoughts, along with empathy and kindness, into a cardboard box, wrap it all up in brown paper, tie it off with string in a perfect bow, and put it away somewhere where they will never accidentally stumble across it again. They think only fools give to charity as they preach down from their outrageously-poor-taste-upper-middle class houses in the suburbs to anyone still bogged down with having nothing, that they should be "happy with what they have" and that they should focus on things that are more important, like having their health, and that they should raise up as their highest priority things like "saving the environment".

They liked to talk down to people telling them that they should be happy that they are healthy enough to endure the ten-hour workdays so that they can actually pay their rent. That they should accept having to pay four times as much for their electricity as they did two years ago, so that they can do their fucking bit to help save the planet. With offhanded gestures, scoffs, and condescending smiles, they liked to disregard and belittle. They stole words like "progressive" and straw-manned them into the assumption that their opinions unquestionably defined progress, instead of just being opinions.

Fucking dolts.

Carbon dioxide is 0.042% of the world's atmosphere and since the industrial revolution, only between 30-40% of that 0.042% has been created as the result of actions by humans — farming, industry, transport, power generation, deforestation — 35% (average) of 0.042%!

So, 0.0147% of the CO_2 in the atmosphere is a direct result of human activity.

Anyone can Google this — it's not like the information is hidden.

These assholes seriously believe that simple working people in Western countries, the people who pay all of the taxes for all of the bills, who provide all of the money to pay for government, infrastructure, services, welfare — everything, should just quietly accept the selfish stupidity of the Zealotribe, this unbearable financial burden imposed on their daily lives, to help 'save the fucking planet'.

I mean, what does that even mean? "98% of scientists agree". What 98%? Where's the list? If you are going to say 98% of something, then you need a fucking list! Where is the complete list of all scientific specialists in that field? You don't have it, do you? No, you fucking don't! Once again, you are just lying, sprouting "your science," manipulating the Complacency Ladder to make sure you keep getting the invitations to those dinner parties and the latest environmentally friendly, gender-neutral, multiracial, vegan book launch.

So what the fuck happens if the 35% of 0.042% doubles magically overnight?

It's okay — I'll do the maths for you.

The percentage of Carbon Dioxide in the earth's atmosphere caused by humans increases from 0.0147% to 0.0294%. That's it! If the carbon dioxide in the Earth's atmosphere caused by humans is doubled to 70% of the 0.042%, then the human impact of CO_2 on the earth's atmosphere increases from 0.0147% to 0.0294%. This would make the total amount of carbon dioxide in the earth's atmosphere increase from .042% to 0.0567%.

The makeup of the other 99.9433% of the earth's atmosphere remains exactly the fucking same!

Carbon emissions declined 22% between 2005 and 2020 after peaking in Britain and most of the rest of Europe in the mid-seventies. The main reason they did not continue to increase on the same trajectory was the transition from coal to natural gas and nuclear power. I mean you've got to ask yourself: why? Why are the people harping on about "climate change," those that are the most opposed to natural gas and nuclear power?

Whenever I find myself in the window seat of a plane and look outside at the world, all I see is trees and forests. It doesn't matter how long I am on the flight for. When I am above the ground, 95% of what I see is green vegetation. I mean, for fucks sake. These assholes go on and on about over-population and the environment, but all they really have for it is disdain. They have no respect at all for nature and her capacity to adapt and thrive. No matter what humanity throws at her, we are just a fucking parasite, and at any stage she can just wipe us out. Their arrogance and pretentiousness are fucking disgraceful. We are only here as her guests, and when she tires of us, she will rid the planet of us — she's in control, she's pulling the strings — not us.

The truth is that, to many people calling themselves Socialists, revolution does not mean a movement of the masses with which they hope to associate themselves; it means a set of reforms which 'we', the clever ones, are going to impose upon 'them', the Lower Orders."

George Orwell — The Road to Wigan Pier

You wilfully ignorant, fascist, fucking ideologues — It's all about global control, sitting there all smug in your diazepam-soaked cloud of moral superiority, your echo chambers of confirmation bias, surrounded by your Climate Action Now! signs.

Fuck you. What? You don't think poor people already value their health? That they are not already terrified — 100% absolutely fucking clear — on the fact that if their health fails them, then they are not just fucked, they're completely fucked? Like sick AND homeless in like one month type fucked?

You self-obsessed assholes weighing decent, hard-working people down with the burdens of your selfish virtue signaling in your endless scramble for more and more social credit.

Anyway, I had escaped all of that — all of them. All of that madness. Since arriving in Thailand, I had been careful with the money I spent — not out of fear, but simple logic. I was actually buying whatever I wanted while living as I always had done, by my 80/20 rule — the last 20% of anything was simply not worth the 80% cost attached to it.

In my world, anyway, this made sense.

To me, it was like an essay in an exam: the first half of the marks were dead easy to get. Just do some general reading, regurgitate some keywords and phrases, and some simple broad arguments; even the first 80% could be achieved reasonably cheaply with a little study. But what is the cost to get that last 20% — to get 100% full marks for the essay? This required a huge "happiness cost", a tremendous amount of study, stress, and worry, and for me, that had just never been worth it. In Thailand, I could have 80% luxury in everything without any financial stress or concerns.

After eventually going back to night school and getting into university, I had taken this concept to the extreme, always trying to get that elusive "Conceded Pass," that magical mark that fell between 47 and 50% for a subject that, for me, defined perfection. If you got a Conceded Pass, you knew you had done the absolute minimum amount of study while enjoying the maximum amount of time partying for the semester. In my opinion, hitting that perfect 3% gap and getting a Conceded Pass was actually much harder to achieve and, therefore, a much higher accolade than falling into that top 15% band you are required to get to receive a High Distinction.

It became an obsession, an art for me.

After arriving in Phuket, I had only stayed at the Baan Laimai Hotel three nights before I had met with a property agent and signed a six-month rental lease on a beach house owned by someone who, as far as I could establish, was a Russian hooker.

Capitalism — you gotta love it.

I liked this hotel, especially this beach-front restaurant and bar open to the public, the atmosphere, the ever-changing parade of humanity that passed by it, and the friendly, polished staff. They reminded me of the clever efficiency of the order takers in the hawker markets in Singapore — seating people, taking orders, upselling chili crab. In fact, I would bet money that, like the guys in the hawker markets, the staff here were remunerated at least in part by performance-based bonuses or commissions — one of those tiny little ecosystems of meritocracy in a world gone mad. I had discovered this place on a stay a few years earlier and really liked the rooms and the tranquil lounges beside the angular granite ponds teaming with their graceful koi fish.

Places like this were getting harder and harder to find though.

The Russian influence really had spread all through Phuket, fundamentally changing the DNA of the place — shrinking its peace and tranquility, the "Thai essence" in it, back. Like the water receding in a drought, what was once everywhere here was now only to be found in puddles, here and there around the edges, overlooked perhaps only by chance. This hotel was one of those places.

The condo came with a small car and had a private pool. It was about a 300 yard walk to the beach and was far enough out of the town, about a 15-minute drive, to be a suitable place to retreat to from all the colours and flavors that Patong offered.

Finally, I had reached a stage in my life when I could have an espresso at 10 p.m. with a cigar by a fire and have no concerns at all about the cigar giving me cancer or the caffeine keeping me awake and making me tired — leaving me to have to struggle through the obligations of the following day.

There were no more obligations. They were all over. Finished, forever.

Partly in gratitude but also to consolidate this new freedom, I had adjusted my life accordingly — begun as I intended to go on — as I liked to say. The afternoon after I had signed the lease on the condo, I had driven into town and purchased some heavy black velvet fabric, a large pair of scissors, and some strong 3M double-sided tape from a haberdashery shop near the Chillva Market. Returning to the Condo, I had blacked out the windows in my bedroom to such an extent that time lost all meaning. I had even run a strip, a black velvet skirt, along the bottom of the door and put a small piece of the heavy foam tape over the little blue LED light on the air-conditioner. I wasn't wearing a watch, and I hardly ever touched my phone — most of the time, it wasn't even charged.

And with that, time lost all significance.

I did exactly what I wanted to do whenever I wanted to do it without any feelings of obligation at all to fit within any of the standardised restrictions or expectations that time had imposed upon me my entire life.

Complete freedom.

If I wanted to sleep, I slept. If I wanted to eat, I ate. McDonald's, eye-fillet steak, sushi, eggs benedict, a cold double chocolate thick-shake at 4am, anything, whenever I felt like it, with zero concern about gaining weight or my health at all. If I wanted a woman, or a glass of wine, or just to lie down and sleep, to feel the sun's rays on my back — let the warmth engulf me — or swim in the pool or the cool of the ocean, whatever it was, I indulged myself completely and entirely.

One time, I even woke up to the sounds of a thunderstorm and, half asleep, had no idea what time of day or night it was or even where I was. I didn't even know what country I was in. I managed to force myself not to think about where I was, and I actually fell back into the deepest sleep without knowing — a sleep that could only come from such a profound feeling of freedom.

But it was not always peaceful.

My goal was simple: to write and to fill in the gaps when I wasn't writing. Once a week, I would video call each of my children —

usually together but occasionally separately — at different times to fit in with their busy lives. The note I had left under my eldest son Tom's keyboard would have broken his heart and weighed him down with a responsibility no 21-year-old boy should ever have to bear. It set out what I was doing and what I needed for him to explain to his mother and his younger brothers. All three of my children were to set up a high-end VPN on their phones and establish themselves on three new email addresses to use for our video meetups, but only on their phones. I gave them all the details they needed to buy SIM cards and establish accounts — to set up and pay for everything in Simon's name.

On one occasion, I logged in for a session expecting my son Liam, but my wife was on the other end. She had clearly been crying. Looking at me, she could not hide her shock at how bad I looked. She wanted to know how I was and said she just wanted to see my face.

People — they're all the same. The way they trample all over the elementary decencies of relationships, of marriage.

The Brothers Karamazov' Fyodor Dostoevsky

You give them hundreds of opportunities to care, to be kind, to focus, but in the end, the only motivation they respond to is being walked away from. I didn't know what to say — nothing new anyway. It made me so sad to see how upset she was. What amazed me about our life together was that even when it seemed the penny had dropped with her, when she said that she "got" it, that she could see what was wrong and that she would work with me to fix it, within as little as a day or two, it was gone. I mean, that's all it took. Vanished completely, as if the conversation never happened.

Unfortunately, sadly, I was done — for me there was nothing more to say.

I was happy that my children were doing well. They all said they understood, but that didn't change the fact that they missed me. Tom started crying in the middle of one of our talks and said he just wanted a hug from me. He said how sorry he was that he had always complained in a joking way whenever I had insisted on a hug from him.

It was heartbreaking.

Sometimes, I couldn't sleep for what felt like days on end, just lying there thinking about my kids, about how they were, about what troubles they were facing, and especially what troubles they would face in their lives in the future and how I would not be there to give them the advice and assistance that a father should. These were the worst times, and I would often end up sobbing, crying myself eventually to sleep.

Occasionally, after finally falling into a fitful slumber, I would wake up in complete terror to pain on the side of my head. It was always the same. I would be dreaming that a revolver was pressed hard into my temple, the clicking scream of the spinning chamber whirring, its vibrations running down the steel barrel straight through the flesh of my temple, through my skull, and into my exhausted brain.

I had left my watch — a Panerai PAM233 GMT with its polished alligator strap — my wedding ring, some pharmaceuticals, my passport, my driver's license, and a few other personal papers in a safety deposit box at CB Lockers near Asok in Bangkok. My plans had me back in Bangkok for the last week of my 365 days, and here, in Thailand, I was Simon. I was still wearing the simple steel keychain ring my son had picked up off the ground and given me so many years ago with an absent-minded smile — a gesture and a gift that had become so utterly precious to me that I couldn't bear to be without it. Anyway, it wasn't the sort of thing someone would want to cut my throat for while I was sleeping. It was valuable only to me.

After a couple of beers, the sun had dropped below the horizon, and — leaving a 500 Baht tip under my empty beer glass — I wandered out along the shops, restaurants, and street stalls of the esplanade, enjoying the sun's last heat for the day, smelling the smells and watching the people.

I passed the guy on a street corner whom I had bought switchblades from over the years. He was one of three I had bought from — the other two were in Bangkok on Sukhumvit between Sois 13 and 15 and at the night markets in Chiang Mai. Although they were illegal in Australia, I had once accumulated a collection of about a dozen of them — all different sizes and designs, after having developed a simple way to smuggle them past Customs back into Australia. I would buy one I liked, and then buy two cheap screwdriver kits from a street stall, and go back to the quiet of my hotel room. There I would press the button to open the knife, use the first screwdriver to remove the two side plates, and then carefully undo the main screw while pinching the two sides tightly together. Then I would insert the screwdriver all the way through from the other side with the tip protruding all the way out, ensuring that the screwdriver took the place of the main screw, holding the internal layers in perfect alignment. This was the most important step because I had learned that if those layers moved out of alignment, the knife was almost impossible to put back together.

Following this step, leaving the first screwdriver in place, I would use the second screwdriver to take out the two fastening screws that held the spring enclosure in place. Because the knife was open with the blade out, the spring was not compressed, and it was easy to just take it out with my fingers. It was then just the simple process of working backwards to refit the two screws over the spring enclosure, then the main screw that the blade pivoted on — carefully pushing it in behind the first screwdriver as I withdrew it slowly out the other side, screwing it in by hand, and then finally screwing the side plates back on. Once the spring had been removed, the switchblade was no longer an "automatic knife" and could only be opened manually, like a standard pocketknife.

The final step was how I made sure that I could bring the spring, separate from the knife, undetected through customs. I would buy a small roll of colourful fabric ribbon, and after winding it all the way around the circular spring like a wreath or garland, I would tie it in a knot onto the main zipper on my suitcase, leaving two 100 mm strands of ribbon trailing. To any Customs Officer, it was just a ribbon on a zip that the owner would have attached to help them identify their bag from hundreds of other similar ones on a luggage carrousel.

But my collection was gone now, thrown out as part of the "great three-month clean-up" I had embarked upon while becoming Simon.

Lost in my musings, I found myself at the entrance to Bangla Road — the so-called "Walking Street" of Patong Beach. Bangla Road was the centre of the nightlife in Phuket, but it was still early, only 6 pm, and things were just starting to get going. I wandered down towards the Taipan Nightclub, which, like many of the night spots in Phuket, looked tired and had obviously seen better days. Government policy around Covid, like in most places around the world, had not been kind to businesses in Phuket. People, in their simplicity, blamed Covid. I blamed the Zealotribe's pathological technocracy and their influence on Government policy. It was a subtle distinction, but I believed an important one. And the Followerati. They were the "Sergeants at Arms" those stupid, selfish people who had been granted a place at a table where they had no natural right to ever be, who had led the Echochamberists by the nose down this path of destruction.

The results of their selfish, grandiose, power-mongering stupidity were nowhere more evident than in places like Patpong or Bangla Road.

Regardless, life went on. Those street-front bars that had survived were starting to fill up with predominantly men whose appearance tended towards being older and who seemed to dress homogeneously, in a sort of uniform: beer-branded singlets, shorts, and rubber flip-flops. It was still hot and humid, and the bar girls in their shiny-silver-miniskirts and tight-spaghetti-string white tops over their cast-iron A-cup-upgraded-to-C-cup bras were just starting work, smiling and encouraging passers-by to come in for a drink. 100 Baht seemed to be the going rate for a cold beer — very reasonable in almost anyone's language.

I was wearing dark-coloured shorts I had had made by my tailors before leaving Bangkok, a blue polo shirt, and a pair of Converse sneakers — copies I had bought at MBK before the Intellectual Property lawyers had shut down that tiny little shop on the ground floor — with low cut white socks. On Bangla Road, I felt almost overdressed.

For over twenty years, I had had all my casual and business long-sleeved shirts and shorts made by my tailor — Ricky's on Sukhumvit. It just made sense. When I thought about the odds of walking into a department store and finding a shirt that was the right size, the perfect cut, the right colour, that was made from a fabric that I really loved, and that was priced at a price I was happy to pay, I guessed the odds were about 1000 to 1. Everything else was a compromise. Having them made by my tailor, I got to choose the finest polished cotton fabrics and linens out of England, Italy, and Egypt, in the colours and designs that I liked and have them cut and made based on my favorite patterns, which Ricky's kept on file for me. Occasionally, I would add variety by asking for a rounded casual hem as opposed to a straight cut or a Chinese mandarin collar instead of the standard button-down Oxford design, or I would add a breast pocket with a separate internal pen pocket or request contrasting mother-of-pearl buttons. The shorts I was wearing were made from an Irish linen that was so soft and hung so loosely — they were just ridiculously comfortable in the hot, humid Thailand weather.

At Ricky's, my request was always the same — no labels at all on anything. I had even made them remove the store's branded pocket label from an exquisite, dark navy 100% cashmere trench

225

coat they had made for me before I would accept it — the guys there knew my preferences by now and apologised for the mistake. The whole point about tailor-made was that it was made just for you; no one else had any fucking claim to it, not even the man with the mouth full of pins and the chalk block and the heavy-worn-edged Toledo scissors who had made it.

I felt like a cool drink and started looking for a bar I might like. I always avoided the "Aussie Bars", the "Kangaroo Bars", and the "Down Under Bars" because when I was out of Australia, the last thing I wanted to do was interact with Australians — somehow being surrounded by Australian expats and tourists was just not something I was ever interested in. Too close to home, perhaps. To memories. Not enough degrees of separation from the sadness and the regrets. There were other bars on Bangla Road, like the Aloha Bar and the Heroes Bar, that I couldn't go into because, over the past few months, I had been banned from them — generally as a result of me opening that door that allowed my drunken rage to come out and deal with some fucking maniac determined to impose his stupidity on me. It never took much.

The Black Rose bar was empty, so I wandered in, sat on the front bench facing the street, and ordered a soda water to quench my throat and a cold Singha beer to sit on. I was always very careful to change the dressing on my neck twice a day — first thing in the morning and just before going to bed. It was ghastly enough without it getting infected. It was important to me that people saw a clean, fresh dressing, that they saw someone who was disciplined and well groomed, not someone who looked like they had given up and didn't even have enough self-respect to look after themselves.

Unnecessarily, romantically, despairingly, I quietly wished — hoped — that people thought it was just a dressing on a new tattoo — something that my drawn, haggard features would have clearly contradicted.

Sitting there sipping my soda water, I started thinking about a dream I had the night before. Like most dreams, there was no context to it. A beautiful girl smiled at me, and we had started to talk. She was about 22 years old with dark hair, long tanned legs and that skin that girls have at that age, perfectly clear, young. She was wearing denim shorts and a simple white 70's looking t-shirt with a caricature of a guy holding a surfboard and standing next to a VW Bug with the words; "Tubeline by Tony Dempsey" underneath it. The design was black and white and lime green and orange. She was relaxed and laughing and staring straight into my eyes. She kept moving closer and closer to me as we stood talking easily together, standing separate in a space that was just ours, somehow completely removed from the world around us. The conversation was so light and friendly, with that underlying feeling of promise — her eyes and lips smiling. Her laugh. To make a girl laugh is a truly beautiful thing. And then she stopped and moved across the last few inches between us so that I could feel her against me, her warmth, and then she kissed me. Like when I was young — soft, intimate lips, tongue exploring. It was so beautiful.

Sitting there, thinking about it, trapped in this 61-year-old body. Contemplating that horrible truth — that that first gentle kiss, the most beautiful thing that can happen to a boy, was gone forever. Why do I even go on? Why does any man go on once this is lost? What on earth is the fucking point? Crazy! It makes no fucking sense at all not to just find the nearest bridge and leap off it once you lose this. It's literally 50% of what's worth living for.

Where I was at in my life was all on me. I knew that. I had made all the decisions that led me here, to this bar, today. My fate, my choices, nothing else. The irony was that I knew, I always knew. It was always the same; the mistakes I had made were when I wanted to say "no", but instead, I had said "yes". And every time I did it, I knew it was a fucking mistake, but I did it anyway.

Choices. My God! Just a few — a handful of decisions defining a life.

They say that "you can't miss what you never had" came back to me, but they never warn you just how much of all of the things you did do, all of the experiences that you have had, that you can miss once they're gone — the other side of that double-edged sword. I had filled my life right up to the brim with these experiences. I was back to my theory of the Yin and Yang in everything and about the choices we make that place us wherever we end up inside those bell curves.

I took a long drink from my beer.

A life of indulgence — full of adventure and risk, how does it end up? You could be forgiven for assuming that all that's left are wonderful, vivid memories of the new and different, of the tastes and smells and excitement and the pleasure of it all.

But you'd be fucking wrong.

Of course, they're there, these memories, but there's no pleasure in them because all they do is remind you of what you once had, everything that's now gone forever.

There comes the point, a devastating moment in time, when you realise that it's all gone. That almost everything new you have tasted is now over. You realise that those opportunities, that anticipation, will never be there for you in the future. And time, that savage adversary, takes every moment it can to remind you just how much you have lost as you sit there, lonely, young, and vibrant — separate from everything — trapped inside an old, worn-out shell of a body.

Just watching a young woman walk past, her beautiful lean body, hair bouncing, her perfumed scent drifting over to you. Watching a young man laughing and flirting with a pretty girl or running past — strong, tanned, flexible, and fit — the sweat on his torso glistening in the summer sun.

Indeed — a double-edged sword.

And to choose the opposite? To choose a life of restraint, one of those banal lives of carefully measured portions, everything deliberately, purposefully weighed and balanced — where does that end up? A deathbed surrounded by loved ones with a contented smile as you die quietly in your sleep?

Maybe, but I don't think so.

A life like that made up of safe choices, of the endless saving and postponing of everything new — of the calculated wasting of time. Is the repetition and routine, the practiced turning of your back, enough to keep everything in life that you've missed out on hidden from you? Forever? Does that choice, that conscious decision to choose to be blind to all of the colour, to insulate yourself from everything beyond the walls of your self-imposed prison, is it enough to hide from you the total difference in experience and joy that exists between being there, actually doing it, and just reading about it?

What is the difference between seeing a photo of a sunset on Railay Beach and actually being there, immersed in one?

Sitting in a borrowed plastic chair.

The back legs pushed into the sand at the end of the beach just up from the edge of the gently lapping ocean.

Next to an old wooden boat that the sand has almost completely devoured.

No roads in, no roads out — long-tail boats only.

That feeling of freedom, of being out of reach, cut off from the system, from everything.

The crystal-clear blue water shimmering under the towering limestone island bluffs, reaching up to the clouds.

Sipping a Negroni, listening to the ice cubes clunking against each other in the plastic cup.

Feeling the pizza oven heat fade back as the sun drops down.

Watching the brightly coloured boats being anchored, immersed in the lazy drift of the locals laughing through the end of the day?

That, or the photograph on Facebook? The two things were completely fucking different, in no way the same.

And that life — to choose that? That life of disciplined, safe repetition, do those choices make for peaceful twilight years? A sunset of grey after a dull, noneventful, long, safe life, without the haunting from the ghosts of pleasures past? Or does it end with a thousand savage daggers of regret?

For me, this was the choice central to all things, the decision that sat above all others, defining everything in life between when it begins and when it ends, absolutely. It was a stone I had carried around in my pocket for my entire life, occasionally taking it out and polishing it — something that was now more than ever in the present, more important than it ever had been.

That safe, protected life. That monotonous, dull existence, full of repetition and routine. The fact that you spend every waking hour looking over the fence at those who made other, braver choices, in a constant, sickening state of longing and resentment, is not important — staring into that photo on Facebook, trying desperately to place yourself there. After all, it's not quality now that matters, is it? It's your total and utter fucking fear of a lack of quality in those latter years of life.

That fatal, poisonous cloud of illusion that most people are immersed in — waiting for life's problems and difficulties to be over before they can decide to be happy.

my friend William is a fortunate man:
he lacks the imagination to suffer

he kept his first job
his first wife

can drive 50,000 miles
without a brake job

he dances like a swan
and has the prettiest blank eyes
this side of El Paso

his garden is a paradise
the heels of his shoes are always level
and his handshake is firm

people love him

when my friend William dies
it will hardly be from madness or cancer

he'll walk right past the devil
and into heaven

you'll see him at the party tonight
grinning
over his martini

blissful and delightful
as some guy
fucks his wife in the bathroom

Charles Bukowski

A life of obligation, of fitting in. A life of excuses, duty, and acceptance. No grins, no screams, no tears. An acceptance of conditioned misery, where to laugh is to lie and where to weep no more than hints at distant emotions that feel only faintly familiar and wonderful, emotions that, strangely, are beyond your grasp. Unchosen. That nagging, annoying suspicion beyond the dusty, dry options that there is something more to life — someone more to life. Something hidden, smothered underneath the endless work of making others happy, of making sure you will always be fed and that you will have enough money to be able to buy gifts on birthdays and at Christmas time.

I guess there is also less chance that you will end up homeless? There's that, I suppose. Shuffling along from one public refuse bin to the next, seemingly oblivious to the world and its standards… or worse still; striding forcefully from one to the other, your face searching, screaming, snarling, acutely aware of every tiny fucking detail of the nightmare you have been completely absorbed by, lost in.

This life of overwhelming prosaic routine that casts the thinnest of veneers over that persistent nagging feeling of lost opportunities, of lost adventures that are always there, just under the surface. Punctuated only by the occasional almost accidental moments of shared companionship, a distraction from the violent assault of life and memories, of childhood and of forsaken dreams — an assault led by the fear stormtroopers: loneliness, poverty, and death, followed closely by the hapless clowns of paradox, fate, and irony.

Smoke-screen-days.

Mechanistically, deliberately imposing concocted, contrived diversions — pushing new, paper-thin scenes across life's raging furnace stage, creating just instants, $17.95-bottles-of-wine-soaked moments of peace, welcomed as distractions from the onslaught of the truth, of anything real.

Sex without hunger — scentless, dry, crumbling in your mouth.

Fuck No. This had never even been an option for me. I had always known I could never bear it. I needed to stay alive, awake, senses pricked — to breathe for God's sake! To find expectations and limits surreal, incomprehensible. To wrestle playfully with danger — hard, confident swordplay against everything determined to push me into the centres of those fucking bell curves. I didn't even care what side I fell on, and I didn't care how hard I fell, as long as it was as far away from the fucking masses, from the middle, from "average" as I could get.

Miserable, lonely, and scared was better than average — every fucking time.

The thought of the rage I would feel if any of these bastards who had settled happily, consciously for fucks sake, into that grey middle space said that something I had done, something about me, a piece of art that I made — this book — was "interesting". The ultimate insult. These people that have no idea that true art can have no value at all unless it costs the artist something — anguish, relationships, peace.

And these assholes were everywhere.

I had come to realise that Thailand was a place where, for me anyway, I should only glance furtively at them — only nod politely, stay determinedly aloof from them, and the mind's fearful warnings they induced. It was a place to be careful not to give them anything more than the most cursory attention as they queued in front of me at a 7-Eleven or sat across from me on the sky train. With steely resolve, I would consciously let them just drift by; strangers on the sidewalk, strangers standing in the shadows — the fucking monsters of consequence.

They can just smell your fear, you know.

They're just waiting for your resolve to crack in a moment of carelessness, ready to pounce with their outrageous optimism —

their faith in "hope", in "tomorrow", with their "happy ruminations of yesterday", or their optimism about "what if". Just waiting for you to weaken and engage with them — to breathe life into them.

Murderous, capricious bastards.

Catching the eye of the barmaid, I held up a finger and ordered another Singha beer.

My time in Thailand, my 365 days, had quickly become a place to be constantly on guard against these bastards, to be ready to identify and completely avoid any contact at all with anyone who nurtured any of these grotesque ideals, who believed in things like commitment, in responsibility, in duty. These people, who were entirely ensconced in this apparatus; this dry-bleached-boned-skeleton of fear wrapped in its skin of sanguinity — like some ugly iron lung machinery, who, as far as I was concerned, had no fucking right to be anywhere near me in my world — who were just passing by, living in their Disneyland haze.

I knew these fucking fuckers could infect me through osmosis, talking about all of the people they loved, and the hopes they had, and their fucking plans and their fucking dreams and all of their commitment to fear and to obligation — their fucking endless rinse and repeat days. People who had no dedication at all to the truth, to ignoring these demons. No fucking Zen at all. No devotion to the moment. No determination at all to giving up, to walking away from the past and from the future, from the lies and the deceptions of aspirations and dreams and commitment. These dullards who had zero interest in seeing the truth, let alone grasping and understanding the fucking terror it brought with it, and embracing it.

We will occupy the minds with the futile and playful. It is good with non-stop gossip and music, to prevent the mind from wondering, thinking, thinking...We will put sexuality at the forefront of human interests. As a social anaesthetic, there's nothing better. In general, we will make sure to banish the seriousness of existence, ridicule everything of high value, maintain a constant apology of lightness; so that the euphoria of advertising and consumption becomes the human happiness standard and the model of freedom.

The Obsolescence of Man — Günther Anders, 1956

Absurd, asinine simpletons. Forever hungry no matter what they eat, where they are, or what they do — emotionally, sexually, aspirationally, endlessly fucking starving. They starve to death without ever even realising they are hungry.

I mean, just think about it. These fucking engagers, this choice of a life of constantly measured restraint, I guess they think they can reasonably expect it to be a long one? Or maybe — just maybe — they don't think it through.

When all of their friends and family have died, each... one at a time, each with varying amounts of gut-wrenching fucking loneliness attached to their fearful, pea soup, desolate, hazed funerals, and they find themselves, finally, all alone, what do they expect then? That their life of restraint and routine, their life of the making of lowest-common-denominator choices, of allowing the scales of measured reason to be their master, of ignoring everything wonderful, enticing, and colourful. That their life of slumping into a comfortable chair at the end of a hopeless day wasted in a hopeless job would allow them to reach that point where they were at best, what? Relatively unscathed physically and financially?

Physically. Well, perhaps they may have jumped the fucking gun a bit here. They might just find that in their perpetually tedious quest to avoid heart disease and cancer, they forgot about strokes.

With all that concentration on absolutely ensuring that they didn't enjoy themselves, all that effort spent resisting the sweet nicotine of a cigar after dinner, or exercising until they couldn't breathe just so that the ageing process only continued at

235

a mildly horrific pace and didn't turn them fat in an instant of relaxed nonchalance. All that racing off to the doctor in a state of fearful denial with every spot that changed shape or colour, or all those women that they encountered where there was a hint of something sweet and wild in their eyes or their smile, but they walked past totally, dogmatically, vehemently, hopelessly fucking safe. All that misery did nothing to prevent the stroke they inherited from their grandfather. You see. These fucking morons don't get it. You can't focus on all of the misery all of the time; no matter how hard you try, something will always get past.

Anyway, let's look on the bright side. This life of abstinence and discipline, if they kept it up, if they stuck to their guns and didn't cheat too often, if they were really fucking miserable most of the time, saved them from heart disease and a plethora of shocking cancers, leaving them with both halves of their body in near perfect health, albeit speaking different languages.

Serves them fucking right.

I was getting quite drunk now and, not wanting to make a liar out of my crazed philosophy of excess and abandonment, motioned to one of the bar girls for another Singha.

And financially? Well! There's always their fucking pension, isn't there? I thought, watching the constant stream of locals and tourists walking past. The crowd was thickening, and of course, it contained lots of these people, these assholes, the Echochamberists, wandering along in their holiday clothes, eking out their holiday money, enjoying the delusion of power and fun as they embarrassed themselves haggling over one dollar with a local who was just trying to get by, just trying to feed her kids. These fuckers always had a pension. Moreover, they usually had a large superannuation payout that some inept government bureaucrat somewhere had fattened up with the theft of taxes from other simple, hard-working people who were never smart enough — or lucky enough — to get their snouts into the pig trough of government ineptitude.

How else did they intend to pay for the outrageously overpriced and utterly depressing sub-standard nursing home that the people who once loved them with all of their hearts, inevitably pushed them into without even a second thought? That place within which they finalise their years of nothingness. Completely alone, save for the occasional visit out of pure obligation from one of their children who the natural current of life has carried far away, and who no longer loves them or really even knows them or cares about them at all anymore — who give their love elsewhere now. Visitors who, when they look at them, are unable to hide the fact that all that they can see is a disconnected montage of eclectic, fractured memories of times together, drawn taut across the bones, the human scraps, of what time has done to them.

Bound to a wheelchair so that they don't fall out, a spittle cup around their neck to catch the dribble, a glazed, painful look on their face as they ponder the incredible paradox between the beautiful, crystal-clear memories of a loved one lost 50 years ago — a chunk of their soul ripped from their heart far too early — and the annoyance of not being able to remember their own fucking name!

Fuck them. These people. These wasters of lives. These malignant disciples of sterile choices. These public servants, the obese pigs, the furtive rat junkies, the accountants adding up everyone else's numbers, the academics rearranging the pages of other people's books, and the lawyers referencing everyone else's words. The timid, pale, wretches with their anxiety-induced-retarded-emotional-musculature, happily locked in their box, peeping through a crack at the truth, safe in their distance from it.

A little girl somewhere, four years old, stands, wearing only a diaper. She is leaning forward, her head hanging over the toilet bowl, and her hands are on the seat as the waves of chemotherapy-induced nausea wash over her. Her brother, only six, stands beside her, a comforting hand on her back, while her father sleeps in the next room of their shabby rented apartment, completely overcome with exhaustion. For fuck's sake, it's easier to get free Wi-Fi than it is to get free water, and people act as if there's nothing wrong with the world.

Life is precious, you fucking bastards! Just because it's not right in front of your fucking face doesn't mean it's not there! Look! Open your eyes! Care, for God's sake.

The bread you store belongs to the hungry. The clothes you accumulate belong to the naked. The shoes that you have in your closet are for the barefoot. The money you bury deep into the ground to keep it safe, belongs to the poor. You were unfair to as many people as you could have helped and you did not.
Basil of Caesarea 364 AD

With all your "more, more, more," and all your "me, me, me." You miserable self-obsessed shallow fucks. Fuck you and everything about you. Thirty-five thousand children die from starvation — from not having enough food in their stomachs — every single, fucking, day. And your focus? Your attention is on sitting there with your dazed expressions, just waiting for the next opportunity to talk about yourself, to show off, and lay bare all of your mediocrity in every word, every sentence that comes out of your mouth. All you're interested in is wallowing in your own miserable, one-dimensional existence — a life so incredibly mundane that it has not even bothered to take the time to show you things, to teach you things.

The doors to your mind slammed shut in your teenage years and were welded closed. Your malignant Disneyland of meaningless reports, of supervising, organising, pleasing, climbing, of negotiating pointless never-ending numbers and activities day after day after day. Your investment properties and your obscene payouts, waiting for you so you can one day "do" Italy and "do" Greece, and "do" the Grand Canyon, and "do" the Catacombs — your face the whole time glued to your phone — desperately punching out endless boasts into social media, taking photos of things that you walk away from having not even fucking seen, desperate to impress people you barely even fucking know. While at the same time, the intricacies of a beautiful piece of street art right next to you, evade you completely.

Very early in their married life he had decided, though perhaps it was only that he knew her more intimately than he knew most people, that she had, without exception, the most stupid, vulgar, empty mind that he had ever encountered. She had not a thought in her head. There was not a slogan, and there was no imbecility, absolutely none, that she was not capable of swallowing.

1984 — George Orwell

Sitting there, watching them. Sipping my beer. The living dead drifting past. The ghouls. The wasters of days, of lives. Carefully avoiding their gaze so that in a moment of relaxed insouciance they didn't inadvertently drag me into their fucking nightmare.

Their astonishing determination to avoid anything original, anything real, with no interest in finding even one thing that they can call theirs, some beauty that they discover that they didn't come across simply by reading a recipe, or a review, or by following the advice or the instructions or the opinions of other people. Days of monotony and repetition, coming home and being anesthetised by reality television and doing it all again tomorrow. Days that mean nothing in the end, except to perhaps permanently ensure that the distain that life has developed for them, and them for it, is inherited by their children. Perpetuating their nothingness into eternity.

I took another long drink from the bottle. And yet, they live. They get to live, and Sam doesn't.

There are women who work in bars, and taxi drivers around the world who work for 14 hours a day, seven days a week, who are fluent in three and four languages, and who have nothing!

239

Simple workers who laugh and taste and smell and feel real things every day, who have never had the chance to travel — not even once — not even outside of the fucking city they were born in, who know so much more about life and people and love and freedom and pain and art and passion and giving than you could ever even imagine! You are the wasters of lives. The NPCs, the pulp people that make up the numbers between these people, the people who live, the people who understand.

Fuck you, you fucking fuckers. I hate you for the space you take up, for your utter ignorance and the bliss you enjoy that goes with it, and for the suffering that goes unaddressed because of it. The suffering of real people; single mothers with disabled kids; young men trying to find their way through the slashing razors of the derision of the world — of people who matter. And let me be clear — you don't! You don't fucking matter. At all! Not. One. Fucking. Bit.

Don't talk like one of them. You're not! Even if you'd like to be. To them, you're just a freak, like me! They need you right now, but when they don't, they'll cast you out, like a leper! You see, their morals, their code, it's a bad joke. Dropped at the first sign of trouble. They're only as good as the world allows them to be. I'll show you. When the chips are down, these... these civilized people, they'll eat each other.

The Joker – Christopher Nolan

Putting my beer down on the counter, I looked over and noticed the bar girl who had served me was looking at me with a curious expression on her face as if she was about to ask me if I was okay. I waved her over, and taking a slow, deep breath I smiled and asked for a triple-shot espresso.

I was so fucking angry. I knew it was crazy. I knew I was crazy. Unreasonable, ridiculously judgmental. Damaged beyond repair. I knew it was all about my little brother, about Sam — the fact that all these people got to live and he didn't. That my beautiful, clever, kind brother was gone, that he had been forced into a corner where the only option, the only option left for him, was to shoot himself. Can you imagine feeling like that? That that was the only path left for you.

I was angry that a good person — a special person — had died so young, while these people, who seemed to see nothing — to feel nothing — these people who passed through life seemingly untouched by it, got to take up space, finally dying of old age without ever meaning anything to anyone. These fucking people and their wilfull selfish ignorance — their deliberate indifferent contempt for the pain and the suffering of others. Their selfish, miserable fucking lives.

> Teacher seeks pupil. Must have an earnest desire to save the world. Apply in person.
>
> Ishmael – Daniel Quinn

But deep down, I knew that was wrong. I knew they shared lives with people who cared about them. That they mattered. But it didn't help. I still fucking hated them almost as much as I hated myself for having let Sam down so badly.

Almost.

My coffee arrived, and, wanting to calm down — wanting to climb out of the dark hole I had fallen into — I took a sip and placed it on the bar in front of me. An hour and three coffees later, I pulled my laptop out of my satchel and, opening up my book, I read back over the last few paragraphs and continued on — through the forest…

Chapter V

Just above the treetops of Cracklewood Forest, a large black raven glided through the cool night air, its deep red eyes glowing like embers. Now and again, its wings swept up and down as Gagglebroth travelled swiftly towards the swamp.

The swamp in Cracklewood Forest was located about two miles northwest of the stump. It was not a large swamp, about one hundred yards long and forty wide. It had formed from a spring that started in the bottom of a large hollow in the forest floor. The water had slowly risen, swallowing the bases of the huge trees that grew there, drowning their roots and eventually killing them.

The enormous dead trees stood grey and silent in the dark, murky water, surrounded by thick green tufts of reeds. Their trunks rose like colossal arms with their sharp, weathered limbs like great gnarled claws reaching out to strangle the sunlight that broke through wherever it could down onto the water. In fact, the graveyard and the swamp were the only two places where the sun actually broke through the canopy and reached the floor of Cracklewood Forest, the trees around the edges partly submerged, clinging to life.

In the middle of the swamp was a small island, bathed in sunshine and covered in long, lush reeds. On this island, amongst the reeds, lived a large toad named Sleash. But for his size and unique ability to speak and walk upright, he was in every way a toad and a very old toad at that, having frequented the forest for over eight hundred years.

The raven slid down through the darkness and landed quietly on one of the branches of the tallest of the dead trees on the edge of the swamp near the little island. And shuffling about on the bough, it studied the swamp below, its deep red eyes searching.

Gagglebroth was looking for Sleash.

Birds looking for a drink were by far Sleash's favorite meal, if only because it was rare for him to catch one, and as such, they offered welcome variety to his usual diet of eels and water spiders. Any bird that was enticed by the water and the promise of food that the swamp held was more often than not snavelled by Sleash's long yellow tongue and swiftly devoured. Gagglebroth was not scared of being eaten by Sleash, for she was far too powerful. However, there was a small chance she could end up in his mouth wrapped in his slimy yellow tongue before she had time to revert to her original form, which would be a decidedly unpleasant experience, even for a Witch, and one she would very much prefer to avoid.

Suddenly, she spotted him. Sleash was in the water, splashing about with something near a tuft of reeds. The raven dropped quietly out of the tree and glided down onto the ground. The splashing stopped. Sleash had heard Gagglebroth land amongst the reeds and was now gliding silently through the water on his belly round to the other side of the island. Gagglebroth knew exactly where the old toad was and stood still, silent in the middle of the island, having returned to her natural state — her eyes shut to conceal their glow in the darkness.

Perhaps a bit of shock value would help with Sleash, she was thinking.

The giant toad slipped stealthily out of the water and up onto the island in search of what it thought was a tasty treat. Even with her eyes shut, Gagglebroth could see Sleash as a dark shape against a darker background. The toad squatted silently, listening, searching. Its eyelids sliding slowly down and up over its large, luminous blue eyes as it blinked. Then Gagglebroth opened her eyes.

"Sleash!" She said sharply. The toad leapt backwards into the water with a scream of fright.

"Sleash? You, miserable excuse for a frog. Get up here!" Said Gagglebroth, the uncontrollable crooked grin on her face at seeing Sleash's fear concealed by the darkness of the night. The toad clambered back out of the water and stood upright on its two hind legs.

"Gagglebroth", said Sleash in a deep, croaky voice, not bothering to try to hide the dislike he had for the queen of the witches in his tone. He walked over to a small stump he used as a seat and sat down. In front of him was a bed of coals from a fire that had long been extinguished. Sleash did not cook his food often, for to do so meant he had to venture into Cracklewood Forest to collect the firewood. Because he had lived in the swamp for over three hundred years, each time he went searching for wood, he had to venture deeper and deeper into the forest, something he did not like to do. He had a very heathy fear of boughglimmbs.

"What do you want?" he asked with the same disdainful tenor, the tail of an eel appearing protruding from one side of his large mouth.

"Don't speak with your mouth full, you disgusting creature! We have a problem."

"We?" said the toad slyly, slurping the last of the eel into its mouth and swallowing it with a squelch.

"WE! You wart-ridden lump of misery! It's Dew", said Gagglebroth impatiently.

"You expect me to mess with Dew after what happened last time!" protested the toad.

Gagglebroth lost her temper.

"Enough insolence frog!" her voice becoming venomous. "Or I'll do more than splash you with salt. I'll bury you to your neck in it and coat your eyeballs in VINE-GAR! Do you understand!" her voice had become a hiss.

"What do you want?" said Sleash a little more submissively but holding onto a hint of the distaste he held for her.

"He has with him a companion by the name of Eugene

Lumpthistle. I want him, at least part of him, in any case. So if you come across him, I don't want you to go drowning him and boiling him up. If you see him or catch him, let me know."

"What makes you think I'll have any business with him?" croaked the toad.

"Nothing. But if you are wise, you may make it your business", said Gagglebroth sharply.

"Should you happen upon him and deliver him to me intact, there's a healthy supply of birds and wood in it for you", said Gagglebroth, a nasty smile appearing on her face.

The large toad reached behind his seat and produced a long wooden pipe. He turned to Gagglebroth, crossing his legs as he placed the pipe in his mouth.

"Do you have a light?" asked Sleash in a non-committal manner, his eyelids slipping back and forth once again. Gagglebroth bent down and picked a twig from the ground, stepped forward, and handed it to the toad. The tip of the twig burst into flame as he took it. He applied it to the end of the pipe and began puffing vigorously at first, then slowing as large plumes of grey smoke drifted up into the night sky.

"Teach me to do that, and it's a deal." Said the toad nonchalantly, taking on a relaxed, confident composure. Gagglebroth bent down to the toad.

"Take heed, wart, lest I skin you alive", she hissed softly, her eyes throwing a red glow across Sleash's face, such was her threatening rage. Sleash felt a cold chill run down his back, a terrifying and unexpected thing for a cold-blooded amphibian.

Gagglebroth stepped back and placed the black feather onto the tip of her black tongue, removed it, pushed it into her matted hair, and closed her eyes. She began to mutter a chant, and her shape immediately began to quiver as she shrank back to a raven. Giving Sleash one last glare with her glowing red eyes, she started flapping her wings and rose upward and back into the night sky from where she had come, leaving him to ponder the error of his ways as he sat, as if paralysed, the tip of his pipe just short of his lips, terrified by her reminder of the magical powers she possessed.

Slowly relaxing from the encounter with Gagglebroth, Sleash sat quietly puffing at his pipe; the morning was close at hand. He pondered the significance of the news of Eugene Lumpthistle. Swallowing dryly at the thought of being buried up to his neck in salt and having his eyes coated with vinegar, or worse, being skinned alive. Gagglebroth was not one for idle threats. But there was an opportunity here for him if he played his cards right, not just the firewood and the birds to feast upon, but to gain favor with the witches would be no small thing. To win them as allies instead of having to be constantly wary of them.

About 50 yards away from the stump in the first murky light that was morning in Cracklewood Forest, Beetlecrunch crouching behind a tree, her pale, green eyes focused on the stump. She was gnawing savagely on a toad stool she had found close by, her thoughts preoccupied with the wrath she felt towards Curdleslop. The anger that Beetlecrunch held towards Curdleslop was only surpassed by her fear of Gagglebroth — the only reason she had the presence of mind to keep her eyes fixed on the stump.

Suddenly, Beetlecrunch stiffened and stopped her rat-like chewing of the toadstool, her eyes squinting into the gloom. She had spotted movement, not at the stump, but amongst the trees off to the left. There it was again. She saw it clearly this time, and then, out from behind a large boobleberry tree thrust the head of a roamer, its large bulbous, almost elongated eyes flitting from side to side and up and down. They were very wary creatures, roamers — only a handful of them were still in existence.

This particular roamer's name was Ziffleweave. Perhaps to state the obvious, they were referred to as roamers for the simple reason that they never stayed in one particular place and seemed to be always on the move.

They had once been a great herd that wandered throughout the Great Northern Forest. A peaceful animal, they had lived in harmony with the Glocks for over 3000 years. Though harmony is probably too strong of a word, it was more like the two groups kept out of each other's way, which was not a difficult thing as the forest at the time had covered an enormous area, and the Glocks stayed put for the most part, unless they were out searching for ingredients.

Meredith Dew had met Ziffleweave only a few times over the years, for as a rule, one did not find Ziffleweave unless he wished to find you. He could move with great speed and stealth if the occasion warranted, and since the witches had moved in breeding and letting lose the boughglimmbs, this speed and stealth had saved his life more than once.

Beetlecrunch stood completely still, for she knew that one movement, no matter how slight, would most certainly be noticed by the roamer, and she desperately needed new information, anything that would help the witches in their quest to find Lumpthistle and, in doing so, help her win back some favor from Gagglebroth.

The roamer emerged slowly from behind the tree, every movement smooth, unstilted, and even though Beetlecrunch knew it was there, she still found it hard to distinguish its shape in the grey-brown darkness on the other side of the clearing. It was not just the light, though — Beetlecrunch, being a Witch, could see quite well on the blackest of nights. It was that the roamer was a tall, rather thin creature whose neck and angular limbs made it blend into the tree trunks, branches, and twigs that made up the mosaic of the forest.

Keeping her eye on the roamer, Beetlecrunch slowly slipped carefully a little farther back behind the Oak tree, but just at that moment, the roamer sprang back into the forest. Beetlecrunch cursed softly under her breath, thinking she had been seen, when, to her surprise, out from the clearing on the other side of the stump waddled one Meredith Dew with Eugene Lumpthistle only a pace or two behind him.

Beetlecrunch licked her pale, thin lips, watching closely as Meredith yawned and Eugene cocked his head to one side, touching at the fury ear that replaced the one Garblebilk had so savagely removed.

"I can hear much better than normal", announced Eugene with a quizzical, and one would have to say, a pleasantly surprised look on his face.

"It's an ill wind", answered Meredith, yawning again, his gold hair glittering brightly in the sun that shone through the hole in the forest canopy.

"What about the witches?" asked Eugene, studying the darkness of the forest about him with a wary air of suspicion.

"Well, they can't get to us in the sunlight, that's for sure", said Meredith, stretching, removing his small leather hat, and looking up at the sky.

"Why's that?" asked Eugene.

"When witches get touched by direct sunlight, they turn into wolves, and they cannot change back until the next full moon. And believe me, they are a lot easier to dispose of in wolf form than they are as witches." Said Meredith emphatically.

Beetlecrunch sneered, wishing she had Meredith's fat little neck in her nobbled, wrinkled hands.

"Still", said Meredith, continuing, "We can't stand here all day, so that fact does not do us a terrible amount of good. For what we are in need of, we can only find further into the forest, so it is there that we must go!" And with that, he replaced his hat and, standing still, suddenly turned his funny round nose skyward and began to sniff the air.

It was at this time Eugene heard a very unusual sound. "BOOLOLOLOP!" Came the high-pitched sound from the forest. "BOOLOLOLOP!" Came the sound again.

"Ziffleweave?" whispered Meredith, but there was no response.

"What's a Ziffleweave?" whispered Eugene in a terrified tone, his thoughts wandering up the food chain to imagine the next level of horrible creature they might encounter.

"Shhhh", whispered Meredith.

Staring into the forest where the sound had appeared to come from, Eugene strained his fox ear in an effort to pick up the slightest noise. Then, to his surprise, out from behind a Booblberry tree, with almost fluid, wary movements, emerged Ziffleweave.

Eugene stood transfixed, unable to take his gaze off the creature standing before him. Staring at it in wonder, it occurred to Eugene that the animal had a stature that was physically the exact opposite of Meredith Dew: tall, thin, angular, with sharp, intelligent eyes that held the expression of the constant appearance of surprise.

"Ziffleweave", said Meredith, sounding surprised and delighted by the visitor who he obviously wasn't expecting to see.

"Meredith!" answered Ziffleweave in a quiet, refined voice as if frightened he may be heard. "I have been looking for you. I have IMPORTANT news!" he said, glancing at Eugene suspiciously. He motioned for Meredith to come and join him out of the light as if the news he had were so important it could only be imparted with a whisper under the cover of darkness. Meredith walked over towards him and the edge of the forest, with Eugene following closely behind him. They stopped in front of Ziffleweave. Ziffleweave studied Eugene closely before giving Meredith a questioning glance.

"He's with me", said Meredith, realizing Ziffleweave's concern, "The witches seek to destroy him, so I guess he's with you as well."

Ziffleweave was about to speak when his eyes returned to Eugene, or to be more exact, Eugene's fox-like ear.

"The witches?" Ziffleweave asked, glancing at Meredith.

"In a roundabout way", said Meredith, shuffling his feet. A knowing look flashed across Ziffleweave's eyes before he refocused back to an expression of seriousness concerning the important news he wished to share. Looking nervously about, he moved slowly in closer to Meredith as if getting ready to impart something of great importance.

"What is it?" Said Meredith anxiously, beginning to become nervous himself.

"The Great Ball!" announced Ziffleweave, quietly but intensely. Eugene thought he also detected a note of fear.

"WHAT!" burst Meredith, seemingly made breathless by the news.

"I have found the Great Ball!"

"What!" Exclaimed Meredith again, looking furtively about at the shadows on the edge of the forest clearing. Eugene, though confused and inquisitive, dared not break the silence that had followed Ziffleweave's obviously very important news.

Hidden in the shadows, across the sunlit glade of the stump, crouched Beetlecrunch. At the news of the Great Ball, her mouth had become instantly dry, and her whole body had begun to shiver with excitement. The Great Ball of power that had once been prized beyond all else by the Glocks of the Great Northern Forest had been lost in the great explosion. It was assumed it had been blown to pieces or shot miles into nowhere, but no one really knew, and all, including the witches, had given up hope of ever finding it.

The Glocks of old had been great miners — iron, gold, marble, emeralds; they mined it all. Twelve hundred years ago, the Great Ball had been found in a marble mine. It was a flawless ruby, three feet across — a perfect sphere. The Glocks soon found that the stone held great magical power, for by placing both hands on it and staring deep into it, one could see things, things that had happened but, more importantly, things in the future, things yet to happen. In fact, if you stared intently for long enough into it, it was possible to see oneself, though not in physical form, but in spirit. Its power was so great that those who looked into it for too long were sent insane, running screaming in terror off into the forest. Some found days later dead from exhaustion as though they had not stopped running; others were never seen again. Eventually, it was forbidden under Glock law for the Great Ball to be used by anyone other than the elders.

The news was of such significance that crouching there, Beetlecrunch had to consciously calm herself so that she could think clearly. The choice she was faced with was critical; should she follow Meredith Dew or hurry straight back to the lair to inform Gagglebroth of what she had learned? Just the news that she already had, she knew, would be enough to return her to Gagglebroth's favor, but if she could find the location of the Great Ball of Power and lead Gagglebroth to it, it would surely mean a grand promotion, and with it far greater knowledge and power than she now possessed.

A nasty grin stretched her thin, pale lips and the wrinkles and furrows across her face as she thought of the power she would have over Curdleslop and perhaps even Elixius. Beetlecrunch had made up her mind, or more precisely, her thirst for power and revenge had made up her mind for her. She would follow the three to find the location of the ball.

After weighing up the news in deep thought, Meredith finally spoke, "Where?" he whispered to Ziffleweave. But in response, Ziffleweave just looked at him and remained silent, effectively answering that he dared not speak the location out loud. Meredith's expression softened, his brow unfurrowing in understanding. Shifting the sack he had over his left shoulder to his right shoulder, he spoke.

"Then we must leave now! Ziffleweave, you lead. Eugene, you next, I'll guard the rear," he said, his nose jiggling in direct defiance of the seriousness of his expression.

They turned their backs on the clearing at once, and Ziffleweave, showing the way, headed northwest back into the forest in the direction of the swamp. With the great ball at his disposal, Meredith would be more than a match for Gagglebroth with her reduced power. He could rid the forest of the witches once and for all.

Behind them, a green-eyed shadow of wickedness followed silently.

10

If I was in Charge

I stopped typing, and closing the lid of my laptop I motioned for the waitress — ordering a double Negroni just as two fat American women wearing matching pink surgical masks wandered in and flopped themselves down into groaning chairs at a table near me.

Like most Americans, they proceeded to speak at a volume much louder than was necessary, almost as if they were addressing the entire room — as if everybody, of course, would be interested to hear what they had to say. Within two minutes of the American women arriving, a group of four Chinese wandered in — two older couples, seating themselves at a table against the wall as three of them simultaneously yelled for the waitress.

"Fú wù yuan!"

The Chinese also spoke unnecessarily loudly, but not out of vanity or self-importance like the Americans did. For the Chinese, I had decided that there were two main reasons why they were always shouting into their phones or speaking at the top of their voices. The first was that this generation was literally stumbling out of primitive darkness headlong into the bright sunshine of modernity — there was nothing gradual about it. I mean, they were literally one set of parents progressed from when everyone bellowed like cows across a paddock or from one bicycle to another out of necessity — just one generation removed from the paddy fields.

The second reason was a little more complex. It was more about a simple lack of awareness or consideration for the privacy or the peacefulness of other people, a pattern of thinking that came from being completely immersed in a system that had no regard at all for the individual — a system imposed upon them by the Chinese Communist Party.

To the CCP, China was all about China — a living organism moving along a time-line across the millennia. The individual was of no consideration at all. Completely irrelevant. Talk about playing the long game. I mean fuck, it was almost like if they really wanted to invade Taiwan, they would simply start walking into the ocean in single file, and their army would eventually emerge on the beaches of Taiwan, walking across a peninsula formed from the drowned bodies of their dead comrades.

Building on the lack of individualism and mass cruelty carried out under centuries of rule by the Chinese monarchy, in the three generations since that murderous lunatic Mao Zedong formed the CCP, the Chinese State had morphed into a monolith of control. Amongst other tyrannies, it enforced its edict through the removal of all privacy and freedom from its citizens not only physically but also mentally and emotionally. The implementation of such an extreme, ordered structure not only kept the people homogeneously unique as a collective in comparison to people from other countries, but by defining and prescribing almost every aspect of daily life at every level—exactly the same for everybody, for "the People", it had also taken away any considerations of the need for individual thought, any considerations for the individual at all, that the people would once have had.

This embedded inability for the individual to think for themselves, in my opinion, was why if ever China found itself at war with Western powers, it would get its fucking ass kicked badly. An army of people who have been controlled and infantised and instructed by Government so completely, across the last two or three generations, who have lost the need to think for themselves

— the ability to evaluate choices, options, assess ramifications, scenarios — to make decisions, would be fucking slaughtered, and it wouldn't take long.

Their army would fail at every single level, from the generals who have been conditioned to just agree with and accept the direction of the State, of Xi, right through the ranks down to the infantry soldiers. Without years of living daily with the experiences of making choices, of practicing and improving the skillset of weighing up alternatives, priorities, options on operational, tactical, and strategic daily-life levels, these soldiers wouldn't have a chance. History shows that indecision in warfare is unforgiving, and to take away the capacity for individual thought from people, to breed that resource out of a whole fighting force, would result in some serious catastrophic shit.

This mentality was obvious to me at the most rudimentary level when I played the computer game *Battlefield* with my sons. Whenever I was on Chinese servers and did something unusual like managing to get in behind enemy lines — a strategy that created a significant advantage, unlike when I was on US and Australian servers, the rest of my squad rarely joined me, rarely ever spawned on me. They preferred instead to remain engaged in the endless face-to-face die-spawn-play-die cycles on whatever frontline had been established between the two sides. Or when I managed to climb up onto a rooftop to get the advantage of height over the enemy, there were immediate complaints in the chat of zhi zhu ren! (Spiderman) and calls to have me kicked from the server — as if there were rules of strategy in warfare and I was breaking them. This never happened on Western servers.

Over the last 70 or so years, this stuff has become deep-seated, like it's in their DNA. Even people who have settled into countries like Australia and the US who hate the CCP — still, for the most part, defend "China" if you ever say anything negative about it.

The capacity to think, to decide, to choose, is the soil from which people grow intellectually.

Privacy is a prerequisite for freedom, and without privacy in a society, the notion of freedom, invariably becomes redundant. Any value or appreciation that the Chinese people might have once had for the virtues of community, privacy, or freedom had just slowly died across the last few generations. It had been asphyxiated by an omnipresent system of suppression and instruction administered through the framework of the all-pervading watchful eyes of flashing cameras and scripted repetitive media, all under the ever-poised-blood-soaked iron fist of Big Brother Xi.

The lack of any form of social security or welfare in China, in my opinion, also played a role. I mean, during these times, if you had no food, your children starved. Living like this, under this threat, would quickly extinguish any notions of things like honesty or the consideration of the welfare of strangers to being concepts that were simply not a priority at all, almost incomprehensible — unaffordable luxuries. If you had no money, you would happily lie or steal from your neighbour to feed your children — I would, I mean, any parent would. Over the last 20 years visiting China, I had had many conversations with Chinese people who had raised questions about this, who were genuinely curious to understand this thing, this honesty, this respect for others, that people from the West seemed to place such a high value on.

In the late 1970s and 80s, the great Deng Xiaoping built on the foundations of Mao's 45 million dead bodies. Adding his clever market economy reforms, he opened the doors to world trade that had allowed China to emerge as an economic superpower — I mean, it was a genuine fucking miracle; Deng Xiaoping, and a few leaders later, Xi, managed to raise 400 million Chinese up out of poverty and into the middle classes. A truly incredible feat.

It was this generation and their children that were now travelling and living around the world. But, regardless of the Western culture and norms that these Chinese are exposed to through the foreign universities they attend, in the business relationships they form, or at the places they travel to — obediently ambling along like primary school children in rows behind their appointed tour guide's flag, they still tend to remain homogeneously separate, somehow immune to the effects of osmosis, insulated from the unique characteristics of those countries, those interactions.

Even those who are fortunate enough to move and live permanently in these Western countries — unlike the Italians, the Greeks, and the Vietnamese before them — they remain "hyphenated" citizens: Chinese-Australian, Chinese-Americans, and so on. The Chinese Government's residual influence over them is part of that, in terms of the constant background threat of violence, the threat of dragging their relatives out of their homes and shooting them in the head in the street. This supreme, overarching authority that the CCP wields over any family members or friends that these people leave behind scares them so much that they probably can't even consider embracing this fundamental shift, to put their adopted country first, to even try to understand these concepts of merit, privacy, civility, and honesty.

I motioned to the bar girl and ordered another double Negroni.

It always annoyed me how the governments of the West and the dumb fucking masses they lorded over didn't seem capable of understanding the unique characteristics embodied in the people from different countries — the way they treated them all the same. Mass migration was clearly destroying the uniqueness, beauty, and character of Western cities like London and countries like Australia — changing what they were, how people behaved, and how they treated each other — and not in a good way. One of the core evils of Relativism and Political Correctness is that it takes away people's right to be discerning — to define the differences between one thing and another, one race and another.

I mean, anyone can clearly see the obvious differences between people from different countries if they bother to look. It's right there. The problem is that even if your eyes are open, if you can see, watch, recognise these differences, Political Correctness tells you to shut the fuck up, tells you not to point out how mass migration from some of these places is just not a very good idea. If you even talk about this stuff, these obvious truths, the masses come at you with flaming torches and pitchforks with screaming accusations of racism, for having the audacity even to question the rubrics of their truths, of their ideologies. It makes no fucking difference if what you are saying is as obvious as the nose on your face; in an instant, you are ghosted, unfriended, cancelled — fucking imprisoned.

In 1992, Denmark gave refuge to 321 Palestinian refugees, and in 2019, the government conducted a study to review what had happened to them. 64% of those who had been given refuge had obtained criminal records. 34% of their children had also obtained criminal records, and the vast majority of the 321 were living on welfare. "X" Nigel_Farage

For fucks sake, what does this tell you about the differences between people based on the lives they have lived, the circumstances they have been subjected to? The way they have been raised and how their particular life has conditioned them?

But fuck it. If you openly discuss the truth about anything at all, you are branded as being just to the right of Genghis Khan politically.

We had a perfectly reasonable and productive immigration strategy and we've ramped it up to a rate that isn't integratable. And we do that because we don't think that integration is necessary. But you know what the opposite of integration is? Disintegration. Its not that hard to figure out man. You could imagine that there's a rate at which the inclusion of new people into your culture is actually invigorating; you know the new ideas that are brought in, the different ideas that are brought in, the different skills. And then you could imagine that there's a rate that if you *exceed becomes devastating. And so its like almost everything else that is complex — if it's done well and wisely then it's going to have a productive consequence. If it's done foolishly and bitterly then its going to be a disaster. And so almost everything we do in this country, especially at the Federal level, is done bitterly, resentfully, and incompetently, and so you don't have to be a genius to figure out where that's leading.*

Jordan Peterson

Just look at the Lebanese in Australia, for Christ's sake. Between 1975 and 1990, the Australian Government under that fucking idiot Malcome Fraser — why the fuck he was on the conservative side of politics still bewilders me, opened Australia's doors to 30,000 Lebanese immigrants — granting them asylum from the horrors of the civil war that was raging there.

These people had been immersed, completely submerged in a daily street-level-explosive-AK47-rocket-fuelled-fucking-blood bath for decades, fucking decades, and they landed on Bondi beach — crowded with the lazy Sunday afternoon shenanigans of everyday Aussies. Pretty girls in bikinis, and young men in board shorts playing volleyball, families playing beach cricket, for Christ's sake! I mean, what the fuck did the Government expect would happen! Violence was all many of these people had ever known; it was in their fucking DNA. To them, all their lives, if you wanted something, then you just took it. You had no choice. I mean, if you are born into this horror, grow up in it, if you're terrified by it and have to get involved in it out of pure necessity to survive and to protect the people you love every day of your fucking life, it's gotta change you, I mean some of it's gotta stick, it's gotta become part of who you are.

Anyway. All anyone in Australia has to do is want to notice, is want to open their eyes, and see what the result was. I mean, just the fucking TV news reports — every high-ranking official of every violent motorcycle gang, and every fucking shooting in the Western suburbs of Sydney since that time has involved the descendants of this decision, this shit-fight you see on the news almost every day. Every single name, whether they are the shooter or the victim, is Lebanese — it's always Hamid Izra who shot Mohammad Mustafa; it's never Peter Smith who shot Steven Johnson.

It's crystal clear. It's right there for anyone, for every one of these wilfully ignorant fucking ideologues to see. It's not "racism"; it's just what it is. It's not somehow hidden, for fuck's sake. I mean, yeah, of course, some of these people — probably the majority of people — will be overwhelmingly grateful and appreciative of our hospitality and go about setting up kebab shops and doing law degrees specialising in migration law, I get that. But you can't only focus on them and completely ignore the significant numbers of them that just burst out laughing at what they see as vulnerability and weakness, see just an opportunity to take advantage of our kindness and accommodation. Like taking candy from a baby, they immediately put their habits of exploitation and violence to work in the drug and prostitution industries — and the effect that has had on Australia and on the Australian way of life is profound.

The media, these assholes, actually glorify it. They get all weak in the knees when they interview some fucking criminal king of Bankstown who's just been cunning and ruthless enough never to have been caught, with their whole bleeding-heart-soft-on-crime-everyone-deserves-a-chance-at-rehabilitation bullshit.

And the same applies to the Chinese. Generational conditioning keeps them separate from Australians, from becoming Australian. They seek out and exploit the gaps between the laws that exist in a civilised society, gaps that we all just take for granted — the places where generally accepted community social norms are all we have ever needed to maintain the civility of mutual respect between people.

I can remember a Pizza Hut in Foshan, China, that had a one-visit salad bar option on the menu. They found that guests quickly started buying one visit for one member of a party of five or ten people, and then that one person would go up to the salad bar and proceed to construct a tower of food on a plate that a structural engineer would have been proud of. They were all generally the same, a circular construction of cucumber slices arranged like brickwork that formed a 30cm-high tube which was then filled with everything else from the salad bar — perhaps almost 5 kg of food on one plate that they would then place in the centre of the table for the whole group to share. I mean, they weren't breaking the law, they weren't breaking the rules, they were just exploiting that space where civility usually sits — in the gaps in the law, between the rules. Needless to say, within a month, the one-visit salad bar option disappeared.

Pissed me off.

It was about 11 p.m. now and Banga Road was pulsing with people and noise and colour. Happy to be just sitting there sipping my drink immersed in it all, I glanced over at the group of Chinese. Their self-focus, their survival instinct to grasp, to take advantage of civility, of what they essentially saw as weakness in our kindness, means, that with the occasional exception, they are almost always just out for themselves, to take as much as they can — even the wealthy ones — especially the wealthy ones. And when a lot of anything is taken from a person or a civilisation, the space left behind has less of it — kindness, generosity, respect, decency.

It changed people, it changed cultures.

I wish I were in fucking charge, I thought — I was getting very drunk again now, slumping forward on my stool against the street bar, dripping, soaked in my introspective misery and contempt. If I was in charge I would make the fuckers tick some extra boxes on their immigration applications, like: If we let you become a permanent resident in Australia, will you promise to let people merge in traffic? Will you teach your children that driving aggressively and tailgating other cars in the black entry-level Mercedes-Benz that you buy them is not how we drive in Australia? Will you not rent a one-bedroom apartment in one of Sydney's best public school zones for six months just so that you send your kids there and can still live in Hurstville?

Fucking fuckers.

I turned my gaze away from them and back out onto the endless stream of passing dullards. Anyway, I thought, it wasn't just an immigration issue, this shit, this deconstruction of civility in the West — in these countries it was actually most evident in the behaviour of big business and the State. I mean, most people still understand right from wrong — with those annoying exceptions, like when you let someone into traffic, and they don't give you a wave, or when they drive down an empty lane and then push in at the end. The people who did this were still a small minority — they weren't breaking the law, they were just being assholes.

Everyday Australians still generally understand and respect civility. But where you really see this stuff in Australia is with big business and government. It's like those parking Inspectors I suggested get subjected to random public floggings. The civility of discretion — of common sense — turning a blind eye to someone using a loading zone to drop their kids off safely at the movies, without hitting them with a $300 fine. Like a hunter setting a trap — some asshole sitting in an airconditioned car taking photos of number plates, fining 10 people in 15 minutes who are just trying to get on with life and keep their kids safe.

They have built this lack of civility into the system; into budgets and operating procedures. Like the ever-increasing number of speed cameras — punishing more and more drivers with fines of hundreds and hundreds of dollars for accidently drifting over the speed limit by five or six kilometers an hour. Strategies focused purely on raising vast amounts of money to feed the voracious appetite of the Pathocracy, all justified under the banner of the disingenuous duplicity of "road safety". If they cared at all about road safety, they would fix the fucking roads that get worse and worse year by year.

There's no civility in that; there's no decency in this stuff.

You're subjected to this same shit every time you're stuck on hold by some huge telco or some government department, and they play that fucking recorded message over and over and over: "We are sorry for the delay; your call is important to us, blah, blah, blah", or the one I hate the most; "Due to an unusually high volume of calls, blah, blah, blah." I mean, fuck off. Just fuck right off. There's clearly not an unusually high volume of calls at all because every time you ring them, it's the same fucking message.

In the end, beaten down by frustration, feelings of failure well up inside you — that particularly miserable feeling of failure — the one that comes when you don't succeed at something that you really needed to achieve, that you were absolutely determined to achieve. When finally, all of your hope has been drained out of you, when you've taken about as much of this shit as you can, and you hang up the phone, it dawns on you.

Your only option left is their website.

You realise that you have been corralled down this path like a dumb fucking cow, and you have no other choice but to go to their website. You know it's a trap. Instinctively you know there will be no answers there, but you can't help but engage with that morbid curiosity — that consciously misplaced optimism, misplaced hope; but what if?

What if, when they developed the outline, the specifications for their website — laughing and lolling back in their $1000 Herman Miller chairs at their carefully-scheduled-just-before-lunchtime meetings, gorging themselves on State-funded avocado and chicken sandwiches cut into perfect triangles — the crusts removed with surgical precision by the pretty girl with the nice breasts at the Lunch 'n Go around the corner. What if, sitting at those melamine-triangular-fit-together tables, their waistlines halved by perfect horizontal lines — their belts separating the two fat lips of their upper and their lower abdomens; what if they had been overwhelmed by an inexplicable determination to be kind, to be civil?

What if there had been a miracle?

Hope builds. You think to yourself, what if they had thought, just for a change — purely for the sake of variety — that they would make a good website, a website that was useful, helpful even? What if the website security protocols were not completely-over-the-top-unnecessarily-complex in their charade of a professionalism everybody knows simply doesn't exist? And what if these protocols actually worked and prevented their all-too-regular massive data breaches? What if while allowing osmosis to spread their soft marshmallow bodies into every contour of their chairs, their faux leather briefcases next to them on the floor, bursting at the seams with stationery supplies stolen to win favor with their nieces and nephews, what if they had actually done a good job and the answer to your question was on the website, there, in plain sight?

With feelings of hope that you in fact find strangely terrifying, and against all your better judgement, you reach for the keyboard.

But. No sooner have you ventured onto their website — your keystrokes guided by the soft glow of your conjured optimism, you once again find yourself cornered. Trapped. Rounded up into a state of confusion by their strategically developed maze of nefarious red herrings, dry gullies, jargon, three-letter acronyms, and belligerent-blunt-instrument circular questions. You stop and stare — you can almost smell the overwhelming cheap deodorants and the conference coffee, almost see their smiles.

You're stuck. There's nowhere else to go.

And the kicker? That fucking question at the very bottom of the screen that asks, "Was this information helpful"? Yes or No? These fucking assholes know full well that their masterfully contrived cacophony of misdirection was about as useful as an ashtray on a motorcycle. They ask this fucking question just to make absolutely certain that you are forced into the conscious realisation that not only have you failed, but that they were completely, deliberately responsible for you failing — for engineering both your hope, and your defeat. Through this question, they force you to understand that the breadcrumbs, that series of seemingly innocuous, binary questions bathed in contrived connotations of concern and interest that they set out for you to follow, carefully crafted to develop the illusion that you were making progress, led nowhere. That they told you absolutely nothing, gave you absolutely nothing that was helpful in any way, while skillfully stealing your time and your morale.

And next to that Yes/No question? That very same fucking phone number that you started with — completing the circle.

The cherry on the top.

These organisations know they have a monopoly or are part of an oligopoly. They know you have no choice but to sit there getting angrier and angrier. They amuse themselves with strategies of misdirection, simplifying, only to then conflate information repeatedly, over and over, constantly insulting you by telling you they care, that you're important to them. Like crabs on a beach, they bury themselves further and further away from you, beyond your reach, down behind recorded messages and pastel coloured pretend help pages, smothering themselves underneath the digital sand of zeros and ones.

All legal, all to save money and labor, and increase profits and budgets, and garnish balance sheets — all just exploiting the gaps, exploiting civility.

They clearly couldn't care less about you. You know that they are lying, and so do they. You know that if they really cared, they would hire more fucking staff so that the wait for customers to talk to an actual person was shorter, or they would make their websites actually useful so that they went somewhere, gave answers, and provided solutions. But they know that your hands are tied, that you're fucked — that there's nothing you can do except get so exasperated that you just walk away and accept whatever insidious fucking injustice they have consciously, deliberately served up to you.

It's pure fucking artifice.

Like with all the essential services — phone, internet, banking, fuel, electricity — clearly, they are oligopolies. I mean, there's almost no difference ever in the pricing or their service levels from one of these businesses to the next. There's no effort to differentiate product or service offerings, to compete between these companies, there's no free market forces at play like the Government is supposed to make sure there is. Prices always all just go up together, and the average punter, you and me? Fucked. Just fucked. There's nothing you can do, you know they are screwing you, and you just have to accept it.

I mean, in a civilized society, having a bank account or electricity in your home are essential services, and if anything should be open to free market forces so the Price Mechanism can do what it's supposed to do, it's stuff like this. The irony is that the government can see all this, and what is their response? To set up more bureaucracy, more formal enquires that pay bureaucrats a fortune and go nowhere, more places you can call or websites you can visit to complain — options that every single person involved knows will be just another complete fucking waste of their time — that nothing will be done, nothing will ever change.

Assholes.

I know what I'd do if I were in charge. I would set up a completely "off-grid" market research company — a company that was totally independent of the market and government and could not be corrupted. That company would have no other function than to conduct both qualitative and quantitative research on an entirely random, large, sample group of customers of every single one of these malignant organisations annually, leading up to the end of the tax year.

Based on the outcome of this feedback, this research company would rank these organisations from 1-10, negative to positive, on the answers provided by simple men-and-women-in-the-street customers to questions like; "Last time you phoned your provider, did they answer your call within a reasonable timeframe?" 1 to 10. "Could you understand what they were saying?" 1 to 10. "Do you feel that they are offering you value for money?" 1 to 10. "Did they provide an actual answer or solution to the question or problem that you contacted them about?" 1 to fucking 10!

The results of these surveys would then be applied to the tax that these fuckers, these organisations had to pay, or if it was government departments, to the funding they received in the next budget. Companies that scored poorly would have a scaled 0 to 30% percent penalty increase applied to that financial year's tax rate, and companies that scored well would get the reverse, a 0 — 30% reduction in their tax rate.

That would bring the competition back into the fucking market — impacting their bottom line. That's the only way.

> It doesn't matter if the cat is black or white, if it catches mice, it is a good cat.
>
> Deng Xiaoping

Impacting on the profits and losses that these companies bring to their annual shareholder meetings is the only fucking way to make them compete with each other, to make them accountable to provide these services that people have no choice but to use, at reasonable fucking prices, to provide these services within a customer service framework that is real, and intentionally helpful, instead of weaponising shitty customer service for profit.

I mean, the companies that actually embraced this system would win so much business from the others — the shareholders would be thrilled with the financials at the annual board meetings, and the rest of us? Our lives would improve immeasurably.

And these government departments! Can you imagine? Them getting their budgets cut savagely and being forced to actually do something, to be accountable, to work for the people? I mean, the only way these lazy fucking assholes can make money is by taking away people's rights and licensing them back to them while at the same time imposing bigger and bigger fines for breaching their ever-growing lists of laws and regulations. These assholes that fail so fucking miserably in managing Australia's more than bountiful water resources and, sneering down their noses, blame the "stupid public" for water shortages — making us put egg timers in our fucking showers and bricks in our toilet cisterns.

The sheer volume of the conversation drew my attention back from the passing streetscape, past the Chinese awkwardly trying as hard as they could to look natural, to fit in, to the two fat American women, with their double chins hovering, wobbling above the chains upon chains around their sweaty-cracked-foundation-caked necks, and their rings upon rings on their fat stubby fingers — all 9-carat-gold-junk jewellery — and their $300 hair cuts.

I looked up, and the same bar girl was watching me. She started laughing. She knew. She understood how fucked up this world was. I mean, why do we have to endure them? Stuffing themselves with fats and lards and sugars and chemicals — always laughing and aggressively imposing their disgusting, sweaty existence on the rest of us. Always with that veneer of contrived-confident-carelessness that defied any fucking logic at all.

I mean, I get it. I don't have a problem with fat people. Really, I don't. I mean food — it's right up there with sex — I love it. It just pisses me off that they expect taxpayers to pay for dealing with all of the inevitable healthcare issues that come with morbid obesity. They can limit what they eat, it's within their control. They chose to be fat. And there are so many people suffering health care issues, life-threatening issues that are not their fault, that they have no control over — problems where that funding could be spent in a far more deserving way.

And why don't they wear clothes that are appropriate? Why make fat a feature? Why on earth do they have to wear those fucking tights and gym gear?!! Do they honestly think it looks attractive? Those rolls and folds, my God! I mean, it's just fucking repulsive. Passive aggression, that's what it is, I'm certain of it. A deliberate act to scream out at the world that they're not ashamed of themselves and that the rest of us had better damn well accept, no, fucking embrace, that their rolls of fat and ridiculous ever-shorter-bob-haircuts are just as beautiful as the pretty fit girl with the ponytail leaning against the bar behind them.

That stupid fake smile that they wear plastered on their stupid-trowelled-on-makeup-faces while they are out in public that I was convinced stayed there just long enough for them to get home in their Priuses and their fucking electric Volvos, only finally giving way to uncontrollable sobs of shame and depression the very moment the door closed behind them and they were alone.

"There is no such thing as a happy fat person", my doctor had once said.

Anyway. These ghastly people never seemed to die from anything, never seemed to even suffer from anything, impervious to the laws of cause and effect, conspicuously living on and on and fucking on forever as they transition from waddling around the supermarket isles in Lycra to that seemingly eternal stage of aggressively pushing their way through crowds on their motorized fucking buggies.

Assholes. Fuck them as well, I thought.

Imagine how much happier they would be and how much money they would save from not desperately chasing dopamine hits from their shitty-cheap-suburban-shopping-centre jewellery and their ridiculous law-of-diminishing-marginal-return haircuts if they just ate sensibly and got some fucking exercise.

I knew what I would do if I was in charge. I would force these lardass bastards to have mandatory legislated annual BMI testing. Then, I'd force them to have private health insurance with the yearly premium weighted, leveraged directly to their BMI. That's what I'd fucking do.

Fucking consequences.

More men die from prostate cancer than women die from breast cancer and yet still, the men's football teams wear pink jerseys in support of breast cancer awareness — and even those efforts, once again, completely ignore men. My uncle died from breast cancer. Men die from breast cancer. Yet 90% of men don't even know that males can get breast cancer — don't have any awareness at all of the seriousness of getting a lump in their chest looked at by a doctor.

Why the fuck should the rest of us subsidise the hospitals and the healthcare system for these gross excessive pigs, while educating and providing support for people with conditions they have no control over, remains perpetually underfunded? What about some funding for men's health – promoting awareness, research and treatment! Here's an idea; why not budget the same amount of money for men's health as they do for women's health? Is that such a fucking crazy suggestion?

Screams of "Misogynist!" from the bleachers by the feminists deliberately misinterpreting a call for actual equality, as an attack on funding for women's health, as they drag themselves out of the self-indulgent quagmire where they have been quietly enjoying the high male suicide rate.

In the West, suicide rates amongst men under 30 have risen by 40% since 2010. Suicide by males now accounts for as many deaths as breast cancer does for women. Did you read that? In the West, male suicide now accounts for as many deaths as breast cancer does in women, for fucks sake! Yet any attempt to put a spotlight on this is quashed either through callous indifference, or deliberately under the ethos of Zero-Sum Empathy. We live in a world where no one; pro-male or pro-female, is prepared to genuinely accept that the other sex has to deal with difficulties, without automatically measuring that cost up against their own suffering.

This ridiculous assumption that any assistance or funding offered to help men and boys, is assistance or funding that must be taken away from helping women and girls.

It's as if the love we have for each other, the care available for people who are struggling in life is seen as a finite resource. It's like both sides are trying to balance some bizarre social justice equation — like victimhood masquerading as arithmetic. It's a fucking catastrophe — just ask the mothers, the fathers, the sisters, the brothers, the boyfriends and the girlfriends of the young men that are killing themselves.

Humanity is an appalling fucking thing.

And these huge fatties sucking up the healthcare spend.

"But doctor, I hardly eat anything", or my favorite, "But I'm big-boned". Fuck off. You never see fat people in concentration camps. Excessive self-indulgent assholes — and Americans seemed to be the worst of them, although Australians were clearly catching up. I mean, go out to any shopping centre in the western suburbs of Sydney — my God, some of these people are fucking purple from the soles of their feet to their knees from poor circulation — wabbling about like penguins chasing the air conditioning, buying crap that they don't need, with money that they don't have. Sitting around all day on welfare, smoking cigarettes, and eating KFC.

Fucking diabetes time bombs.

I know what I'd do if I was running the fucking country. I would shut down that section of the Department of Social Security responsible for unemployment benefits and set up a company that had the sole purpose of implementing clever environmental initiatives for Australia.

If you became unemployed, there were no handouts every fortnight — if you didn't want to starve or end up homeless, you went and got a job at this company. There would be jobs for everyone who needed them — everybody from environmental scientists to kitchen hands, to accountants to bulldozer drivers and mechanics, carpenters, labourers, cleaners, truck drivers — the list would be fucking endless. Whatever you wanted to be, you could be, simply by applying yourself. There would be real jobs, apprenticeships, on-the-job training programmes, six and seven-figure salaries to attract the very best people into strategic roles.

There would be no fucking excuse for second and third-generation welfare families.

All the money handed out in unemployment payments, and all the money spent on buildings full of paper-shuffling fucking zombies administering those payments, would be poured into an organisation that fixed the rivers and the streams, and planted the forests, and built the new water storage and management solutions and state-of-the-art recycling facilities. Environmental solutions that actually worked in a way that made fucking sense — like what Singapore does. Everyone involved paid industry wages, going home at night full of pride and self-respect.

That's what I'd fucking do.

Looking at the American women, I smiled thinking about that Monty Python skit, where the American keeps interrupting the Grim Reaper, and the Grim Reaper finally loses it and tells them to, "Shut up! Shut up, you American! You Americans, all you do is talk, and talk, and say 'let me tell you something' and 'I just Waana say.' Well, ya dead now, so shut up!"

"Can I help you?" In my drunken haze, I must have been obviously staring at the two American women, and one of them was looking aggressively at me now for an answer.

"I doubt that. Fuck off", I sneered, turning my gaze away from them and back out to the constant stream of people walking past — letting their indignant mask-muffled objections fall rattling to the ground — exactly where they belonged in a place like this.

Grenouille broke out in a different jubilation. A black jubilation. A wicked feeling of triumph that set him quivering and excited him like an attack of lechery. And he had trouble to keep from spurting it like venom and spleen all over these people, and screaming exultantly in their faces that he was not afraid of them, that he hardly hated them anymore but that his contempt for them was profound and total.

Perfume – Patrick Süskind

The bar girl who had been laughing earlier had seen the exchange and walked over, asking the women if they would like another drink in an effort to diffuse the situation. "Two Manhattans on ice with a twist of lime" was the answer, although it took the fattest of the two women three attempts before the girl could understand her order because her voice was so muffled by that stupid fucking mask she was wearing.

Fucking morons.

11

The Albanian

September 29, 2025

I opened my eyes and the first thing I saw was the old Indian man.

I blinked, thinking I was seeing things, but he was still there! Real. He was in exactly the same position, sitting on the edge of his bed, staring straight at me with those beautiful, old, kind eyes. It was as if, apart from the slight rocking forward and back, he hadn't moved at all.

How long had he been there? I closed my eyes and listened to his voice, that soft chanting that seemed to be falling above, somehow just in front of the mechanical, electronic beeping and humming of the hospital room that had become my world. It was some kind of repetitive mantra, but very strange. It was as if he was breathing the words more than he was actually saying them.

All of a sudden, I felt a hand holding mine, and I opened my eyes. It was the old man, but it made no sense because I hadn't heard him move. How could he have gotten to the side of my bed so quickly? Perhaps I had drifted off — most of the time, with the drugs and the pain and the monotony, I found I was struggling to be certain if I was even awake or if I was dreaming. He was so close to me now, blocking out everything, that I had no choice but to just stare at his face into those eyes — sitting there in a chair beside my bed, holding my hand.

Where had the chair come from? What the fuck was he doing? Where were the nurses?

As if on cue, a nurse's uniform drifted into my peripheral vision, past behind the old man, and after opening the curtains, appeared over his shoulder, standing behind him, smiling at me.

"You are very lucky, sir. He is the Vishnu Parshad. He is one of India's most famous spiritual leaders. He speaks for the god Shiva. He became ill on his lecture tour here. He is praying for you. You are very lucky, Sir. Very lucky", she said again, shaking her head as if in disbelief at how lucky I was.

I looked back at the man, directly up into his eyes. There was so much peace there, his body rocking forward and backwards ever so slightly as if in tune with his melodic, whispered chanting. Clearly, the nurse hadn't thought it was odd — him sitting in a chair holding my hand. And why was there no pain? Staring into his face suddenly made me feel as if everything was ok. I hadn't felt like that for so long. I closed my eyes, listening to his voice, the soft, smooth skin of his warm hand holding mine. Peace. Sleep.

April 26, 2025

Sitting at the kitchen bench in my Phuket beach house, sipping a glass of merlot. Looking outside through the sliding glass doors that led from the lounge room out onto the patio by the pool. I guessed it was probably quite early in the morning. There was a girl lying down on her back on the couch in front of me, completely naked, a half-eaten butterscotch doughnut resting between her breasts. It was one of six I had purchased yesterday from John Donut on Thalang Road. The butterscotch sauce had oozed out, running like a golden-brown river down the centre from her chest across her flat stomach, pooling into a perfectly circular puddle in her belly button. Like most Asian women, her pubic hair was light and assiduously manicured; and her breasts sat perfectly on her small frame.

She worked at the back of the laundry station on the esplanade near the entrance to Bangla Road, where I got my laundry done. Before I met her out last night we had never spoken, only smiled at each other on occasion. There were the remnants of the icing sugar dust from the donut on her lips and what I guessed was cocaine under her nose as well as on the glass coffee table next to her, along with my black HSBC Visa card, a vial of PCP, and a variety of half-full and empty glasses of various shapes and sizes. On the floor next to her was a red glass bong shaped like a large cock with the brass cone set in between the balls, and a half-full bowl of Pink Panther weed I had bought from Juicy Buds in Patong a few days earlier.

It had been a good night.

Halfway through an evening of what I could only describe as wild sexual exploration, of touching and licking and sucking and fucking — a blur of flesh and sweet scents, someone had produced amyl nitrate. The three and four-minute explosions of sexual intensity it brought on were beyond anything I had ever experienced, something entirely new for me. A treat, I thought as I remembered, smiling. Looking around, I could see the empty, broken capsules, two different brand tubes of lube, a dildo — even a stun gun. I mean fuck, the things we'd done! At the other end of the room was a tangle of three people in various states of dress, all sound asleep, lounging across two large bean bags in front of another set of sliding glass doors that opened up the wall next to the wooden front door.

One of the glass doors had been smashed, and the glass was all over the polished concrete floor, mixed with semi-dried pools and splashes of congealed blood — sparkling red in the morning sunshine — the results of a severe altercation with the Albanian that had occurred during the evening.

The Albanian was a cunt. The two girls, Li and Mae, all tangled up with "Princess" on the beanbags in deep sleep, limbs in all directions, both topless, didn't like the Albanian at all — because he was a cunt.

The girls and I, along with Princess — a ladyboy friend of theirs, had become close over the last few months. Princess was a scream; she was smart, outrageously precocious, and fantastically animated — exaggerating everything she did, she was always making me laugh. All three of them were happy for the reprieve from having to offer up their services to the endless stream of strangers and the occasional pent-up sociopath who visited their club on Bangla Road to rent them.

They had said that they found most customers were generally nice — grateful even, but that you never knew what you were in for once the hotel room door closed behind you.

They both agreed that the general rule of thumb was it was the plain ones that were the worst — the most dangerous — the clean-cut, straight-looking ones, the ones without any of the tattoos or the long hair or the beer bellies — who were dressed in simple conservative clothes and looked like they worked in some government department. The Albanian was like that — scrawny, furtive with lank hair that looked like it needed a good wash, a greasy cow's lick fringe swept across his brow. He could have been a government accountant in his beige-checkered-button-down-collar short-sleeved shirts and cream coloured trousers. The girls had an endless list of terrifying stories, of things that had happened to them working in the clubs — but the worst by far was a story Li had told me that had involved the Albanian.

I hadn't had much sleep, and staring at the broken glass in the sunlight was mesmerising, sharp splashes of red from the blood dancing between the refractions of every colour of the rainbow as the sunlight turned each cube of the safety glass into a prism.

I took another sip of my wine. Now. Where was I? That's right. That fucking Albanian. Sitting there, I could just imagine that bastard in a chair next to me, drumming his fingers on the kitchen benchtop, waiting for me to give him some words, his next direction — something to do in this story. Fuck you, I thought. You're a fucking Albanian, go out and rape someone.

I know, I know — I'm supposed to say that I'm sure most Albanians are probably really nice people and all that shit, but fuck it. Him, this Albanian, the stories about him, what I had seen — I couldn't help myself but dislike the entire fucking race that had produced him — couldn't help but resent the fact that they had not had the foresight to cut his fucking throat at birth.

Anyway, Li, Mae and Princess were just wonderful — so much fun. It amazed me how resilient, how strong these girls were. How they could go through so much in life and yet still be so sweet and happy, so much fun to be around. I guessed it wasn't all Thai girls, but these three were just fantastic company. I was outrageously generous with them, which I am sure helped a lot.

One day, as a spur-of-the-moment thing, I had flown them to Bangkok with me for a four-day change of scenery, staying at the luxurious Mandarin Oriental. At my suggestion, we went shopping at the Siam Paragon, where I happily spent a little over 50,000 Baht on clothes and jewellery on each of them. It was not a huge amount, and they were genuinely thankful in their appreciation of it as a gift and not a payment for services rendered. It was always kept deliberately ambiguous the payment side of this "girlfriend experience" these beautiful young Eastern women offered — as far away as possible from the distasteful prostitute/customer relationship expectation of these transactions in the West.

The games people play.

This way, everybody got to keep face, and it became all about both parties giving, not taking — that was the key, and in the end, both walking away with their pride intact and a new friend's number in their phone. If you were lucky, occasionally there was actually some truth to be found in these relationships, some honest, caring connection there, a momentary real dedication to each other which was beyond the unmentioned financial transaction that was all the cynical sanitised observer inevitably viewed from the outside with ignorant skepticism. It was found in the words and the actions that weren't required, but that happened anyway. Little kindnesses, moments of tenderness and fun and understanding that could come from no other place than from an honest emotional bond between two people.

They behaved as if they just loved life and seemed to be just grateful for the peace and quiet of the fun times we were having together, as one day blended into the next. They would even insist on helping me change the dressing on my neck twice a day — like clockwork — a task that I am sure was not pleasant but something they did religiously with honest, gentle care, and kindness.

Li's story about what the Albanian had done to her friend Na was just fucking terrifying.

The Albanian had given a tuk-tuk driver money and instructions to go to the club the girls were working at and to pay the bar fine for both girls (numbers 19 and 28) — the girls in the pole dancing clubs all wore numbers so that they were easily identified. The tuk-tuk driver had then taken the girls back to outside the Sultan's Grill just off Thawewong Road, where the Albanian was waiting for them. He had then walked with them back to his apartment that was nearby. However, when telling me about it, Li had pointed out that they took an unnecessarily long route, which she thought was weird. Later, when the police went to check her story, they discovered there were no CCTV cameras along the path they had taken.

The evening had started out fairly normally.

After they all had some drinks sitting around the table, the Albanian moved over to the couch and sitting back, drinking a mix of vodka and Red Bull, he had instructed the two girls to take off each other's clothes and make out on the carpet in front of him. I remember Li had said that the only thing that was kind of weird at that stage of the night was how precise he was with his instructions. She said that at one stage, he got really angry with her because she had only inserted one finger inside Na and not three as he had instructed. He had also become furious when he thought Na was not being rough enough, aggressive enough, massaging Li's breasts with the baby oil he had given them. Li was a little unusual for a Thai woman, with natural, quite large C-cup breasts that looked fantastic on her small frame.

Anyway, eventually he had laid down on the couch and asked Na to come over and straddle his face so he could eat her pussy while telling Li to go down on him. According to the girls, this was all pretty standard for them — although he had grabbed Li's hair and forced her to let him come down her throat, which had pissed her off. She said she usually only allowed regulars that she actually liked to do that.

When this was all over, he had gone to take a shower and returned carrying a Monopoly board and a bottle of Mekong, insisting that they all play. Continuing into the kitchen and pouring two glasses of Mekong for the girls — he returned, holding a glass in each hand and the bottle under his arm. During the game, the girls described how they would be laughing and talking when, all of a sudden, he would get really angry — accusing one of them of cheating or saying that something wasn't fair. She said it was really scary because there was no warning when this happened, and the change in his attitude was so sudden, so extreme — it was like he went instantly "crazy." She said when he was having one of these outbursts, his eyes would narrow, and he looked like he was going to get violent with them.

About halfway through the game, Li said she suddenly felt really weird, like extremely tired and confused. She said she remembered looking over at Na, and it felt like she had been looking at her for an hour, the whole time struggling to look back at the game board. It got worse and worse, and Li remembers the Albanian had started laughing weirdly and gotten up and left the room.

It didn't take long for Li to realise they had been drugged, and although she knew they were in serious trouble, there was nothing she could do about it. They could hardly move. The Albanian returned with a roll of heavy electrical tape, a camera on a tripod, and a large roll of clear plastic tubing with a diameter of about 50mm over his shoulder.

By this stage, Li said she was terrified.

She said he then dragged two kitchen chairs into the lounge room and lifted Na, who was still naked, sitting her up in one of them. Li said Na's head was lolling about, and the Albanian kept laughing and referring to her as his "sexy little meat puppet". Li said he then dragged her, also still naked by the hair across the room — which she said she didn't feel at all, probably because of the effect of the drug — and propped her up on the floor with her back against the front of the couch — directly side-on to the chair Na had been placed in. He then set up the camera on the tripod so that the field of view would be across the front of Na on an angle to Li sitting on the floor against the couch. Li said that when he had done that, he had stood there for a moment looking at the scene and that after changing the position of Na's seat so it faced the camera just a little more, slightly more away from Li, he seemed pleased with himself.

He then grabbed the roll of electrical tape from the table, walked over to Na, lifted one leg up, placed the sole of her foot on the chair, and used the electrical tape to tape her ankle tightly to the arm of the chair where it joined the seat. Once done, he did the same with the other foot. Li had said that she could see the fear in Na's face, in her eyes, but there was nothing she could do.

Li said the Albanian then walked out of the room for less than a minute and came back with a bundle of clothes under his arm and an expression on his face that Li said looked as if he had just snorted something — his eyes were just crazed and his grin menacing, insane. He seemed very pale all of a sudden.

After standing there, grinning at them both, clearly proud of his work, he started to undress and, once he was completely naked, put on the clothing he had brought out. Li said it was a Nazi uniform adorned with swastikas and SS emblazoned on both sides of the collar. She said it even had about six medals with ribbons pinned across the chest and it seemed to fit him perfectly.

Once his costume was complete, he picked up the coil of clear tube and, with a switchblade he took out of a pocket in the uniform, cut off a length of tube about eight feet long. He then walked over with the piece of tube while licking the end of it and stood directly in front of Na sitting — her legs spread wide, unable to move with her feet right up on each side of the seat cushion, her ankles taped to the chair. Leaning over Na, he inserted the end of the tube he had been licking between her legs quite roughly, pushing it deep inside her. He then reached backwards for the second kitchen chair and, dragging it closer, placed the other end of the tube on it so that it rested on the seat and traveled up at an angle, with the end resting on the top of the back of the chair.

What happened next was just fucking appalling. He left the room again, and when he came back, he was wearing a latex cartoon pig head mask — the final terrifying piece of his costume — and carrying a rat in a shiny golden cage.

Li said that they could both see what was happening and realised, at the same time, what the Albanian was going to do. Despite the effects of the drugs, both girls had started to scream, although all they could manage was a quiet, more of a high-pitched moaning sound that no one would have been able to hear outside of the room.

Li said that Na's eyes were nearly round, actually almost coming out of their sockets in fear.

She said that their reaction clearly excited the Albanian, and he unzipped his trousers and started to masturbate. He then walked over and turned on the camera, checking the digital screen viewfinder twice to make sure it was capturing the whole scene — Na in the chair on a slight angle, almost facing the camera, and Li on the floor with her back against the couch in the background. He then walked over to the table, picked up the golden cage, moved over to between Na and the tripod, and held the cage up in front of the camera, slowly turning it around for about thirty seconds.

Sill masturbating, he carried the cage back over to the table, opened a latch on the top, and carefully removed the rat holding it by its tail. He then walked over to directly in front of the camera, again letting the rat hang there, wriggling and squirming, clawing the air for his imagined audience.

Finally, he turned and walked back to the chairs, and with a flurry, almost as if he was imagining himself as a magician doing some great magic act, he lowered the rat into the tube head first. Li said that the rat was reasonably large, and for a moment, she had hoped that it wouldn't fit — but it seemed to narrow itself out and scampered into the tube quite easily.

Clearly terrified just recounting the story, Li said she must have fainted because she had no memory of anything that happened after that.

The next thing she knew, was when she was woken up in the park at the northern end of Patong Beach at 9 a.m. the following morning by a friend of hers who thought it was strange that she was there. After Li's hysterical account of what had happened the night before, her friend took her to the police station on Sainamyen Road, where the police, realising the seriousness of what had happened, took her directly to the Sainamyen International Medical Clinic for a check-up before she was asked to make a formal statement.

Li said that, miraculously, the doctors had informed her that physically she was uninjured and gave her some Valium to calm her down. The police took her back to the station, and she gave a detailed account of everything that had happened — the first of three she was asked to provide over the course of the next month. She said her blood test results had come back the next day, showing nothing for her to be concerned about, as did the same tests she did two weeks later as requested by the doctors.

Li said she never saw Na again. No one did.

The police interrogated the Albanian, as did special investigators who had been brought down from Bangkok. In the end, although the authorities suspected the two women had been victims in the making of a snuff movie and that Na had most certainly been murdered by the Albanian, after a four-month investigation they did not have enough evidence to bring charges against him. They found no evidence of the girls having been in his apartment, which they said had been thoroughly cleaned with a heavy ammonia-based solution. They found no uniform, no camera or tripod, no pig mask, no Mekong — and they couldn't find the tuk tuk driver, who Li said had picked them up from the club.

The Albanian had gotten away with it.

I took another sip of my wine, remembering back to last night. At some time during the evening, Li received a phone call from a friend of hers who had asked if she could borrow her motor scooter. Li had said yes and given her the address of my condo, but after she hung up, she commented that her friend sounded weird. About twenty minutes later, Li and I were sitting at the table when we heard the sound of a tuk tuk arriving outside the condo. We assumed it was Li's friend. Just as I had finished doing a line of coke and Li had finished snorting a line of PCP, everything happened at once.

At precisely the same time as the drugs exploded into our brains, lighting up every sensation like a Christmas tree, we both looked up to see the Albanian's white face suddenly appear pressed against the glass, looking into the room from the outside — an expression of drunk menace about him.

In the moment it took me to realise what was happening, Li had already left her chair and was across the room to the four-foot length of galvanized steel pipe that I kept resting against the wall in the corner behind the front door. The adrenalin hit from the PCP, and seeing the Albanian's face seemed to give Li superhuman speed and strength, and before I was even out of my chair, she had smashed the Albanian's face with the pipe straight through the glass door. By the time I reached her, she had hit the now unconscious Albanian at least three more times in the head with the pipe as he lay on the floor where he had fallen forward into the room. Snatching the steel pipe from her, I dropped it backwards behind me, terrified she would kill him and end up in prison for the rest of her life.

She was hysterical, and I grabbed her and, wrapping my arms around her, held her tight, telling her she was safe and everything was okay, just trying to calm her down. After about two or three minutes she stopped screaming and was just muttering and crying. Mae had then taken her upstairs, staying with her after she had put her into a warm shower.

With the sound of the smashing glass and all the noise from Li's screaming, it wasn't long before the police arrived. Fortunately, Princess, who only ever smoked a little weed and didn't drink at all, had had the presence of mind to put the PCP, the cocaine, and the amyl nitrate capsules in a bag of frozen peas in the freezer and cover the residue left on the coffee table with a tea towel from the kitchen as a makeshift tablecloth.

After an ambulance had taken the Albanian away, the police interviewed all five of us. The warm shower had calmed Li down, and although she insisted on taking full responsibility for what she had done, the police knew her, and they knew the Albanian — and most importantly, they knew the history between them; what Li had claimed the Albanian had done to her and her friend Na. In their minds, it was self-defense, and they didn't seem to think anything more would come of it. In fact, they seemed almost disinterested, even pleased, with what had happened to the Albanian.

Dragging my gaze up from the sparkling crystal-red mess on the floor, and away from the all-but-naked human tangle on the beanbags, and taking one last look at the girl and the butterscotch doughnut on the couch in front of me, I took another sip of my wine. Pulling my laptop across the kitchen counter towards me, I opened it up and started to write.

...Chapter IX

Back at the fire, far away from Beetlecrunch, Elixius relayed the new orders to Garblebilk and Curdleslop that Gagglebroth had given to her, and the three, excited by the task at hand, made ready to leave for the town of Applecreek Grove.

Once preparations were complete, they started off, Elixius in front, then Garblebilk followed by Curdleslop, who carried the small cauldron containing the potion of "Confusion", the mixture having solidified into a thick clear goo as it cooled. They moved swiftly, weaving through the forest like three black shadows. After half an hour or so, Elixius held up her hand, and they came to a stop. Garblebilk moved forward in front of her and peered through the last of the brambles and bushes at the ghostly road that ran along the front of Cracklewood Forest and into the town. Confirming all was quiet, they stepped out from the forest onto the road, hurrying the last mile to their destination.

On the opposite side of the road was an apple or-chid. Row upon row of apple trees stretching into the night. Not one leaf rustled, for the night was as still as can be, with not a breath of wind save the mist from the Witch's breathing as they made their way along the narrow dirt road through the frosty night air. Up ahead, they could see where the rows of apple trees stopped and the houses began.

When they reached the houses, the trio slowed, moving off a little to their left to merge with the shadows cast by the forest. They stopped in front of the first house and, crouching, gathered around the cauldron. Taking their turns, they all dipped their right hand into the goo, scooping out a handful. For no apparent reason, Curdleslop began to giggle, something that Garblebilk put an end to with a sharp crack of her left hand across Curdleslop's head.

Standing up and with Garblebilk giving the direc-tions, they split up and began running from house to house, wiping small amounts of the goo onto the door handles and the tops of gates and latches. Dogs be-gan to bark as the three moved along with surprising speed.

The road forked to the right offering up houses now on both sides. Handles of carts and wheelbarrows were also smeared in the goo whenever they presented themselves, and in fact, handles of any sort for to work, the potion had to be touched. Once it had been touched, the person became confused in any number of different ways, making any organisation of thoughts, logic, or commonsense almost impossible.

At Garblebilk's signal, they stopped and, having covered most of the town, hurried back the way they had come, Garblebilk pausing behind the others for a moment to place a small black box, about three inches square, in the middle of the road in the town's main intersection, before hurrying along behind the others. The potion would only retain its magic for twenty-four hours, and the box would help start the clock.

Scuttling silently back up the road past the orchid, they could hear the sound of barking dogs becoming less and less as, one by one, they gave it away as a waste of time till only the one persisted before it yelped and became silent.

Turning off the road, they went back into the forest at the same place they had emerged. Once back in the camouflage of the forest, they stopped, and closing her eyes, Garblebilk muttered a verse in witch tongue. Back on the road in the middle of the intersection, the lid popped off the little black box, and up rose the specter of a brightly coloured circus clown waving about with a drum strapped to its chest and with a whistle in its mouth.

For a moment, it just floated about above the box in the dark, wavering ever so slightly before suddenly springing to life, beating the drum with much gusto and blowing the whistle with mindless enthusiasm. The dogs in the neighborhood immediately all started barking at once again.

Lamps in windows began to light up as the people all around woke and set out to investigate what the racket was all about.

Mrs. Pompleshore opened her front door and looked out. Still half asleep, she stood in the doorway, astonished at the scene that greeted her. Directly opposite her house, waving around in the middle of the road, was a clown beating a big drum and blowing a whistle. She could see it wasn't a real clown as although it was very bright, it was somewhat transparent, and it seemed to taper down to a single point on the road. She stood transfixed by its colourful, noisy display, so much so that she did not even notice Mr. Pompleshore trying to get past her for a better look. He gently moved her to one side and made his way down the front steps. From across the road and from houses up and down the surrounding streets, people began emerging to see what was happening. Quite a crowd had formed a circle of at least six people deep around the strange spectacle when all of a sudden, the clown stopped banging the drum and blowing the whistle, let out a shriekish laugh, and then was suddenly kind of sucked back into the little black box on the road.

After a few seconds of stunned silence and almost as if it was an afterthought, the lid that had been lying on the road next to it, so far unnoticed, suddenly flipped up and back onto the top of the box, startling everybody into gasping and jumping backwards all at once.

And then there was silence; even the dogs had stopped barking.

Everyone was standing perfectly still around the box, watching, waiting with puzzled anticipation to see what would happen next when suddenly it exploded, splashing every colour of the rainbow into all directions like a giant firecracker. Everybody that had been standing around it once again leapt into the air at once, falling all over each other.

After gathering their wits and dusting themselves off, the townsfolk began returning to their homes, mur-

muring amongst themselves as theories were developed and discarded, more than one of them wondering if it had all been a dream.

Murrey Mooblemyer, publican of one of the two taverns in Applecreek Grove, lent lazily against the gate post at the front of his house. Dressed only in his long — johns and a pair of gum boots, he stood stroking his puggy, unshaven chin with his free hand as he watched his neighbors return to their respective dwellings. The Mooblemyer family had been part of the town from the very beginning. His great, great Grandfather, one Wendel Mooblemyer, had been part of Edward P. Fizzlebub's expedition and had built the first tavern in Applecreek Grove, called "The Flaming Arrow", which was now run by Murrey.

Having been such a significant part of the town's history with such close connections to the Fizzlebubs meant that Murrey knew just about as much as anybody, and quite possibly more, about the legends of Fizzlebub and the witches. And it was witches that he was now wondering about as he lent against the gate post.

The tavern he owned and ran, as well as its signature drink, had been named the Flaming Arrow because legend had it that one way to dispose of a Witch was to shoot a flaming arrow into its heart.

As if to give some credence to this theory, there had been, for as long as he could remember, a crossbow hanging on the back wall of the cellar beneath the tavern, and next to that hanging in an old leather quiver, six slender hardwood bolts each with decaying oily rags wrapped around the shafts just below their steel barbed tips.

Unbeknown to him, his hand now rested upon a generous smear of Garblebilk's potion that was slowly being absorbed through his skin. After what he had just witnessed, he could come up with no better explanation other than that there were witches about, and thinking of the crossbow, he decided he would make for the tavern as quickly as possible. However, by the time he had returned to his house, the potion had begun to have its effect, as it had on many others in the street, including Mr. Pompleshore, the town barber, who at that very moment was trying his very best to convince Mrs. Pompleshore that if she would not let him go out and mow the lawn, then it was rather a matter of urgency that he give her short back and sides and a shave, though he would not hear a word of the two bits he normally charged.

Murrey Mooblemyer emerged from his house under the distinct impression that he was dressed for the occasion, the occasion being to take his horse and buggy down into town and open the tavern for business – regardless of the fact that it was one o'clock in the morning. He had quite forgotten all about the crossbow as he strode down his front steps dressed only in his hat and a jacket over his long johns and gum boots. He waved to his neighbor three doors up, Mr. Pompleshore, who was busy crisscrossing his lawn with his mower, the steel blade whirring to a holt at the end of every pass. Mr. Pompleshore waved back with a friendlier-than-usual grin and continued to mow under the moonlight.

Hitching up his horse and buggy, Murrey Mooblemyer started off towards the centre of town, informing everyone he passed that the tavern would be open for business in half an hour and that the drinks would be on the house. As he went down the road, he passed Mrs. Brackabrook imploring her next-door neighbor, the town's schoolmaster, Mr. Weedlepeck, to "stop ringing that infernal bell!"

By the time the three witches had returned to their lair, the trouble had quite certainly taken hold of the little town of Applecreek Grove. The "Flaming Arrow" had now been open for an hour and was creating such a noise that Wilbur P. Fizzlebub, having been woken from an unusually troubled sleep, was now standing at his study window looking down at the tavern with a sleepy, bewildered expression on his face.

When the pub's doors had been flung open by Murrey Mooblemyer, of all the people at the pub, only about a quarter of those there had come in touch with the "potion of confusion". But as the drinks were free and being drunk with gay abandon, it was not long before everyone there had shaken hands with everyone else at least twice, spreading the potion and its confusion like wildfire.

Standing on the bar at one end stood Ethel Vanderbule, a feverish look dancing in his eyes. He was passionately expounding the virtues of a world where a man could grow his nose hairs as long as he liked to a small group of confused and intoxicated, but nonetheless seemingly very interested, listeners.

"A world where no one would comment, even if they were to dip occasionally into one's bowl of soup", he added with conviction, his listeners becoming prouder and more certain of the merits of his idea as he plundered every sentence for everything it had.

At the other end of the bar, seated on a bar stool, was Henry Mapleton, who was sprouting poetry in a loud, pompous voice, though no one seemed to be listening.

They seek him here,
they seek him there,
I shot an arrow in the air,
Where it landed, I don't care,
for am I sitting on a chair,
my thirst is quenched, and my knees are bare,
if I had a frog, I'd take him there,
and when…

This was where his fourteenth poem for the evening ended, as he was smashed over the head with a half-empty bottle of Applecreek Whisky by the chap who was sitting next to him, who had decided that enough was enough and thought this was the best option as opposed to moving and having to give up his seat. He was greeted with a smattering of applause, and the festivities continued.

The line in the poem about the arrow had been overheard by Murrey Mooblemyer, who, having just knocked back his sixth straight Flaming Arrow, stood up and disappeared out through the back door and down into the cellar beneath, leaving his station behind the bar in the capable hands of his cross-eyed nephew Lewis.

At the bottom of the stairs that led down into the cellar, a very drunk and quietly confused Murrey Mooblemyer fumbled about with a box of matches and a lamp, all the while trying to remember what he was supposed to be searching for, if indeed, he ever managed to get the lamp alight. With what he found to be quite a surprising glare, the match he had been repeatedly striking suddenly flared up into life.

Weaving the match towards the wick, the lamp was eventually lit, and holding it up in front of him, he gazed about at the racks of bottles of wine, spirits, and kegs of beer that were stacked neatly around the cellar.

The muffled rabble upstairs was suddenly interrupted by an almighty cheer before it bubbled back off again on its chaotic course. Unbeknown to Murray, Henry Mapleton had just regained consciousness and, upon resettling himself on his stool, had resumed his fourteenth poem for the evening at the exact spot he had left off before he had been rudely interrupted by the whisky bottle. The chap next to him, not having the heart to strike him again and conceding to himself that it would altogether be in bad taste to do so, decided to relinquish his seat and go join what had by this time become quite a large audience in front of Ethel Venderbule, who was still extolling the virtues of a world where nose hairs could; to quote Mr. Vanderbule; "Grow wild and free".

Below, Murrey Mooblemyer, weaving his way around and past the wine racks amongst the shadows they cast, was under the impression he would know what he was looking for once he saw it.

Eventually, his meandering brought him to the back wall, and looking up and seeing the old crossbow and the bolts, was suddenly gripped by an inexplicable fear.

"The witches", he gasped out loud. "They are here! Upstairs!" he gasped.

Placing the lamp on a keg of beer, he removed the crossbow from its hook and grabbed a bolt. Putting the crossbow upside down in front of him and with his foot in the stirrup used all the strength he could muster to pull the wire back and cock it. Lifting it up, he inserted the bolt into position before raising the glass on the lantern and lighting the oily rag at its tip.

It was at this very moment that a tall, gaunt, and altogether stalky-looking fellow of about fifty years of age was closing in on the tavern with long, purposeful strides. With his head thrust slightly forward, held there by his excessively long, tenuous neck, his sharp, angular features gave him a cadaverous appearance in the moonlight. He was dressed in a white shirt and black suit with highly polished black leather shoes. Clasped in his right hand was a bell, for it was none other than Mr. Weedlepeck, the schoolmaster, determined to find out why everyone in the tavern was not in school for his Latin lesson.

Back in the cellar, Murrey Mooblemyer was hurriedly weaving his way back through the wine racks toward the stairs. The lantern clutched in his left hand, the crossbow clutched in his right. Replacing the lantern on the empty keg at the bottom of the stairs, he blew it out and started up. The flickering flame on the end of the arrow lighting the way.

Bursting through the door, he came out behind the bar yelling, booming at the top of his lungs, "The witches are back! The witches are back!" The crossbow in his hands waving wildly about in front of him. Suddenly, all the noise fell away, the silence only broken by the solitary sound of the school bell ringing fervently and getting louder.

Murrey Mooblemyer, his eyes full of fear, had just had time to raise his bow and take aim at the doorway when Mr. Weedlepeck, with one deft kick, sent the left-hand door swinging back, hitting the wall strode through, all in the one movement. There was a flash as the arrow was let loose. An astonished expression on his face, Mr. Weedlepeck stood perfectly still, his head lowered, just staring at the arrow protruding from the left-hand side of his chest, his mouth slightly open. A full three seconds passed before the bell slipped smoothly from his right hand and fell to the floor with a clang, shattering the silence. He swayed ever so slightly backwards, then ever so slightly forwards as if he were considering his options, and, apparently having made up his mind, fell slowly backwards out through the door landing with a thud on the timber porch of the tavern, from his knees down left protruding through the doorway and into the crowded bar…

12

Alone and Palely Loitering

October 1, 2025

My eyes opened to the sound of a conversation. Disoriented, it took me some time to realise where I was. The pain in my leg seemed to have faded back to a dull ache. Both the old Indian man and his bed were gone — replaced by nothing between me and that wall. Strangely, I felt disappointed. I missed him. I was sad that he was gone. I felt somehow that his visit had changed me, that everything was in some way different. I couldn't explain it, even to myself.

Someone had propped me up slightly on an angle, and I could see two people talking between me and the top part of the window and that brick wall beyond.

"Try to manage it with morphine, but I think that perhaps we will have to go back to pethidine before the end of your shift. In either case, just write it up, and I will review it in the morning."

"Yes, doctor."

The younger of the two women turned and walked away out of my field of vision as the nurse turned towards me with a smile brimming with sadness and pity — a smile utterly devoid of anything positive or encouraging. Strangely, my mind forced time to stop, and I just gazed at her, studying her. An empty space of consciousness that I held onto for a few seconds — no thoughts, just nothingness.

"Good afternoon, Sir," she said, looking into my face. "Sir… I am sorry to tell you, Sir, but we have had to amputate your leg. It was very badly infected, Sir, we could not save it."

I just stared.

My mind turned this news over quietly, analysing it from all angles — as if I were someone else, as if from a distance.

I completely ignored the natural urge to settle on the contrived responses of shock and sadness that wandered out into the spotlight on my mind's stage to present themselves, because they thought that this was where they were supposed to be — what was expected. Familiarity had fed my contempt for them over the years, and I disregarded them easily, watching them with a cold gaze as they turned slowly and walked off the stage back into the darkness. For me, the news was almost irrelevant.

To die, piece by piece, I thought. It seemed reasonable, somehow honest, almost, the next natural step.

The nurse smiled that uncomfortable smile at me again, turned, and walked away.

Closing my eyes, I drifted off into an uneasy sleep, only to wake sometime later to a new pain, an intense pain that seemed to engulf me completely, that seemed to have no specific location. I was whimpering. Scrounging around in my mind for peace, for relief. The detailed fabric of the nurse's uniform appearing inches from my face again, a rough cold rub, a needle, falling gently down through the metal framed bed into oblivion.

September 12, 2025

Day 360. I flew from Chiang Mai into Dom Mueang Airport. After a particularly enjoyable taxi ride with one of those drivers you occasionally get who is just simply "happy", and a short stop off at CB Lockers, I checked in to Lebua at State Tower in Bangkok as myself.

Simon's role in my life was finished now.

I had spent the last three months in Chiang Mai at the CM White House — a small guesthouse off Soi 5, at 12 Rachadamnoen Road. My health had not been good, and I had really enjoyed Chiang Mai's cooler temperature and slower pace.

I had stayed at the Lebua at State Tower a few times before, and it was one of my favourites, with its full suites, outrageous luxury, and the attention to detail the staff offered. I mean, they had the ingredients for Bloody Marys — including a bottle of "Jewel of Russia Ultra Black Vodka" on the breakfast bar, for God's sake.

When I first stayed there in about 2015, I had come down for breakfast at the Café Mozu on the second morning, and after seating me, my hostess had said, "Triple shot latte on cream in a piccolo"? The place was packed, and she had remembered my coffee order from the morning before. Amazing.

The other reasons I was here were the private balconies off the suites and the Distil bar, a cocktail bar located on the 64th floor overlooking the Chao Phraya River that served the very best whiskeys and cigars. With an amazing outlook across the Bangkok skyline, it held a very special place in my heart for one evening I spent there enjoying the breeze and the views with my wife.

But that was many years ago, before she had wandered, lost, in tired curiosity down that path where there are no signs, just a dark, overgrown entrance that smells of moist, evil decay. She had groped her way forward in the dim light, threading carefully through the wet, rancid branches of dreams, memories and regrets — their thorns dripping with black poison. Eventually, she had strolled far enough to reach a place where she had stopped and realised all of a sudden, that she would prefer I was dead.

On a video call with my wife, she had asked me why I went away and how I could leave my sons. I replied that there was only one thing worse than the pain I felt walking away from my children, and that was being reminded every single day how little she really cared about me. The way there was never any pain or sadness at all in her eyes. The way everyday she couldn't help but allow the happiness, the relief that she felt with what was happening to me, shine through the cracks in the clumsy mask of pantomime concern that she wore on her face.

You don't need words — there are a thousand different ways to let someone know that you don't love them anymore.

8 am September 17, 2025 — Day 365

And when nobody wakes you up in the morning, and when nobody waits for you at night, and when you can do whatever you want. What do you call it, freedom or loneliness?

Charles Bukowski

I woke up and just lay there staring at the ceiling. The bed was huge, its size reminding me of just how alone I was.

My whole life, I had loved solitude — but not the solitude most people craved; sitting in a park, or leaving their home and going for a walk. For me true peacefulness could only really be found in big cities like Rome, London, and Bangkok. In big cities, you are still exposed to all the colour and the smells and the tastes and the beauty of life, but no one you encounter ever talks to you, no one ever tries to engage you in conversation. In places like these, you are completely alone — isolated by people's self-actualised disinterest, and their urgent egocentric obsessions. Contrastingly, in the suburbs, all you had to do was walk out onto the sidewalk and some well-meaning benign bastard would engage you in mindless conversation about the weather, or your dog, or their socially coalesced ignorant theories about some political issue they had gleaned from the mainstream television news. There was never any peace in suburbia. These "communities" — they were a fucking nightmare.

To be free, really free, you have to be alone. Without solitude, true freedom is not possible, and if you do not love being alone, then freedom is not something that can be important to you. But, lying there in that huge bed, for the first time that I could remember, I did not want freedom. Instead, I found myself craving the company of the people that I loved, longing to be completely ensnared, bound up by the warm embrace of all of the complications and the impositions of their lives; by their needs and their wants and their happiness and their opinions and their failings.

Eventually, I slowly got out of bed and had a long, luxurious shower. I found myself thinking about each of my children, one at a time. Going over their lives from when they were born, times I could remember when they were growing up, the things we had done together. Their hugs and their smiles. When we had walked across England along Hadrian's wall as a family — putting one foot in the North Sea and one in the Irish Sea at the other end. When we had climbed the Eiffel Tower together, and when we had had breakfast in the jungle in Borneo, and the orangutan came down from the canopy and watched us from only meters away. Memories of Thomas eating a croissant in Edinburgh — covered in crumbs; Liam buying an antique bayonet in Barcelona; Ethan beside me, swimming with a whale shark in Exmouth. Kate, my beautiful wife before we had lost each other, me and her, driving around the mid-north NSW coast in her old Mercedes convertible with our German Shepherd, Loki, in the back.

All the good bits.

My beautiful wife, and the way we were. My children becoming adults — building their lives with girlfriends and driver's licences and strong harsh, defiant words back to me; weight training; studying; chasing dreams; sitting quietly with me alone — crying, asking for help, and laughing hard staring into their eyes at the dinner table; and showing me something on an iPad; or playing *Battlefield* with me; or showing me an engineering assignment that was at a level of complexity I couldn't even fathom; or a beautiful drawing or painting they had made; or discussing some complex philosophical potentially life-altering theory; or watching a tennis Grand Slam together; or showing me a new knit shirt they had just purchased.

Eventually, I turned off the faucets, stepped out, and after towelling myself dry with one of those outrageously thick, fluffy, huge white towels, dressed in a pair of blue jeans, my Converse kicks with white low-cut socks, and a beautiful new pink linen shirt I had picked up from Ricky's the day before. There were still faint white chalk marks on it from the man who had set the pattern before cutting it out.

I was once again wearing my wedding ring. Regardless of everything, I still loved my wife, and it felt nice to be wearing it. Life and emotions are complicated things.

Three nights ago, I had met up with Waan. She was back in Thailand again on holiday, and we met for dinner at the Limoncello restaurant — that fantastic homage to the Italian Amalfi coast — just off Sukhumvit Soi 11, for one of their incredible pizzas. We had shared a bottle of wine, "Vernaccia di San Gimignano". It was one of my favorites, not so much in its flavor, but in its history. It was a wine drawn from the same grape — from the very same vine in Tuscany that Dante, when he wrote his Divine Comedy over 700 years ago, had condemned Pope Martin the XXIV into Purgatory for his sins of gluttony over — his excessive consumption of that exact same drop.

Like I, too, had been condemned. For me, drinking this particular wine felt somehow correct — prophetic, providential even — and I savoured every last drop.

Although Waan's eyes were full of sadness and concern as she looked at me, we had had a lovely evening, rounded off by the kindness of her insisting on paying the bill and travelling back with me in the taxi, dropping me off at the hotel afterwards. The following night, I had met up with an old friend, Somchai — someone I hadn't seen for years — at the British Club, that amazing oasis of English stiff-upper-lip-grandeur right in the heart of Bangkok. Talk about old-world colonial! Fucking cricket nets in the middle of Bangkok! It was so nice to see him again.

But last night, I had chosen to order room service and have dinner by myself in my room, politely dismissing the room service waiter who had seemed insistent on standing off to one side with a folded napkin over one arm at his waist while I ate my meal, should I require his service.

I felt like being alone with my thoughts, with no distractions.

Today was my last day, and, for perhaps the first time in my life, I felt lonely in my own company.

The memories of the last twelve months were now just that, memories — things in the past that had no relevance to today, things that had no real meaning for me at all, really. Twelve months, a snap of the fingers. Were they even real? Was any of the past ever really real? What difference was there between things you had only dreamed about and things you had actually done, once they were in the past? The weight of the decisions I had made, the "opportunity cost" of the last twelve months, had been growing in my mind and was now almost unbearable, smothering me.

> You can avoid reality, but you can't avoid the consequences of avoiding reality.
>
> Ayn Rand

The twelve months had been a cascading waterfall of colour and flesh and flavours, and deep intoxication, and satisfaction, and pain, and sleep, and sadness, and loss and pleasure — and above all, rage. I went into the bathroom and did the best I could to change the dressing on my throat — it was horrific now, covering almost one entire side of my neck. I took three Endone and three Panadeine Forte and wandered down to breakfast.

A short, very strong latte — a triple shot and a double shot espresso on the side that I would add once the level got down far enough. Toast, monitoring the Chinese magpies, flipped eggs. Bacon — crispy. Fresh orange juice. More than one sad smile from other diners; a middle-aged Caucasian woman, two small children staring.

I must be looking dreadful, I thought — another coffee.

10 am September 17, 2025 — Day 365

After breakfast, I went for a walk down Silom, past all the bulk silver jewelry shops, the 7-Elevens, the tired massage shops with their generic beautiful Thai woman and Lotus flower livery — all still closed, and the piles of rubbish bags out for collection. Eventually, I found myself staring at the desolate, post-apocalyptic streetscape that is Patpong in the early morning — the scrawny soi dogs all-four-legs-straining at the concrete as if to bunch it up like a carpet in their effort to shit — finally ending up sitting in the Burger King on Silom Road just before the intersection at Lumphini Park.

Sipping an orange juice, I ceremoniously cut up all evidence of me as Simon — manually shredding his passport, driver's licence, and other documents using a pair of scissors I had bought a few days before from the Tokyu department store in MBK.

Without Simon, I would not have had the peace, the distance, and the freedom over these last twelve months to ignore everything that had mattered so much to me leading up to my time in Thailand. Strangely, I suddenly felt somber; a great feeling of indebtedness to him for his help came over me. I wondered if he was okay. I carefully mixed up and separated the shredded pile into three plastic bags, each tied in a knot. Thanking the staff as I left, I dropped each one of the bags into a different rubbish pile along the sidewalk as I walked on to the Sala Deng skytrain station where, after putting some coins into the machine, I travelled back along Silom to the hotel.

The day before, I had posted four packages from the Phat Phong Post Office, a slight detour from the same route I had just walked. The first three contained photocopies of all the documents that had established me as Simon: his passport, driver's License, Medicare card, and bank account details. I had included three letters I had written, one each to my brother, my sister, and my wife and children. A final goodbye. In the package to my brother, I had also included my PAM 233 as a gift, and in the one to my sister, our mother's engagement ring that I knew she had always been fond of.

In my wife's package, I had included proof that my "Life Insurance Policy — Natural or Accidental Death" was paid up to date, along with a copy of my novel that I had finally finished writing.

In the letter to her, I had done my best to make her feel ok, not to blame herself. I loved her, and I told her that.

The fourth package was a blank "Happy Anniversary" card containing $5,000 cash, addressed to Simon at the shelter where I had met him.

11:45 pm September 17, 2025. Day 365

Sitting on the bed in my room, sipping a 21-year-old single malt, The Glenlivet, from a small crystal glass — gazing at the bottle I had purchased that afternoon that was now a little under half full. I stood up slowly and took my wallet out of my pocket. It was packed full of me, bolstered fat with evidence of who I was: my driver's license, Medicare card, even a Bangkok City Library card that I had established in my own name purely for this purpose, happily paying the 50 Baht fee. Pouring the last of the whisky down my throat, I placed the empty glass next to the bottle on the counter under the TV and, walking over to the cupboards, punched the six-digit security code into the room safe. Checking to make sure my passport and other documents were still there, I closed and locked the safe again.

I then walked over, opened the sliding door onto the balcony, and stepped outside into the warm evening air. I just stood there, staring out at the view from the 56 floor, sparkling lights, the freeway traffic — the black ink of the Chao Phraya river. With my wallet still in my hand, I walked over to the edge of the balcony, and leaning over and down as far as I could, very carefully, I lobbed it about a meter onto the outside ledge of the balcony balustrading of the unit next to mine. It landed perfectly — just out of reach. I had practiced this 1,000 times in my room over the back of a chair that was approximately the same height as the balcony, onto my copy of "Meditations" by Marcus Aurelius which was about the same size as the space the wallet needed to land on.

Standing upright, I took a step into the centre of the balcony and leaning forward again, half lying down, hugging the heavy concrete balustrade, I carefully climbed over, one leg at a time. Standing now on the small ledge, staring out at this city I loved so much and down at the road below — the warm Bangkok breeze on my face. The Chao Phraya River — beautiful.

It's not a big deal, really; it's just that sometimes my voice catches when I'm talking.

I am sure it's nothing, but patients I have had in the past have turned out to be right about things like this, so you should persevere — let's send you to an ENT specialist.

As a specialist, I can say it is common for one tonsil to be bigger than the other — perfectly normal.

As long as it's not cancer, then I don't care.

No, it's not cancer.

The night sky, the beautiful lights of the buildings, and the headlight snakes of traffic. The warm, moist, scented breeze.

Well, it's been a year, but if you're still concerned, let's get another opinion.

There is no need for you to stress about it — I give it less than 5% that it is cancer.

Ok, if it's still worrying you, let's just remove the tonsils.

Slowly falling forward now.

I'm sorry, Alex, it's cancer — but it's quite treatable, which is good.

Yeah, fucking great.

No, I mean the treatment is very effective against this type of cancer. We achieve a 90 - 95% success rate.

...seven weeks — pinned by my fucking shoulders and my face to a table by a hot moulded plastic mask, smelling my own flesh burning in my throat from the radiation... vitamin shakes, no food, no beer, trying to drink water that felt like it was full of sand... and then that fucking feeding tube down my nose...

Floating, turning gracefully, completely relaxed.

It's over. Your treatment was textbook. In our experience, you have a 95% chance of a full cure. You are a standard garden-variety cancer survivor. Stop worrying that it will come back, and just get on with your life! *Huge fucking smiling face*

Drifting, turning, sparkling lights.

I'm sorry, the scan shows it's back, and it's spread. We need to do it all again.

... But first, you need some surgery. We need to cut into your throat and carve some of it out so that you can never talk again...

....and so children in supermarkets will recoil in horror at the sight of you...

Blah, blah, blah, words, blah, blah, blah, words, blah, blah, fucking blah.

Floating. Sam's face. The realisation for the first time that everything was there, the answers, all in his eyes, his expression for me to have seen the truth, to have understood his story completely.

Why hadn't I?

Loud wind whistling.

Nothing.

6 am October 3

Waking up to the sounds of urgency — the sounds of beeping, of metal trolleys being manoeuvred around my bed. Metal bashing against metal, hitting the sides, the bed jolting, people's voices, urgent yelling. But it was all slowly fading away, along with the pain and the smell of disinfectant.

Gone now. Silence.

I opened my eyes. The wall was gone, replaced by another different, vaguely familiar wall. Silence. It was so strange; it had been so long since everything had been quiet.

Had they moved me to another hospital ward? Without even thinking, I rolled over onto my back. That's odd, I thought. I was sure I couldn't do that. The ceiling light was different but looked really familiar.

Looking around, it was a dream. I suddenly realised — I was in my childhood bedroom.

I just lay there, not daring to move, terrified of breaking the spell. Looking around the room, my cupboards, the louvres above the sliding door, my desk — just the way it was when I had moved out of home more than forty years ago. It was incredible — so real, so wonderful. I was fighting with all my strength not to wake up.

After what felt like an hour of lying perfectly motionless, I was still there — looking around the room, remembering. I started to think how strange it was, how unusual it was to be in a dream for so long, especially when nothing was happening — just lying there. I actually felt like I was awake. The room felt real.

I slowly pulled back the covers and swung my legs over the side of the bed, fully expecting to wake up. But I didn't. I just sat there feeling the carpet under my feet. Everything felt so immediate, so now, it didn't feel like a dream. It was light outside, perhaps early morning. Standing up, I walked over to the wardrobe, each slow step revealing some other object, some other detail in the room that I remembered from when I was a child. How could I remember all of these things from so long ago? Reaching the wardrobe, I opened the left door — the one with the mirror on the inside. I just stared.

I was looking at myself when I was twelve years old.

How did I know I was twelve years old? Wearing pajama pants, no shirt. My body was so lean, so young, my skin so pale and flawless — there was a silver marijuana leaf hanging around my neck on a leather strip tied in a knot. I could clearly remember getting Mum to help me tie that knot only a few days ago. I could distinctly remember my older brother Daniel telling me how stupid it looked just yesterday. How? My hair was a shock of curly blonde ringlets. I just stared. I wasn't scared. I was just amazed and confused about what was happening, how real it all felt. I was barely able to breathe. I just stopped and stared and listened. A sound, a storm bird in the distance. It felt like summer.

My body was ringing with all this, with where I was.

I needed to understand what was happening to me. I walked over to the desk and bracing myself, starting to get frightened now and determined to wake up, I kicked the underside of the bottom drawer hard, immediately falling to the floor from the pain in my shin. I lay there holding my shin while the pain faded back. How could this not be a dream? How could this be real? I could feel the scratchy carpet against my body, see things, trivial, unimportant things, things I should have forgotten decades ago, should not have been able to remember at all.

It made no sense. Clearly, it was real — undeniably, impossibly real.

Lying there, I heard the sliding door upstairs directly above my room open, as I had heard it a million times before growing up in that house. "Alex, time to get up, son, time for school", my dad's voice sounded down from the verandah above. I looked up from where I was lying on the carpet, holding my leg, looking at my reflection in the mirror again, remembering every aspect of my father's funeral almost fifteen years ago. Slowly standing up, I turned around and walked over to the door, limping a little from the pain in my shin.

Sliding back the silver barrel bolt I had fitted to the frame so long ago and turning the handle, I walked through the doorway and out into the brown-tiled hall. Mesmerised. Looking up the hallway towards the green door, I could see Daniel's closed bedroom door on the left and Sam's on the right. At just that moment, the handle on Sam's door turned, and the door opened, and he walked out. He was so young, only seven years old, so innocent and heavy-eyed and beautiful. He looked at me.

"What was that bang?" he said sleepily.

Looking at him, I could feel tears coming to my eyes.

"Morning", I said as casually as I could manage, my mind racing. "Sorry, I dropped a book". My voice sounded ridiculous, so strange, so young. Turning slowly, I walked back into my room. Closing the door behind me, I looked down at the bruise already starting to form on my shin, fell forward slowly onto my knees, and started to cry. Soft, quiet sobbing, my mind racing.

It was real. I knew I was twelve years old. I could remember what I did yesterday as a twelve year old, but I could also remember my wife, my children, my 50th birthday, my mum in that nursing home, my dad's funeral. I could remember standing on the balcony of my room at the Lebua at State Tower in Bangkok just yesterday.

How?

Suddenly, it came to me. I drew myself up off the carpet onto my knees. The old Indian man! Surely not?? But how else? Who else? I knelt there, racking my mind. The old Indian man was the only answer I could find. It must have been him — something he had done. Somehow, I was twelve years old with 62 years of lifetime memories, at the same time.

Kneeling on that carpet, I could feel all the years of sorrow and pain and regret, all the anger and resentment and rage leaving me; I could physically feel it lifting out of me. I felt so light, so strange, so full of peace and joy I thought I would just melt into the happiness of it all, that it would take me over completely.

Sam. I had a second chance — I could fix it.

I would fix it all.

THE END

www.thebeatingroom.com
author@thebeatingroom.com

Epilogue

Whatever comes our way by chance is unsteady, and the higher it rises the more liable it is to fall. Furthermore, what is doomed to fall delights no one. So it is inevitable that life will be not just very short but very miserable for those who acquire by great toil what they must keep by greater toil.

They achieve what they want laboriously, they possess what they have achieved anxiously, and meanwhile they take no account of time that will never more return. New preoccupations take the place of the old, hope excites more hope and ambition more ambition. They do not look for an end to their misery, but simply change the reason for it.

Essay De Brevitate Vitae (On the Shortness of Life) – Seneca

Acknowledgments

Thank you to my beautiful wife. Without your patience and support, I would never have finished this book. And to my brother and my sister for always being there for me.

Finally, thank you to my brother Jim for giving us Meredith and his adventures. I hope and I pray that I do it justice.

Book List

The Beating Room

Meredith Dew and the Witches of Cracklewood Forest
(*Coming soon*)

Printed in Dunstable, United Kingdom

71654692R10181